I WILL PAINT THE NIGHT

I WILL PAINT THE NIGHT

SAM MULLER

ISBN: 979-8-88785-023-8 (Paperback)
ISBN: 979-8-88785-024-5 (Hardcover)

Library of Congress Control Number: 2023943387

Any references to historical events, real people, or real places are used fictitiously. Names, characters, and places are products of the author's imagination.

Book design by Allison Chernutan.
Cover florals by lukasdedi on Freepik.

Printed in the United States of America.

First printing edition 2023.

emily@fracturedmirrorpublishing.com
Fractured Mirror Publishing
Knoxville, Tennessee

www.fracturedmirrorpublishing.com

FOR PEGGY,
A WORLD

"Three things have you taught me—to labor, to suffer, and to love. I am more learned than the Immortals."

The Good Thunder – A Japanese fairy tale

BOOK
ONE

1

DEATH DOESN'T KNOCK

"That night, Liminalin, One God, appeared to them in a dream. His four heads were crowned with gold diadems. His loincloth was of silver, and his cudgel iron. He said, Follow me, and I will lead you to your future. And his voice was the roar of a thousand black-lions."

Song of Sallonia — Book One

MOTHER DIED AND TOOK THE MEMORIES WITH HER. No trace of her existence remained in the castle, other than me. And the painting in Father's study. Framed in smoked silver, she sits under a blooming änge tree, flame haired and ebony skinned, one hand holding a yellow änge sprig, the other resting on an open book.

In the painting, she is smiling, happy.

Bellizza too looked happy when she first came to Sallonia

to marry my father. I was six then, and my new stepmother eighteen.

Stepmother; was there ever a word more seeped in myth, laden with tradition? One hardly ever heard of evil stepfathers, but which stepmother wasn't evil?

Experience soon disabused me of that inherited fallacy. It was to Bellizza I ran when I was seven and believed the ground would open up and suck me into the bottommost hell because I had asked why One God had four heads and only two hands. It was with Bellizza I shared my secret dream of becoming a plant explorer. She had backed me when I demanded permission to study herbalism and praised my translation of the great classic, *On the World of Plants*, from High Pegalian to Sallonian. I did it as a birthday gift to Father. His response had been a polite smile and a stilted thank you.

Fourteen months ago, she helped me escape a marriage that would have been worse than the hell. Much worse.

The rose-apples were a thank you. Bellizza loved rose-apples, but they couldn't survive in Sallonia, with its seven months of scorching heat and seven months of unrelenting rain. I had begun my experiment of growing them in my indoor garden with little hope of success. But two seedlings survived into adulthood and one bore fruits, soft and luscious, pentagons in pink.

Bellizza was in the sunroom thread-knitting, when I went in with the rose-apples. She smiled in greeting, smiled when she put down the thread-knitting to accept the fruits, smiled as she bit into one. But her eyes remained lost in whatever desolated landscape her mind inhabited these days.

I wanted to grab her by her shoulders and tell her that

not being able to give birth to a living son wasn't the end of the world. I didn't. It wasn't the lying part that stopped me, but the useless part. I would have lied with every word if it gave Bellizza even a thimbleful of comfort.

It wouldn't have. We both knew better. The *Song of Sallonia* left no room for arguments. Kings ruled. Queens produced sons. And princesses kept their blasphemous thoughts to themselves.

"This tastes good, Allii." Bellizza's voice had a lilt in it.

I grinned. "Truly? You aren't just being nice to me?"

"I swear, by my sister."

Thirteen months and thirty four days of working the soil, of struggling to control temperature with ember curtains in the rainy season and water screens in the dry season had not been in vain. I kissed her cheek. "Thanks, Belle."

This time the smile reached her eyes. In that moment, she looked like the Bellizza in the picture on the red mahogany table, eyes alight with love, blue hair rippling in the wind, one hand on my father's arm, the other hand clasping mine. The picture had caught her joyous smile, the proud lift of Father's head, the skip in my step—happiness imprisoned on a canvas.

Bellizza munched more rose-apple. "You really are magical with plants, dearest."

I grinned again. "Maybe I have witch-blood in me." Most Sallonians were undecided on the existence of witches, but every Sallonian knew what they were like—nasty, evil, and green-fingered.

In Sallonia, we said, *Like the touch of a witch, killing men and healing trees.*

Bellizza's breath was a gasp. "Allii, don't say such things."

I knelt and caught her hand, my copper-collared fingers stark against her pearly-skin. "Only to you, Belle. You know I mind my tongue as a rule."

"Not even to me. You never know who might overhear."

My eyes darted around the sunroom. Who could overhear us in this glass cage devoid of living things, other than the two of us?

Perhaps Bellizza meant One God. With his four heads, he certainly had enough ears for it.

"Won't do it again," I said, standing up, giving the skirt of my robe a vigorous shake.

Bellizza's blue brows formed a delicate arch over her blue eyes. "You are leaving?"

"There's a little something awaiting my attention."

Her eyes twinkled. "A new plant?"

"A fern, a green beauty with silver whorls." I laughed in anticipation of the joy awaiting me.

Bellizza nodded, reaching out for the half-finished thread-tree and the silver needles. Her smile was like the pale gleam of a distant star.

I closed the door wondering what twist she'd add to the white thread-tree. Would it be a branch curling like a scimitar or noose-like roots? The last time she did a thread-tree, she gave it a fruit like a screaming mouth.

Thread-knitting was how Bellizza had escaped the stupor of despair after her final stillbirth.

Bellizza conceived every year. Each pregnancy ended in a dead baby. After her ninth attempt, Doktoras Poll said she wouldn't be able to conceive again. She emerged from the birthing-chamber a week later a wraith. Her eyes were blank, her smiles grimaces. She ate little, spoke less, and rarely left her apartment. I spent as much time as I could with her, shoving plants under her nose, reading to her from books I hoped would interest her, telling her a woman's worth was not in her womb.

She responded only once. "If you hire a singer, you expect her to sing,"

I bristled. "You are not father's hired singer. You are his wife, his queen."

Her fingers clenched on the arms of her chair. "A royal marriage is a contract, dearest. I've failed to fulfill my part in it."

The maids whispered the king no longer visited the Queen's Apartment. I had sense enough not to ask Bellizza about it, but I did ask Nana.

Nana's lips tightened.

Nana, Dame Nanarina, personal maid and surrogate mother, helped birth me, nursed me, taught me my first lessons, scolded me, and loved me. When she folded her lips, a lecture was bound to follow, a wave of words cresting on an appropriate quotation from the *Song of Sallonia*. Curiosity featured at the top of Nana's Sin List, on par with disobedience and levity. *A curious mind stinks worse than a sewer*, she'd mutter, a frown darkening her mud-brown face. *Curiosity leads to hell*, she'd add, her frown vanishing, her eyes turning into green pools of tears, as if she was visualizing me in that insalubrious place, imps pulling out my unruly tongue with fiery pincers.

But there had been no hurling of sacred quotes that day. Nana had nodded her head, her old eyes sad.

That memory made me shiver, even though the hallway was warm with the heat from ember curtains. I told myself not to be a fanciful ass and rapped on the silver-studded door leading from the Queen's Apartment to the entrance chamber.

The door glided open.

The Queen's Guards had changed during my visit with Bellizza. I smiled at the new pair. Kiko brought plants for me whenever he visited his home in the Dollz Mountains. Terrii lived in the capital-city, Pinckossia. Though he stood as straight as his ceremonial lance, his eyes were red-rimmed and pouched. Even his moustache drooped.

"Is the baby sick again, Terrii?" I asked.

His smile was rueful. "She's teething, Highness."

I've never encountered a teething baby, but the books were clear on the subject: one afflicted infant could deprive an entire village of its nightly rest. "Grounded star-roots with honey would help," I said, "or some mashed…"

The door leading out to the private stairway opened. Father strode in, followed by Lord Sherriz, the Chief Minister. They must have come from a formal occasion. Father wore a state-robe, crimson with silver work. The Ring of Sallonia gleamed on his right hand. Sherriz tripped at his side, an eager insect.

I bowed, trying to think of something interesting to say. Alone in my room, I could conjure up long conversations between Father and me. Reality was another world. "Good afternoon, Papa," was all I could manage.

Not a bit interesting, and he wasn't interested. He nodded in my general direction, and resumed listening to Sherriz, his brown head bent to catch the short man's murmuring.

They headed towards the King's Apartment.

"Allii, aren't afternoons your plant-time?" The voice was deep and warm, with a hint of a smile.

I turned around, focusing on the unadorned magenta robe of the speaker, giving myself time to put together an answering smile.

At twenty-seven, Cousin Tygyrin was only nine years older than me. But he was already a member of the Governing Council, a general in the army, and a lay attendant of One God. I was certain he was the son Father would have liked to have in my place. Had he been less kind I could have hated him.

"My rose-apple tree is bearing fruits," I said. "I took some for Belle."

Tygyrin kissed my cheek. "I knew you would succeed. And how are you faring with my humble offering on desert plants?"

This time, the smile came unbidden. "Finished it yesterday." When I did, it was as if I were plucked from a boundless space of sun and wind, and dropped back into my limited world of routine, etiquette, and tradition.

Tygyrin's brows went up. "Your birthday was thirteen days ago and that book has 705 pages."

"I read in bed." Until Nana caught me and gave me a scolding as long as the *Song of Sallonia* for ruining my eyes.

Tygyrin laughed. "Would you like some of those plants

for your herbarium?" I must have looked like a bubble of excitement for he laughed some more. "The next time one of my agents travels to…"

"Lord Tygyrin, His Majesty is waiting." Sherriz managed to sound both unctuous and smug, a signature trait. His smile was apologetic, but for a second, the pale blue eyes gloated in the baby-smooth face. I once told Bellizza he must use a pot of face paint every day. She shushed me, but only after we finished giggling.

"In a minute, Chief Minister." Tygyrin's voice was cold.

Sherriz cleared his throat. "The discussion on the blueprint can't wait."

"Will you excuse me, Allii?" Tygyrin lowered his voice. "It's a new weapon, an important matter."

I nodded, keeping my eyes on his long fingers, on his totemic ring, a black lion on a red field.

Tygyrin's lips brushed my head. "I hope to see you in Aunt Bellizza's room in the evening," he murmured and was gone.

I turned around and headed towards the stairway. I should tell Terrii how to make the concoction to reduce his baby's teething pain but I couldn't bring myself to look at him or Kiko.

Pity could sting more than unkindness. I knew.

Terrii would be here in the evening. I'd tell him then.

Once alone on the stairs leading up to my apartment, I balled my hand into a fist and hammered the banister, wishing the polished wood was Sherriz's smooth face. Hurting myself as a way of taking revenge on Sherriz might have made some obscure sense when I was seven, not at seventeen though. I knew it, just as I knew, in some dark seldom-visited crater in my mind, that Father's indifference enabled Sherriz's insolence. Still, my mood lightened with each burst of pain.

Had Nana seen me, I would have got a scolding. "Princesses never show their anger," was another of her precepts, probably the three hundred and fiftieth. "Remember, you are Princess Albalia, the daughter of King Walterin." She never said King Walterin and Queen Filliana.

No one talked about Mother, not even Uncle Bernii, who talked about everything under the sun and the three moons.

I entered my apartment and went straight to my work-room. It housed my most prized possessions: herbaria, book collection, plant presses and the enlarging glasses. I removed the snowflake fern from the plant-press and examined it through the enlarging glass. There was no discoloration.

The rest was routine—don soft cotton gloves, open the herbarium onto a blank page, pick the right brush (quarter-inch for this one), apply the fish-oil paste on the back of the fern, place it on the blank page, write my observations on the facing page.

The next two hours would pass in happy oblivion. I'd be free from Sallonia, wandering among root systems, vegetative shoots, leaves, nodes, and apical buds.

The moth rose was as big as my palm. I held it to my face, relishing the satiny feel of its grey petals, the musky smell.

A scream rang out, long and sharp, like Bellizza's thread knitting needles.

The castle was a place of hushed voices. A full-throated scream was as alien in it as the howl of a cloud-wolf or the screech of a pink-owl.

The scream stopped, as if cut with a knife. Silence returned. A different silence, like that line in the Song of Sallonia:

The silence that comes
After the end, and before the beginning.

One moment I was glued to the stool, moth-rose crushed in my clenched fist. The next moment I was running, out of my apartment and down the stairs.

A crowd milled on the landing, lords and ladies, menservants and maids, even a few officials in their gray robes. Wordless whispers hissed through the air. The door to the royal apartments stood ajar. A guard kept the crowd at bay, using his ceremonial lance as a bar.

I patted my hair to ensure it was where it should be and assumed a sedate descent, one step at a time. Running was one more thing Princess Albalia was not supposed to do, ever, not even if the castle were on fire and the said princess was about to be roasted alive.

The crowd parted for me. The guard bowed. I had no memory of seeing him before.

The entrance chamber was empty. The guards at the door to Father's apartment stood still, eyes fixed on the middle distance. Terrii and Kiko bowed. Terrii opened the door to Bellizza's apartment.

I thanked him. His hands shook worse than my words.

A knot of women huddled by the entrance to the sun-room. Lady Nellin, Bellizza's chief attendant, stood over them, like a malevolent spirit.

The deep carpet swallowed the sound of my hurrying footsteps, but Lady Nellin turned around, her face hardening into a polite mask. She stepped forward in a rustle of red silks and bowed.

"What's wrong, Lady Nellin?"

"One of the maids screamed." Nellin's tone was as expressionless as her face.

I pressed my sweaty palms against the folds of my robe. "Why did the maid scream? Where is the Queen?"

Nellin pursed her lips and pulled the door shut.

The nebulous fear vanished, leaving me in the all too familiar territory of anger. *How dare she, that icicle of malice?*

I reached for the door. Nellin's hand shot out, diamond-glass bangles clinking. I raised my brows. Nellin opened her mouth and closed it. Her hand dropped to her side. She squared her plump shoulders and stepped out of my way.

I opened the door.

A shaft of light struck my eyes, blinding me. The rain had ceased. The kind of sun rarely seen in the wet season had broken through, bright as gold.

I blinked and the room came into focus in slow motion: bay-shaped glass wall overlooking the garden, the red mahogany table, the two chairs…

Bellizza was neither sitting on the chair knitting nor standing by the glass wall staring.

Something glittered on the floor. I looked down.

Bellizza lay sprawled on the flowered carpet.

"Belle!" I dropped on to my knees and cradled her head. "Belle, Belle…"

"Princess…"

I glared at Nellin. "Why are you just standing there? Have you called Doktoras Poll? Get me some pincha leaves and a glass of…"

"She is beyond help, Princess."

"But she…" The words died as I looked and saw.

Bellizza's placid expression was distorted into a grimace. Her midnight blue eyes were glassy. A touch of foam spotted the perfectly shaped lips. Blood-infused saliva traced a delicate line down the chin.

The body I cradled was still, with the kind of stillness that had no place in life.

A hand jammed into my mouth forcing the scream down. It took me a while to realize the hand was mine. It shook, like the rest of me.

I waited till my teeth ceased chattering. "What happened? When did…" A sob rose, choking me. I allowed my head to fall, to hide my brimming eyes.

Nellin's voice had no life in it. "Her maid and I came with her tisane and found her dead."

Dead—the word slashed my innards.

"How?"

"Doktoras Poll is on his way."

"My father?"

"Chief Minister Sherriz has been informed. He will apprise His Majesty."

I smoothed the disordered blue waves and kissed the

cooling brow. Bellizza's familiar scent, the subtle perfume of moon-lilies, enveloped me. I laid her gently on the carpet and stumbled to my feet, almost slipping on a silver needle.

Bellizza had been knitting when whatever happened to her happened. The red and white thread-tree, now three-quarters finished, lay close to one awkwardly angled arm.

I staggered to the glass wall and leaned against it, wrapping my trembling arms around my shuddering body. The sunroom was warm. The cold came from inside me.

"What is this? What is this?"

Doktoras Poll had not come alone. Father was with him, and Sherriz.

I said, "Papa, I'm sorry." Or tried to. The words were unintelligible even to my own ears.

Perhaps Father didn't hear. He didn't look at me, but stood gazing down at his wife of eleven years. His usual earth-brown color had vanished, his face was drawn.

The sun disappeared behind a gray counterpane of clouds. The room sank into shadows. My eyes moved aimlessly, like fluttering moths, from Father's blank face to Nellin's tormented one, Doktoras Poll's kneeling-form, the flowery carpet, the white and red thread-tree, the picture from the past, the thread-box, the white and red…

A mist blanketed my eyes. My head began to spin in a crazy whirl. I reached out for something unmoving…

A hand caught my elbow in a firm grip. "Highness, you are in shock. You must retire to your room." Doktoras Poll's voice was kind. "You need rest, sleep."

I tried to smile. Poll had been my mother's friend. He had known me all my life, since he delivered me.

He turned to Father. "The Princess has had a shock, Sire. She needs to rest. And, er, I'd like to examine Her Majesty, if you would give me leave."

Father nodded, his hands clenching and unclenching at his sides.

I said, again, "Papa, I'm sorry." This time I could hear my words.

Father bent his head to listen to Sherriz, a muscle on his left cheek twitching.

Suddenly Nana was there, cuddling me. "There, there, my Allikin, come away, love. You need sleep." Her tone was a lullaby.

I hesitated and gave in. I'd talk to Father later.

I woke up to a room dappled with shadows.

The sheer curtains offered a glimpse of a gray sky. Morning or evening? Morning. Coiffure-birds chattered outside, and they only sang in the morning.

The stone-light on the bedside table created a golden halo. Nana dozed in a chair by the bed. Her face was deeply lined, like the bark of an ancient tree. Her breath wheezed through her half-open mouth. With her piercing eyes closed, she looked strangely fragile.

Nana had been the biggest staple in my life, whose presence I never questioned, like the sun or the rain. Seeing her thus, devoid of her aura of authority, made me realize she wasn't an eternal force of nature, but an old woman who would one day die—

Like Bellizza.

A memory flashed, me at six, kneeling on a chair by an upstairs window, craning my neck to catch a glimpse of my new stepmother. The silver carriage coming to a stop by the main entrance of the castle; Bellizza stepping out, her blue hair flowing down to her ankles, like the waters of the Sky River…

The memory segued into another memory, of Bellizza lying dead, her head cushioned by her hair.

Bellizza once told me that she never saw her marriage contract. It was signed by her brother and my father. Her brother undertook to secure the north-eastern trade routes for Sallonia. Father agreed to sell Sallikan to Bellizza's brother at a fixed prize. They were both keen on the marriage. Trade routes were vital to Sallonian commerce; Sallikan— a metal of exceptional strength and suppleness, an essential component of mechanical pigeons, mechanical bulls and mechanical carriages—was available only in Sallonia.

Bellizza was the sealant of the new alliance.

Married at eighteen, dead at twenty nine; eleven years of wedded bliss in between, marked by nine failed pregnancies.

That shouldn't have been your life, Belle.

I closed my stinging eyes and wished for yesterday, any yesterday except the last one. I'd go to Bellizza's room after breakfast. We'd spend the morning together. I might read something to her or she might have some news of her favorite sister, the one who ran away from an unwanted marriage to become a stargazer.

A hand caressed my cheek. A voice muttered a prayer to One God.

I opened my eyes and looked into Nana's red-rimmed ones, not sharp anymore but blotched with fear.

"Sherriz wants to talk to you." Something in Nana's voice reminded me of the screeching of ulliina, the little brown bird of death. "Wanted me to wake you up. I said no, he'll wait till you woke up in your own time, urgent or not."

I sat up in bed. "Nana, they'd want to talk to me about Bellizza. Tell them I'll be with them shortly."

A knock rang, sharper than any I could remember. The door opened and Nellin walked in, wrapped in a dull green robe, the color of mourning. Her face had lines that hadn't been there yesterday. She bowed to me but addressed Nana. "You informed the Princess?"

I cut in. "She did. And I've already given my answer. Now if you'll excuse me—" I got up and walked to the bathing-chamber. As I closed the door, I caught a glimpse of Nellin's expression. No known poison could have come close to its venom.

I paused by the door to the anteroom, holding my head high and my back straight. I didn't want Sherriz to see how shaken I was.

It wasn't Sherriz who awaited me, but old Minister Ekko, leaning heavily on his black and silver walking stick.

I smiled a greeting and sat down, indicating he should do the same. He stood there for a few seconds, gazing at me. Tears started trickling down his thin, parchment like cheeks and he let them. It was as if he didn't realize he was crying. I wanted to put my arms around him, to comfort him. But such a display would violate royal protocol and probably embarrass him as well.

"The queen's death is a great loss," I began, my voice quite steady. "I saw her maybe an hour before..." The memories lashed at me. I stopped, battling my own tears.

"Highness, Princess—" Ekko swallowed and started again, this time in a slightly steadier voice. "The queen was poisoned."

I fell back in my chair.

Poisoned, poisoned, poisoned, poisoned...

Minister Ekko was droning on. I forced myself to listen. "—nivati."

Nivati. I tried to remember what I'd read about nivati plants. But my memory was gone, like Bellizza.

"According to Doktoras Poll, it's a fast-acting poison. He says paralysis would have set in within seconds. She wouldn't have suffered."

I tried to murmur a prayer of thanks. The familiar words eluded me.

Ekko had been studying the carpet now he addressed it. "The poison was administered through a rose-apple."

"I took the queen two rose-apples from my indoor tree—" I stopped, touched by a ripple of dread. "Did you say the poison was in a rose-apple?"

Ekko swallowed. His eyes never left the carpet, and he continued to address himself to it. "Yes, Highness."

I have no clear recollection of what happened next, between the time Minister Ekko said his fateful words and the time I was escorted to my room by royal guards—the only suspect in the murder of my stepmother.

Did I protest my innocence? Did I ask to see Father? Did I demand a chance to clear myself? Of any of it, I retained no recollection.

All I had were three memory fragments.

Minister Ekko muttering, his voice tremulous, "They are saying you hated the queen because she took your mother's place."

Nana wailing, "My baby, my baby, she killed nobody. My Allikin—" Until her was voice was cut off, as if by a knife.

Lady Nellin storming into the room, face crusted into a mask of hate, voice throbbing, "Why did you kill her? I thought you were clever. Didn't you know you were safe only so long as she was there? Why did you have to kill her?"

2
DRAMATIC INJUSTICE

*"They strove, over oceans and forests, valleys and hills,
never despairing, for their faith was as pure as crystal."*
Song of Sallonia – Book One

MOON MOTHS CREATED BLOTCHES OF SILVER ON THE
bedside table, on the carpet, even on the bed.

Nana must have forgotten to close the curtains. The
moon moths would have streamed in through the open
window heading for the stone-light on the bedside table,
and death.

Death.

Bits of memory fluttered like moth wings. Is Bellizza
dead? Did someone accuse me of killing Bellizza?

I cried, "Nana—Nana," And bit my tongue to stop the
scream.

Closely spaced grilles barred the windows.

I sprang out of bed and rushed about my apartment trying door after door. The doors leading to my dressing chamber, bathing chamber, sitting room, and the anteroom were unlocked. The doors leading to my workroom and the passageway were locked, from outside.

Every window was barred with gleaming silver-iron grilles.

My rooms were on the third floor. Did whoever who ordered this horror think I could climb down a marble wall, with not so much as a reedy vine or a minute crack to help me?

I rang the bell for Nana, rang and rang. There was no Nana.

No books either. The bookshelves on the flanks of my writing cabinet were empty.

Fear was clogging my mind. I knelt before the frieze depicting One God in his seven manifestations and tried to pray. The words came out in a jumble. I gave up and focused instead on his image as Lawgiver. Scroll in the right hand, cudgel in the left, right foot resting on the back of a supine figure, presumably a wrongdoer, it was an effective antidote even for mindless panic.

Soon I discovered another antidote—getting dressed on my own.

I managed the underskirt and the slippers, but tying the bodice and buttoning the robe proved to be superhuman tasks; at least they required superhuman patience. Attempts to achieve my usual braided-topknot constituted the greatest of my list of failures. Eventually I settled for a plain topknot, jabbing pin after pin to keep the wobbling mass in place.

I emerged from the dressing chamber to find a meal awaiting me in the sitting room, together with Lady Nellin and two strange women dressed in the brown trouser-blouse uniform of castle maids.

"They will attend to your needs." Lady Nellin paused and added, "Highness."

"Where's Nana?"

"Dame Nanarina is indisposed."

I clenched my fingers inside the pockets of my robe. "What's wrong with her?"

"She is being treated."

"I want to see her."

"I'm afraid that's impossible." Nellin's voice was polite, yet insolent. It was as if she were daring me to stamp my foot, raise my voice, throw a tantrum…

Inside the capacious pockets, my fingers twitched. I turned to the ornamental mirror hanging above the silver-inlaid half table and made a show of examining my hair, watching Nellin from under my eyelids.

"The maids will be outside." Nellin's voice was as flat as the dusty plains of southern Sallonia. "They'll come when you ring the bell."

I toyed with a stray copper curl, tucking it behind my ear, studying the effect as if nothing else in the world mattered.

Nellin glared at my back, before flouncing out, followed by the two maids.

Once alone, I inspected the food, a pot of hot pomegranate juice and a plate of toasted honey-cheese—mid-morning fare. No marsh-clouds, the soft green sweets made from mallow plants. I had come to dislike marsh-clouds, and ate them only to please Nana. Now I ached for them, just one piece, soft like moth wings, like Nana's touch, like Bellizza's voice—

I crammed some food into my mouth and sat at my writing cabinet. Whoever took away my books had been considerate enough to leave me some writing paper and two pens. I wrote to Father, begging for an opportunity to clear my name and for permission to attend Bellizza's funeral.

When I rang the bell, the maids came in.

I smiled at them. "Are you two new here? What are your names?"

There were no answering smiles or answers.

I held out the letter. "This is for the King. Can you please make sure it reaches him?"

One of them, taller and thinner than the other, took the letter.

Afterward, I sat on a chair and watched the air-clock on the writing cabinet.

Two hours and eight minutes later, a knock sounded. One of the maids entered and said the Chief Minister would like to see me.

Was Sherriz Father's answer to my plea for help?

Rage came first, followed by despair. Then they were gone, leaving me empty, bereft.

I forced myself out of the chair, went to the dressing room and examined myself in the floor-length mirror. My topknot wobbled every time I moved my head. I inserted a few more hairpins at random and smoothed away a crease in my robe. About the sickly gray pallor discoloring my coppery face I could do nothing, not without a pot or two of war paint.

Sherriz and three other ministers were waiting in the anteroom. Their bows had the usual depth. I inclined my head and sat down. Sherriz perched on the other chair. The retinue ranged behind him.

"Why am I being detained in this manner?" I asked, pleased my voice didn't shake the way my insides did.

Sherriz cleared his throat. "A mere formality, Highness. The demands of justice must be met. It mustn't be said the laws were bent because of your high position as his majesty's beloved only child."

The sarcasm didn't escape me, but I felt relieved. It made sense. The law had to be the same for everyone. It would protect me because it protected innocents.

Sherriz consulted a paper. "Highness, may I ask you some questions?"

"Please do. I'm as eager as you are to discover who killed the Queen." My mouth started trembling at the thought of Bellizza. I bit my lip hard, stilling the tremor.

"What sort of relationship did you have with the queen?"

I blinked and stared. "Would you mind repeating the question please?"

"Highness, what sort of a relationship did you have with the late Queen Bellizza?"

I knitted my brows. "We were friends, as you well know, Chief Minister."

Sherriz jotted down something. "Did you feel Queen Bellizza was coming between you and your father?"

Either my ears were playing tricks, or Sherriz had lost his memory. This time when I answered, my voice was taut with suppressed anger. "You know the queen did everything in her power to bring my father and me closer. And I don't understand the relevance of these questions."

He scrawled again, the pen moving over the paper with ponderous dignity. "Did you resent your stepmother for taking your mother's place?"

That did it. One of us had to be mad. "I didn't resent my stepmother. I loved her." *Stop shrieking, Allii.* "Shouldn't you be asking me about this supposedly poisoned rose-apple? That's why I'm under suspicion, isn't it?"

"Highness, I will decide on the manner of this proceeding, not you."

I glared at Sherriz, trying not to scream at him. "I want to see my father."

Sherriz flashed a thin smile. "His Majesty is in mourning. He is not seeing anyone."

"Other than you." The words were out before I could stop them.

His thin smile widened a fraction. "Indeed, Highness. Now, are you refusing to answer my questions?"

His eyes caught mine and held them. There was a challenge in his gaze. I looked away first. He held all the cards. I was not just powerless. I was also in the power of this man who for some reason had never liked me.

I tried to cover myself with the tatters of my torn dignity. "I have no intention of not answering your questions."

Sherriz bowed. "What did you feel about your father's marriage?"

"I can't remember. It was a long time ago."

"Did you fear that your prospects would be adversely affected by a sibling?"

I took a deep breath, steadying myself. "Since Sallonian law doesn't permit a queen-regnant, your question is irrelevant. Why aren't you asking me about the supposedly poisoned rose-apple?"

Sherriz's pale blue eyes met mine. "May I remind you that you are not in a position to make demands?"

"I'm demanding justice."

"You will be given justice."

My hands clenched. I unclenched them. Princess Albalia thumping Chief Minister Sherriz on his lying mouth would be deemed unseemly. Plus it wouldn't do me any favors. And I had a favor to ask.

"I want to pay my last respects to the queen, Chief Minister, to be present at her funeral. I would be most grateful if you could arrange it."

Sherriz rolled the papers into a neat cylinder. "The queen's last rites were performed at dawn, Highness."

There was a story I loved as a child, of a giant trapped in a cave. He ate whatever he could find, rodents, slugs, ferns-A few holes on the roof brought in breathable air and a hint of the sun. To keep track of the weeks, months and years, he made marks on the walls with a nail he pulled out of his own boot, one dash per day.

In the end, he ran out of places for his dashes.

My prison was my suite of rooms. Maids brought my meals from the royal kitchen. They did my laundry, made my bed, dusted, swept, took away used stone-lights and brought back re-powered ones. They didn't return my smiles and ignored my greetings and thanks.

Nellin accompanied them often. Though her tongue remained silent, her grief-haunted eyes continued to accuse me.

Every morning my interrogators descended on me. Sherriz asked the same questions, again and again. After they left, I was on my own.

I spent the crawling hours writing letters. I wrote to Father begging for justice and permission to visit Bellizza's grave. I wrote to Nana asking after her health, telling her how much I missed her. I wrote to Prince Bernalin (Uncle Bernii, Father's cousin and heir, and my favorite relative) explaining my predicament. I wrote to Doktoras Poll assuring him the poisoned rose-apple couldn't have been mine. I wrote to Cousin Tygyrin asking for books. I wrote to Minister Ekko reminding him that both entrances to the Queen's Apartment were guarded, and requesting him to obtain for me a list of all those who were in the Apartment at the time of the murder or came in from outside.

I had no idea whether the letters were even delivered. Still I wrote.

※

On the fifth day of my imprisonment, Sherriz's questions turned into statements.

"We have been informed that two days before the queen's arrival in Sallonia, you cried and said you hated her."

I shrugged.

"Three days before the wedding you said if your stepmother tried to mother you, you would," Sherriz looked at the piece of paper in his hand, "you would pull her blue hair until she was blue in the face."

I resisted the urge to stamp my foot and shrugged again.

When they were gone, I strode about the room, driven by memories.

The wedding festivities for Father and Bellizza had lasted seven days, as dictated by Sallonian traditions. The ceremonies would begin with dawn and continue late into the night, well past my bedtime. Each night, a pageant was staged depicting a portion of Sallonians' epic journey to their new homeland. It was followed by one of the seven traditional Sallonian dances: water-pot dance, peacock dance, red-mammoth dance, fire-pole dance, planting dance, harvesting dance, and winnowing dance.

On the first night, I tossed and turned in bed, wishing I was down there watching the fun. Suddenly there was a murmur of voices in the antechamber, and a knock on the door. It opened and Bellizza peeped in.

"May I come?"

I nodded, trying to smile.

Bellizza closed the door, walked over to the bed, and placed a silver box on the bedside table. "Cocolade balls, infused with honey."

My mouth watered. Cocolade was a luxury even for a princess.

Bellizza smiled, "In my land, there are Cocolade trees."

I gulped. "Cocolade trees?"

"Well, trees with pods from which cocolade is made." A shadow that had nothing to do with the dim light in the room fell over her face. "I'm going to miss them."

I looked at Bellizza, saw the darkness in her eyes and realized she would never see her own home again. She'd have to spend the rest of her life among people who looked so very different to her, people with yellow or brown hair and brown skins, other than me of course, with my copper-colored hair and copper-colored skin. The only time Bellizza would see a blue-haired, pearl-skinned person would be when she looked in a mirror.

Would that make her lonely, sad? Did Mother feel the same way? She too would have been the only red-haired, black-skinned person in the entire realm.

The thought disturbed me, for a reason I didn't understand. So did the silence eddying around us.

I asked in a rush, "Are you going to be my new mother?"

Bellizza had been staring at a painting on the wall. She turned towards me. There was no smile on her face. She looked solemn. "Do you want me to?"

A no was impossible. I said nothing.

Bellizza nodded. "You have Nanarina to mother you. I'd like to be your friend. I'd like us to be friends."

Bellizza had kept her promise. I hadn't. Had I stayed with her that afternoon, instead of seeking the more exciting company of my plants, I could have saved her. The murderer wouldn't have been able to poison Bellizza with nivati—

Nivati.

I had a nivati plant in my indoor garden, bush-like with long satiny-green leaves and yellow flowers. Its berries killed slowly, and painfully, after hours of agonizing convulsions.

The way Bellizza looked in death was etched in my mind. Her body bore signs of some pain, but not convulsions.

Bellizza was poisoned, but not with nivati.

Doktoras Poll would know the properties of nivati. Even if he didn't he could have checked it in a book.

What he said about nivati was no honest mistake, no accidental error. He, who was my mother's friend, who was present at my birth and her death, lied to pin Bellizza's murder on me.

Why? Why? Why?

Panic washed over me in unrelenting waves. I began saying plant names out loud in alphabetical order. By the time the list was over, the evening was advanced, exhaustion had obliterated panic, and I could think.

My plight was not due to my usual bugbears, Sherriz's malice, Nellin's spite, and Father's indifference. It was the result of a conspiracy, which involved Poll, Sherriz, and probably Nellin. The whys of the conspiracy still eluded me, but its implications were all too clear. I was alone, surrounded by people who wished me harm. To expect any justice from them would be lunacy. I had to find my own way out.

The grilles barred one way out. Even if I managed to overpower the maids and get out of the door, I wouldn't go far.

I had my casket of jewels. Nellin wasn't bribable, but the

maids might be. Perhaps if I made a show of compliance, my enemies would relax a little, and the maids might be less hostile, more open to persuasion—

As flimsy as a moth's wing.

I brushed the thought aside. The plan had enough holes to double up as a sieve, but I could think of nothing better. I'd pretend to be compliant and bide my time.

Maybe I'd even learn something to my advantage, as they say in the books.

I wanted to laugh, laugh until there was no laughter left in me.

※

At first, responding to outrageous statements with polite words was teeth-gritting tough. But with each new day, the pretence became easier, more natural.

As I became more docile, Sherriz turned friendlier. On the eleventh day of my imprisonment, he shifted the interrogation onto a new track, from Mean Princess Albalia hated Good Queen Bellizza to Evil Queen Bellizza detested Innocent Princess Albalia.

"Highness, were you aware that the queen disliked you?" Sherriz's tone was sympathetic, even friendly.

Was my plan working? I conjured an ingratiating smile. "The queen didn't hate me."

Sherriz shook his head. "You were too trusting, Highness." His voice was sad and a little stern, almost a parody of Nana's. "Did you know she was trying to ruin your prospects?"

I opened my eyes as wide as possible. "I can't believe she would do such a thing."

"The king found a great match for you. She persuaded him to abandon it."

I had been staring at my hands, which I always kept folded on my lap. At those words my head shot up.

Sherriz watched me, his eyes as wide and as guileless as an excited baby's.

I closed my eyes.

Soon after my sixteenth birthday, an emissary from the Kikilonian Empire had arrived with a proposal. Nana had wept with joy. "I knew my baby-princess was destined for greatness," she said, holding my face in her cupped hands. "You might even be an empress, my love."

I laughed. "It's the fourth son, Nana, not the heir."

Nana's expression hardened. "One God can make many things happen."

That evening, I went to Father's library and looked in the books. I don't remember being happy or unhappy about the proposal. I just wanted to know everything possible about the country which might become my new home. "Knowledge can spare you much trouble," Uncle Bernii used to say.

On the second day of reading, I discovered a fertility rite still practiced in the Kikilonian Empire. Every royal bride had to live one year in isolation, in a special palace. Her only duty was to rear a newly-born yellow ram. Once the year was up, she had to sacrifice the ram by beheading him at the temple of One God. The consummation of the marriage would happen that night.

The book slipped from my fingers. I ran to Bellizza.

Bellizza was in the Green Room, a large chamber filled with artificial trees and mechanical birds, relaxing on a day-bed. Nellin sat on a low chair, watching her.

They looked up when I went in, Nellin's frown darker than a thundercloud. Bellizza held out a hand. "Allii, what is wrong?"

"May I have a word alone?"

Bellizza signaled to Nellin who threw me a murderous glare before closing the door behind her.

I sat by Bellizza. "I don't want this marriage."

Bellizza frowned. "But why, Allii? It's a good match. You will occupy a position of honour."

I told her.

Bellizza's eyes caught mine and held them. "Is this horrible fertility rite the only reason you don't want this marriage? You haven't formed an attachment to someone?"

I laughed. "As if I have the chance, Belle! Or do you think I'm spoilt for choice between Sherriz, and Doktoras Poll, and Chief Priest Pena?" I stopped noticing the anxious expression in Bellizza's face. "Belle, I swear, when I dream, it's about roaming the world looking for new plants."

Bellizza's stare had continued, as if trying to read my innermost thoughts. Then she had given a lopsided smile. "I'll talk to your father. He is unlikely to refuse me." She had placed her hand on her heavy stomach, and added, "Not for a week or two."

Tears were misting my eyes. I blinked them back and touched my forehead. "May we stop for today, Chief

Minister? My head is aching."

Sherriz stood with alacrity and bowed.

I nodded my thanks and hurried to my bedroom.

Stars die, Bellizza once told me. They are born, they live, and they die like us. Bellizza had been like a new star when she came to Sallonia to marry my father, young, beautiful, shining with happiness and hope. A decade later, she resembled a dead star, still young, still beautiful, but with a beauty dulled by grief and despair.

Through the barred window, I watched a flock of rainbirds circling high above the lawn. Suddenly the birds folded their wings allowing themselves to drop. They dipped so fast, I feared they had died or lost their minds. But a few feet from the ground, they spread their wings and soared, higher and higher.

I tried to count them, but they were too fast for me.

The fourteenth day of my imprisonment began with a knock on the door. One of the maids entered saying Lord Pena begged the favor of a word.

Pena, Chief Priest of One God, a man who ignored me whenever possible. What did he want? Question me? Spy on me?

I nodded assent.

Seconds later, Pena strode into the room. He was probably the only person in the castle, other than Father, who didn't color his age-blackened hair. Father's few black hairs were almost invisible amidst his deep brown crop.

Pena's age-blackened strands streaked his thick shoulder-length yellow hair in neat stripes.

He bowed to me, his expression grave. "Lord Tygyrin wanted me to convey his warmest regards, Highness."

My heart leaped. "Why didn't he come?"

"You are not allowed visitors, Highness. Even I had some difficulty obtaining permission to see you. But your religious needs must be attended to, as the Chief Minister was compelled to concur." He smiled a little, baring stained teeth. "I also wanted to reassure you about Dame Nanarina. She is worried, almost out of her mind, about you. I want to place her mind at rest by telling her I saw you with my own eyes and you are as well as you can be in these difficult circumstances."

I struggled with an urge to burst into tears. "Thank you for your kindness to Nana, Lord Pena."

He bowed. "I visit her often, Highness, to pray with her and provide her what succor I can."

I wiped my eyes with the back of my hand. "I wrote to her many times."

Pena cleared his throat. "If you have any message for her, Highness, I promise to convey it word to word." He paused and added, in his usual brusque voice, "Whoever has forsaken you, Highness, One God has not. Now shall we pray for your safe deliverance from this troubled sea?"

On the nineteenth day of my imprisonment, Sherriz had a new question.

"Highness, we know the queen corresponded regularly with her siblings, except the sister who ran away. We are informed that she shared the contents of those letters with you. What can you tell us about them?"

I kept my eyes on my clasped hands, hoping he didn't notice the instinctive jerk of my head. "She told me news from her home. About births, marriages, illnesses, and deaths." I looked up with what I hoped was a sweet smile. "If you ask me specific questions, they might jog my memory and help me answer."

Sherriz evaded my eyes, swallowed and moved on to a standard groove.

Once Sherriz and his attending officials were gone, I paced about, trying to make sense of what I heard.

Sherriz didn't know that Bellizza corresponded regularly with Kummizza, the sister who ran away to become a stargazer. That could mean only one thing. They didn't use mechanical pigeons for their correspondence.

Why? Mechanical pigeons were faster and more reliable than human couriers. And the letters Bellizza had read out to me seemed rather innocuous.

No, the parts she read out to me were innocuous. Perhaps other parts were not.

What happened to those letters? Did Nellin hide them? Or did Bellizza destroy them?

Suddenly I remembered the bundle of candles I saw inside a drawer of Bellizza's writing desk. I had been looking for a pen for her and barely glanced at the candles. Now the memory blazed before me.

Candles were used by people who couldn't afford stone-lights, not by queens in castles where massive stone-lights turned night into day.

Candles had one advantage over stone-lights, though. They could be used to burn things, such as not-so-innocuous letters.

I walked up to the window and gripped the grille.

Bellizza had told me that she and Kummizza had no secrets from each other. If Bellizza knew or suspected she were in danger, she would have shared that information with Kummizza. Kummizza might have kept those letters. Even if not, she'd remember the important parts. If I could reach her, I might be able to discover who or what Bellizza feared.

To do that I'd have to escape—

I had not thought about escaping for days. At some point my pretended docility had turned real. I had given up on freedom, on myself.

It was like waking up from a long fervid sleep.

Docility was dangerous, to me. I needed a new plan.

Ж

The next day, I informed Sherriz I will not answer any more questions.

Sherriz stared, as did his minions. One of them, I'd no idea who, made a sound which could have been a muffled cough or a suppressed chuckle.

I got up. "Don't bother to come again. If in a week I'm not put on trial, I'll starve myself to death." I smiled politely, said, "I wish a good day to all of you," and left.

They wouldn't allow me to starve to death. They couldn't. It would look bad. So they'd have to put me on trial. I had no faith in their justice. But to put me on trial, they'll have to take me out of this place. That might give me a chance to escape.

Of course, they'd try to break my resolution by piling me with all my culinary favorites. Suddenly I was assailed by memories, the sharp scent of lemongrass pies, the way starberry cakes would crumble at the touch, the taste of honey-infused cocolade balls especially brought down from Bellizza's land—

I clenched my hands. I will resist whatever temptation they throw my way. I must, for myself, for Bellizza.

I will not be a moth flailing against the light. I will be a firefly guided by her own light.

And I will paint the night in the brightest colors I could find.

Three days passed. Three days of absolutely nothing. No Sherriz, no news.

On the fourth evening, the maids set the dinner table under Lady Nellin's supervision and left. I sat down and unfolded the linen napkin. Something fell out, a small piece of paper.

At first I stared at it, my mind a blank. Then I grabbed it with a shaking hand. It took me a while to read, as the words gyrated before my eyes.

Be ready tonight.

No name. Just the three words. The handwriting was

unfamiliar, but that meant nothing. I wouldn't know the handwriting of most people in the castle.

I read the note again and again, until the paper was drenched with my sweat. Then I tore it into the tiniest possible pieces, and dropped each one out into the open through the grilles.

The wind and the rain would take care of them.

When the maids arrived to remove the dishes, I studied them while pretending to be immersed in painting my finger nails. Which one would have taken the risk of secreting the note? After all, if the woman were caught, she'd end up in a far less comfortable prison than mine. Why take such a risk? The note-bringer might have been bribed, but who did the bribing? Why? Could it be a trap? Am I being set up?

I'd know soon enough.

Once the maids were gone, I hurried into the dressing room, tore off the robe and put on my riding costume of trousers and long tunic, the thickest socks I could find, walking shoes, and my favorite hooded cloak. I pulled out various undergarments from drawers and made a bundle with a blanket. Then I unpinned the topknot and braided my hair, to keep it out of the way. Finally I rummaged in a drawer of my writing cabinet for the pair of silver thread-knitting needles Bellizza had given me years ago. I put them in my pocket, sharp reminders of a life lost and promises to keep.

Waiting was a form of torture. I forced myself to sit, forced myself to count the seconds. I had reached two hundred and fifty six when I heard the soft knock.

My stomach started churning so much I feared I was going to be sick.

The key turned. The door opened a crack. A figure stepped into the room. The gait was familiar, as well as the stick clasped in one hand.

"I should have known it was you," I told Minister Ekko softly.

Ekko's smile was watery. "Not just me, as I told you. Once you are out of here, head for the Great Southern Road. Prince Bernalin will be waiting for you."

"Uncle Bernii," I whispered, my voice throbbing with joy.

Ekko took a bulging pouch from a pocket. "The only thing I can give you, my dear princess. Money."

I took the pouch. "You are giving me my life."

"I promised your mother I'd look after you."

I said, "Papa…" and stopped, not knowing how to continue.

Ekko avoided my eyes. That was answer enough.

"Is Nana well?"

He nodded, even though he still avoided my eyes.

I put my arms around Ekko in an awkward embrace. It violated the court etiquette, but I didn't care. He hesitated and returned my embrace.

A figure in a hooded cloak stood in the passage. I almost laughed for joy. Panda the forester, a friend who had introduced me to many a rare plant.

Panda bowed. "Highness, please come with me." He turned around and started walking with silent steps.

I was about to follow when Ekko caught my arm. "Trust no one, Princess," he whispered, his voice urgent. "Trust no one, I beg of you. No one."

3

A NIGHT IN A FOREST

"As the sun appeared in the eastern sky, they reached the summit of the mountain and looked down upon a land as fair as the new dawn. As one, they knelt and gave thanks."
Song of Sallonia — Book One

I THOUGHT I KNEW THE CASTLE FROM THE ATTICS TO THE cellars. But where Panda was taking me, I had never been. The staircases were narrow, corridors uncarpeted, walls bare and everything ill-lit. The strangeness of this familiar place added another layer to the sense of unreality that had possessed me since the day of Bellizza's murder. It also kept fear at bay. It was like being in a dream where danger was illusory and life didn't end with death.

Panda opened one more door and the sense of unreality ended. We were outside the castle, in a walled kitchen garden. The rain lashed at me, its taste on my lips slightly bitter. The wind whipped at the trees making them bend, the way courtiers did when they came into Father's presence.

We hurried through the kitchen garden into the wide lawn that lay between the posterior of the castle and the royal wood. I stopped and looked up at the second floor. Darkness reigned, except for a single flickering light. Was Father still up? What was he doing? Reading an important document? Pacing? Thinking of Bellizza? Thinking of me?

I wanted to run back, to tell him I loved Bellizza and would have never done her harm. If I could talk to him face to face, if he listened to what I had to say, he'd have to believe me wouldn't he?

Wouldn't he?

The hope was as fragile as a moth. I'd never reach him. I'd be caught and locked up, again. And Father wouldn't lift a finger to save me. He didn't do so all this time. Why should he act differently now?

I also had to consider the people who were risking themselves to help me. It was one thing to be stupid and get caught, quite another thing to let my friends down.

I sighed and turned away.

Panda had been standing still, as if the wind and the rain were things that happened to other people. He didn't tell me to hurry, just resumed walking, silent and sure-footed as a nocturnal animal. I followed, struggling with the absence of light and with a terrain that had been transformed by the rain into a bog. The howling of the wind drowned out the sounds I made as I slid and stumbled.

We reached the royal woods without being spotted.

Panda avoided the walkways, taking paths only he could see, until we reached an unguarded exit.

He fetched a small stone-light from his pocket and gave it to me. "Go that way, Highness," he said, pointing with his hand. "Soon you'll reach a fork. Turn to the left then. It's the Great Southern Road." His voice turned a little diffident. "It's not far, and there aren't any wild creatures. I wish I could go with you. I wanted to, but was told I mustn't."

After the hostility and indifference of the last several weeks, Panda's concern for my safety made me want to cry. I held out my hand. "I wish you were coming with me too, Panda. Thank you for helping me. I'm more grateful than I can ever say."

He mumbled something, but didn't take my hand. For an ordinary Sallonian man, touching a royal woman was a crime punishable by flogging.

I smiled at him. "I'm no longer a princess, Panda. I'm a fugitive. You have been a friend to me, when I needed a friend the most."

He took my hand, looking at me directly for the first time. "I never believed you killed the queen. There are many who don't. Someday, you'll be back, Highness. You have more friends than you know."

I reached the fork in the road sooner than I expected.

The Great Southern Road was an arterial road connecting the Sallonian capital, Pinckossia, with the Sapoo mountain range which marked the kingdom's southern border.

Where the other road led I had no idea. I've heard rumors of course; maids whispered about a dangerously mysterious forest where a young woman—why was it always a young woman?—could meet with a fate worse than death, whatever that was.

In my case, a fate worse than death would be an encounter with Sherriz at the head of a troop of guards, baby blue eyes twinkling with malicious triumph.

I turned to the Great Southern Road and hurried. Soon the nightmare would be over, and I'd be with Uncle Bernii, safe. From there I could make my way to Kummizza. Perhaps Uncle himself would take me.

The wind rose. Giant trees—mice-ears with their red and white patterned bark, and cannonballs, their trunks dotted with yellow fruits—writhed. Crow-nettle bushes lined the roadside, their thin branches covered not with leaves but with thorns. Thorns long and sharp like Bellizza's thread-knitting needles.

Bellizza.

I stood still as if wind and rain weren't happening.

Bellizza was killed not by a stranger, but by someone she knew, and possibly trusted.

Minister Ekko's warning echoed in my ears. *"Trust no one, I beg of you. No one."*

What did he mean by that? And before that—before those cryptic words, when I thanked him, he said there were others involved. He said, *as I told you.*

The only way he could have told me about anything was through a letter. And the only note I received contained no such information or any information. Just three words.

Realization was louder than a thunderclap. Ekko's explanatory letter had fallen into the wrong hands. I was headed not towards Uncle Bernii and freedom, but a trap.

I looked around wildly, trying to think of a plan. My panic-ridden gaze fell on a crow-nettle bush—and I knew what to do to escape the trap.

I took off my hooded cloak, threw it over the bush, and started pulling at it. The thorns were tenacious; with each pull, the cloak tore. I counted to twenty and let go, allowing the bush to take the torn cloak. I ran back until I reached the fork, and turned right.

The path I wasn't supposed to take was more a mud track than a road. It wended through a dark forest, like a corkscrew. I had no idea where it was taking me, no plan about what I should do. My only care was to put as much distance between me and the castle.

The rain slowed to a drizzle and stopped. The wind ceased howling. The clouds parted to reveal a sliver of Nila, the blue moon.

When I first heard the sound, I thought it was the trees. But the trees were still; not a leaf moved.

I tapped off the stone-light and listened.

Someone or something grunted.

Terror gripped me with icy claws. A maid's whispered tale came to my mind, about monsters lurking in the forest, waiting for unwary females, yearning for new blood and young flesh. I strained my ears and heard words, a muttered curse.

Skin off a Muffie.

Not monsters. Worse. People.

I shoved the stone-light into my tunic pocket, hurried off the path, and crouched behind a half-wall of leafy bushes.

"—mistake, I tell you." The voice was hoarse, as if its owner had a sore throat. "She took the big road."

"Have to follow orders." The second voice was reedy. "If they find her there they'll sound the horn. We look here until then."

I peeped. The men were soldiers, though not of the castle guard. Their uniform was unfamiliar. In the flittering moonlight, I glimpsed an insignia, some animal or bird.

Behind the leafy rampart, I began to shiver, a shiver that had nothing to do with my sodden clothes or the chill in the air. The back of my neck started to itch. I longed to scratch it. The next thing would be a sneeze, the way it always happened in books.

"What I don't understand is..." the hoarse voice continued, "if she could get out using magic, why didn't she just fly away? Why'd she have to kill that poor sod—"

A wordless cry assaulted my ears. I barely recognized my voice in it.

Silence fell, rock-heavy, broken by a muffled noise.

The soldiers were leaving the track, entering the forest in search of that sound.

Panic welled inside me. My legs wanted to run. I stilled the urge. They'd outrun me easily. Even if I slipped through their hands, it would be of little use. They'd have arrow-guns, and long-distance horns to summon reinforcements.

I knew what panic did to hunted animals. Better to stay where I was and hope they'd somehow not see me.

My universe became reduced to sounds. The squelch of boots in mud. A curse as a foot slipped. The slash of a blade clearing bracken. A hoarse cough, hastily stifled.

Then silence.

"Got her!"

Hands, like vices, grabbed me, held me. The stink of stale sweat clogged my nostrils.

My arms were trapped but my feet were free. I kicked, connected with flesh, heard a groan, and kicked again.

A lightning-bolt of pain coursed through my leg. I screamed.

Then I was falling, crashing onto ground, the taste of brackish leafy-mud in my mouth.

I rolled onto my back, trying to peer through the darkness. The soldiers stood almost within touching distance, two silhouettes as unmoving as stone, the deep silence broken only by the rasping sound of their breathing.

Facing them was a shadow, in a half-crouch, readying to spring.

A voice spluttered, "A wolf!"

The wolf leapt, its growl vibrating through the forest.

The men fled.

For a while my ears were filled with sobbing breaths, booted-feet crashing the undergrowth, desperate bodies ramming into anything in their path. Then the sounds and their echoes died. Silence returned.

The wolf moved in my direction.

I scrambled to my feet. At least I tried to. But my leg gave way, and I was back on the mud, clutching at my ankle, sobbing with pain. Fleeing was impossible, not with an injured leg. The only option was to act submissive. Hopefully the wolf wouldn't regard me as food or threat, would lose interest and go its way, whatever that way was.

I burrowed into myself and waited.

The animal was close now.

It didn't seem so big, or so menacing. And its tail, its plumy tail, started wagging.

It was…it was a dog.

My galloping heart slowed down to a canter. I extended my hand, palm up. The dog sniffed at it. I said, "You saved me."

The dog uttered a low bark, turned around and set off into the dark heart of the forest.

My mind was fluttering like a whisper of moths. I forced myself to focus. The soldiers were bound to return soon, with reinforcements. If I tarried here I'd be caught. I'd be better off with the dog, than alone. True, he could be a creature of some monster, but at this moment I didn't care much.

The dog barked again. For a moment, it was as if the bark contained a word—*Come.*

I shook my head. Perhaps my recent experiences were unhinging me.

"Please wait. I think I've sprained my ankle." I stopped, biting back a bout of hysterical laughter. How idiotic it was to expect a dog to understand my words.

Perhaps he did. He sat down, his eyes two orbs of red.

I removed the muddy shoe and the woolen sock and touched my ankle. It was swollen and hurt worse than a toothache. Tears pricked my eyes. How was I going to walk with an injured ankle? I needed treatment, rest, Nana's care.

The memory of Nana brought back other memories. If I sat here feeling sorry for myself I'd be caught.

Putting the shoe and socks back on was impossible. I abandoned the effort, and got up carefully, resting my weight on the uninjured leg, focusing on what I needed to do as a mental-antidote to the tearing pain in my ankle. The ground was littered with fallen branches. I hobbled around until I found one sturdy enough to be used as a walking stick. My bundle had been trodden into the muddy ground. The clothes were probably useless, but I didn't want to leave any of it behind. Perhaps I could get it all washed, once I was safe, whenever and wherever that might be.

The dog barked and resumed walking. I clutched the stick and limped after him, biting my lip to keep in the moans of pain. About the tears, I could do nothing.

As we moved deeper and deeper into the forest all light vanished and a darkness, unlike any other darkness I had experienced, descended. The stone-light, even at its strongest, was a mere firefly against it, but the dog's eyes shone through, like two beacons.

I wondered where the dog came from and where he was taking me. I didn't much care. My mind had other concerns.

The murdered guard, who was he? Who killed him and why? Was it to make me look like a murderess twice?

Was Uncle Bernii waiting for me down the Great Southern Road, as Ekko and Panda told me? Or was he pottering about in his castle, unaware of my fate? Did the plan belong to my friends or my enemies?

Immersed in my thoughts, it took me a while to notice

the difference. I was no longer chilled, because the air was warmer. My foot didn't get sucked into the mud, because the forest floor had ceased being a bog.

This part of the forest had not been pounded by rain for months.

I stood still leaning on the stick. My darting eyes fell on a pool of light ahead.

Through a gap in the interlaced canopy, the three moons, Nila, Peetha, and Lohitha, shone in their full glory in a cloudless sky.

I clung to the stick to stop myself from falling. The triple full moons happened once in a decade. The phenomenon was not due for three more years.

Was I hallucinating, like those people who imagined that One God visited them? Nana said these visions were true. Safely out of her hearing, Tygyrin disagreed. "If One God appeared, it would be to his true descendants, Cousin, not to peasants," he once told me.

I closed my eyes, counted to ten, then ten more, and opened them. The moons, three perfect orbs of blue, yellow, and crimson, looked down upon me with majestic indifference.

I had no idea where I was. But wherever I was, I was beyond the reach of Father's soldiers. That much I knew.

For now, that sufficed.

The dog barked, as if telling me to hurry. I gripped the stick tighter and followed him.

Sometime later, I had no idea how long or short, dawn began to break. Gradually the forest changed from dense shapes into trees and bushes. When the dog turned around to wait for me I could see him clearly, a largish black and white animal with a wispy beard.

Suddenly, I felt as if I couldn't take one more step, couldn't keep my eyes open one more second. A massive tree with a smooth silvery trunk looked too inviting to resist. I slipped down into a huddle by it, telling the dog, "I need some rest."

He stared for a moment, a strangely thoughtful look, as if he were considering the merits of various options. Then he sat down, facing the forest. I knew he was telling me to go to sleep, that he would wait for me.

I said, "Thank you," just in case my crazy surmise was right and he did understand me.

He didn't turn, but the plumy tail thumped the ground, once.

I leaned back against the trunk of the tree and closed my eyes.

⋈

A bird trilled somewhere, its song a strangely melodious mix of the wind's whistle and a cat's purr. I tried to place the sound, and failed.

The attempt at identifying the bird dissipated the mists of sleep. Memory flowed in starting with Bellizza's murder and ending with the question, voiced by a man with a hoarse-throat, directed not at any particular person but at the incomprehensible fates: *Why'd she have to kill that poor sod?*

The words were like burning coal inside my head.

I'd never be able to escape their fiery grip, not until I uncovered the name of the murdered man and the name of his murderer.

With that thought, another memory returned.

The dog. What if he had left me and gone?

My eyes flew open. The dog sat a few feet away, regarding me with a measured expression, like a conscientious judge.

I smiled at him. "Sorry about that, falling asleep for hours and hours. I didn't mean to. I must have been more tired than I realized. You must be thinking I'm a lazy layabout." I stopped, flushing. Here I was babbling, my voice high-pitched, excusing myself to a dog.

The back of my neck was stiff, my spine hurt. The pain in my ankle had settled into a dull ache. My swollen foot looked like a rotten jak-melon.

I grabbed the stick and hauled myself up, careful not to put much weight on the injured foot. The sun was almost overhead. The sky was a symphony in blue. There was something gentle, something soft, about this land.

My spine tingled. What had begun as a flight seemed to be turning into an adventure, like in the books. Whether the adventure was good or bad remained to be discovered. The uncertainty heightened the excitement, making me eager to press forward, to discover more.

I examined the tree that had sheltered me. It seemed like a *devamara*, except the silvery trunk was patterned with whorls. I looked around. The other trees too displayed the same combination of familiarity and strangeness.

A bank of ferns with white shell-shaped leaves made me think of my herbarium. I bent to uproot a plant and stopped, smiling at my idiocy. I had no herbarium, not even a piece of paper.

The dog barked and resumed walking. I plucked a single fern, placed it carefully in my pocket, and limped after him.

The gnawing in my stomach reminded me I had not brought any food or water with me.

"Are you hungry?" I asked the dog. "I wish I had something to give you."

The dog ignored me. He seemed intent on getting somewhere.

The forest was peopled with strange creatures: a rat with gossamer orange wings; a pair of grey and purple butterflies, so big they seemed like birds; a deer-like creature, white with black spots and massive green antlers; a frog glowing like a lump of gold and croaking like a lark; a jet black bird with a towering crest containing within it every shade and sub-shade of blue.

I wanted to see more of the creatures. I yearned to study the strange plants and trees. But whenever I stopped, the dog barked, an authoritative sound needing no translation—*Hurry*.

We stopped only once, near a brook. I nearly fell into the water in my eagerness. Having downed the water with as little ceremony as the dog, I tried to wash the patina of mud and dirt off myself. I would have liked to linger, maybe take a proper bath, but the dog wouldn't let me. When I ignored his bark, he turned around and stalked off, leaving me with no choice but to limp after him.

The sun rose, peaked, and started waning. The forest continued, as did the dog. He seemed immune to hunger or exhaustion.

I wasn't. My head felt as if it were full of needles, my foot ached, my body was sore, and my stomach a ceaseless rumble. I wished for the hundredth time that I had had enough sense to bring some food with me. Once, the world spun so fast, I had to lean against a tree and wait until it settled. I dragged myself in the dog's footsteps like a tired old woman, telling myself even the strangest forest had to end somewhere.

The forest did end, with disconcerting suddenness. As a dying sun turned the sky into a medley of red and gold, I followed the dog through a thick wall of vegetation and emerged onto a meadow of unruly grasses and red and yellow wildflowers. A single dead tree, its branches twisted into bird-shapes, stood like a sentinel over a small stone and timber cottage. I took in the curtained windows and the smoking chimney. The cottage was inhabited, probably by the dog's owner. He had led me not to fresh danger, as I had feared once or twice, but to his own home.

I turned around to thank the dog. He wasn't there.

Fear prickled my throat. I licked my dry lips with a sandpaper tongue. Where was the dog? What did his absence mean? Did the cottage represent refuge or danger?

I wanted to flee. But there was no place to flee to. No ability either. Fleeing on an empty stomach was conceivable; fleeing with an injured ankle wasn't.

I fingered the fern in my pocket, feelings its contours, its texture. Then I squared my shoulders and limped towards the cottage.

4

A NOOSE OF LIGHT

"The fair land welcomed them, as a maiden welcomes
her lover."
Song of Sallonia – Book One

THE DOOR WAS PAINTED WHITE. THE DRAGON-SHAPED
knocker gave not the rat-a-tat sound of my expectation but
a muffled boom.

The door glided open, as if it had a life of its own.

A woman in a sack-like dress, which could have been
black or brown once, peeped out. Her hair was black
with age, her night-dark face lined. There was something
familiar about her, even though I had no recollection of
seeing her before.

She smiled, turning the lines on her face into grooves.
"Lost your way?"

I nodded. Through the open door came a smell that

filled my dry mouth with saliva: the scent of fresh bread.

The woman's smile broadened. "Happens sometimes to folks." Her eyes rested for a second on my makeshift staff. "Injured your ankle?"

I gulped a few times. "Yes."

"Would you like me to take a look at your foot? Or would you like to eat something first?"

Nana's voice reverberated in my head. "A princess must smile politely when she is sad inside or angry. She must never seem hungry or bored or even scared. People are watching you all the time, Highness. If you do anything you shouldn't..." Nana always ended her homilies on a cliff-edge, as if the consequences of unseemly conduct were a fall beyond words.

I managed a smile. "I'd like to eat first please, if it's no inconvenience."

The woman opened the door wider. "Come in then."

I bowed. "Thank you so much."

The door led to a little kitchen. A laden table stood near the window. I struggled with the urge to fall on the food and eat until the rumbling cavern that was my stomach was full.

The woman indicated the table. "Eat."

I forgot the mystery of the dog, forgot Bellizza, Father, Nana, the murdered guard, the throbbing pain in my ankle, and my uncertain future. Food was the only thing I saw, felt, tasted, and thought about. I would have gone on eating even if a yale burst in, red eyes blaring, horns gleaming.

The woman stood by the table and watched.

I gobbled down one more chunk of sesame-and-nut cake (sprinkled with red sugar and finely-grounded puhulan nuts, just the way I liked it), picked up another mushroom-roll (creamy on the inside, crisp on the outside, again just the way I liked it), and realized my stomach was full to the point of bursting. Putting the roll back was not polite. I nibbled at it, allowing my eyes to assay my surrounding.

Wooden shelves lined the walls. They held metal and ceramic crucibles, different-sized mortars and pestles, two glass alembics, and several other glass, metal or wooden equipment. Massive stone jars, capacious enough to hide a baby or even two, stood in corners. Bunches of herbs hung from the wooden beams as did two glass globes filled with a reddish liquid. Pots with strange plants occupied the windowsills. Mushrooms shaped like red lotuses sprouted from a round clay pot. There was a normal oven and an athanor. I smelled goat's foot, ran-awara flowers, and black mist.

The kitchen was a space used not only to cook but to make other concoctions, perhaps medicinal, perhaps not.

I turned to my hostess and almost cried out. The woman no longer looked old or homely but tall, thin, and angular, with the sharpness of knives.

I gripped the table with both hands and stood up. Raw pain shot through my leg and a red mist clouded my eyes. I fell back on to the chair with a groan.

The woman continued to stand as if turned to stone, doing nothing, saying nothing.

I took deep breaths, struggling with fear and pain.

Calmness streaked in, and with it a memory. The dog had looked like a wolf the first time I saw him, a shadow on the cusp of a leap. It couldn't have been just my rampaging imagination. The soldiers wouldn't have fled had the dog not looked like a wolf.

Perhaps transformations back and forth were the norm in this strange place.

I managed a smile. "Thank you for helping me. You sent the dog to me, didn't you?"

"I asked him." The woman's voice too had changed. It carried a hint of steel. "He was good enough to oblige me."

So the dog wasn't anyone's pet but a free agent. That fitted with the way he behaved.

"Will you please thank him for saving me?"

The woman pulled a chair and sat down. "Don't you have a question or two for me, Princess Albalia?"

I tensed, then relaxed. If this woman knew I needed help there was nothing surprising in her knowing my name.

"Allii, please call me Allii." Questions I had, a quiverfull; the problem was where to start. Perhaps with basics, like names?

"I don't know your name or who you are."

The woman made a dismissive gesture with her hand. Her nails were long and slightly curved, like claws. "My name's Roaziyan. As for who I am, a witch is what your people would call me. Your father's people, that is."

To prevent my voice from rising to a screech was hard work. "Are you really a witch? I mean a real witch?"

"Names, Albalia, can mean anything, everything or nothing. Witch, forest-spirit, wise woman, they can denote the same or opposite. Let's say I'm a descendant of the original inhabitants of this land."

My mouth fell open, a hooked fish gasping for breath. "Your people owned my father's kingdom?"

"No one owns land. Most humans think they do. But the more you think you own the land the more the land owns you."

Any other time, I would have dug deeper into Roaziyan's statement. Now I had more pressing considerations. "If you're a witch, do you know magic?" *The Song of Sallonia* and other holy texts excoriated witches at length. In Sallonia, magic was either dismissed as a hoax or punished as a crime. Nana said magic was evil. Tygyrin said magic was a lie. Uncle Bernii said one man's magic was another man's religion.

Roaziyan's upper lip curled, making her look like a bird of prey. "If you mean can I turn you into a moth or make the cake of your choice appear on the table, no. But my people can understand and manage nature, and communicate with each other without using words. We have heightened senses, long lives, and longer memories. We can live outside space and time to some extent. We…"

A tiny white bird with a black beak landed on the window sill, chirping. Roaziyan leaned forward to take a piece of cake. As she did so, I caught a flash of red amongst her age-blackened hair and knew why she had looked familiar.

Roaziyan placed the crumbled cake on the window sill and returned to her chair, arching an eyebrow at my flushed face.

I forced myself to speak calmly. "Please pardon me if I'm being rude. I can't remember my mother. I've seen just one painting of her. It hangs in my father's study. In it she has red hair and black skin, like you. I wrote a poem for her when I was small. *Are you lonely up there, lady of fire? Is it sadness I see in your*—Sorry, it's a terrible poem." I drew a deep breath. "My mother came from the Island of Conches. You said your people were the original inhabitants of Sallonia. Are you connected in some way?"

Roaziyan didn't reply. Her stare reminded me of the door to Father's treasury, shut, bolted, and triple-locked, a storehouse accessible only to the select.

"Forgive me for persisting. Did you know my mother? Was that why you helped me?"

"You want to know why I helped you? Because you were being persecuted for a crime you didn't commit. Because your father's people are the enemies of my people and subverting their plans appealed to me. Because you were alone without anyone to take your part. All of this, some of this, none of this—take your pick."

"You didn't know my mother, then?"

"I knew your mother. But not well enough."

I waited for more. There was nothing. I decided to try a different track. "What is this place? I saw many strange things, and the weather is totally different."

"This is a microcosm of what the land was like before Sallonians occupied it."

"Including the trees and animals and birds?"

"Ah, yes, the ones Sallonians drove to extinction. Cut, cut, kill, kill—that was ever their way." Roaziyan's smile made me shudder. "Think of this place as a space beyond time, a bubble invisible to the human eye. No one can come here, unless I allow them in."

"Why did you let me in?"

"Because this is the only safe place for you in the entire kingdom. And like you, I want to get to the bottom of your stepmother's murder."

"Why? Why do you care? You don't…didn't know Bellizza?"

"Let's say I like to know what happens in my enemy's realm." Roaziyan paused as if considering her next words. "What do you know about the history of this land?"

I've never cared much for history, though the fundamentals had been dinned into me. "The books say Sallonians were the descendents of One God. He bequeathed this land to us, I mean the first Sallonians, because they were his chosen people. When the First Hundred Families came here, the land was a wilderness. There was a tribe of monkey-people, fearsome and cannibalistic."

Roaziyan's stare made me want to cower. I resisted the urge, and continued, in a determinedly light voice, "Not that I believed the *descended from god* part. People claim all kinds of ancestors, don't they? I've read about people who think they are the descendants of unicorns or dragons or even lightning. I liked that story best, how lightning fell in love with a tree and embraced her, and out of the tree emerged this particular tribe." I drank some water. "What I didn't know was Sallonians had invaded anyone's land."

Roaziyan folded her hands on the table, a bird of prey in repose. "Your Song of Sallonia is a lie concocted to justify what your father's people did to mine. No god guided the invaders. They came because we were renowned for our prosperity, our culture, and our lack of weapons."

"But the monkey people…"

"There were no monkey-people, just us. We are called Muffics. We never ate any flesh, let alone human flesh. We used the land gently, and the land treated us well. That unwritten covenant with land was the keystone of our lives. We understood nature, we could communicate with trees and animals, we knew the mood of rivers, we could predict storms, earth-heavings, and floods. We wrote books, staged dramas, and painted pictures. We mused on life and studied the stars. But we were not versed in the art of killing, which Sallonians excelled at." Roaziyan's folded hands clenched. "They took our lands and expelled us. We were confined to the most unlivable areas of what became the Serene Kingdom of Sallonia. Because my people still retain their ancient knowledge, they manage to eke a living but it's a hard life."

Goosebumps dotted my arms. "Was my mother—was my mother a Muffic?"

Roaziyan nodded.

All my life I had believed mother was from the Island of Conches, an orphan who came to Sallonia to escape the clan war that turned her home into a wasteland. That was what Nana told me.

Nana couldn't have lied to me. Nana would never lie to me. It wasn't possible. It just wasn't possible.

Then came the memory of a long-ago incident.

Kiko, the guard who used to bring me plants, once

told me his mother had the breathing-disease. She had contacted it by living close to a Sallikan mine as a girl.

When I told Nana about it, she had glared at me. "Who told you such lies, Highness?" When Nana was angry with me, she invariably called me Highness.

I had shrugged. "I heard someone saying something." I had mastered the art of lying long before I learnt the basics of sewing or music or painting.

Nana's eyes had bored into me, as if trying to dig the truth out of me. "Sallikan is One God's gift to us. Of all the lands of the world, only Sallonia is blessed with Sallikan. It is a sign of One God's favor, because we are his chosen people. Those who spread such lies about Sallikan are being blasphemous." She had caught my hand in hers, her eyes no longer sharp, but anxious. "Don't repeat such lies. Ever. If you do, you'd be breaking the law. Do you understand me, Allikin?"

I had nodded, worried by her worry.

I didn't talk about it again. But I thought about it a lot. I found it impossible that Nana would tell me an untruth. But Kiko had no reason to lie to me either. And both of them couldn't be telling the truth.

About two weeks later, I caught Kiko alone and asked him about Sallikan. His eyes darted around. He licked his lips. "I know nothing about Sallikan, Highness. You must've been mistaken."

I didn't pursue the matter. There was no need to. His denial, and his manner, convinced me he had told the truth the first time.

If Kiko had told the truth, then Nana had lied to me.

The thought was unbearable. Nana was my anchor, the keystone of my life. She had to be true.

I had done the only thing possible for me, perhaps for any ten-year-old with no mother, and a father who didn't care a moth's wing about her, banished the memory into a far corner in my mind, until now.

Nana had lied to me about Sallikan. Or she told the truth as she knew it. Did it mean she had misled me about other things too?

I turned to Roaziyan. "None of the books mention Muffics."

"Oh, books! Books can be made to lie, just like tongues. Only approved books are allowed into your country anyway."

"Why would everyone lie to me?"

Roaziyan's answer was a seemingly unrelated question. "Who will inherit the throne if your father has no sons?"

"Father's cousin, Prince Bernalin," Uncle Bernii. Had my escape plan not been sabotaged, I'd have been with him now, safe and as ignorant as ever about history: Sallonia's, Mother's, and mine.

"Why not you?"

"I'm not a son."

"You didn't care about the injustice of it?"

I shrugged. "It's the law." I didn't care anymore, but I had once. When I was very young, I had just assumed I'd inherit everything Father had, including the crown. One day, during an argument with Nana, I had shouted, "When I'm queen, I'll make friends with anyone I want." Nana had sat me down and explained why I could never be queen.

It had rankled for a while. Then I became absorbed in plants, and the lure of a crown had diminished. Learning that there had never been a queen-regnant in Sallonia made acceptance of my own disinheritance easier. Injustice is easier to live with when it dons the garments of tradition and creed.

Roaziyan's smile indicated she knew—or guessed—some of my thoughts. "You can't inherit because of what you are."

I gripped my hands on my lap, out of sight of her probing eyes. "And what am I?"

"A Halfling."

The headache was different from any headache I've ever experienced. It was as if something inside my skull was expanding, building up pressure. I dug my nails into my hands trying to focus on that bearable pain. "What is a Halfling?"

"A mixed-breed, like you. A product of a union between a Sallonian and a Muffic. Such unions are banned by Sallonian law and by Muffic tradition. Halflings are considered polluted by Sallonians and Muffics. They are accepted by neither side."

A little more pressure and my skull would explode. I wanted it to.

Was that why Nana was always telling me to be careful? When Nana admonished me to behave like a princess, did she mean don't behave like a Halfling?

Did Father ignore me because he was ashamed of his Halfling daughter? If he didn't want a Halfling child, why did he marry a Muffic woman?

My skull still hurt, but my curiosity acted as a balm. "Did my father know my mother was a Muffic?"

Roaziyan's voice sounded distant, as if it were coming from a faraway place. "Your parents were too much in love to have sense or heed reason. They were in a world of their own and wouldn't let reality intrude into their fantasies. They ran away. Your grandparents might have tried to separate them by force, had your father not been the youngest son. So they let him be."

Very much in love—the words twirled around in my mind. What had Father been like then when he was so much in love?

The pressure inside my skull was easing. I tried to remember the way Father was in the first years of his marriage to Bellizza. He had been friendly and approachable, almost happy. Almost: why did I use that word? Did it mean he wasn't really happy? What made me think so? Was it because even when he laughed, his eyes had a distant look, as if a part of him existed in a different place?

Roaziyan watched me. Something in that gaze made my skin crawl.

"Then your father's two older brothers died within three months of each other. By that time your parents had been together for several years and your mother was with child."

"Me?" I murmured.

"You." Roaziyan's voice was like thorns. "Your grandfather never recovered from the death of his two older sons. He died four months later. Your father left your mother and returned to Pinckossia and was crowned king."

The food I had eaten with such joyous abandon started

to roil inside me. "I thought he loved her—" my words came out in a choky whisper.

Roaziyan's voice was knife-sharp. "He loved his kind more." She folded her lips. It reminded me of Nana. That was what she did when she wanted to refrain from speaking.

Another long-ago memory surfaced. Something Tygyrin had told me. I couldn't recall the context, but I remembered the words. "Your father is a great man, Allii. He sacrificed his happiness for Sallonia. That's what great men do. They put their land and their kind before themselves. You are fortunate to have such a father."

Roaziyan tapped the table with a fingertip, a strangely rhythmic sound. "Let's return to your current predicament. What do you plan to do with yourself?" Her voice was a noose, catching my vagrant mind, forcing it back to the present.

I took a deep breath. "I want to uncover who killed Bellizza."

"Why?"

I splayed my hands. "Because I loved her. Because I owe it to her. Because her murderer has to punished. Because I can't think of any other way I can prove my innocence." I wanted to imitate Roaziyan and add, *one of this, some of this, all of this*, but didn't.

She knew though. Her glance turned dagger-sharp, but she said nothing.

"Killing Bellizza was such an evil thing to do. She never harmed anyone. She was kind and loving…" And I left her to die alone, because I was in a hurry to get back to my herbarium, because I was beginning to find her unending grief tedious. I tried to blink back my tears. "Another person was killed, a guard. The soldiers pursuing me called him a poor sod. They think I killed him. I don't even know his name." I stopped, my voice breaking "I don't even know his name."

The tears rushed out, choking me. I cried for Bellizza, for myself, for Nana, and for the poor murdered guard whose name I didn't know. Roaziyan made no effort to comfort me, just waited in silence until my tears were spent.

I wiped my face with the sleeve of my tunic. "Sorry."

Roaziyan waved a hand. "It is no matter. Tell me, how do you propose to find Bellizza's killer? And the killer of this unknown guard?"

I answered slowly, taking time to untangle my thoughts and ideas. "Had I been free, I could have talked to the guards and Bellizza's ladies and maids. Since I can't I'll have to use a roundabout way. I want to meet Bellizza's sister, Kummizza."

Roaziyan's left eyebrow went up until it melded with the hairline. "The stargazer living atop Mount Mäga? Why?"

"Bellizza wasn't allowed to visit her family, but she wrote to them regularly. She wrote mostly to her sister. Sometimes she used to read out bits from her sister's letters to me." Bellizza would hold those letters as if they were the most precious things in the world—

Roaziyan's voice dissipated the memories. "You surmise the letters Bellizza wrote to her sister might contain information germane to her eventual fate?"

"It's more than a surmise," I said, and recounted the incident with Sherriz.

Roaziyan continued to tap the table with a finger, strange background music for a stranger conversation. "You might be correct, or not. Either way, you must leave your father's kingdom. So you might as well go to your stepmother's sister. All things considered it's not a bad choice. Your father's people won't think you went there. My advice is to keep your destination secret. Don't tell anyone, including any friends you might make on the road."

I stared. "Do you mean I'll be pursued beyond Sallonia? Why?" I had thought of myself as a fugitive but not a fugitive with soldiers in hot pursuit. It didn't seem credible. And even Sherriz wouldn't be able to commit soldiers to such a task without Father's permission. And Father would never consent.

*Father would **never** consent.*

"You are a Halfling, but you are also your father's daughter. He brought you up as a Sallonian princess. You can turn yourself into—or be turned into—the rallying point for those who are discontented with the way Sallonia is run. That makes you a loose end. Powerful men don't like loose ends."

I shook my head. "I think I'd be safe once I'm out of Sallonia."

Roaziyan's eyes snapped, but when she spoke her voice was strangely mild, almost pitying. "Amongst the soldiers who were pursuing you last night, there would have been one entrusted with the task of putting an end to you. Fortunately, you decided not to head in the direction your spurious saviors told you to. That shows you are not completely devoid of intelligence. Cling to your illusions if you must, but don't let them blind you. Most humans would do anything for a crown. Add Sallikan to the equation and no infamy becomes too much. Whoever controls Sallonia controls Sallikan."

Sallikan, the most valuable metal in the world. The wings of the mechanical messenger pigeons, the bodies of the mechanical carriages, the legs of the mechanical farming-bulls, they all needed Sallikan. And Sallikan, in sufficient quantities, could be found only in Sallonia.

"Sallonia is courted even by the great empires because of Sallikan," Roaziyan said. "All Sallikan mines are owned by the king. They are heavily guarded. The miners, all of them pure bred Sallonians, live like prisoners. They are hired for a certain period and can't leave until that period is over. Very few of them survive anyway."

I stared at Roaziyan in horror. "That can't be true. You are…" I stopped, remembering the mining songs Nana had taught me, so haunting, so full of feelings of loss and longing, melodious lamentations.

Roaziyan nodded, almost as if she could read my turbulent thoughts. "Weighted against Sallikan, your life would be worth less than nothing. That is why you will have to be on the run long after you've escaped Sallonia." She stood up. "Now, shall we take a look at your ankle?"

5
RIVERS FROM THE PAST

*"Before they could claim the land given to them
by Liminalin, One God-True-God, the evil that
possessed the land had to be vanquished. And the evil
was powerful, because it was born of witch-power,
beings of darkness anathema to One God,
he bearer of light."*
Song of Sallonia – Book One

THE NIGHT CRAWLED. IN ROAZIYAN'S SPARE BEDROOM,
I tossed and turned like a boat caught in a storm. Sleep
eluded me not because the bed was lumpy, the pillow hard,
or the bedclothes coarse. After all, I had had no problem
falling asleep with my back to a tree.

What kept me awake was the one question I didn't ask
Roaziyan.

How much did Father know about the plan to kill Bellizza

and remove me?

I didn't ask that question because voicing those words to a stranger seemed an act of unpardonable betrayal. And it would have opened a door I wanted to keep locked, the key thrown into the depth of the deepest ocean where it would never be found.

Escaping my own mind was far harder than escaping soldiers. The more I tried not to think about the question, the more it pricked me, demanding acknowledgement and answers.

If I get to Kummizza's, if I read Bellizza's letters, what will I discover?

Sallonia was a small country. But Pegala was a large world. I could just lose myself in it, become a different person and build a new life. I had enough money for it.

Discovering a new plant species and naming it after my-self had been my dream. Now I had the chance of turning it into reality.

Well, only the finding part. I'd never be able to name if after me. My name, my real name, would remain disgraced, the princess who killed her stepmother.

No, I had to clear my name. And avenge Bellizza. And the poor murdered guard whose name I didn't know.

Sallonians believed the murdered couldn't be reborn so long as the killer was at large. They turn into moon-moths forever seeking light. Uncle Bernii had called it a myth. He was probably right, but I could see a point in the myth. The murdered, if they had any choice in the matter, would want their killers to be revealed and punished.

I had to find Bellizza's killer. What would happen

afterward, I had no idea. I couldn't see that far, and I didn't want to.

One brush stroke at a time, Allii, that's the way to go, if you want to paint the night.

My throat felt parched. There was a bench by the open window with a pitcher of water on it. I stood up carefully, flexing my injured foot. The swelling was gone, and it didn't hurt anymore.

Roaziyan had set it right, with one twist.

She had placed my injured foot on a chair and examined the ankle, holding the heel with one hand and the toes with the other. Suddenly, she twisted the foot. A bolt of pain shot through the leg. My body whipped up. A scream escaped me. I clamped my teeth together to prevent another scream and realized there was no need. The pain was gone.

Roaziyan wiped her hands on a handkerchief. "Stand up. Put your weight on that leg."

I didn't want to, but there was no disobeying that voice.

There was no pain and my leg was back to normal.

Roaziyan cut short my fervent thanks. "That was not magic, but learning and practice. Healing was another thing my people did well."

I frowned. "If your people had so much power, why didn't you fight back when Sallonians occupied your land?"

For a second, Roaziyan's mouth had reminded me of a beak. Then she had shrugged. "The first rule of what you call magic is that its power cannot be used to deprive any living being of life. That, unfortunately, includes humans."

I mulled over those words as I sipped from the earthenware pitcher. The water felt cool and clear. The water at home, even after several rounds of purifying, was heavy on the tongue, and in the stomach.

The breeze from the narrow window was unfamiliar in its softness. Back at home, the wind was hot during dry months and chilly during rainy months. I peered at the night sky, spotting the Constellation of the Leaping Fox and the bright yellow Dragon Star. The familiar sight comforted me; this place and Sallonia existed under the same sky, some of the time.

I returned to bed, struggling once again to make some sense of what I'd heard this day.

The first conclusion was obvious. Everyone in my life, including Nana—no starting with Nana—had lied to me. The lies were probably motivated by affection and concern. That somehow made everything worse and not better. How people like Nellin and Sherriz would have laughed at me behind my back, as I went about safe in my make-believe world. I cringed. I, who was so proud of my intelligence, had been everyone's dupe.

Bellizza wouldn't have liked the deception. She would have gone along because that was what she did. Go along, pretend nothing was wrong. She never enacted scenes, never complained or protested.

Not even when Chief Priest Pena insulted her publicly.

Every time Bellizza became pregnant, a prayer-ceremony was held in the palace-temple to seek divine blessings for the queen and the unborn baby.

The entire court, led by father, had attended the first one. The temple had been filled to overflowing. Chief Priest Hiro had presided over the ceremony. As I sat down, he had caught my eyes and winked.

I loved Hiro. He handled my religious instructions and responded to my questions about One God with indulgence. Nana used to mutter he didn't respect anything much—tradition, history, or god.

Seven months after that first ceremony, Bellizza's baby, a son, was born, premature and dead.

Bellizza was pregnant again the next year. Once again, there was rejoicing and thanksgiving. Until she gave birth to another dead baby, a girl.

At some point—I couldn't quite remember when—father stopped attending the prayer ceremony. His absence was taken as a signal by everyone else. Each year, attendance at the ceremony dwindled. Bellizza was accompanied to the last one by just the members of her own household, Nana, and me.

By that time, old Hiro was long dead. Pena was the Chief Priest, younger, full of zeal. He had thundered about women who failed to perform their primary One God-mandated duty—bear children. Living ones, he repeated.

I gritted my teeth, holding Bellizza's cold hand tight.

"In our well-run farms, there is a time-honored practice." Pena paused for a second, his cadaverous form looming over the altar, his piercing eyes directed at Bellizza. "Those female animals incapable of giving birth to new life are sent to the chopping block."

My rage was no longer containable. I sprang to my feet but was yanked back. Bellizza said one word.

"Please."

I sat, glaring at Pena. A silence, bristling with words no

one wanted to utter, filled the temple.

After the ceremony, I escorted Bellizza to the sunroom. Once she was settled, I went in search of Pena. He was talking to two acolytes in the temple courtyard. When he saw me, he came over and bowed.

"That remark," I said, drawing myself to my full height, which still made me at least a foot shorter than him, "was execrable."

Pena's eyes were hooded, his voice polite. "Your comment is noted, Highness."

Then he stalked away, his robes flapping against his sandaled feet.

Afterwards, I had tried to forget the incident. I had convinced myself it was nothing important, just the outcome of one man's malice.

I tried to reconcile that Pena, a creature of unwavering piety and hard malice, with the Pena who visited me in my prison. It was difficult. The Pena who visited me had seemed sympathetic, concerned, almost a friend. But that didn't fit in with the Pena who had said those terrible things about Bellizza.

Perhaps that was the answer. He disliked Bellizza, because to his narrow mind she was a failure. Perhaps he was happy Bellizza was no more and didn't care who killed her.

I shook my head. That didn't explain why he came visiting. Was it out of concern for Nana? Or was Nana too an excuse? Did he visit me as a friend or a spy?

Suddenly other memories started flowing, rivers from the past. I felt an urgent need to write them down. But I had no writing implements. Perhaps Roaziyan did.

I picked up the stone-light, opened the door slowly, and went out. The kitchen was empty, so was the parlor. I stood wondering what to do.

"Looking for something?"

I whirled around. In the semi-dark, Roaziyan's black clad form was visible only in outline. Had she been in the parlor all the time? Or did she follow me there?

I swallowed. "I'm sorry. I wanted to ask you for some paper and a pen."

Roaziyan's eyes glittered for a second. Then she walked to a door hidden in the shadows, opened it, and went in. I followed her, after a few seconds' hesitation.

The door led to a room lined with books. A small writing desk stood in the middle. A shaded lamp sat on the desk bathing the room with a golden light.

Roaziyan opened the desk, took out a sheaf of papers, picked up a pen from her pen-stand, and held them out to me. I took them, mumbling my thanks.

Her brows went up. "Is there anything else?"

I steeled myself. "Can you see in the dark?"

"Yes, night and day are same to the likes of me. Anything else?"

I swallowed. "How do you become proficient in magic?"

"The way you become proficient in anything. Hard work. You study. You practice."

"So you are not born with it?"

"You are born with the potential. It must be honed and harnessed through sheer grind. Anything else?"

My courage had gone into hiding. I shook my head.

Back in my room I studied the paper. They were of a

different type than the ones I knew, smoother, with almost a silken texture and a subtle smell. They were bound securely together with a thin yarn.

This will serve as my memory book. I'll write down the past as I remember it. That way, I might be able to see clues I had missed or ignored, clues to my own identity as well as to Bellizza's fate.

When I was small, Nana invented games to keep me amused during the rainy months. My favorite was a word-game. Nana would say a word and I had to come up with a matching word before Nana could count to three.

Nana never said mother. But she did say father. My invariable response was busy.

After a few times, Nana stopped saying father too.

Busy was my earliest memory of Papa. Busy with ruling and its attendant pursuits, hunting, feasting, and visiting various parts of his realm. When he was at home, I saw him once a day. After breakfast, Nana would take me to the audience chamber where he received his ministers and high officials. An attendant would open the door and I would go in, my hand clasped tightly in Nana's. Papa would be seated on a simple wooden chair, the table next to him piled high with papers. We would wish each other well for the day. I would look at him and he would look at a point above my head. He would ask me how I was doing. I would say I was well. He would nod absently, his attention already on whatever work he was engaged in.

That had been the sum total of our regular interactions.

I saw rather more of Papa during the first years of his new marriage, when Bellizza was bright and laughing, and the days were full of long rides, leisurely picnics and small informal parties. Bellizza had included me in all these, and for the first time in my remembered-life, I had actually spent an hour or two in Papa's company. He had asked me questions about my studies and seemed interested in my answers. He had even smiled at some of my remarks, as if I were witty and amusing, like the clever princesses in the books.

The hope of an heir faded with each miscarriage. Bellizza's smiles vanished and her brightness dimmed. As Bellizza and Papa grew apart, I found myself in Bellizza's company. It wasn't a matter of choice. Papa went back to treating me with polite indifference. Bellizza needed me. My friendship with Bellizza grew with each passing year, and with each passing year, Papa became more of a stranger.

I have more and better memories of my two cousins, Tygyrin and Kollarin, the youngest and the oldest sons of Papa's objectionable cousin, Uncle Rokkrin and his even more objectionable wife, Aunt Amberlina. Tygyrin taught me riding, gave me books on plants, and got me specimens for my herbaria. Kollarin built me a tree-house, took me on expeditions to the royal woods, and told me hair-raising tales of adventure and horror.

How did I become a lover of plants? Was it through Uncle Bernii who cultivated rare plants?

When I visited him we used to have our meals in a chamber overlooking his massive herb garden. The windows would be open and the wind carried the scent of the herbs into the room. Whenever a scent wafted in, he would ask me to name it. At first I couldn't. But as I learned more and more about herbs, I began to be able to whiff-out the names.

"Monkey-warts," I'd say, smelling a thin, sharp scent.

He'd clap his hands. "Good. Now tell me what monkey-warts are used for."

"Insomnia," I'd say, relishing the word because it was still new to me. "Tiredness and grief."

And it would go on.

Father's main castle, where I lived, was in the plains, in a broad valley at the southernmost end of Pinckossia, the capital city. Bernii's home was nestled in the Asha Mountains. When I was small I visited him often for long stays.

I loved those visits.

When the mechanical carriage bearing Nana and me reached the castle gates, Uncle Bernii would be waiting, his robe crumpled, the sun turning his bald pate into a golden saucer. The backdoor would swing open and uncle would be there, arms held out, smiling from ear to ear, eyes shining and chins wobbling. He'd catch me as I tumbled down the steps, and swing me high in the air.

Did Papa ever hug me like that? Or swing me up in the air? If he did, I have no recollection of it.

After the long hug, we'd take a good look at each other.

"You've grown, niece," he'd say with mock solemnity.

I'd try to assume a serious expression to match his. "You have not, uncle."

We'd both fall into gusts of laughter. It was silly. But I loved it. No one ever laughed like that back at home.

Nana would frown. The free and easy ways at Bernii's didn't please her. She muttered he was turning me into a ragamuffin.

The visits became less frequent after Papa married Belle. They stopped altogether a few years later. Uncle Bernii and I wrote to each other, but we met rarely, because he hardly ever came to see us. He and Belle disliked each other.

How do I know that? Did someone tell me something? Or did I notice anything?

But if so, during his last visit to the castle less than three months ago, why did he tell me to arrange a picnic because he wanted to talk to Bellizza alone?

What did they talk about when they went for that long walk amongst the blooming samia trees?

6

A PINCH OF MAGIC

"They prayed to One God-True-God, for guidance. And One God heeded their supplication. He appeared bearing the fire sword and the lightning lance. He drove out the evil and purified the profaned land so his chosen people could live in it for evermore."
Song of Sallonia – Book One

I opened my eyes to two incessant sounds—the twittering of birds and the echo of a memory.

Why'd she have to kill that poor sod?

I stumbled out of bed. The voice in my head receded as the cacophony of birds filled my ears.

The narrow window faced an orchard. Roaziyan stood by a tree, putting food into a bird-feeder.

I turned away and started making the bed. It didn't look

very neat when it was done. But it wasn't too bad for a first attempt.

A knock sounded. The door opened a second later and Roaziyan walked in carrying a pair of shears. She pointed to the low bench by the window, saying, "We need to make you look different, so the hair has to go. Sit down."

Sallonian royal ladies always had their hair long. By the time Roaziyan was done, my thick waist-length tresses lay at my feet in coppery whorls.

I sniffled a little. I had been proud of my hair.

Roaziyan gathered the coppery strands, saying in a conversational tone, "Did you know birds and rodents use human hair to line their nests and lairs? I'll keep this under a tree and soon it'll be gone. The bathhouse is outside. I've left some clothes for you there." She fetched two vials from an inner pocket, one filled with a colorless liquid, the other containing a creamy yellowish paste. "Once you have your bath, apply these. The liquid is for your hair. The cream is for your face and your body. Do the applications while you are still wet from the bath. Wait until they dry. They'll make you look like a pure-bred Sallonian." She almost spat the last two words. "Don't forget the nape of the neck and the back of the ears."

I examined the vials. "Are they magic?"

Her voice could have sliced stones. "Herbs."

The bathhouse was a primitive affair with only one type of water, icy cold. I had never seen a hand pump before and found the task of using it arm-aching hard. But at the end of it I felt a sense of achievement, as if I had passed the first real test of my new life.

Once the bath was over, I opened the bottles and smelled them. Perhaps I'd be able to identify some of the ingredients from their scents.

Both were odorless.

I rubbed the liquid into my chin-length hair and applied the thin paste on my face and body. I was ready for a long wait, but they dried in a surprisingly short time.

Perhaps there was a pinch of magic in them, after all.

The clothes hung on a nail in a dull tangle. They were of coarse cotton—undergarments, trousers, and a blouse. Underneath stood a pair of boots made of the bark of meeya tree. I had seen Sallonians dressed like that on the road and in books—though in the books the clothes had seemed brighter and softer.

The blouse was too big, the trousers a little short. Both had a threadbare appearance. There was no mirror in the bathhouse. I was glad. Shorn of hair and in ill-fitting clothes, I was bound to look terrible.

The sound of birds greeted me as I emerged from the bathhouse. Roaziyan had placed my hair under a banoa tree teeming with blue and white flowers. Birds crowded around it, chirping excitedly. Roaziyan watched them, occasionally saying something, to which they seemed to respond.

The sight brought back a memory that had lain dormant for years.

The swan.

The incident had happened before Father's marriage to Bellizza. I must have been about five. I had wandered into one of the kitchen-gardens and found a swan in a cage. She had begged me to release her. She said the cook would kill her otherwise. She had babies waiting for her. Without her to care for them, they'd die.

I released her. She flew away.

That day I had lunch in one of the formal chambers with Father and several others. Tygyrin was there, as well as his parents and his middle brother, the unbearable Tawnilin. Aunt Amberlina was very partial to swan meat, and the swan was meant for her.

When the dessert was brought, she gave her tinkling laugh (like gravel inside a tin) and asked whether swans were in short supply at the moment. I remember Tygyrin frowning. Even Uncle Rokkrin looked a little embarrassed. Only Tawni giggled.

Father's face was rigid with anger. I knew inquiries would be made. I didn't want a cook to get the blame for what I did.

I said I released the swan because she didn't want to be killed.

There was something rather strange in the silence which followed my words. And Father's face. It scared me. He didn't look angry. He didn't look sad. He didn't look anything. His face was bloodless, like the face of a dead man.

Tygyrin broke the silence. He asked me about my studies and promised to get me a book I had been wanting. He asked Father about an impending military ceremony. Even Uncle Rokkrin chipped in, talking about his newest castle. Theirs was a valiant effort but it didn't work. Nana was summoned, and I was sent to my room.

Nana asked me what happened. I told her.

She knelt by me. "You have grieved your father. Only people possessed by demons talk to animals. Normal human beings don't. Tygyrin is a decent young man, but those parents of his, not to mention the pest Tawnilin, they'll tell everyone you talk to animals. If you continue like this, there'll be trouble. People will get angry. They might even attack the castle and kill us all. Do you want that to happen?"

I shook my head. Nana's fear was more frightening than anything she could have said or done to me.

"Your father wants a good daughter. If you behave badly, he'll think I'm not capable of looking after you properly. He'll send me away and get another nurse for you."

Horror had possessed me. I had hugged Nana and wept, and promised I'll do anything she wanted me to so long as she stayed with me.

A bird flew down, perched on Roaziyan's head, chirping. She said something in reply, turned around and walked toward me.

I smiled. "Thank you for the clothes. Were you talking to the birds?"

"And listening to them. Listening is as important as talking, perhaps more so. You'll need to learn how to listen if you are going to succeed in your quest."

I drew a deep breath. "Can I learn to understand birds and animals?"

Roaziyan looked me up and down as if I were a horse and she a prospective buyer. "You might be able to."

"Can you teach me?"

"No."

"How do I learn then?"

Her voice was laconic. "I just told you. Listen." She strode towards the house saying over her shoulder, "There's a mirror in the passage. Go and look."

The mirror was not a full-length one, but the image it portrayed more than sufficed. I looked a study in dullness. My hair was a patch of withered brown grass chopped with a machete. My skin was brown too and had a mottled, uncared-for look. My faded clothes added another layer of gloom.

"Awful is how you must look." Roaziyan's voice at my shoulder made me jump. The woman could move as stealthily as any wild animal. "Looking too awful to merit a second glance is the way to safety."

"What'll happen when I get caught in the rain?" After all, it'll be rainy season for many more months in Sallonia.

"Nothing, not for about three days. Then the colors will fade gradually. In a week you'll look your normal Halfling self. By that time, you'll be long out of here."

I hoped so.

"Your father's soldiers will be looking for a single female. To complete your disguise, I'll give you a companion."

"A companion?"

"Yes, the one who helped you the night before."

"The dog," I cried. "I've always wanted to have a dog."

"Have implies ownership. You can't have him anymore than he can have you. You will be companions. He is only a part-dog. Dogs are good if you live in your corner of the world. A wolf would suit your purpose better."

"But people are frightened of wolves."

"Some people should be frightened. The dog who saved you is a daemon-dog. He can assume certain shapes when in need. Such as that of a wolf."

So that was how it worked. "It'll be good to have him as a companion."

Roaziyan's lips curled. "Whether you'll be in the same mind after you've had his company for a few days remains to be seen." She leaned out of the kitchen window and emitted a long clear whistle.

In a surprisingly short while the door opened and the dog came in. He walked up to me with firm measured steps and sniffed at my outstretched hand with a disdainful air. I knelt and looked into his reddish eyes. He stared back, look for look.

"Thank you for saving me and for agreeing to come with me," I told the daemon-dog. I turned to Roaziyan. "Would you mind telling me his name?"

"He doesn't have one. Animals need names only if they associate with humans. He'll be your companion. You can give him a name. But remember to ask him if he approves."

I thought of a dozen names, but none of them would fit this strange dog.

"Spooky?" I ventured at last, my voice tentative. In Bellizza's language, *spookih* meant friend.

Roaziyan turned to the daemon-dog. "How do you like the name, master?"

The dog barked. I remembered Roaziyan's advice and tried to empty my mind of all other thoughts and focus on the bark.

It still seemed a bark.

Roaziyan's withering voice broke my concentration. "He doesn't mind the name."

I gave a weak smile, feeling stupid.

Roaziyan walked to the store chamber and emerged with a bag and a palm frond umbrella. "You'll find a change of clothes in here and some food. The umbrella won't keep the rain out, but it'll complete your disguise."

I accepted the bag and the umbrella. "Thank you."

"When you leave this place you will find yourself on a road, the one your people call the Great Eastern Road. It will lead you to the Crow Mountains. Cross the mountains and you will be out of your father's kingdom. Along the way you might come across people and even soldiers. Have a story ready, a convincing story."

I nodded. The Crow Mountains marked Sallonia's Eastern boundary.

Roaziyan walked to where the dog was sitting, his attention focused on a buzzing humming-bee and began a conversation with him in a voice too low for me to catch. The dog listened, oversized ears perked, head tilted.

I turned away pretending to adjust my clothes, wondering about the many things Roaziyan left unsaid.

Minister Ekko's final words, both plea and advice, came to my mind.

"Trust no one. No one."

Was the dog just a companion? Or a spy as well?

BOOK TWO

1

A GIRL CALLED BÄNGE

"Sallonians first arrived in this land they now call their own as supplicants, seeking food and nights of shelter."
Histories – Roaziyan the Younger

IT WAS THE KIND OF DAY I HAD NEVER EXPERIENCED IN Sallonia.

The sun was a warming fire not a burning furnace, the breeze as gentle as Nana's touch. Birds twittered and bees hummed in an endless symphony. The heady scent of wild flowers and tender grass filled the air.

A mauve-fox lay under the flowery canopy of a yellow-bell tree watching her gamboling cubs. One cub, more adventurous than her siblings, started running in my direction. The mother sat up emitting a deep growl.

The world then changed, as if I had walked through an unseen door into a different reality.

The sun-warmed meadow was gone. In its place was a barren plain. Rain slashed. Wind roared. I dragged the palm-frond umbrella out. By the time I unfolded it, I was drenched. The umbrella wouldn't have provided much protection had I been faster with it. Even a palm-thatched roof might not have sufficed against this rain.

I was about to put the umbrella away when I remembered another rainy day, watching the world through the glass-covered window of a mechanical carriage. The few people on the road carried palm-frond umbrellas held lengthwise. Everyone, old and young, walked with their upper bodies bent.

That posture had intrigued me and I asked Nana about it. Nana had explained it was the best way—the only way—to gain some protection from the slashing rain.

I tried to imitate those figures. The new posture protected my face, my chest, and even my back from the arrow like raindrops. It also slowed me down. Soon my spine was screaming in protest.

The dog didn't seem to mind the rain. He strode ahead, pausing occasionally to throw me impatient glances, as if he suspected me of dawdling deliberately.

I tried to keep pace with him with little success. My clothes were slugs slithering on my wet body. Mud covered my feet like a second skin. Hunger came and went. I toyed with the idea of eating something, but couldn't summon the energy. Though I had no way of knowing the time, I sensed the night might not be far away. Where I'd spend it I had no idea.

After a while the rain slowed to a steady drizzle. The road

still ran through the barren plain, though with occasional rises and dips. When the clouds parted for a few moments, I could see the Crow Mountains outlining the far horizon, rocky and bare of vegetation, the tallest peak shaped like a bird in mid-flight. The mountains didn't seem as if they were scalable. But I'd need to scale them if I wanted to get out of Sallonia.

The road rose again. Below lay a village, beyond it a dense forest.

The road dipped and evened out. Soon the first dwellings appeared, huts that looked as if they'd fall at the touch of the wind, mud walls unpainted, thatched roofs dark with age, totally unlike the pictures of pretty cottages I had seen in a book titled, *The Sallonian Countryside.* The only well-maintained structure was the temple of One God, brick walls freshly plastered, roof-tiles gleaming a bright blue, bronze spire reaching out to the grey sky.

Ahead of me, a crowd milled, men, women, and children, necks craned, eyes fixed on something to their right beyond my line of vision. A deep silence hung in the air, as if everyone had been struck with the mute-malady.

The dog bared his teeth at me, and ran in the direction of the crowd. I didn't know whether he wanted me to wait for him or to follow him. I compromised by walking slowly after him.

A scream shattered the silence. Suddenly all was noise, people crying, dogs barking, horses neighing.

The crowd parted. An officer, young and mustachioed, rode through, on a tall grey horse, and turned to the main road, towards the heart of Sallonia. A troop of soldiers followed. Their silver-on-blue uniforms were crumpled and muddy, but they marched in perfect formation. Walled between their ranks was a group of young men in ragged clothes rather like my own. They dragged their feet, as if invisible chains held them back. One wept openly; several looked as if they too wanted to cry.

I slipped into the crowd. There was no danger of being recognized. Still it made sense to be careful.

The cavalcade was followed by a band of men, women, and children. They wailed and called out names. Some made supplications to One God. Every so often, the three soldiers bringing up the rear would turn around and brandish their arrow-guns at the villagers straggling behind them.

An old woman clutched at one of the soldiers with a scrawny hand. He pushed her away. She would have fallen had not an even older looking man caught her.

I tried to make sense of what was happening. The young men looked like conscripts, extremely unwilling ones at that. But the Sallonian army wasn't a conscript army. The books were clear on the matter—people joined the army for glory, employment, or adventure.

None of these young men looked as if they wanted to join the army for any reason.

The books must have lied about the nature of the army too. Why not? Obfuscating the truth, rather than revealing it, seemed the main purpose of books in Sallonia.

The crowd straggling behind the troops stopped at the edge of the village. The soldiers marched on, taking the young men with them.

From the huddled villagers, the figure of a girl emerged. She veered past the marching soldiers and reached the rank of conscripts. A soldier tried to grab her. She ducked, evading him. Another soldier caught her arm. She tried to break free. He twisted her arm. She screamed and kicked him. He yelled a curse and pushed her away. She fell.

One of the conscripts, a yellow-haired young man in a grubby grey smock, swerved and ducked, trying to reach the girl. He held out a hand to her, screaming a word over and over again, a name.

"Bänge!"

The girl sat up and held out her own hand.

The officer shouted something.

The two hands were within touching distance when the soldiers grabbed the young man. He struggled like someone demented.

For a moment, I had a crazy desire to shout at the villagers, tell them to help the girl and her young man. If all the villagers got together, we could defeat the soldiers. Then I remembered the arrow-guns. What if the soldiers fired them? Would Sallonians shoot at other Sallonians? A few hours ago, such an idea wouldn't have occurred to me. Now I wasn't sure.

And what if no one heeded my cry? What would happen to me then? I'd be arrested, and taken away. Sooner or later my identity would be uncovered. That would be the end of my quest, and of me.

So I said nothing. Like everyone else, I watched as two soldiers grabbed the young man, watched as a third hit him on the head with an arrow-gun, watched as he slumped, and watched as he was dragged away. I was angry, burning angry inside. Still, I did nothing.

The girl, Bänge, tried to stand up. A soldier kicked her. She crumpled back into the mud. He spat at her. She lay unmoving like a stillborn fetus.

The troops resumed their journey.

When a bend on the road hid the marching company, the dogs started barking, loud mournful howls.

I blinked and looked around me.

Suddenly the villagers were everywhere. Many rushed to where Bänge lay. Prayers and mutterings mushroomed.

"As if we're Muffies."

"They say we are all Sallonians but treat us worse than they treat Muffies."

"War's fine. But who's going to till our land when the young are taken?"

"Poor Bänge."

"We should complain."

"To whom?"

"The king. Perhaps he doesn't know."

"Ay, and a tiger thinks the deer want to be eaten."

A few people looked at me as if noticing me for the first time. They didn't seem friendly. Soon there would be questions. That was a situation I didn't want to face.

Spooky detached himself from a pack of dogs and came up to me. He didn't bark, but the message in his eyes was somehow unmistakable. He thought we should leave. Now.

He loped towards the forest and the mountain range. I followed. Soon we were out of the village and walking through a rain-drenched wilderness.

The keening sound seemed a part of the wind at first. The dog stopped, his ears cocked. I stopped too and listened. A few seconds later I heard the sound again and recognized it. Someone was weeping.

The weeping indicated someone in trouble. And I knew all about being in trouble. Perhaps I could help—

The dog must have sensed my intent even as I was marshalling my thoughts. He bared his teeth, emitting a warning growl for emphasis.

I decided to play conciliatory. No need to make him more irked than he was. "I have to go and see. Please understand."

He growled again. Clearly he wasn't willing to understand.

I hesitated, torn. The sensible thing would be to listen to him, and try to reach the mountains before the night descended or the rain resumed. But I couldn't get rid of the memory of my own incarceration, how I longed for a friendly word. Added to that memory was a sense of guilt. I had watched a horrible injustice being committed, without a word. That inaction probably saved me; it also made me feel wretched.

Ignoring the dog's bristling anger, I plunged into the forest. I expected the dog to bark, bar my way, or even take a bite out of my ankle, but there was nothing.

A short distance away, in a tiny clearing, I came across the weeper, huddled on a fallen tree trunk, head bent, shoulders heaving.

My jaw dropped. It was…Bänge.

I said, "Good evening," and wanted to bite my tongue.

Not the right greeting for someone who was obviously having a very bad evening.

Bänge looked up, dashing a thin hand across her tear-filled eyes. Her facial muscles tightened and her brows drew together. "Who are you? What are you doing here?" Her voice was taut, with a sharp edge to it.

I wished I had listened to the dog. It was too late now. I had to answer Bänge's questions before she raised alarm. I had decided on a name for myself and a tale during my walk. I struggled to remember, but my mind seemed a blank.

Bänge's expression hardened into hostility. "You…" She stopped, staring at something behind me.

I turned around to see the dog walking into the clearing. I hardly recognized him. His tail was wagging, and his mouth hung open in a wide dopey grin. He ignored me and headed straight to Bänge, greeting her with a bark oozing with affection. She held out a tentative hand. The dog gave it a hearty lick. She patted him on the head. He gazed up at her, his tail wagging so much I thought it would fall off—and I wouldn't have minded if it did.

Ever since we began the journey, he had been treating me like a troublesome gnat. Here he was making a fuss of a complete stranger. I knew why he was doing it. Still it set my teeth on edge.

As the theatre of affection continued, I studied Bänge. She seemed to be about my age. Her brownish yellow hair was cropped as short as mine; two dimples danced in and out as she smiled at the dog.

"What a nice dog," she said at last. "Is he with you?" She

gave the dog another pat. He capered around her in a fair imitation of joyous delirium. "What's your name? Where are you going?"

"This is Spooky," I began, trying hard not to stammer as I moved from fact to not-quite-fiction. "A few days ago, I lost my way and became stranded in a forest. He found me and helped me to get out. I thought he'd go back to wherever he came from but he didn't. I think he has sort of adopted me. I was lonely, and it was nice to have a companion." I avoided looking at the dog, but still felt his disapprobation. He clearly thought I was doing a bad job with my ramshackle story. He certainly didn't approve of the picture I painted of him—rescuer of lost damsels.

My delivery must have been convincing because Bänge bowed her head and brought her palms together in a traditional Sallonian greeting. "I'm Bänge. Who are you? What are you doing here?"

I took time with my own greeting, trying to remember the story I had prepared. I could sense it hovering at the edge of my memory. But every time I reached out it slipped away.

Bänge's face tightened a little. Her friendly gaze started changing into an intense stare.

Sweat trickled down my back, despite the cold.

A memory flashed, not the one I sought but of a conversation I overheard once, between Nana and Sherby, one of the younger maids. Sherby had been begging Nana's help to rescue her sister from her master. Nana must have succeeded in eliciting Bellizza's intervention because Sherby's sister joined the queen's household as a junior maid.

Genii, a mousy little thing who looked as if she was terrified of her own shadow.

"My name is Genii, I'm…I'm running away." I held out my hands. "Please you mustn't betray me."

Bänge waited, her body stiff with wariness again.

"My parents are…are dead. I'm a servant. I worked for a warrior's family. My master…my master…" I tried desperately to think of something awful my supposed master did that would warrant me running away. What had Genii's master done to her? All I could remember were a few stray words like trouble and bother. "He bothered me…" I stopped, realizing what the word meant in this particular context.

"You poor thing." Bänge's voice was as soft as the wind in Roaziyan's land.

I looked down flushing, feeling guilty about the lie.

"I'm right glad you escaped," Bänge said, her light brown face darkening with anger. "We hear awful stories about bonded servants. My father says it's real terrible, Sallonians treating Sallonians so bad. As if we are Muffies."

Muffies that word again.

I knew it, a slang-word meaning uncivilized and stupid. Calling someone a Muffie was the ultimate insult. Once when we were small, Cousin Tawni called me a Muffie. Nana had boxed his ears. He had complained to Tygyrin and got his ears boxed again, much to my loud delight and Nana's quiet satisfaction.

Now I understood. Muffie, short for Muffic, Mother's people. My people too, just as Sallonians were my people.

Tawni, like everyone else in Sallonia, knew. How he

must have laughed at me. I thought of his other name for me, Copper Princess. I had always believed the name was sourced in my reddish-brown coloring. But copper had another meaning, cheap, insignificant, third rate; the lowest coins were cast in copper.

Why did I allow myself to be fooled so easily? Why? Why didn't I look deeper and reflect more? When Nana refused to answer my questions, why didn't I ask Tygyrin? He would have told me the truth. He might even have waited for me to reach out to him, to turn to him for answers. I remember him telling me twice, to come to him if I was confused about something. I didn't. When something confused me, and plenty did, I'd push it to the back of my mind, focusing on a plant until I forgot.

Bänge was saying something. I heard only the two last words—Crow Mountain. She must have asked me if I was headed there.

I nodded. "I want to get out of Sallonia. I was walking through your village and saw what happened to you and your friend."

Her brown eyes darkened. "Anonian. We grew up together. The king's men came this morning. We had no warning till they started hammering on doors."

Questions crowded my tongue but I didn't ask them. Ignorance like mine would be abnormal. Bänge might wonder which hole-under-a-stone I emerged from.

"Do they take young men often?' I asked. That seemed like a proper question. After all, I was a stranger to this area.

"A few join, for money. Most don't. We're farmers here,

not soldiers. They come once a year for the levy. This year they came twice. I suppose it's because war's coming."

I frowned, trying to remember whether anyone said anything about an impending war back at home. I was sure no one had. Roaziyan hadn't either.

And what levy?

I chose my words with care. "Where I was, we didn't hear much. We lived in the servants' quarter. When the work was done, we were too tired to do anything other than sleep. It was like being in a different world."

Bänge shook her head. "Here no one's talking of nothing else. Everyone's sure the war'll come soon. Maybe even this year."

"But with whom?"

"Muffies of course."

This time I couldn't control the gasp. "Muffics?'

Bänge nodded, blinking nervously.

"But why? I mean I know they are…they are fearful. But why go to war with them?"

"Some people say it's got to be done, 'cos they own all the best land." Bänge gave another doleful sniff. "My father says they just do better in worse lands, 'cos they've magic. Until they took Anonn away, I wasn't bothered about the war. Now he's been taken, and I don't want war. What good will a war be for folks like us? The king will get everything, and we'll just get dead bodies."

"Can't you complain to the king?"

Bänge's gaze turned withering. "What do kings care about folks like you and me?" She made a dismissive gesture with her hand. "Now the queen's dead, he'd be looking for a new wife. He has to, with only a Halfling daughter. He'd be busy with ceremonies and the like, not with you or me."

I tried to nod. My mind felt like a maze. It seemed as if I knew next to nothing about not just my own country's past, but also its present.

The sky split open in a flash of lightning. Rain poured. The wind wailed as it whipped against the branches.

Bänge turned to me, shouting to be heard over the storm. "Come home with me. You can stay with us and set off tomorrow."

A dry room, a crackling fire, warm food; I almost gave in. But there'd be questions. Bänge hadn't noticed any holes in my patchy tale, but her folks might.

"It's too dangerous. I don't want to be caught." We were standing very close, and I was literally yelling in her ear.

"We've helped runaways before. We Sallonians must stand by each other. As the Book says, we're the leaves of the same divine tree."

I hesitated. The danger of harboring a runaway bonded servant might not be much, but a runaway princess, and one accused of murdering the queen? The soldiers could come here, a day, a week, a month from today. If by some mischance they discovered what happened, these people would be in serious trouble. The risk of such a mischance might be minimal, but I didn't want to take it, not after what I saw today.

Bänge gave my hand a reassuring squeeze. "Sometimes masters offer a reward. But you can trust us. We'll not betray you."

I shook my sodden head. "My master is very powerful.

I've defied him. If he fails to capture me, it would set a bad example. He caught a runaway servant after two years, and got him hung."

Bänge looked doubtful and worried. "I can't leave you here…" Her face brightened. "There's this abandoned hut that belonged to a woodcutter. He died months ago. We used to go there, Anonn and I…" Her voice wavered a little. "It's dry inside. You'd be safe there."

It seemed a better option. I gave in.

The dog didn't growl. I decided to take his silence as a sign of approval.

The walk to the hut was not long, but we had to battle our way through thickets and over fallen branches. The rain pelted us without mercy. The wind roared, like a hungry beast.

When we reached our destination, I felt the trouble was worth it. The hut was indeed dry. A palace couldn't have pleased me more.

Bänge stood staring at the blank wall, as if she saw something else there. Suddenly she turned towards me, her eyes too bright. "What about your food?" There was a slight tremor in her voice. I pretended not to notice it.

"An old woman I met on the way gave us some food."

"I'll come tomorrow morning and show you the best way over the mountains." Bänge's voice was firm, but there was an almost pleading look in her eyes. "There's a pass at the knee of one of the hills. It's not known to outsiders. If you take it, you'll be out by nightfall. Otherwise you'd have to climb for about two days."

I gave in, again. It should be safe.

After Bänge left, I unpacked the food. Spooky gulped down his meat and curled into a tight ball by the door. I removed my muddy footwear, cleaned myself as best as I could, and ate my sesame patties, pickled onions, and fried treacle cake, savoring each mouthful.

Afterwards, I took out the stone-light and my Memory Book.

Genii was bonded to her master, like a slave.

The books painted a different picture of bonded servants. They were depicted as hardworking but happy, eager to labor, earn, and become their own masters, a kind of apprenticeship. The first step in a ladder that leads up and up.

Lies.

Sallonia is a divided country, vertically between Sallonians and Muffics, and horizontally, between rich Sallonians and poor ones, between the ones with power and the ones without.

Perhaps instead of studying plants, I should have studied people.

Genii's master had harassed her; no that's the wrong word. He had tried to molest her or had molested her. No wonder the poor girl looked so terrified.

I felt sorry for her and was kind to her (What did my kindness entail other than a smile on the rare occasion I saw her?). But I never bothered to learn her story, didn't even wonder whether she had a story. Why didn't I? True, no one would have told me the truth even if I asked. The point is, I never asked.

Are bonded servants used in Sallikan mines as well?

Sallikan was One God's gift to us, Nana claimed. An accident of geography, Uncle Bernii cried. Something we must use for the betterment of our people, Tygyrin said.

Bänge mentioned an annual levy. Levy means a tax, in gold or in grain or some other material. Or so I thought. Can levy also denote a tax in men? Could the king make families pay by taking sons for the army?

Papa, Uncle Bernii, Tygyrin, Minister Ekko—they are all good men. Why did they let such injustice be when they could have done much to make things better?

2

ONLY A SHE-WOLF

"We greeted the Sallonians with courtesy, and allowed them to camp out on the fallow fields."
Histories – Roaziyan the Younger

By the time I woke up next morning, the rain had stopped. The sky hung with grayish purple clouds, promising more rain, soon.

Spooky had gone out, probably in search of food. I brushed myself down and peered into the little mirror Roaziyan had given me. The dye still held. Once satisfied that I looked like a proper Sallonian, I started clearing the hut of any telltale signs of last night's stay. I was almost done when I heard Spooky's bark. Understanding its welcoming nature needed no effort on my part.

Bänge came in, flushed and flustered. "The soldiers are here."

"They've come to take more young men?" This seemed an unending nightmare.

"No, these ones are different. They've come from Pinckossia, searching for a Halfling who'd killed two people."

I started, a ghostly finger tracing icy cold lines up and down my spine.

"They say she's about seventeen, has coppery hair and coppery skin, like most Halflings, I guess. We told them we've not seen any Halflings here."

"Did you tell them about me?" I demanded, trying to keep my voice steady.

Bänge shook her head. "No, but some of the villagers had seen you. They'd told the soldiers. Now the officer wants to talk to you."

"But…but I'm not a Halfling."

Bänge smiled. "Of course you're not. I know colors, don't I?" She dropped her voice. "But I've heard some Halflings are almost brown and have brown or yellow hair, just like us. Anyway, they probably want to ask you if you'd seen this Halfling."

Panic was taking over. All I wanted to do was run. I grabbed my pack, trying to speak calmly. "I didn't see any Halfling. I can't talk to the soldiers. If they suspect I'm a runaway, they'll arrest me and return me to my master. Please go away and forget you saw me. That way both of us will be safer."

Bänge caught my hand. "I'll show you the way to the pass." She took out a small packet from her pocket. "Here's some food. Eat. Then we'll go."

I shook my head. "No. We can manage. Please just don't

mention you ever saw me."

"I'll take you and Spooky to the foothills, Genii," Bänge insisted, her fingers stroking the dog's spine.

I was about to say no when the dog barked. It seemed as if he was telling me to do as Bänge suggested.

I blinked to clear my head. How did I know that?

Bänge got the food out, flatbread and a paste of grounded onions, tomatoes and yellow chilies. The flatbread was dense and the paste hot. But they filled my stomach and made me feel more able to face what might await me.

Bänge led us deeper into the forest. The absence of rain made walking easier, even though the ground was boggy. Now and then, Bänge gave the sky an interrogative look, as if trying to fathom the hour of rain.

We were within sight of the foothills when we heard the voices, far enough still but coming closer.

Spooky growled.

Bänge said, "Soldiers." She grabbed my bag from me, caught me by the other hand and ran, Spooky at our heels. She was fleeter of foot and soon I was gasping for breath like a drowning woman. But terror spurred me on, giving me a few more ounces of energy every time I thought I'd spent the last one.

Bänge stopped finally and pointed through the tree-line at a rock with a flat-top, rather like a table.

"Go round that rock. There'll be a narrow path heading up. You'll have some hard climbing to do, but head for the ledge. It's straight up. It'll lead you to a notch. Cross it, and you're out of Sallonia. I'll throw your umbrella into the stream over there. That way they'd think you had fallen in."

She took out the palm frond umbrella from my bag and held the bag out to Spooky. He took it in his mouth.

I touched her arm. "I don't know how to thank you. Will you be able to get back home in safety?"

Bänge nodded. She bent down to give Spooky a kiss. I watched the easy interaction between them.

Then Bänge was sweeping me into a kind of embrace that reminded me of Uncle Bernii. "Go in safety. I hope we'll see each other again."

I returned the embrace. Perhaps, when all this is over, I'll return and tell her the truth…

Bänge vanished into the forest. A low growl made me turn around. A grey wolf stood by me, his gold-flecked eyes flashing. The next moment he was running up the scree towards the rock with the flat top, carrying my bag in his mouth.

I scurried after him.

The path wound between scraggy bushes and towering boulders, more like the bed of a dried-up streamlet.

The voices got closer, the clamor made by many people talking at the same time. How did they know where to look for me? Did some villager tell them about the secret path?

Spooky growled. It was as if he were telling me to focus. He began to climb the path, as sure-footed as any mountain goat.

I wasn't as sure-footed as a mountain goat though. Not even close. I had done some climbing during my visits to Uncle Bernii, but that had been like sauntering on level ground compared to the kind of climbing I was faced with currently. These slopes were not vertical yet, but they were heading in that direction. Soon I'd have to give up walking and start crawling upwards, like an ant. And there was precious little to cling to for support, other than rocks.

The path vanished into a boulder. Walking ended and crawling began. I stopped my mind from straying and focused on each foothold and handhold. The wind carried the voices of my pursuers, but I forced myself not to listen. I kept my attention on each rock, testing whether it was capable of holding my weight before taking the next step. My heart thudded painfully against my ribs, my body ached, and my hands felt bruised. A cold wind whipped around me, yet I was drenched in sweat.

The clouds hung low. If rain descended suddenly, the rocks would turn too slippery to hold. I tried to pray to One God, but the words wouldn't come.

The rock seemed solid until I put my weight on it. Then it was gone. The cry of terror escaped before I could stop it, followed by the sound of the rock hitting a boulder below. Another rock fell, taking my other foothold with it. And my feet were kicking at air.

I clung to the stone with both hands. Sweat was raining and my fingers were slippery with it. Breathing hurt, each breath was a gasp. I forced myself not to look down. I looked up instead, at the glowering sky and at Spooky. He was staring at me with horror in his face, a grey wolf with a bag in his mouth.

Suddenly I felt lightheaded, assailed by an urge to laugh and cry.

Somewhere below a voice shouted. "Capt'n, the rock-fall, that's her."

The unseen soldier's voice steadied me by reminding me of the greater peril. If I fell I'll have a quick death. What would happen to me if they caught me, I had no idea.

I stopped kicking at nothing, clung to the stone harder, and heaved myself up.

And found a foothold, and then another.

I started to crawl again, inch by inch.

A different voice, with a note of command in it, said, "You two, go up the track. Corporal Cyclo, go round."

Spooky hurried up the mountainside, reached the ledge, and was gone. A new fear stabbed at me. Was he abandoning me?

The sound of another rock falling almost made me lose my grip. I thought it was my doing until I realized the sound came from somewhere else.

A voice cried, "It's a dog. I told you I saw a dog there below. He must be with her."

Spooky howled.

"You halfwit," the commanding voice shouted. "Are you blind? That's a wolf."

Spooky howled again, an eerie sound that filled the air.

The narrow ledge was close. I reached it with a final heave and huddled on the flat surface, racked with silent sobs. My hands and legs were bleeding. My body ached like one unending sore. Still, I was safe for the moment, even though I had no idea what was happening to Spooky. He had obviously kicked down a stone in the hope the soldiers would think he was responsible for the earlier rockfall as well. But what if they shot at him?

Almost on cue the commanding voice shouted, "Don't

shoot, you cretin. Wolves live in packs. You'll bring down the whole lot on us."

Someone replied, in a tone which was both unctuous and sullen, "They have to be up there, capt'n. We have to get her. They told us she's a killer…"

The commanding voice cut in. "Are you trying to teach me my job, soldier? Even if the Halfling came this way, the wolves would have finished her. Put your weapon down. That is a command, soldier, not a request."

I heaved a gust of relief. Spooky was safe, for now.

That was when I saw him: a soldier, a young man, standing on the rocky plateau, looking up at me. As I sat hugging the ledge transfixed with shock and horror, he waved a reassuring hand and walked away. I stared at him, unable to make sense of what happened until the jutting rocks hid him.

Silence reigned for a while. It was broken by a new voice. "Nothing there Captain, except I think a she-wolf."

"They are the worst," shouted the voice of the commander. "Get going. We have wasted enough time here. Those villagers lied. She must have headed in the other direction."

I felt faint with relief.

Spooky was beside me, still in his wolf form, still carrying the bag. He gave me a satirical look, turned around, and started running. I followed him. As Bänge said, the ledge was a narrow circuitous path leading to a notch in the ridge. A few more minutes and we were on the other side, out of Sallonia. I staggered to a patch of grass and collapsed.

The dog, still in his wolf form, watched me.

"I need a rest," I said, holding out my hand for the bag. "Just a few minutes."

He dropped the bag near my outstretched hand. I took out the water gourd, drank some water, broke the remaining flatbread into two pieces, and gave one to Spooky. He growled.

I started munching the flatbread. I was almost done when the word came to me.

Trash.

I swallowed the last mouthful and choked. Coughs racked my body. I pressed my hand to my mouth to keep the noise in.

Trash.

It was fantastic, unbelievable. This was the way I had felt when, after struggling for months, I began to understand Bellizza's language.

I caught the dog's eyes. "You said trash, didn't you, when I gave you the flatbread?" I smiled. "I hope you were referring to the bread and not to me."

We stared at each other in silence. Eventually the dog growled. At first the growl was just a sound. Then it had words.

I repeated, "Bread, stupid"

Excitement gripped me. The joy of discovery was intoxicating. I felt as if a whole new world was opening up. I forced myself to curb my bubbling emotions. If I didn't concentrate, the new understanding might slip from my still tenuous grip.

I also had to be careful of the dog's reactions. He wouldn't approve if I capered about whooping for joy.

"I'll ask you some questions, Spooky. If you answer, I'll repeat your answers to you in my language. If I'm right, will you thump your tail once?" I added, in an even politer tone, "If you don't mind, that is."

The dog made no sound. But his expression indicated a reluctant willingness.

"Why did you call me stupid?"

Another long silence followed. I sat back, listening to the wind. Eventually the dog emitted a series of growls.

I closed my eyes, honing in on the sound. The thrill of discovery possessed me again. I said, "Because I've been understanding you for a while without realizing it?"

The dog regarded me, his expression unreadable. Then he thumped his tail, once.

"I suppose you are right," I said wonderingly.

He growled.

I focused. It was easier now. "You said we must go." The first rain drops hit me. I smiled at Spooky. "We should indeed."

His glance rested on my chopped hair. He barked something and loped off. As I followed him at a run, the meaning of that bark became clear, drawing a chuckle from me.

"More sense than hair, thank the wolves."

3
THE TALE OF THE THREAD-TREE

"On the first solstice of every year, we held the ceremony to honour Earth-mother. Sallonians begged leave to stay for it. We were happy to grant their request."
Histories – Roaziyan the Younger

DESCENDING A PATHLESS MOUNTAIN WITH RAIN LASHING behind and ahead was far harder than walking through a rain-infested forest. Yet I felt light-hearted. I was out of Sallonia, able to walk without looking over my shoulder, and sleep without wondering what enemy was lurking in the shadows.

Spooky, back in his dog form, hurried ahead, growling at me to be careful. But his tone indicated more concern than irritation; it took the sting out of the rain and made me feel less alone.

A chilly night edged out the grey evening. Twice I

slipped on the treacherous mud. The second time I would have fallen had I not clutched at a ragged bush.

My stifled cry made Spooky stop and turn around. In the advancing dark, he seemed more like an outline of a dog rather than a flesh and blood creature. But his eyes glowed red.

He barked. It took me a few seconds to turn the sound into words: "Can't you…see…see in the dark?"

My teeth were chattering from cold and from fear of that almost-fall. I shook my head.

"Roaziyan can."

"I seem to have got the short end of both sticks."

His growls throbbed with annoyance. "Why didn't you tell me? Wait for me. Don't…move." He paused, probably to give me time to comprehend him. "Do you understand?"

I nodded. My knees gave away, and I sank into a huddle.

The rain battered me. The wind moaned as it found its way through crags and crannies. The wet clothes clung to me like an unwanted embrace. I tried to occupy my mind with practical things, like hunger. There was food inside the bag. As soon as Spooky found a shelter, we'd be able to eat. I imagined a dry cave and a crackling fire.

That was when I became aware of the stinging pain in my palm. I must have injured it when I clutched at the bush to prevent my fall.

"Just lick the wound." Uncle Bernii once told me when I injured my finger on a nettle while on a walk.

"Why?" I had asked.

"Because it's a small wound and saliva has healing properties. That's what many animals do when they are injured."

Blood.

I wasn't huddled against a rock on a dark mountainside with rain beating down on me. I was in Bellizza's sunroom staring at her prone figure, knowing that something was not right without knowing what.

Now I did.

When I visited Bellizza that afternoon, the needles had been threaded in white silk, and the half-finished thread-tree was white. The three-quarters finished thread-tree I saw by Bellizza's lifeless body was red and white, more red than white.

"Allii!"

The bark vibrated with irritation, as if Spooky had been barking for quite a while.

I muttered a hasty, "Sorry." I could see nothing of him. Only his ember-eyes.

He growled. I forced myself to concentrate on his words. "Did you fall asleep?"

I shook my head.

"You look as if you've seen a roomful of ghosts."

"Not a roomful," I said through clattering teeth. "Just one."

"Why are you sitting in darkness? Where is your stone-light?"

The stone-light. How stupid of me to forget it.

I took out the stone-light and followed Spooky. The footpath circled the mountain for some distance and ended at the mouth of a shallow cave with a sandy floor. There was barely enough room, but it was blissfully dry.

When eating was over, Spooky asked, "What was the

ghost you saw?" This time I understood most of what he said without making a conscious effort.

Tygyrin once told me that relearning something was easier than learning. I must have inherited the ability to understand animals from my mother. I was taught to forget it, but the ability remained dormant. Perhaps that was what Nana meant when she muttered there was no need to sharpen a nettle.

"My stepmother's," I said. "Not her ghost of course. Something that had been bothering me, I suddenly realized what it was."

"Now you are talking in riddles."

I took out the Memory Book and started writing. This way I'd be able to arrange my thoughts and tell Spooky a coherent tale. If it were cogent enough and convincing enough it might wipe that snarky look off his face—hopefully.

Thread-knitting: Bellizza's favorite sister Kummizza had called it an art designed for women who had no real work to do.

Belle disagreed. She said thread-knitting had been designed by royal women to keep themselves sane.

"Think about it, Allii. If you are a daughter forced into a marriage you hate, a wife tied to a husband you can't love, a mother who has seen her children turn against each other, what can you do? You must find a way to live until you die."

"Daughters and wives can always run away."

"Where to? And to what end? A life of manual labor in the fields or in the mines? To marry a poor man, and suffer

privations all your life? It is not as if royal females are taught any useful skills."

"There are other options," I objected. "Your sister ran away and became a stargazer."

"She has a passion for stars. She lives atop a mountain, staring at stars, calculating their lives. I'd go mad if I have to live like that."

"So, you thread-knit. Is it better?"

Bellizza smiled. "As long as I do this, I'm at peace." She held out the figure she had just finished. A bull-crane in yellow. It was exquisite.

"The beak should have been red," I said.

She shook her head. "No, thread-knitting should be done only in a single color. That way the mind gets absorbed and you are taken away from the present into a place where there's no time, no other people, just you and the joy of creation."

Then there it was: Belle's final creation, a tree, three-quarters finished. The needles were threaded with white silks, not white and red. I saw it.

The red had to be blood.

So how did the thread-tree get blood on it?

There was no blood visible anywhere in the room, other than on the thread-tree. That means a small injury, maybe even a prick. Was it her finger? What caused the injury? One of the needles? A pin? Was it an accident or not?

Is there a connection between the blood and the murder or are they unrelated?

I read out what I had written and ended with a lame, "I don't know what you think…"

Spooky growled.

I heard no words. Panic covered me in a cold-sweat. Am I losing the ability to understand him as soon as I discovered it?

He must have sensed something. He gave a short, sharp bark. I forced down my panic, listened, and heard. "Focus."

I nodded.

He growled again. I listened, brushing all other thoughts aside, and heard. "You might be right about the bloodstain, Allii. But is it relevant to the murder?"

"I think so."

"She might have pricked her finger while knitting."

I frowned. "Bellizza was an expert knitter. An accident can't be ruled out even so. But if she pricked her finger accidently, how did the thread tree get bloodstained?"

"She touched it?"

"She wouldn't, not with a bleeding finger, not Bellizza." I bit my lip, trying to string my thoughts in proper order, scowling at the gaps I could sense. "Call me stupid, if you will. I think Bellizza was pricked with something poisonous. That was how she died."

"You mean someone jabbed her finger with a poisonous needle? And she let them?"

I flushed a little at his tone. "No, of course not. Maybe she didn't see. It must have been someone she trusted." Doktoras Poll framed me for the murder. He would have had a hand in the murder as well. A man I had trusted completely. But then, I suppose, it wasn't all that hard to deceive me. I didn't see, because I didn't want to see.

When my cousin Tawni called me a Muffie, I almost

scratched his eye out. I knew Muffie was considered a profanity and I was furious he used such a vulgar word on me. I never wondered why he did so.

I didn't realize I had spoken the words out loud, until Spooky asked, "Who's Tawni?"

"My cousin, the middle son of my uncle, Prince Rokkrin."

"Was this Rokkrin the one who was supposed to rescue you?"

I stifled a giggle at the thought. "No, he would have been thrilled I was locked up. He never liked me." Now I knew why he, and people like Sherriz, disliked me. They must have hated having to treat me like a Sallonian princess instead of the Halfling I was.

"So who's Rokkrin?"

"He's my father's cousin. He and his wife Amberlina have, well had, three sons—Tygyrin, Tawnilin and Kollarin. Kolla died years ago. He was my special friend. Tygyrin has always been kind to me. Tawni and I've had a lifelong tiff." I used to call Tawni my personal wasp. Nana, while reproving me for being rude, agreed life was more peaceful when Tawni was absent from it. She liked Tygyrin though. They shared an interest in Sallonian history and in the study of religious texts. He had a habit of seeking her opinion on the meaning of an obscure passage from some arcane tome. His trust in her ability gratified her.

"Weird family you have." There was a laugh in Spooky's growls. "Could any of them have killed your stepmother?"

"I'd love to think Uncle Rokkrin did it or better still Aunt Amberlina. But they were not in Pinckossia when the murder happened." I frowned. "They hated me. They must have hated my mother even more and feared her too." How lonely she must have been, especially after Father abandoned her.

And then the memory came. I grabbed my book and started writing.

I think I must have been about five. I had been wandering around the castle. The room was on the fifth floor. There was no dust there, or cobwebs, or a musty smell, so it was cleaned and aired regularly. Maybe a maid forgot to lock the door afterward.

The room was full of boxes, towers of boxes, some reaching as high as the wood-lined ceiling.

Towards the centre of the room, the boxes were in ones and twos. I opened the nearest.

Books.

I took one. It had a green cover and looked old and well-thumbed. The flyleaf contained a single word, a name: Filliana.

The book had belonged to Mama. The elegant handwriting must have been hers.

I put it aside and took another one; Filliana again. I glanced through the book. Sentences and phrases were underlined. Words were written on the margins in that same elegant hand. I checked the other books. They had all belonged to Mother.

I wish I had committed at least one title to memory.

I might have paid more attention to the books had I not been diverted by another discovery, a rectangular leather case containing two metal tubes, with glass at both ends, one tube slightly larger than the other. A distance-seeing glass. Uncle Bernii had several.

I fixed the two tubes together. The room had a single window. I fixed the distance-seeing glass to my eye and looked out.

The world came to my fingertips—leaves, flowers, birds, clouds.

I suppose someone noticed the open window. And told Nana. I was studying a blue-winged crow when she stormed in.

She put away the books and the distance-seeing glass and locked the room. She took me to my room, made me sit on the bed, knelt by me, and kissed my palms, first one then the other. There were tears in her eyes.

"You want your father to love you, don't you my Allikin?"

I nodded, confused.

"Then don't go to that room again. Don't tell anyone you were there. Don't talk about what you found there. Don't ask any questions."

I immediately asked a question. Come to think of it, when I was a very young child, I asked a lot of questions. Tygyrin used to tease me saying that the first complete sentence I uttered had to have been a question.

"Why would Papa not love me if he knows I've been to that room?"

"Because he doesn't want anyone to go in there. He wouldn't like his orders to be disobeyed."

"But those are Mama's things in that room, aren't they? Why can't I look?"

Nana hesitated. Now I wonder whether those brief hesitations were inadvertent preludes to lies.

"When you are old enough, your father will take you there and show you everything. You must learn to be patient, Allikin." She frowned. "If you are disobedient, your father

will send me away and stop caring about you. Then horrid people like Rokkrin and that wife of his would be able to do whatever they want to you. Remember that. If you are good and obedient, you will be safe and happy. If not…"

I looked up from my writing. Spooky was curled up near the mouth of the cave. I was wondering whether to call him and read out what I had written when he lifted his head and said, "Try to get some sleep. We have a long day ahead of us."

I put the book away, tapped off the stone-light, and lay down, two questions buzzing inside my head like a hive of demented bees.

Who killed Bellizza? Why kill Bellizza? Who? Why? Who? Why…

On the cusp of sleep at last, a memory came to me, something I had seen on the few times I had been out of Pinckossia. Men and women walking, weighed down by the sacks on their backs. I used to wonder how long it would take for them to reach their destination and lay down their burden.

How long would it take for me to be rid of my own burden?

4
GHOSTS THAT LIVE

"The ceremony to honour Earth-mother brought together Muffics from every part of the land. It was an occasion of joy. There was dancing and singing and great feasting. So it had been every year and so it was that year."
Histories – Roaziyan the Younger

WE MADE THE DESCENT TO THE FOOTHILLS UNDER A glowering sky. As we reached the lower slopes the terrain started turning green. By midday we encountered our first fruit trees. I gobbled clumps of red-star fruits, sour skins and all.

Soon we were on a mud-caked and pitted road snaking through a dense forest. Rain fell in fits and starts, though its virulence diminished as we moved further and further from Sallonia.

Around early evening, we came within sight of a tall

wooden fence circling either a large village or a small town. Relief made fatigue vanish. I had enough money thanks to Minister Ekko's generosity. We'd be able to buy ourselves some decent food, maybe even find an inn. I smiled at the thought of spending the night safe from elements in a warm room.

"Allii!"

I emerged from my dream of a cozy fire and a soft bed to find Spooky glaring at me.

"What? Did you say something?"

"There are men with weapons at the gate."

I peered. All I could see was a throng of people near what had to be the entrance to the village.

"I'll take a look." Spooky's growl had a worried timbre to it. "Get off the road and wait for me."

I did. This forest seemed less inhospitable than the forests of Sallonia and full of new wonders. I was inspecting a bush with spindly red and yellow flowers and tiny green berries when Spooky came running. He was panting, his voice more panicky than I had ever heard it.

"The soldiers are Sallonians. I recognized the uniform. They are looking for you."

"What?"

"There was also a man wearing a grey robe."

"A castle official." My voice sounded as if it belonged to someone with a dreadful hoarse throat.

"He had a picture of you as you, in a pink robe with your hair up. They were questioning every female who entered or left the village and…"

I walked up to the closest tree and ran my hand over its

trunk. Underneath my palm the bark was smooth, as if had been polished. The tree had round leaves and grey flowers with a pungent smell. Perhaps I could pluck a bloom and ready it for my herbarium. I'll need to know its name though.

"Allii, what are you doing?"

"I don't know its name. I wish I did." I picked a bloom from a low-hanging branch and held it out to Spooky. "See, the flowers smell sharp. If it bears fruits, they'll be tangy and not sweet. Better for a relish than a dessert."

"We must get out of here."

I looked around. There didn't seem to be any ways out. Just dead-ends.

"Where?"

"As far away from the soldiers as possible. Deep into the forest."

That made sense, just walking with no destination. Sometimes getting lost was the only way left.

Spooky strode ahead, ears cocked, tail stiff. I followed him.

Once or twice, he asked me to wait for him while he went ahead to explore. I stood still until he came back. There was nothing of interest, no new kind of trees or plants. The third time I spotted some tall grass of a green like that of a peacock feather. I crouched on the ground for a closer look. The grass had a satiny touch to match the satiny gleam.

If only I had brought my herbarium and maybe the smaller plant press—

"Allii," Spooky sounded as if he'd had a bad day. "I found a cave. We can spend the night there."

"Just see this grass…"

"For wolf's sake, we are not on a plant-discovering expedition. There are soldiers out there looking for you. Understand?"

I blinked.

Roaziyan had warned me I might be pursued beyond Sallonia's border. I hadn't taken the warning seriously. Sherriz would need Father's permission to commit soldiers to chase me beyond Sallonia. I had been certain Father would never give his consent to something so preposterous. He was unable to free me from my prison, but he'd be glad I was free, or so I thought.

I was wrong.

I followed Spooky into a cave, broad, shallow, and full of light. Darkness would have been better.

Spooky growled. It took me a while to figure the words. "We need food."

Food.

"I can hunt a mouse-rabbit or a grey squirrel. Would you eat it raw or would you like it roasted? Are princesses in castles taught how to skin rabbits?"

The words conjured images of a poor rabbit, all torn flesh and bloody. "Don't kill rabbits," I cried. "Don't kill anything for me. I don't eat flesh or fish." Nana had been appalled when I decided on my new diet. She had tried hard to make me change my mind. Nana's tears generally worked, but not that time.

"Like your mother's people." Spooky's eyes glinted. "I know. I thought the idea of dead rabbits might bring you back from the dead."

"You don't understand…"

"I do, a little. You can't give in. If you do, you'll die. Either they'll kill you or you'll wither away."

Oblivion was the only kind of afterlife there was, Uncle Bernii used to say. Oblivion seemed good right now. Quite good.

"Allii!"

I barely saw Spooky. Other images were there, Father, Bellizza, Nana, Uncle Bernii, a faceless corpse in a uniform…I had to find that poor man's name. I had to meet his family and tell them I didn't kill him.

"There is a stream outside," Spooky said. "I noticed some fruit trees."

I hauled myself up. "Thank you."

The stream was cool and clear. In the soft light of the blue moon, it glittered like the waters of the Sky River, like Bellizza's hair. I lingered, allowing the gentle ripples to bring some calm to the maelstrom raging inside my head.

We resumed our walk early the next morning.

I didn't think about the mystery I had to solve. I didn't write in my Memory Book or discuss ideas and theories with Spooky. I turned the walk into a plant-finding expedition of a kind. There was plenty to find—trees, bushes, grasses, vines, water-plants. Some I recognized from my herbaria or my reading. Most I didn't. Since taking samples was not practical, I plucked leaves and flowers and sketched them in my Memory Book when we stopped for the night.

The world of plants helped me to disremember the world of men.

One such evening, I started drawing a leaf shaped like a splayed hand. I completed the blade and peered at the stipule. It was even more intricately veined. I picked up the stone-light to hold it over the sprig. It felt cold to the touch.

The stone-light had gone out at some point. The cave was clothed in darkness. But I could still see its walls, the book on my lap, the leaf on my palm, the trembling of my fingers—

A bark of laughter made me look at Spooky. "You've been seeing better and better in the dark and never realized it. No wonder everyone could deceive you."

I looked at him, at the forest outside. He was right. My night-sight had improved, and I didn't notice it.

I hadn't got the short end of both sticks after all.

From then on, I started to pay attention to myself and made other discoveries. I could understand the natural world around me better, especially the growls, squeaks, and tweets of animals and birds. I could also recognize which fruits and leaves were edible and which were not from their smell and texture. It was nothing definitive, nothing I could explain even to myself; just a sense that something was good to eat and something else wasn't.

"You were born with those abilities and trained to forget them," Spooky said, as he watched me smelling an orange-colored fruit shaped like a tear drop, feeling it was safe, and taking a cautious bite.

Several days later we reached the end of the forest. Ahead

was a towering mountain range. Spooky's plan was to walk along the foothills for a day and cut across the forest in a northerly direction until we reconnected with the road leading to Mount Mäga. I agreed.

We walked along the foothills until nightfall. A cave cut deep into the mountainside was our place of rest.

I woke up from my nightmare-ridden sleep early next morning to find Spooky deep in conversation with two bat-eared mice.

The mice might have been unsure whether he was just after information or breakfast as well and were relieved to see me up. They jumped onto my outstretched palm, chattering. I tried to understand what they were saying but the voices were too fast. "Slowly, slowly," I said, "I'm still a learner."

The mice had a story to tell. On the other side of the mountain range was a little valley inhabited by two humans and a dog. The woman talked with animals and birds.

"What does she look like?" I asked, excitement rising inside me.

"Black like night," one mouse chattered.

"Hair like fire," the other mouse cheeped.

I looked at Spooky and saw my own excitement mirrored in his eyes. "And the man?" I asked.

"Brown like earth, with straw hair," both mice cried.

"Looks like the woman is a Muffic and the man a Sallonian," Spooky said.

"They must be like my parents." I could barely sit still. "I want to meet them."

I expected Spooky to object but he agreed without a

demur. "Let me get the exact directions from this pair of gibber-gabbers."

Getting the exact directions turned out to be a long process. At the end of it Spooky looked as if he'd like to murder every mouse he could lay a paw on.

"Remind me never to talk to a mouse again," he growled. "These cheeping idiots, for your information, had never seen this couple. They've heard the story from other mice."

I grinned. "A mouse-vine, you mean?"

"Whatever. They've never been to this valley. And its location seems a little more complicated than the other side of the mountain. First we must find a tunnel through which an underground river runs and get out of it through another tunnel. Or so they've been told by other mice. Are you certain you want to try this? It might not even exist."

"You mean something like a mouse-myth?"

"Whatever. Even if it does exist, it might not be safe."

The amusement drained away as the real world returned. I shrugged. "Is anything safe?"

Spooky flapped an ear. "If you are willing to chase a mouse's tale, it's fine by me. We'll have to find more precise information though."

Later that morning we found the information we sought from a pair of green-crested magpies.

After two more days of walking and climbing we reached a pass leading to a lush valley. A wide stream meandered between banks of pink and white wildflowers and disappeared into a cavern. Spooky led the way into its dark depths and I followed. The stream widened as it rushed along the high tunnel, probably fed by subterranean springs.

The sound was soft at first, almost elusive. It increased with each step we took until it grew into a thunderous roar—as if invisible giants were pounding colossal pestles inside my ears and my head.

Spooky exited the cave first. I followed him, and stopped, my cry lost in the tumult of the waters.

We were on a narrow horseshoe-shaped ledge studded with dark grey rocks veined in black. Eight caves, like the one we had traversed, opened up to the ledge. From each a river gushed out and tumbled down to the unseen depths in cascades of silver. Above the ledge cliffs rose, steep and unwelcoming; below the visibility ended in a cloud of mist. Rainbows weaved in and out of the waterfalls. The spray from the tumbling water filled the air. Caught by sunlight, they turned into tiny pearls before vanishing.

An entire landscape of waterfalls! Who in the relative safety of their family, would believe the world could hold so many wonders?

After a while, we found the cave the birds mentioned, the one aligned east. The opening led to a tunnel with another stream running through it. Unlike the one we had traversed before, this tunnel was narrow. I had to walk sideways for long stretches while Spooky waded in the stream.

The tunnel ended in a small sunlit valley. The stream tumbled through a meadow of tall grasses and wild flowers, ending in a pond shaded by spider-web willows, and livened by white star-lotuses. A woman knelt on the bank, washing clothes.

Spooky wagged his tail, not the way he had done with Bänge, but in a stately manner. "Good evening. May we speak with you?"

The woman turned around, her eyes widening in surprise. She stood up in a curiously fluid movement and walked towards us. She was very tall and had the same fiery hair and ebony skin as my mother. She looked young, though there was an ageless quality in her. Her eyes were deep wells of gray on gray, calm on the surface but swirling with hidden currents. I could feel those eyes catching me and pulling me into their depths.

A voice, deep and melodious, brought me back to reality. "Welcome."

I blinked. The woman's eyes didn't look like depthless pools of swirling grays anymore. Just ordinary gray eyes.

She smiled. "I'm Patriana and I live here with my mate and our dog. Welcome to our home."

I bowed. "Thank you. This is Spooky. My name is Allii and I'm a fugitive." Spooky would probably flay me for that indiscretion. But I didn't want to lie, not to this woman.

Patriana nodded. "So you are Princess Albalia. My mate will return shortly. He'll be delighted to see you. Relieved too. Ever since your escape plan was betrayed, we've been fearful for you." She smiled, and for a moment her eyes glimmered like stars. "Call me Pattii. What would you like to do first? Sleep? Eat? Bathe?"

My mouth had fallen open at the mention of the escape plan. I closed it. Spooky too looked shaken.

Patriana smiled. "You must be wondering how I know about your escape plan."

I opted for a nod, not trusting my voice.

"It's a long story. It would be better if you heard it from

my mate." The gray eyes became twinkling stars again. "He'll enjoy telling the story more. Would you mind very much waiting until he returns? I hope you will accept my word that you are among friends."

I sneaked a quick look at Spooky. He answered my unasked question with a bark. "Indeed we do."

Patriana's smile reminded me of moonlight. "Thank you. Now let me repeat my question. What would you like to do first? Eat? Sleep? Bathe?"

Spooky cocked his ears. "I don't know about Allii here, but I'd like to eat something. That is assuming you have something I can eat. I suppose you don't eat meat or fish?"

Pattii laughed. "You suppose right. But I can give you plenty of cheese. Bread too."

Spooky emitted a heart-rending sigh. "Ah well, milk and cheese it is. And bread."

Pattii took us past a natural windbreak made of a row of trees into a small stone cottage. Soon Spooky was lost in a plate of a cheesy concoction, and I was gobbling sesame bread with chunks of cheese.

"Do you keep animals here?" I asked in between mouthfuls.

"No, but there are mountain goats and they allow me to milk them."

We were coming to the end of our meal when I heard the sound of a commanding bark: "Put me down."

Pattii smiled. "Our dog doesn't like the life we lead here. Her puppyhood was spent in a castle stable. She thinks she has come down in the world."

We went out. A man was walking towards the cottage,

carrying a load of wood, a dog at his side.

From the peremptory bark and Pattii's description, I had expected a large and ferocious animal. The dog was no bigger than a house cat, oblong-shaped with stick-thin and bandy legs, a porcine head, and a little curly tail.

A king couldn't have appeared more regal or looked more disdainful.

The dog reached us first, her manner both curious and unwelcoming. Pattii picked her up and kissed the top of her head. "This is Her Imperial Majesty Bandikutz the Great."

"And behold my majestic kingdom," growled the dog.

Pattii laughed, and held out a hand to the man, "Allii, this is my mate."

I stared at the man, taking in the curly yellow hair, the golden brown eyes, the lean face with a day's growth of stubble. Was fatigue making me see things?

The man grinned, his eyes glinting with mischief. "Welcome, little cousin."

I gaped. What I was seeing couldn't be.

I didn't believe in ghosts.

The man laughed. "You don't remember me?"

"Cousin Kollarin?" I stammered. "But…but you are dead." I remembered Nana, face distraught, telling me Kolla had died in a boating accident. The river had been swollen with months of rain, the current treacherous. No body.

He held out a hand. "Flesh and blood, I assure you, Allikin."

I gulped several times. "They told me you died four years ago. Nana took me to visit your memorial. We placed flowers there."

Kolla put his arm around Pattii's shoulders. "When you love the enemy, you are dead to your people."

Pattii's smile was a little awry. "So you are looking at two ghosts, Allii. Two people who are dead to their own kind."

"You mean because you two got married, Uncle Rokkrin and Aunt Amberlina told everyone you were dead?"

Kolla nodded. "Yes. But first tell me what happened to you. Ever since Panda sent word to us about the mishap, we've been worried sick. Pattii had been sending out her generia, but we have had no word about you."

I blinked. Panda? You mean the forester? Do you know him?"

"I used to see him around. I thought he was just a forester, though an uncommonly knowledgeable one. Later, when I fell in love with Pattii, he talked to me. That was when I discovered the rest of his identity." Kolla smiled. "He is a Halfling."

"What?"

Kolla nodded. "Panda and I made our own plans to rescue you, Allii. Then Minister Ekko summoned him and ordered him to get you out of the castle. He was told that a rescue party would be waiting for you on the Great Southern Road. He had just about an hour's notice and had no choice but to go along. He was told to go to his cottage afterward, and not come out, whatever happened. Still, he kept his ears open for any unusual sounds, and heard nothing. No alarm was rung."

I frowned. "Where did the soldiers come from? They were not of the household guard, at least the two I saw. They had a different uniform." There was something familiar about that uniform, but I couldn't place it.

Kolla's eyes were grim. "They would have been brought from the provinces and stationed outside the castle. Ekko summoned Panda the next morning and told him that something had gone wrong with the plan. The old man was beside himself with worry. So was Panda. He looked everywhere for you, but found no trace. How did you evade the soldiers?"

Spooky said, before I could reply, "She suspected a trap, and took another way. I was out and about on an errand and thought she could do with some company."

Pattii repeated Spooky's answer in Sallonian.

Kolla turned to me, brows drawn together in puzzlement. "What made you suspect a trap?"

"Minister Ekko said he sent me a letter explaining everything. I didn't get a letter. I got a three-word note that explained nothing"

Kolla's face was taut. "So someone found out about the plan, someone who hated you enough to wish you dead, because…" He stopped, running a hand through his hair.

"Because I'm a Halfling. The secret everyone knew other than me."

Kolla flushed a little. "You are angry with me for not telling you. But it was what your father ordered."

I threw him an accusatory look. "I thought you were my friend."

Kolla's eyes didn't waver. "Had I told you, would you have believed me?"

I thought about it. "No, I don't suppose so."

"Exactly. You would have run to that terrible old woman, and I would have been in serious trouble."

"What terrible old woman?"

"Nanarina."

"Nana is not terrible. How dare you, Kolla? She's the kindest, most caring, the most loyal person on earth."

Pattii placed her hand on my arm. "From what I've heard, Nanarina was nothing but good to you, Allii, a second mother. Kolla had a different experience with her. She was virulently opposed to our union. She hates Muffics and Halflings. She is a descendant of the First Hundred Families who invaded Sallonia. She's very proud of her origins."

"She loves me," I said in a hard little voice.

Pattii's smile was gentle. "Yes, but she also dislikes Halflings. She loves you, so in that love she was able to forget your mixed origins. And didn't she try to turn you into a perfect little Sallonian princess?"

"Yes, but…" I stopped, unable to continue any longer. Nana did her best to kill the Muffic part in me. And she did lie to me.

"I never doubted Nanarina's love and loyalty to you," Kolla's voice was earnest. "No one did. No one could. She was like a lioness with one cub where you were concerned. Panda always said we didn't have to worry about your safety so long as she was there." He held out his hand. "Friends, Allii."

I took it, smiling. "I'm so happy I found you again, cousin."

His fingers tightened on mine. "So am I. Now tell us what happened to you."

I did. "I thought I'd be free once I was out of Sallonia," I added, trying to keep my voice steady. "I thought…"

Kolla's eyes hardened. "They can't afford to let you go free because they know your value. You see, Panda is organizing other Halflings."

"Organizing other Halflings?" I repeated, feeling stupid and lost.

"They are planning a rebellion. You, Allii, are at the heart of their plans."

5

QUEENS AND PAWNS

"Sallonians mingled with us freely during the public part of the ceremony. When it came to the time for secret rites, we courteously requested them to withdraw, and they with equal courtesy complied. They informed us they will be leaving on the morrow and thanked us for our hospitality. We bade them a safe journey."
Histories – Roaziyan the Younger

IT WAS THE MOST RESTFUL NIGHT I HAD EXPERIENCED since the day of Bellizza's murder. I fell asleep almost as soon as I closed my eyes, didn't dream of being chased by shadowy figures over dark landscapes, and woke up with an unfamiliar sense of wellbeing.

Silence cocooned the cottage. The sounds from outside—chatter of birds, gurgling of water, and rustling of leaves—blended into that silence. I lingered on my bed of soft spade-grass thinking nothing, worrying about nothing, planning nothing—until a blue beetle decided to subject me to a close inspection.

The cottage was empty. I went out. Spooky sat on a rock sunning himself.

"Our hosts have gone out, the dog too," he said. "If you want to ask me something confidential, you can."

I sat down next to him. "What do you think of, well, you know, everything?"

His eyes gleamed with mockery. "You mean the plans to make you queen?"

I nodded glumly.

"I thought you'd be over the three moons."

"Why should I be thrilled? I don't want to go against my father."

"Think of the good you could do."

"Think of the harm I might do." I looked around. We were alone, still I dropped my voice. "This plan to make me queen is no different from my father's plans to get me married off to some prince in a faraway land, probably with a suitable supply of Sallikan as dowry. I'm being used by others for their purposes. Nobody bothers to ask what I want. They want me to do what they want."

Spooky yawned. "You don't want to be queen?"

"No. Yes. No. I don't know."

"Let me ask the question another way. If the choice is all yours, what do you want to be?"

I stared at the faraway mountains, their peaks lost in whorls of mist. "When I was small, I dreamt of being a plant explorer. I was going to discover a new plant species and name it after myself. My stepmother convinced me it wasn't an achievable ambition." I swallowed a sudden constriction in my throat. "Dreams linger, even after you've accepted their futility. Once I find who killed Bellizza and why, then I'll decide what I want to do with the rest of my life. Maybe I'll become a plant explorer. Maybe some other thing. Whatever path I take, it will be mine. I will not be anyone's pawn, again."

"That makes sense."

I stared. "You think so?"

"I do. But may I make a suggestion? Instead of delivering your 'I don't want to be anyone's pawn' line to your cousin, with your long nose in the air for emphasis, I suggest you try to discover as much as possible about what's happening. Right now all we know is the Halflings are planning a rebellion in your name. I think there's a lot more to it than that."

I nodded. "Does Roaziyan know anything about this rebellion?"

Spooky busied himself for a while, checking his paws, biting the tip of his tail, a trick he used when he wanted to buy himself time. "Bound to," he said at last. "Mind you, I can't be certain. Still, this I can tell you. Roaziyan is as proud of her unsullied bloodline as any of your father's people. I don't think she'd be thrilled with the prospect of Halflings ruling the land she still considers hers."

"You mean she doesn't like Halflings? But she was kind to me."

"That's different. Roaziyan is made of layers. It'll take you several lifetimes to get to the bottom of who she is."

He got up and gave himself a thorough shake. "While we are on the subject of Roaziyan, better keep her name out of any conversation with these excellent people. From what I know, she is a controversial figure even among Muffics." His mouth opened in a wide canine grin. "She's not the popular kind."

"Tell me how the two of you met," I asked Pattii and Cousin Kolla that night.

With unspoken consent, we stayed away from the topic of Sallonian politics, especially the Halfling rebellion. We talked about other things—like Cherry Dancers circling the central stone in intersecting ovals.

Pattii fed the fire with a handful of kittirik, the pungent herbs used to keep nocturnal insects at bay—blood moths, buzzing flies, and oil ants. "I had a brother, my One. He and I wanted to learn about mechanics. Our elders have banned such learning. They equate mechanics with Sallonians, and reject both, though in other parts of Pegala, witches have been leading inventors for centuries." She fixed those depthless eyes on me. "The first mechanical messenger bird was invented by a witch. Witches invented stone-lights and water-clocks as well. There's even a book called The *Mechanics of Witchcraft* by a renowned witch, Meaya of Sammalore. We used to point that out to our parents and argue that by rejecting all mechanics we were rejecting a part of our own heritage." A smile flashed and was gone. "You'll realize, Allii, that Muffics can be as obdurate as Sallonians when it comes to received truths and age old traditions."

Kolla shook his head. "But the truly insurmountable problem, the one that makes our situation so intractable, Allii, is the Sallonian conviction that mechanics is the solution to all of life's problems." From his tone, I guessed this was a replay of a longstanding debate between the two of them. "Sallonians equate nature with Muffics, and harm both, though you wouldn't know it from the permitted books. Over several centuries, Sallonians wiped out our entire population of rat-bulls, and then invented mechanical oxen to plough the fields. But only the wealthy can afford mechanical oxen. The poor have to kill themselves doing their own ploughing. Mechanical oxen need Sallikan. The mining is destroying the rivers. Do you know that certain parts of southwest Sallonia are turning into deserts, Allii? Our obsessions are hurting Sallonians as well. We are too wedded to myths and traditions to see it."

Pattii smiled a little. Unlike my excitable cousin, there was an inner equanimity in her; whether this was her real core or merely a layer masking a core of turbulence, I had no idea. "He is right, Allii. But Muffics too cleave to their traditions as stubbornly and as ruthlessly as Sallonians do. Sometimes I think we, Sallonians and Muffics, are the two sides of the same hidebound, intolerant coin."

This conversation was veering too close to topics I wanted to avoid for now. I decided to put it back on a safe track. "You still haven't told me how the two of you met."

Pattii smiled, almost as if she knew what I was angling for and why. "When my brother and I insisted on studying mechanics, we were treated like criminals. We ran away, disguised ourselves as Sallonians, and began studying under a Sallonian master-mechanist." The grey eyes were abysses. "The disguise has to be maintained, with the help of unguents. My brother was remiss sometimes; he forgot little details."

"Like the back of the neck and the ears?" I asked, remembering what Roaziyan told me. "People always do, when they disguise themselves," I added, in response to Pattii's questioning glance. "The books always warn about that."

Pattii nodded. "Exactly. I used to keep an eye on him, but that day he left for the market ahead of me." She stopped, as if she had encountered an invisible obstacle. Her eyes moved to the mountains ringing the horizon and stayed there.

For about a minute, the only sounds were the crackle of fire and the distinct rustle of the heart-shaped leaves of an elephant ear tree.

Pattii resumed speaking, her words coming slow. "I saw this hive of people, heard them shouting 'a witch.' He reached out to me with his mind, begging me to run. I ran towards him shouting his name, but I never saw him." She turned her gaze from the faraway peaks to her clasped hands. "The mob began chasing me. Then your cousin came…"

Kolla had inched closer to Pattii until their shoulders were touching. "Do you remember Liizz, Allii, my mare? She saved us. You should have seen the way she stood while I grabbed hold of Pattii. Then she ran right into the mob, screaming. That was how we got away." He paused, his finger tracing a pattern on Pattii's palm.

I let out the breath I had been holding. "And?"

"When they heard about Pattii, the family went crazy. Mother and father raged. Tygyrin froze. Tawni had hysterics, elegant ones of course. Pattii couldn't go back home. She and her brother had been cast off as polluters. That was when Panda talked to me. He said he heard the rumors and offered to help."

"Didn't you talk to Papa?"

"I did."

I waited for details, explanations. There was none. Instead Kolla said, "So we ran away with Panda's help. We lived in a small village in the Kingdom of Chootzia first, until we heard that a tracker-assassin pair has been set on us."

Tracker-assassins, hired killers used to hunt exotic animals or to track and eliminate fugitives. They were called human blood-hounds because they rarely failed to get their prey. And their charges were exorbitant.

"Was it—was it Uncle Rokki?" I asked.

Kolla shrugged.

"How did you find out??"

"One of your father's generals sent me a message. General Soodda. He had helped me earlier too."

I stared. "Why would someone in his position do something like that?"

Kolla's smile had no mirth in it. "Perhaps he felt pity for us, though pity is not an emotion I'd associate with that type. The likeliest explanation is that he is an opponent of my father. Court rivalry can produce strange results. We are still alive thanks to him. We fled, again and again, until we found this place."

A silence fell, the kind of silence that comes when a conversation had moved beyond words. I realized the story told to me had more to it, more loss, more grief, too intense to be shared. The unspoken words, and the underlying emotions, hung in the air like tongues of flame.

"Are you certain you are safe here? What if they trace you to this place?" My concern was real. I also wanted to escape the raw eddying of emotions round me. They felt too deep and strangely disturbing.

It was Pattii who answered. "Trackers, like Muffics, possess inborn powers. These powers are sourced in nature, the earth, the air, the water, the sky. The powers are not evenly distributed. They are weak on oceans, in deserts, and below ground. We think we are safe here, because the only way here is through the underground cavern."

I nodded, then asked the question that had been churning inside me. "Did my parents face the same kind of persecution as you two?"

"Uncle Walterin was your grandmother's favorite son. She protected him. Your parents had to leave Sallonia of course. They settled down in a house close to Sallonia's northwestern border. Then your father's two older brothers died. Your grandparents summoned your father and told him he had to accept the crown."

"And he came, leaving my mother and me behind." The bitterness came from a place I didn't know I owned.

"From what I heard, you were a bone of contention. Your father wanted you. Your mother didn't want to give you up. Don't think Uncle Walterin abandoned you. On the contrary. He insisted you should be accepted as a princess of Sallonia and granted all privileges of that position. He made his coronation conditional on that."

I blinked back the tears. So he had stood up for me. But why didn't he stand up for Mother? Why did he abandon her? Was protecting me an act of love or expiation? If he went to such lengths to get me, why did he treat me with indifference? Did he regret his decision? Did I turn into an embarrassment, a living embodiment of a mistake he wanted consigned to oblivion?

Pattii leaned forward, looking into my eyes. "Don't see the world in black and white. It is rarely that. Someday, talk to your father. Alone. Ask him all the questions you want to ask. Give him a chance to tell you his side of the story. Don't judge him until then."

Her words were sensible, too sensible in the light of recent discoveries. "Is there going to be a war against Muffics?" I asked. "Is Papa planning to destroy Mama's people?"

Kolla and Pattii looked up in surprise. "How did you hear about it?" Pattii asked.

"When I was escaping Sallonia, a girl helped me. She told me. I saw men being taken away to join the army."

"We've heard rumors. The army is being expanded, probably for that reason, though it is not the work of your father."

I frowned. "Then who? He is king, isn't he?"

Kolla smiled, the same way he used to when I was small and bewildered by something that was obvious to everyone else. "Even kings have to compromise sometimes. I think the expansion of the army is the work of one of the three factions in the court."

I frowned. There seemed to be no end to my ignorance. "What factions?"

Kolla sighed. "You know there's a crisis of succession?"

I groaned inwardly. Ignorance should have been my middle name. "I thought Uncle Bernii would succeed father."

Kolla's smile was grim. "Officially, yes. Unofficially nothing is settled. Don't forget this is a crown we are talking about. That brings out the worst in people. Add Sallikan to the equation and what you get is something unimaginably toxic. Whoever controls Sallonia controls Sallikan. Whoever controls Sallikan has a reach beyond Sallonia's borders. Even the great empires court Sallonia because the more lethal weapons cannot be made without Sallikan—flame-balls, fire-throwers, skin-burners, weapons which kill not one or two at a time, but tens or even hundreds. To return to your question, Uncle Bernii possesses a greater claim because his father was next in age to your grandfather. But in most Sallonian eyes, he has two disqualifications. He has no sons and his mother was a commoner."

I stared. "She was a Sallonian, wasn't she?"

Kolla glance was half-quizzical, half-exasperated. "You are spectacularly ignorant of the reality of our country."

Spooky's bark would have been a guffaw in a human.

I gave a deprecatory smile. "I'm sorry."

"No, it's not your fault. They told you nothing. You had no way of finding out on your own because Veracity Inspectors censor books. Those who are caught reading banned books get locked up."

I frowned. "You mean what they did to me they are doing to the entire country? And everyone in Sallonia goes along with it? They don't realize they are being lied to?"

Kolla's eyes held mine. "I suppose they sense the discrepancies, the inconsistencies. Most don't ask questions because it's safer to keep some doors closed. That was what I did until I met Pattii." His gaze deepened. "Wasn't that what you did, Allii, until Aunt Bellizza was murdered?"

I said, slowly, "It's not an act of will. It just happens. By the time you are old enough to think through things, not looking too deeply has become a habit." I had ignored the gaps in the cocoon of lies I lived in, because deep down I sensed that outside lay insecurity and loneliness.

I had been one more coward in a land of cowards.

Kolla nodded. "To return to what we were discussing, Uncle Bernii's mother wasn't a member of the original hundred families." His lips curled. "The First Hundred Families as they call themselves, with enough pride to move mountains. Whether the initial migration consisted of one hundred families, or not, is anyone's guess. But that is the religious truth, the official truth, and the traditional truth. Sallonian aristocrats always looked down on Bernii and his mother. The Peddler King—that's what Tygyrin calls poor Bernii. The second claimant is…"

I cried, "Uncle Rokkrin."

Kolla grinned. "My father. Now you know why he exploded about Pattii. I'm only a younger son, but me aligning with a Muffic is a huge blot on his otherwise pristine reputation."

"So they told everyone you were dead. How could they?"

"The lure of a crown. I told you it brings out the worst in people. My father wants to be King Rokkrin the Second. In his eyes, he has everything Bernii lacks: a mother and a wife from the First Hundred Families, and two sons to follow him. Tawni would beggar the treasury in months. What kind of king Tygyrin would make is as unfathomable as the man himself."

A very proper one, I thought, pious, kind, and probably a bit boring. Tawni would covet a crown because he'd think it'll look good on him. Tygyrin would accept a crown because he considered it his duty. I didn't voice my thoughts though. For some reason, Kolla and Tygyrin never got along.

"So your father heads one faction. Tell me about the other two."

"The second one is the Bernalin faction. Minister Ekko is a part of that. They want a change in succession laws to enable you to succeed your father. They also want Muffics and Halflings to be treated the same as Sallonians.

"The third is the Sherriz-Pena faction—most of the top officials and priests belong to that. They don't want Bernalin because they think he is too unorthodox. They don't want my father because they know he'll be a disaster. They want your father to marry again. They were pressuring Bellizza to go away."

Bellizza's face, pale and drawn, flashed before my eyes.

"She agreed to go away?"

"No."

Suddenly I heard Bellizza's words in my head. "When you hire a singer, dearest, you expect her to sing." And knew the bit she kept to herself, because she was loyal to father even through his disloyalty—if the singer couldn't sing, she'd be sent away.

What happened when the singer refused to go away?

One more truth that had been staring at me in the face. One more truth I turned away from because of what its acceptance would entail.

My stepmother was murdered so my father could get himself a new wife. As plain as a wolf's fang, yet I never saw it because I didn't want to. I chose to be blind and stupid, because I was too much of a coward to face the truth.

How much did Father know? Did he merely fail to protect Bellizza, or did he have a hand in her murder?

Pattii had planted three varieties of bamboo. One was edible. She made clothes and paper out of the other two. There was a row of trees with seed-pods shaped like four-burner lamps. Pattii didn't know their name, so called them lamp-pod trees; the pods, once dried, were used as oil lamps. There was a vine with a delicate grey flower shaped like a moth. A row of bushes with flowers that changed colors according to the time of day—from white in the morning to pink in the afternoon and a deep gold in the evening—were called sky flowers by Pattii and clock flowers by Kolla.

I wished I could spend all my time studying these new wonders. Unfortunately I had problems to think through and decisions to make. I still wanted to uncover who killed Bellizza and the guard. But I wasn't sure about my chosen path. Was there any point in seeking Kummizza? Could Bellizza's letters tell me anything more than Kolla had?

But then, Kolla had been officially dead for four years. What he knew, he knew second hand. Bellizza lived at the heart of the court. She would have known more. Whatever she knew or suspected, it would be in the letters to Kummizza.

Going to see her still made sense, I decided.

Once I made up my mind, I discussed the matter with Spooky. To my surprise he raised no objection. His sole response was a question. "Are you going to tell our hosts?"

"Of course."

"They won't like it. Especially your cousin."

"But we can't sneak away without a word."

He yawned. "We can. You won't."

"He will understand," I said, though I felt far from convinced.

Spooky yawned again.

That night, I told Kolla and Pattii about Kummizza, the letters, and my plan.

"I see your point, Allii," Kolla said, once I was done. "But for you to roam all over Pegala is dangerous. What if something happened to you? There's too much at stake."

I could feel my expression hardening. "I'll be careful."

Kolla's mouth was a thin line. "The risk is too great. To succeed, the rebellion needs you. When you vanished, our plans became mired in debates. There was no consensus about how to proceed. Now that you are here, everything's on track again. I don't want any more upsets. The rebellion matters more than anyone of us."

My fingers clenched into fists. "I have to go."

Kolla spoke slowly, as if he too was trying to keep his emotions under control. "Do you have any idea the kind of horrors normal Halflings are subject to?"

I shook my head.

"There are far more Halflings than most people realize. Officially they don't exist, because officially Sallonians can't have 'any commerce' with Muffics. But laws can't prevail against life. In many of the border areas only a penetrable forest, a fordable river, or a low ridge separates Sallonian villages and Muffic settlements. People from the two sides interact with each other. They buy, sell, and exchange. Sometimes they form a passion, even fall in love. When there are children, they are hidden, even abandoned by their own parents. Halflings don't have a sense of belonging. Most leave their unwelcome birth-villages and go to towns and cities. If they are not easily recognizable as Halflings they can manage, like Panda. Others end up in prisons or dead."

I shivered. I had lived a life of ease atop a mountain of injustice and suffering.

Kolla's eyes were on me. "You have a chance to end all that, Allii. Become the queen regnant and change Sallonia for the better."

"I'm not interested in the throne," I muttered.

Kolla leaned forward, staring into my eyes. "Allii, if you are the queen-regnant, you will be able to unite your father's people and your mother's people, and usher in an era of peace. As the daughter of your parents, as the only member of the royal family with Sallonian and Muffic blood, that's your destiny."

"You sound like a storyteller, Cousin Kolla—the princess unites the warring clans and everyone lives happily ever after."

Pattii gave a short mocking laugh.

Kolla's expression was reproving. "Sometimes life imitates stories, like the persecuted princess who becomes a vagabond. You mustn't think I'm some kind of dreamer unmoored from reality. I'm not. And Panda is as hard-headed as they come. I'm not asking you to become queen for your sake. I'm asking you to do it to end millennia of injustice."

I swallowed, but my mouth was dry and my throat hurt. I looked at Spooky. He sat staring at a paw with intense concentration. There would be no help from him. This was my decision and I'd have to make it alone.

Kolla leaned forward. He spoke softly, putting emphasis on each word. "Allii, you can either stay here or you can go to Bernii."

"But the rebellion will take years…"

Kolla's eyes were like closed doors. "The rebellion will *not* take years."

I looked at his face and saw the truth staring at me. This time I faced it. They intended to launch the rebellion before Father made his next marriage.

If I wanted to help others like me, I had to become a traitor to Father. I had to do to him what he did to my mother, and perhaps to Bellizza. I had to put my duty to the people I belonged to above my loyalty to the persons I loved.

Would I do it? Perhaps. Perhaps not. But first I had to complete my own quest. If I gave up now, there'd be no justice for Bellizza, and no closure for me. This was between Belle and me. This was something I had to do.

All my life, I allowed other people to make decisions for me. Not anymore.

"I'll come back," I said. "I swear by Nana, I'll come back. But first I must go. Please don't stand in my way."

Pattii gave her gentle smile. "I think it's a good decision. Go, do what you must do, and return."

Spooky wagged his tail, once.

Kolla's eyes were narrowed, his jaw set into a hard angle. I readied myself for an argument. Suddenly he laughed. "I can hardly keep you a prisoner here. May I make a suggestion though? A faster road to Mount Mäga?"

"What's that?"

"Stargazers need distance-seeing glasses. They can get them from only one place."

"Brunelles the dragon," I cried.

Tales of Brunelles had enthralled my otherwise sedate childhood. Brunelles the dragon had saved Uncle Bernii's life and they had been friends since then. Bernii had an unending store of Brunelles stories which he regaled me with when I used to visit him. At the end of each tale, I'd cry, "I wish I could meet him."

Bernii would rub his chins. "Well…"

"Does he eat little girls?" I'd ask, dropping my voice to a dramatic whisper.

"Only for breakfast and dinner. Visit him at lunch and you'd be perfectly safe."

We would burst into laughter. If Nana was around, she'd mutter.

I looked from Kolla to Pattii smiling. "I always wanted to meet Uncle Bernii's Bruni." And see the Red Dome Hills, and the Forest of Dwarf-Trees. They were names that made my childhood dreams.

How could I resist?

Pattii had sent her messenger bird, a generia, to Panda seeking information, including about the identity of the guard I supposedly killed. I agreed to stay until the bird returned.

It was a precious interlude.

I helped Pattii and Kolla with their work, carrying buckets of manure and bringing in firewood and perfumed-grasses.

Bandikutz, the little dog, often followed me around. "When you become the queen, I'm willing to be your royal dog," she'd say. An emperor couldn't have been more graciously condescending.

"If I didn't know better, I'd think she is Panda's secret agent," Kolla would say, watching with a grin on his face. "She wouldn't deign to look at him though. After all, he is just a forester."

I also spent hours reading Pattii's collection of books on Muffic history and literature, lost in words both beautiful and bitter, in the company of minds who had only a past.

My reading provided me with answers, and questions.

Pattii was engaged in making paper from snake-bamboo. I'd sit with her, doing what I could to help while plying her with questions.

"Muffic power," Pattii would say, as we cut bamboo sheaths into squares, "is sourced in nature. Understanding nature is the key to unlocking the power. The divisions in Muffic society are based on this gradation of power. The greater your power, the higher you were placed."

"So you had your haves and have-nots?"

"What society doesn't, Allii? All the rhetoric about one tribe or one people or one kind, that's just talk, a necessary cover. Greater the celebration of oneness and unity, deeper the divisions hidden in plain sight."

"The Muffics had a highly developed civilization before Sallonians came," Pattii would remark, as she boiled powdered herbs in water and added bamboo sheaths to it. "Painting, music, books. Most of it was destroyed. My mother had this piece of pottery, a vase, something that had been handed down from mother to daughter. It depicted a dance in a grove of trees. I wish you could have seen the beauty of it, the grace. It was more than an heirloom. It was a piece of memory, a reminder of greatness gained and lost."

"The Muffic name for Sallikan was Vinyasa, meaning destruction," Pattii would explain, as she removed a bamboo sheath from the pot, rinsed it in cold water, and pulled at it, separating it along the grain. "Muffics knew extracting the ore would poison the rivers and destroy the land. They made a conscious choice not to."

"Did they know of the uses of Sallikan?" I asked.

"They did. Yet they decided that the damage of extracting the ore and purifying it would far outweigh the benefits. Legend has it that Sallikan once existed in other parts of Pegala, especially the land now known as the Dhanus Plain."

"The great desert?"

She nodded. "According to legend, that was once a fertile valley, fed by two rivers, and the home to an ancient kingdom. Extracting Sallikan on a mass scale first raised the kingdom to great heights and power, then cast it down to drought and starvation. Some of our people believe that place was the original homeland of Sallonians. It's a legend, not fact, yet to be proven, or disproven."

"Deriving power from nature also imposed limitations on the use of those powers," Pattii would remind me, as she removed the pot from the fire, allowing the bamboo to cool. "Muffics couldn't use their powers for destructive purposes. For us, taking life, any life, was the first taboo. Those who broke that taboo were driven out of society. According to another legend, the dreaded tracker-assassins originated from those outcasts."

"Was that why you never fought against Sallonian occupation of your land?"

"Actually, Allii, we did, twice, during the first hundred years of the occupation. The rebellions were rather tiny, going by what the oral and written histories say, but they still happened. Both ended in defeat. Most Muffics withdrew into themselves afterward and focused on survival."

Like Roaziyan, I thought.

"Halflings, on the other hand, are not subjected to that taboo. They can kill if they want to." She looked up, her gaze piercing me, like gray lances.

The messenger-bird arrived on the sixth evening, not a mechanical one but a real bird, a generia, with gray feathers and a pink crest. He landed on Pattii's outstretched arm.

Kolla pulled me away. "He always speaks to her alone. Come Spooky."

I followed him to the edge of the valley, with Spooky bringing up the rear. We sat on a rock and watched the sun vanish behind the mountains until Pattii called us.

I reached her at a run. "How is Nana?"

"Panda says she is being confined to a room."

That meant Nana was a prisoner, like I had been.

"And the man who was killed? Does Panda know who he is?"

Pattii bit her lip, her eyes shifting from one end of the horizon to the other. "He was a palace guard. His name was Terrilian."

My legs felt as if they were made of paper. I took several careful steps away and sat down. If I didn't, I might have fallen.

Terrii.

Terrii with his tired eyes and his teething baby.

Terrii and the other guard, Kiko, would have known who went in and out of Bellizza's apartment that fatal afternoon. If an outsider came in, they would have known that. If no outsider came in, they would have known that too.

Terrii might have been indiscreet about his knowledge.

Hot tears stung my eyes. I forced them back. I had cried enough. There'd be another time for tears, but not now.

I turned to Pattii. "What was the other news?"

"According to Panda, this Terrilian had told a couple of

people that you were innocent. Panda thinks that was why he was killed. Another guard, Kikolan, had been pensioned off. The rumor is he had been given a large sum of money and ordered to return to his village."

"Anything else?" I asked. I knew there was more. I could see it in Pattii's face.

"A new marriage is being arranged for the king and is expected to take place as soon as the six month mourning period is over." She paused. "Since finding a princess from somewhere else might take time, he has agreed to marry a suitable lady from the First Hundred Families. Many say the bride is already chosen. The name is yet to be revealed."

I had expected Father to marry again. Even so, it deepened the crater in my heart.

"That is the direction you have to take," Kolla said. "Just walk toward the east until you reach the road. It'll take you to Lion's Pride. Join a caravan that goes past the Red Dome Hills."

Kolla, Pattii, and Bandikutz had accompanied Spooky and me on the first leg of our journey. We stood on a ridge looking over a broad plain.

I stared at Kolla. "Why call a town a Lion's Pride?"

"The place was once home to a pride of rare gray lions. The town's founders were welcomed by the lions and allowed to build a small settlement, or so it's said."

I smiled. "I've always wanted to see gray lions."

"The lions were hunted, driven away, as the settlement expanded."

"But I thought…" I began and stopped. Of course, a town and a pride of lions couldn't exist side by side.

Kolla ruffled my hair, the way he used to do when I was a toddler hanging on to his arm. "Humans have this unique capacity to mix ruthlessness with sentiment, to use the latter to conceal the former, even from themselves." He looked at the sky. "If you hurry, you'd be able to get there before sunset."

I embraced Kolla and Pattii, trying hard not to cry. Now that I was about to return to the world beyond, I thought longingly of all the things I had taken for granted in the last fortnight—sleeping and waking up without fear, walking without looking over my shoulder fearing every shadow, friendship, affection, laughter.

Bandikutz suffered my farewell embrace with good grace. "You won't forget to send for me when you are queen?"

I held her face in my hands. "If ever I become queen, you'll be the first dog of the land, and eat out of a gold plate. But I must tell you, no palace can be happier than where you live now. Believe me, I know."

When I glanced back for one last look, Kolla had his arm around Pattii. She was leaning against him, cradling Bandikutz.

My heart lurched. I hoped power wouldn't sunder their lives as it did my parents'.

6

THE WILDERNESS OF A TOWN

"Early next dawn, Sallonians attacked us. They slaughtered many and drove out the others. They claimed the land as their own, a gift from their vicious god. They proclaimed one of their number king, and began abusing the land we had protected for millennia."
Histories – Roaziyan the Younger

THE ROAD TO LION'S PRIDE TEEMED WITH PEOPLE AND pack-animals. There was even an elephant caravan, the huge brown beasts moving with the majesty of kings on parade.

A high wall ringed the town. Two lions in gray marble reared on either side of the massive iron gates. Inside were more gray lions, some as large as life, others small enough to fit inside a pocket, some made of marble or smoke-silver, others of painted clay or colored paper. They ornamented buildings, skulked on street corners, and occupied shop windows.

It was a town haunted by a memory of an ancient wrong.

The main street seemed a two-way river of humans and animals. The din was deafening, the smells ranging from irresistible to nauseous. I tried to push and wriggle my way through, until, in trying to avoid a woman carrying a child on her hip, I collided with a man juggling several baskets. I started to apologize, but my voice was drowned in the man's vituperation, and the shouts and grunts of people streaming past us.

"Here."

I ran blindly in the direction of Spooky's bark, ignoring the jostles, the shoves, and the curses, until I reached a smaller, less crowded street.

"I'd rather climb any mountain than that," I muttered, once I got my breath back.

Spooky looked amused. "Where to now?"

Our plan had been to find the starting place for caravans. But I felt too battered and bruised to make the attempt immediately.

A sudden breeze brought with it an enticing scent.

"Food," I sniffed, but the mouth-watering smell was gone with the breeze.

"Good idea," Spooky said. "This way."

Soon we were outside an eatery. Copper pots lined a long wooden table. I bought cooked meat for Spooky and a plateful of fragrant-noodles topped with a reed-mushroom stew for me. The owner, a woman built on generous lines, her hair a mass of green curls and her skin a clear golden yellow, poured a generous portion of liquid cheese over the stew.

The place was busy. I sat at the only unoccupied table. The owner came over with some more meat for Spooky and a drink for me. Like the food, the drink was unfamiliar, a concoction of cream, sugar, and grounded nutmeg.

When I went to pay, the woman asked in broken Pegalian, "Sleep?" Her accent robbed the word of any meaning for me. I wouldn't have understood what she meant had she not accompanied the question with a sleeping gesture, pillowing her head on her hand.

I nodded and smiled.

The woman made a series of hand gestures. I mimicked them—go back the way we came, take the first turn to the left, then the second turn to the left. She smiled and said a word that might have been, "correct."

I thanked her, hoping my accent wasn't as incomprehensible to her as hers was to me.

The directions were easy to follow and led us to a small inn on a quiet lane, the now familiar gray lion, done in clay, crouching by the half-open door. An elderly man seemed to be its owner. After a conversation of hand gestures and scattered words, followed by the requisite payment, I got a room for the night.

The room was small and clean, its single window looking out onto a cluttered backyard. I sat down on the bed, removed my shoes, and rubbed my aching feet.

Spooky sniffed every corner and turned to me. "You should be safe enough here. I'll go out a bit. Bolt the door just in case."

I bolted the door after him, stretched out on the bed, and opened my Memory Book. Time to bring some order out of chaos.

Myths, I remember reading somewhere, can matter more than reality. Sometimes they even supplant reality. That was what happened to me. I was told a farrago of lies about everything, my life, my parents, Sallonia.

This complicates the task of discovering who murdered Belle and Terrii. If everyone lied to me about everything, how can I believe anything anyone said? I must start by not taking anything or anyone for granted.

<u>Facts</u>
1. Belle was murdered.
2. The blame was pinned on me.
3. Sherriz tried to browbeat me into implicating myself.
4. A trap was set for me: allow me to flee and ensure I'm killed while 'resisting recapture.'

<u>Who would gain from Belle's murder?</u>
1. Bernalin faction would gain nothing.
2. Rokkrin faction too would gain nothing. (If they need to remove someone, it would be poor Uncle Bernii.)
3. Panda and Kolla (Halflings rebels and their Sallonian allies) too gain nothing by removing Belle.
4. Sherriz-Pena faction—What are they opposed to? A King Bernalin, a King Rokkrin or a Queen Albalia. What do they want? King Walterin to be succeeded by a son. So...

I paused, pressing a hand to my throbbing temples. It was no use. The pain surged.

You know what to do, Allii. Stop writing, stop thinking, and you'd be fine. Just leave this mess behind and go and build yourself a life.

A new life, your kind of life.

No.

I grabbed the pen and started writing frenziedly.

What about Papa?

Papa would have stayed above the factions, or given the appearance of doing so.

Did he, in reality, lean towards one? Did he form shifting alliances with them, favoring one now and another next, never in public, always behind the scenes?

Or was one of the factions actually his?

How much did he know about the plans each faction made to further its objectives and interests?

Why didn't he do anything to save Belle?

Why didn't he do anything to save me?

What does his inaction mean? Ignorance? Weakness? Or—

My spine tingled. I looked up from the Memory Book. The doorknob was turning. Slowly, like a snail.

I froze, eyes riveted on the brass knob. It was no longer turning. Perhaps I imagined it.

The doorknob turned faster, in a blur of dull yellow.

A friend or a stranger would knock. This was the work of an enemy. Who? A robber? A man who regarded a single female as easy prey? Father's soldiers still pursuing me?

I grabbed my bag, shoved the book and shoes inside, and scrambled onto the window sill. Squeezing out took an effort but the months of hard-walking had turned me into a wiry scarecrow. I wriggled through, jumped into the cluttered backyard, wrenched open the small back gate, and fled to the sound of the door crashing.

The lane was deserted. I ran the length of it and found myself in another lane, equally deserted.

Running heedlessly across an empty space with no cover would be stupid. I crouched behind a lonely bush and waited.

My spine tingled, again.

Earlier in the room, I had sensed the doorknob turning before I saw it. Now I sensed the footsteps before I heard them. They were confident and measured, too silent for a soldier.

I put my hand into my pocket, my fingers closing on Bellizza's thread-knitting needle. When the footsteps were close enough, I sprang up and jabbed with the needle.

The intruder reeled, a ghostly shape in the weak light of a single moon. I had aimed for the eye but got the cheek instead. The man uttered a muted cry, more like a growl, but didn't let go of the two-toothed knife. He lunged at me. I evaded him by a couple of inches and ran, screaming at the top of my voice for help.

An assassin wouldn't want any witnesses to his deed.

The scream worked. Several people from nearby dwellings rushed out in response. I stopped, casting a quick look back. There was no sign of the assassin. He must have melted into the shadows. I had no fear he'd be among the people gathered round me, not with a bleeding cheek.

My would-be rescuers were all talking at once, clearly asking me what was wrong. I indicated my bag, and waved my arms around, allowing the fear I had kept at bay to appear on my face.

Some of the men and women spread about, peering into dark corners. Others, using smiles and hand gestures, assured me I was safe.

A woman asked in broken Pegalian, "You where?"

My mind raced through my options. Going back to the inn was out of question. I could go to another inn or perhaps even beg for` shelter from one of my rescuers. But the assassin might skulk around till morning and follow me out of the town. My best option was to lose myself in a street full of people and wait for Spooky to find me. Hopefully his sense of smell was up to the task.

I whispered in Pegalian, "Main Street."

My rescuers brought me to Main Street. I thanked them and walked for a while at random, weaving my way in and out of the unceasing river of people and animals, allowing myself to drown in it. Here I was truly anonymous, one of thousands.

The smell came suddenly, the subtle scent of moon-lilies. For a second, I was transported back to my lost life, sitting with Bellizza in the sunroom, working on my herbarium, being cosseted by Nana, begging Tygyrin to teach me how to row a boat…then the scent was gone, I was back in the present, alone with peril.

In that moment, I would have given anything to regain the safety, the security, the orderliness I once had and lost.

Anything.

After a long while of being jostled and pushed, I went into a shop. I needed to think of a way to meet up with Spooky and to get out of Lion's Pride without being discovered.

The shop sold an array of glassware. I picked up a gray lion and pretended to contemplate it, my mind busy. Was the assassin working alone? Who set him on my path? How did he find me? Did someone betray me? That wasn't possible, because only Kolla and Pattii knew about my destination. They would never betray me.

Still the question remained. How did the man find me?

Fear and loneliness clogged my heart. I closed my eyes and thought of Spooky, wishing he was around.

And felt the words, the way a fish might feel the ripple of a distant wave.

Get out of the town. Two men ransacked your room. One went out. I'm following him. I opened my eyes, returning from wherever my mind had taken me.

The shopkeeper, a portly man in a turban, asked in Pegalian, "Are you all right?"

I nodded and walked out of the shop, still feeling unreal. How had I reached out to Spooky? How did it happen?

Then I felt words again.

This man is like an animal tracking a scent. Reminds me of me.

My feet stopped moving. Someone bumped into me from behind, cursing. I reeled and clutched at the nearest arm. An angry voice hissed, "Are you drunk?" I let go of the arm, mumbled an apology, and resumed walking.

Could the men pursuing me be a tracker-assassin pair? Am I being hunted by the same human bloodhounds who chased Kolla and Pattii?

What do I know about tracker-assassins? They kept their operational details secret, though many claimed they used some item of clothing that belonged to the target.

Who paid a small fortune to set them on me? Who gave them an item of clothing that was mine? Who—

I forced myself to stop. Now I must act. The time to think would come later, if there was a later.

I quickened my steps, studying the shops. Within minutes I found what I was looking for—a clothier. I went inside and made my choice, a pair of trousers and a tunic in soft linen and a shawl. It took longer to explain to the shopkeeper that I wanted to change out of my old clothes into new ones. Eventually the woman understood and took me to a pokey little backroom.

I changed, stuffed my old clothes in my bag and went out.

Finding the posterior of the town took some while and several wrong turns. I didn't mind. As I traversed the bowels of the town, rabbit warrens flanked by decrepit houses and shops, I hid my recently discarded clothes in backyards and drains.

Eventually I reached the town's posterior, a small wasteland for the residents' detritus. Piles of garbage were everywhere. Their stink made me gag. The competing odors created mental pictures I tried in vain to banish. There was no gate. But the wall was not so tall here, and there were plenty of trees.

I circled a steaming pile of something and reached for a scalable tree. I heaved myself onto a low branch, crawled up until I reached the wall, and jumped, landing stomach-first on a bush.

A narrow dirt road ran alongside the wall. There were hiding places aplenty, bushes and trees, even a dry-ditch. I picked a particularly bristly bush, wide of girth and tall of height, and squeezed into the niche between it and the wall.

I sensed Spooky long before he reached me. Without that pre-warning, I would have embraced him. Probably wept too.

The shock hit me. I bit my lip hard to stop my teeth from chattering.

Spooky butted my head with his, gently. "Calm down."

I nodded. "A man tried to kill me."

"One of the men ransacking your room had a bleeding cheek. Was that your doing?"

I nodded.

"Good work. Didn't think you had it in you."

"I think they are tracker-assassins."

"Like the ones who chased your cousin and Patriana?"

I nodded again.

"Unpopular, aren't you? We'd better get going, though it'll be hard to put them off the scent once they are on the track." He glanced at me impatiently. "Don't just sit there, Allii. Come."

"No, wait. Do you think you can find where the caravans start from?"

Spooky stared at me, as if he thought I had lost all senses.

"Are you mad? We mustn't go with a caravan."

I took off the shawl, wiped my sweaty face with it for good measure. "I know. But this should. Can you get this on to a cart heading in the direction opposite to Red Dome Hills?"

He studied me for a second, his expression unreadable. Then the canine grin dawned. "Interesting mind you have."

I smiled back. "Thanks."

He took my shawl in his mouth and set off.

My bag had fallen when I jumped down. I bent to pick it up and noticed an angry looking scratch on my arm, just above the wrist. The bush I landed on must have been a thorny one.

I watched as a single drop of blood welled, like a tiny red pearl. And realized what killed Bellizza.

Kolla had maps. I had studied the different routes to the Red Dome Hills from Lion's Pride. The easiest was the one lying parallel to the Pooza-Mooza river.

Spooky led the way. We ran through the night, stopping for short breaks, when I neared collapsing point.

The next morning, we stopped for a rest. As we gobbled our food, I told Spooky about my new surmise.

"Think of it. The killer enters the room, maybe on some errand. Belle doesn't suspect anything because the killer is someone she knows and trusts. The killer waits for the right moment and pricks Belle with a poison thorn. Belle feels pain…"

"She doesn't see? What's she doing? Sleeping?"

"Perhaps it is one of her ladies, arranging her hair…"

Spooky's nose twitched. "She doesn't cry out?"

"Maybe she does. Perhaps she thinks it's an insect or an ant. She touches the spot instinctively. But the pain is already over. She resumes her knitting, thereby smearing the thread-tree accidently."

"Poison thorns don't grow on every tree." Spooky bit a paw. "And it seems too risky. Anyone could have walked in,and discovered murder being committed."

I continued to pursue my own thoughts. "No man, apart from Papa, could walk into the queen's apartment. Others had to make appointments. Even Doktoras Poll and Chief Priest Pena had to go through Nellin. They would have had to use someone else to commit the actual murder, probably a member of Belle's household." Bellizza was a kind and a considerate mistress, and her women loved her. Still bribes, threats, or a combination thereof could have been used to subvert someone.

Spooky's voice interrupted my thoughts. "Let's go. We've bigger problems now. Once those men discover you are not with the caravan, they'll get on to the right track."

For two days we walked and ran, with short breaks for eating and sleeping. Ordinary every day things had to be abandoned, like washing or changing. I was drenched with sweat and coated with grime. My own smell made me gag. Inadequate sleep and exhaustion rendered conscious thought impossible. My mind seemed to have shut down. I was operating on instinct, like a mechanical creature with a fixed idea—escape.

I would have bought a horse, or even a donkey, had I the opportunity. But the road ran between the river and a forest.

On the afternoon of the second day, Spooky stopped suddenly, raised his head and growled, "Tracker-assassins."

I panted, trying to catch my breath. "Where?"

Spooky sniffed. "A day away at most. Come."

We ran, and ran, until I collapsed in a heap.

Spooky stood over me, hackles rising. "Get up, Allii."

I shook my head, or tried to.

"You run or you die, Allii."

I wanted to tell him I'll never be able to outrun the tracker-assassin pair. My voice was gone. I searched for words, and came up with a memory instead.

Spooky snarled, "Get up, Allii."

I tried to reach his mind, but the ability seemed to be gone. "Red Dome Hills are too far by the road," I panted, the words part-slurred by my wheezing breath. "Pattii said in some places a tracker's power is weak, like deserts. The Hills border a desert. If we cut across the forest in an easterly direction, we might be able to reach it."

Spooky said nothing.

"Well?" I asked at last.

"We don't have much of an option, do we?" His voice was terse. "It should be all right." I had to strain to hear the last sentence. He sounded as if he was talking to himself not to me, and as if he was trying to reassure himself not me.

7

CHASING MIRAGES

> *"Words, how much can be done and undone through them! Our fall began with their weapons. But it was completed with their words, holy texts and prayers, laws and decrees. They wrote a new past for themselves and built a future on that."*
>
> *Histories – Roaziyan the Younger*

WE RAN, GUIDED BY THE SUN DURING THE DAY AND THE Great Northern Star in the night.

The forest was thick. There was no path. We had to find a winding way around trees and bushes. That slowed us down. Part of me was glad; it gave me an opportunity to breathe.

Around the evening of the next day, the density of the forest started lessening. That night, as we stopped for a brief rest, I realized the air was heavy with heat.

Hope inundated me. "I think the desert is close."

Spooky made a sound that had no words in it.

We ran for a while and stopped for a short break. All I remember was sitting under a tree. I woke up to Spooky's snarling words. "They're here."

I scrambled to my feet. Spooky was already running.

The forest was a shadow land under the light of a half-moon. We corkscrewed our way, pursued first by an empty silence, then a silence throbbing with menace.

Unlike me, the tracker-assassins made no noise. Still I could sense them gaining. I ran, as if I were born to run. The increasingly dry wind on my face spurred me on. The desert was close, and with it, safety, perhaps.

I took another sharp bend round a spindly tree. There was no Spooky running ahead of me. My eyes darted around, trying to catch a glimpse of a furry tail. Then something hard barreled on to me. I managed not to cry out, but I couldn't break my fall.

An object whizzed through the space my head would have occupied, had I not fallen.

A wolf-shape leapt and landed.

A man was on the ground. Spooky was on him. Through the trees, I could sense another presence, nearing. I grabbed the stone-light from the bag.

The second man reached the huddle on the ground with swift silent steps, a knife gleaming in his hand, aimed at Spooky. I threw the stone-light at the assassin's head. The man must have sensed the danger. He straightened up, his eyes catching me in a noose. The stone-light hit him on the shoulder and sent him reeling. Then Spooky was on him, felling him to the ground.

I was searching desperately for a stout stick when Spooky howled. "Run."

He streaked past me, still in his wolf shape. I ran after him, driven by fear and a strange sense of exhilaration. I wanted to shout in joy, even laugh. When I first spotted the plain through the trees, I did laugh.

The pre-desert was a dusty space with a few scraggy trees. We ran through it most of that day, reached the desert close to nightfall, and stopped for a break.

"I couldn't kill them," Spooky said. "I aimed for the throat, but they were wearing metal guards."

I shuddered at the regret I sensed in his voice. Then I remembered my own sense of exhilaration earlier in the day and identified its source. I had thought Spooky killed the men. My joy, my excitement had come from my own blood lust.

What was I turning into?

I wasn't just my mother's daughter. I was also my father's daughter. The killer instincts were in me. Circumstances could turn me into a killer of humans and a hunter of animals. There were no inner taboos to guard me against such a fall. I'd have to create my own barriers.

Spooky's terse voice interrupted my thoughts. "If I could have killed them, we could have returned to the road. Now we can't avoid the desert." He had changed back to a dog without my noticing. The transformation made him seem less strong, more vulnerable.

"It doesn't look too bad," I said. The desert seemed a thing of beauty, a sea of golden sand, the dunes undulating like velvet waves from afar. The air was sharp but clear. The sun was a white ball surrounded by a golden nimbus. The sky was streaked in pinks and purples. Everything felt strangely soft and peaceful.

We sat watching the sun set, waiting for the stars. Going by what I had read, we'd have to take as our guides the dragon star and the constellation of the archer.

Once the two markers appeared in the night sky, we resumed our journey. It was slow going at first. Walking in the sand was a bit like wading in shallow water.

Before the night was over we reached a substantial oasis, with a large pool of clear water and plenty of trees. I dumped the bag on the grass and jumped into the pool without bothering to take off my clothes. Spooky followed. We gamboled in the water like a pair of puppies.

Afterward we had a meal. Spooky stretched himself on the muddy bank while I inspected the trees. There were treacle palms, squat and spindly; sun-berry bushes; and nettle-thorns with their tiny fruits which helped to keep thirst away.

We swam and rested most of the day and resumed our journey after nightfall, under a dark blue sky studded with stars.

"Do you sense the tracker-assassins?" I asked Spooky as we readied for our journey.

He shook his head, slowly.

I smiled with relief. "Then they must have given up.

When we were on the road, you sensed them two days away." I shouldered my pack. "Pattii was right. The desert obviously is anathematic to them."

Spooky said nothing.

I set off humming a tune, my eyes on the two heavenly markers.

I've always wanted to see the desert. Thanks to Tygyrin's book, I'd learnt a lot about desert plants and their uses. An opportunity to put that learning into practice thrilled me. When we reached an oasis, I'd rush to point out the plants to Spooky, naming them, detailing their uses. He didn't seem impressed. He'd snarl something, heading for the shade.

It took me a few days to discover that following stars was not as easy as I thought it would be. We might still have managed, had it not been for a night of heavy cloud-cover. The next evening, I stared at the dragon star and the constellation of the archer, and realized they were not where they should be—or rather we were not where we should be. The fault was not in the stars, but in direction we had taken the previous night.

"What shall we do?" I asked, trying to keep my panic under control.

Spooky grunted. "Get our direction right."

I nodded. "I'm sorry, I should have been more careful."

Spooky grunted again. "It wasn't anyone's fault."

We started following the stars again. Spooky was disinclined to talk, so after a couple of efforts, I subsided. We reached a small oasis just before dawn and spent the day there.

The oasis had a pond and several trees. Yet as the day advanced the heat became unbearable, even in the shelter. The wind had a burning quality to it. I wondered whether we'd have to walk close to the primal heart of the desert to return to the right path.

I looked at Spooky, wanting to share my fear with him. He was seated under a leafy palm, eyes closed, panting.

"Spooky."

He opened his eyes and the words died on my tongue. He looked distant, as if an invisible wall separated us.

"Nothing," I mumbled, not quite understanding my own response. "Nothing."

The day passed in silence. When the sun set, we resumed walking.

By next morning I knew my fear was correct. The dragon star and the constellation of the archer was taking us deeper and deeper into the desert. With the sun beating down, and the heat rising from the ground, it was like being cooked by two fires. The wind was scorching. Sand was in the air we breathed; it stung the eyes, laced the tongue, and clogged the throat.

Another day passed, confronting me with a new problem: water. We had two water gourds. So long as oases were many and verdant, that had sufficed. But where we were now, oases had become meager affairs, just a waterhole with brackish almost undrinkable water and a scraggy bush or two.

Food was another issue. I had some fruits left and some hard cheese. In the early days, Spooky hunted for small animals. As the heat grew, his hunting stopped.

"Only poisonous lizards," he snarled, when I asked him why he didn't hunt.

Spooky was changing. He seemed irritated by even the littlest thing, and ripped into me for no reason at all. Soon I started snarling back. We walked slowly, slept badly, and barely spoke to each other. It was as if we had stopped being a team and become two separate creatures, each preoccupied with its own problems.

This sense of disconnectedness from both reality and each other bothered me a bit, but not too much, until the day I noticed Spooky's pace was slower than mine.

I looked at him, really looked at him, and noticed other changes. He seemed to have become thinner, more like a bag of bones. Beneath his constant panting, I could hear faint whimpers, as if he were in acute pain.

I too must have lost weight, but I didn't think I had turned skeletal. I too panted and every inch of my body hurt, but I was certain I didn't whimper, except in my sleep.

"Is anything wrong?" I asked hesitantly.

Spooky's expression was withering. "Apart from the desert, you mean? How about stupid girls asking stupid questions?"

"You seem more tired than I am."

"I'd be even more tired if I have to keep answering you."

I subsided, dashing a hand across my brimming eyes. Whether the tears came from concern for Spooky or self-pity, I didn't know.

The wretched stalemate continued for almost two days, until the night Spooky collapsed after no more than an hour of slow walking.

And the real nightmare began.

Spooky neither admitted nor denied his condition. He refused to discuss it. He didn't even snarl at me, just turned away and pretended to sleep.

I wanted to hold him in my arms and beg him to tell me what was wrong, but feared his reaction.

I sat down as close to him as I dared, trying to make sense of what was happening. We were both suffering from lack of food and water. We were both sick from the heat. But he was sicker, way more than me, as if…as if he were dying.

I told myself not to be idiotic. He couldn't be dying. Animals were hardier than humans. It was just thirst, and hunger, and heat.

We rested for several hours and managed to reach the bare shelter of a large rock before dawn. I hoped a long sleep would help Spooky to revive.

It didn't.

That evening, he looked at me with eyes that seemed dead, and said in a voice trembling with pain and exhaustion, "Leave me. Go."

I stared at him, shock paralyzing me. Spooky was indeed dying. If I stayed with him, I'd die too. The only way I could survive was to do as he said and leave him.

Suddenly I didn't want to die. I wanted to live. Not for the quest, but for myself. I wanted to escape this sandy hell. I wanted to look at a proper tree, feel cool water on my body. I wanted to eat, drink, love, enjoy. Live.

A memory flashed before me: Bänge and her Anonn being hammered by soldiers. I had been appalled by the horror and the injustice of it. I had wanted to intervene, but didn't. Whenever that failure haunted me, I told myself I didn't intervene because I had a higher duty, to discover who murdered Bellizza and Terrii.

That was a lie. I didn't intervene because I didn't want to risk myself.

I still wanted to live, desperately. With death so close, the need to live turned into an overpowering greed, an irresistible lust, a flame that turned every other feeling and consideration into ashes.

Without the burden of Spooky's presence I'd be able to travel a little faster, reach the next oasis and the next. The water and the food would last longer. Once I made it out of the desert and into the dragon's castle, I wouldn't need Spooky anyway.

It wasn't as if I'd be abandoning Spooky. He wanted me to go. He told me to go. It made sense. Of course it made sense. By going, I'd be obeying him.

I'll make him comfortable, wait till he's asleep, and leave. That way he wouldn't know I had left. He might even slip into a coma and die, without realizing I had taken his very sensible advice, and left him alone, abandoned him, the way I abandoned Bellizza…

The fire welling inside me fizzled out.

I crawled to his side and touched his head. "We live or die together."

I waited for him to get angry, to rave at me, to call me stupid. He didn't. Instead he said, in a surprisingly clear voice, "Roaziyan is your grandmother."

I blinked trying to bring the name into focus.

Roaziyan—then memory returned and I croaked, "What?"

"Your mother's mother. Promised not to tell you. Doesn't matter anymore."

No it doesn't, I thought.

Spooky turned away from me, as if he were done with me. I sat next to him, listening to his whimpers, making plans. I'd wait for him to fall asleep and carry him as far as I could until we reached a better shelter.

A sound woke me from the fitful sleep I had fallen into. I opened my eyes. It was still night and I was alone.

"Spooky," I squawked. There was no answer. I stumbled out, forcing myself not to run heedlessly.

Spooky lay in a heap a few yards away.

At first I thought he was dead. Then I noticed the rise and fall of his chest. It was barely visible, but there.

I picked him up and started walking, keeping an eye on the dragon star. He had lost weight, but I too had become weaker. I stumbled many times, but managed not to fall.

Dawn broke. Streaks of light, yellow and orange, red and pink, began to bleed into the night sky. The heat rose, every new second warmer than the previous one. I looked around desperately for a shelter, but there was nothing. Soon the stars would cease to be visible.

I tried to walk faster, using the fear of being caught in the blistering sun without any shelter whatsoever to spur myself on. But my feet sank deeper into the sand with each step.

The dragon star disappeared into a streak of pink light. The constellation of the archer followed.

I stopped, looking around desperately. And caught sight

of something. Was it a glimpse of an oasis or a mirage? There was only one way to find out. I'd have to turn left. If the glimpse turned out to be a mirage, we'd end up not just shelterless, but lost.

The sky was beginning to clear, white replacing the colors. If I failed to find a shelter soon, being on the right track geographically wouldn't matter a bit.

I heaved a deep, scorching breath, and hurried in the direction of reality or mirage. The air was already shimmering with heat. I kept on walking, until something caught my unwary foot and sent me sprawling.

Whether I lost consciousness or just blacked out for a few seconds, I've no idea. When I opened my eyes, the first sight I saw was green.

I blinked, trying to focus. Realization dawned. I was still clutching Spooky to my chest. And what I had glimpsed hadn't been a mirage. We were in a tiny oasis, a stunted tree, a few bushes, and a mud-hole.

Still I wasn't certain, because I had experienced how life-like mirages could be. Clutching Spooky with one hand, I reached out for the bush with the other. My trembling fingers touched not air, but a leaf.

A delirium of relief was threatening to take me over. I forced myself to be calm, crawled to the tree, and laid Spooky under its shelter. Then I staggered to my feet, and stumbled up to the waterhole. The water was almost black, but tasted sweeter than honey in my parched mouth.

I filled a gourd, knelt by Spooky, and called him. He didn't respond. He lay still, thin and bedraggled beyond belief. I wetted his muzzle, forced his mouth open, and wetted his tongue. Then I emptied the gourd over him, kept on doing it, until he seemed a little less dead.

Afterward I took stock.

There were two choices: waiting here until Spooky recovered or resuming the journey in the night. Both seemed fraught with danger. I had no idea what ailed Spooky. He might need the help of a physician. Just staying here might not save him.

But what if we moved and were unable to find a shelter by the next sunrise?

Perhaps if I can find a desert creature, I might be able to get some information—

I ventured out a little distance several times, seeking an animal or a bird, but there was no sign of life. Just light, and heat, and sand, painful on my sore eyes, my aching body. The fourth time when I turned back, I realized I had gone further than I intended.

I could still see the oasis, three of them.

Terror overwhelmed me. I stumbled in the direction of the nearest oasis. The closer I got the further it seemed to be.

I forced myself to stop. Many oases beckoned me. I examined each carefully. All of them were havens of greens and blues, except one that didn't look so verdant. I walked slowly in that direction. The sun beat down on me and the world started whirling around. I could barely see, but managed to reach a real bush, before everything gave away.

I was brought back to wakefulness by a jarring voice screeching one word repeatedly: *Food.*

I opened my eyes. A brown bird dappled with gold sat a few feet away regarding me.

A guppy-vulture.

He came close, step by step, until his hooked beak was inches away from my outstretched hand. Then he moved a few steps back and said in a regretful tone to himself, "Not dead yet."

"No," I rasped. "But will be soon."

The vulture's head snapped back. He took a cautious step towards me, his clear blue eyes fixed on me. "You understand me?"

I gave an infinitesimal nod and dragged myself up to Spooky. The momentary improvement I thought I saw in him earlier had vanished. He looked almost dead. I grabbed the gourd, crawled to the waterhole, filled it, drank some, and poured the rest over him.

The vulture pointed with his beak at Spooky. "Looks like a daemon-dog."

"He's dying," I muttered, my voice shaking.

"Of course he is. Heat kills his kind. What's he doing in the desert?"

I tried to shake my head. It made sense now, the reason for Spooky to sicken in this way. Was that why he insisted I leave him? Was that why he made a last desperate attempt to leave, to free me from the burden he had become?

Suddenly hope blazoned like a benevolent sun. I scrambled onto my feet, picked up Spooky, and laid him in the waterhole, holding his head up with one hand.

Was it my imagination or did his breathing turn slightly less ragged?

Another vulture landed, the female partner, going by the gold crest. The male said, "The human can understand us.

The daemon-dog's dying."

The female looked hard at us, and cawed in an unexpectedly kind voice, "There's a mountain several days' walk from here. Trees, water, people. You'd be able to manage it, human. Leave the daemon-dog here. We promise not to eat him."

I glared at the vultures. "I'm not leaving him behind."

"Fool," said the male.

I ignored the pair and watched Spooky. No, it wasn't my imagination. His breathing was a bit better. If only I could get him help, medicine, a physician—

Brunelles. If I can send him a message…a message—

I turned to the vultures. "Do you know the Red Dome Hills?"

"Yes."

"Sometimes there are good pickings there," the male chipped in. "Whole humans."

Hope lapped at me. "Beyond that lives a dragon. His name is Brunelles. If I give you a letter, can you take it to him? Please."

The vultures looked at each other. Eventually, the female said, "I'll go."

"Oh, thank you, thank you." Hope flowed, a river of cool, cool water. I dragged Spooky onto the muddy bank, rummaged in my bag, tore a piece of paper from the Memory Book, and wrote a note, introducing myself, begging for help.

The female took the note in her beak and flew away, after adjuring her mate to keep an eye on us.

I laid Spooky back in the waterhole, holding his head

up with my hands. It would be the ultimate irony, if he drowned in a desert.

To keep myself awake, I studied the meager vegetation of this place. The tree seemed to be a dwarf version of sweet-juche. The leaves and the patterns on the trunk were the same, but the red and white fruits that gave the tree its name were absent. The bushes seemed sand-kutzis, a version of a plant used as insect-repellent in Sallonia. Unlike its less toxic cousin, this desert version had a sap that was poisonous not just to insects but also to larger life forms, according to the book Tygyrin gave me for my sixteenth birthday.

My sixteenth birthday, celebrated by Bellizza with a small party in her apartment. She had ordered all my favorite food—frozen sandberries with coconut cream, tiny thorn-pear cakes, lavender biscuits. And flagons of cool, cool drinks…Father was too busy, but Tygyrin was there. After we had refreshments, Bellizza played the qanun, and Tygyrin and I danced. I teased him, saying I didn't know he could dance. He laughed, lifting me up and twirling me.

Nana had watched us, face inscrutable…

The sun peaked and turned. It must have been close to evening when the female vulture landed next to me. "The dragon is here," she said.

I dragged Spooky out and laid him on the ground. Standing up was hard. The long hours of crouching by the waterhole seemed to have done something to my legs. In the end I managed, swaying like a drunk.

Just outside the oasis, there was a new shade, caused by a gigantic black shadow.

I squinted. The shadow came from a giant copper-colored rock that was somehow new to the landscape. Maybe another illusion? I squinted some more. The rock started assuming a shape, a huge head, a long neck, a body…A pair of bright green eyes regarded me with interest.

"Brunelles!"

The dragon's voice sounded like thunder, in a purring mood. "So you are little Allii. Always wanted to meet you. Think you can get the daemon-dog and yourself in here?"

In here was a large cage-like contraption on the dragon's back. I nodded.

"Good. There's an ice blanket inside. Cover the dog with it."

I had no idea where the energy came from. I carried Spooky to the contraption, laid him on the floor, and covered him with the ice blanket, a thick piece of cloth so cold it burnt. I scrambled down to get my bag and bid a grateful goodbye to the vultures.

My last memory was curling up next to Spooky and closing my eyes.

8

THE DRAGON WHO DOUBTED

"An ancient Muffic myth tells the tale of the angry hills. The hills were the guardians of a metal more precious than gold, more dangerous than poison. When men tried to extract it, the hills were angry. They cried, Touch it not, because its name is death."
Histories – Roaziyan the Younger

I woke up to the feeling of soft sheets and feathery pillows. Light streamed in through tall windows, illuminating a wall covered with a three-dimensional painting of a dragon flying over a lush-woodland.

Memory returned like a thunderclap. I bolted up crying, "Spooky!"

"Here."

Spooky sat by the door of a chamber that made my room back at home seem small and drab by comparison.

He still looked like a bag of bones, threadbare and sagging. But the sick look was gone and his eyes sparkled with life.

I fell back on the bed, weeping.

After a while, I felt a tentative lick on my hand. Spooky was standing by the bed. I tumbled down and hugged him. He licked my wet face.

"Thank you."

I wiped my eyes. "Have I been sleeping long?"

"Two days. Consider yourself lucky. I was locked up in an ice-house until this morning."

I smiled, only for a second. "Why didn't you tell me that extreme heat is lethal to you?"

Spooky's manner was blithe. He was going to try to brazen it out.

"I thought I'd be able to manage it. There was no other way to go, and…"

A red mist covered my eyes, blocking my vision. I wanted to slap Spooky, shake him until his bones rattled. "How could you?" I cried. "I agree we didn't have many options. But if you had told me, we could have prepared a little better. At least I would have known what was happening. How dare you make such a decision without even a word to me? If I did something half—no, no, one hundredth as stupid—you'd never have let me forget it. You were beyond stupid, beyond thoughtless, beyond idiotic…"

Spooky listened, until I ran out of words, ran out of breath.

The silence hung between us for a few moments, laden with memories. Then Spooky said, in a tone I had never heard before, "I deserve all that—and more, though I'm glad your vocabulary ran out. You can't blame me even one tenth as much as I blame myself. I almost got you killed." He paused, and said, in a strange voice, "Did you ever wonder why I agreed to come with you?"

I shook my head, feeling shamed. I had never bothered to think about what life Spooky had before he joined me, what his family was. Had he been a human, I would have wondered about all of it. I didn't, because he was an animal. I had called him my companion, while regarding him all the time as an appendage.

And I didn't know about daemon dogs and extreme heat partly because I never bothered to ask questions about him or his kind. He wasn't the only one responsible for that near disaster. I was too…

I tried so smile. "I'm sorry, I didn't think about it earlier. I do now. Will you tell me?"

"I had only one litter-mate, a sister." His voice was hoarse, perhaps from residue weakness. He didn't look at me, but stared at a point beyond my shoulder. "We did everything together. She was the feisty one, curious, bold, always adventuring. One day we were out and about when we heard the sound of a hunting party. I wanted to get back to safety. She wanted to stay a bit more, look. We argued. She wouldn't listen to me. In the end, I left. She never came back."

I didn't know what to say. So I pulled Spooky to me, hugging him tight. And he let me.

After a while I said, "I too have a confession to make. In the desert, when you told me to leave you and go, I almost did."

He looked at me, his eyes unreadable. "You almost left me, but didn't. I almost went after my sister, but didn't. Almost has no value. What matters is what you do, or don't." He pulled himself out of my embrace and stood up, shaking himself. His eyes gleamed, in his old manner. "Get ready and come down. I'll tell the dragon you are up."

Brunelles was nothing like the painted or carved dragons I had seen. His scales gleamed like polished bronze. His wings were so translucent they seemed like glass. He wore a tiara of fire-opals, an emerald necklace, and an array of pink diamond bracelets.

He greeted me warmly, brushing off my thanks. "Once is enough, once is enough, Brunelles is such a mouthful. Call me Bruni. Your uncle loved it. Bruni and Bernii, he called us. He used to say that had I not been a dragon and he a prince, we could have become a pair of travelling performers. Now sit down and eat. You must be famished."

I had spent most of my life in a king's castle. Yet, I had never beheld anything like the dragon's table. The food was a riot of color. The varied scents were an olfactory symphony. Most of the dishes I'd never seen before.

"Enough to feed a whole army for a month," muttered Spooky.

The food didn't seem too much once the dragon started making inroads into them. He talked as much as he ate. 'I doubt,' was his motto and experimentation his passion. His latest effort was a cloak that would make its wearer more visible. "I'm wondering whether to call it an anti-invisible cloak or an extra-visible cloak. I can't decide which one sounds better. What do you think?"

I thought anti-invisible would be better. Spooky opted for extra-visible.

"Who'd want a cloak that'll make them more visible?" I asked.

The dragon shook his head, like a reproving teacher. "If you are an experimenter, then you experiment. You don't waste time thinking whether something is useful or not. You just think whether it can be done or not. It's another human trait," he said in an admonitory tone, "To think the world is there for them, and only what is of use to them is of value. That is what the dragons thought when they ruled the world. See where we ended up."

"Eating and talking?" Spooky murmured.

"Eating and talking, my dear daemon-dog, is much better than killing." Brunelles emitted a puff of blue smoke, probably a sign of excitement. "Once, so long ago that no human remembers, dragons ruled the world. Like any species enjoying absolute dominion, we made many mistakes and committed even more crimes. I was born millennia after that time, so I have only the memories of others to go by. There are many discrepancies in these narratives, but on one count they all agree. We became hated by all other living beings. Then humans, who were in the infancy of their development, made an alliance with many different species to rid the world of our pernicious rule. In the end, my kind lost. By the wrongs we did, we had isolated ourselves. We were pitiless when we had power.

When we fell, none would pity us."

"I'm sorry," I mumbled. It seemed the only possible response.

"Don't be, don't be," Brunelles cried. "We deserved to lose. Our rule was a scourge. I wish we could have been overthrown with lesser bloodshed. But that's war for you. Once you start it even for the best of reasons, it tends to gain a life of its own."

Spooky looked up from the massive bone he was gnawing. "What happened then?"

"Those dragons who survived retired to various corners of the world. Most of us found consolation in philosophy and experimentation, simple hobbies and high arts. Eating and talking too. We became keepers of records and inventors of new things. I like to think we are happier this way. We certainly do less harm to ourselves and others. Someday, my kind will cease to exist. We'll become a dim memory, a character in a story, a picture in a book."

I frowned, thinking over his words. "Do you think humans will die out too?"

"Why not, Allii? Why-ever-not? The world is older than your kind or mine. It managed perfectly well before we came along. It'll manage equally well once we're gone." He waved a finger making the bracelets jingle. "Dragons and humans are both taken up with themselves. We believe we are the pivot of existence and the world was made for us. We think the world of ourselves, but the world thinks nothing of us. The world won't notice when we're gone."

It seemed a rather doleful prospect. But a very possible one.

Brunelles drained his glass of frothy honey-cream, smacked his lips, and turned to me. "Now, tell me your story and how I may help you. I know about your stepmother's murder and your incarceration. I know Bernii planned to rescue you. Something went wrong with the plan and you vanished. That's what I heard from him. I sent word to him telling him you are safe with me, since I knew he was going out of his mind with worry."

Spooky and I told our story, taking turns. Brunelles listened in attentive silence. Once we were done, he said, "I'm glad you found out about your mother. Who told you?"

"Roaziyan." A memory crashed into my mind and I choked on a piece of dhal cake. When the coughing was over, I turned to Spooky. "Did you…did you say Roaziyan is my grandmother?"

He grinned. "A dying confession. I'm surprised you didn't suspect. You have quite a look of her."

I gaped, beyond words.

Brunelles stepped into the breach. "I never met your mother, though I know of her, because of Bernii. He and your mother were friends. They had shared interests. The pursuit of arcane knowledge, experimentation, things like that. Your mother stayed in his castle for a while. That was how your father met her."

"I suppose Grandmother Roaziyan was as opposed to their marriage as my other grandparents?"

The answer came from Spooky. "Don't judge her too harshly. Whatever she might have felt about your parents' union, she cared enough to save you from the soldiers and to send me with you, so that you wouldn't be alone and unprotected, especially in those first weeks. I didn't want to come. She gave me no choice. I owed her a favor, and she called it."

I flushed a little. "I'm grateful, Spooky. But I want to know what happened between her and my mother."

Brunelles studied the bracelets circling his arm. "Roaziyan expelled your mother, declared her a traitor to Muffics. That meant she couldn't go back, ever."

"You mean like Patriana? She said any Muffic who leaves can't go back."

Brunelles nodded.

"But it wouldn't be much of a problem, would it? I mean, Mother wouldn't have wanted to go back?"

"At first yes. She was happy and had no intention of going back. Then your father became king, and everything changed." He hesitated, as if mulling something, and gave a massive sigh. "Your father wanted you, and your mother didn't want to give you up. She knew the only place she'd be safe from your father's reach was your grandmother's bubble. She fled there with you. I know this because she sent Bernii a letter. That was the last he heard from her. Then he heard your mother had died in a carriage accident. He thought she might have been refused access by Roaziyan and was fleeing towards the nearest border."

I imagined the woman in the painting, the thoughtful features distorted by fear and despair, clutching her baby and searching for a refuge. How terrified, how lonely she would have been.

What did Roaziyan feel when she heard about the fate

of her daughter? Did she feel a wedge of responsibility, a twinge of guilt? Was that why she intervened to save me? Because I too was fleeing, just as her daughter had.

Did Father keep the painting of the woman he rejected, whose death he caused probably unwittingly, out of guilt?

Spooky's voice intruded into my musing. "I told you Roaziyan is made up of layers. Grief is one. I believed she was grieving over the lost land. Perhaps her grief was for your mother as well."

Brunelles rubbed his hands. "As for your suspicion, that your stepmother was killed with a thorn, I can't venture an opinion. I'm no expert on thorns. But you can check in my library. There should be enough books there on plants, including poisonous plants. In the meantime, I'll send a message to the Stargazers, seeking leave to bring you along when I go there with their order of long-distance glasses." He got up, all eagerness and bustle. "Make yourselves at home. Recover from your near-deaths. Read. Explore. There is much to see."

✗

Brunelles was right. There was much to see.

The Red Dome Hills were what the name implied, dome-shaped, and red in all its differing shades, from crimson so dark it looked black from afar to pink so pale it was almost white. The colors came from sand as fine as sieved-flour. Here and there, rocks reared, blood red, sharp-toothed and translucent.

Below the hills, lay a miniature forest consisting of

diminutive trees, rivers, lakes, hills, waterfalls and even mountain ranges. The tallest trees barely reached my knees. The mountains were no taller than Spooky. Paths crisscrossed it, so narrow that I had to walk on tiptoe.

It was an ancient dragon art, Uncle Bernii had told me.

Spooky was not impressed. "What's wrong with that dragon? Hasn't he got better things to do with his life? If he wanted a forest, there are plenty around."

"Well, this is a living work of art," I responded, stopping to admire a valley full of flowering shrubs. "I think the real reason is dragons live more than a thousand years."

Spooky sniffed. "I suppose a dragon's got to fill his time."

The dragon's castle was a wonder in itself. His library left me speechless, a universe of books.

"We have a copy of every book ever written," the librarian told me proudly. Master Sabha had a thatch of white hair, stooping shoulders, and a gentle manner. He had been a questing prince once-upon-a-time. He had turned up at the castle to rescue the beautiful princess the dragon was said to be concealing. There was no evidence, but he believed it because it was common knowledge. After encountering Brunelles, he understood common knowledge lied. He settled down in the castle and, before long, discovered a new passion—a desire for knowledge. He resumed his travels but this time in search of cerebral experiences.

"When I became too old to travel, I came here," he told me as he placed several volumes on a table. "Now I do a different kind of travelling, through books. I go farther and faster this way, even to the stars."

Brunelles had a huge botanical garden in which he had reproduced the traditional gardens of the many lands he had visited over a long and peripatetic life. My favorite was a section where a crystal clear stream ambled in a green dale shaded with cherry trees. Pebbles of varying shapes and colors lined the stream-bed. Larger craggier rocks were placed at artful intervals on the banks. A curved ornamental bridge crossed the stream at its widest point. I spent most of my mornings there, reading and making notes about poisonous plants with thorns.

On the thirteenth day of my arrival, I looked up from my notebook, rubbing my weary eyes. Spooky, who was enjoying his morning sun-bath, gave a sigh of contentment. "You should take a break. All that reading can't be good. Frankly, you look sick."

"You sound like Nana." I closed the notebook and stretched my legs. "I wonder how Bänge is doing. And Kolla and Pattii and Bandikutz."

Spooky snorted. "That animal is a sourpuss, not a dog. I bet her bite is poisonous."

I choked on my own saliva. A dark patina covered my eyes, blinding me, yet I'd never seen more clearly.

"Allii, are you sick?"

I blinked and physical sight returned. "You've given me an idea. I need to check something."

I ran to the library. Master Sabha looked up from his book when I burst in.

"Allii, my dear, is anything the matter?"

I shook my head, panting. Excitement robbed me of both voice and coherence. It took me a little while to make myself understood.

"You want books on manmade poisons?" He asked, his brows knitted. "A strange request. Still, I'm certain you aren't planning to poison anyone in the castle."

I managed a weak laugh at his attempted sally.

In a few minutes, I was in my room with a tall pile of books. I locked the door, sat down, and started reading. I read through the day. Spooky and Brunelles came up to summon me for meals, but I begged and pleaded to be excused. In the end, trays of food were sent to me at mealtimes. I had no appetite but crammed the food into my mouth.

It was close to dawn when I came across a thin book, its green cover illustrated with a tree. It somehow felt familiar. The title didn't ring a bell. It was just the cover. I touched it and the feeling grew. I had definitely seen this book before.

"What's a kutzi thorn?" Spooky asked, licking his muzzle in search of a stray piece of egg.

Brunelles frowned. "Kutzi is a mildly poisonous plant. It can kill insects, not humans. We grow them here."

I nodded. "We have them in Sallonia too. There is another version of it, sand-kutzi, grows only in deserts." I pushed the book towards Brunelles. "Read page thirty-one."

The dragon fixed a pair of gold-rimmed spectacles on his nose. "*A Guide to Hidden Poisons* by—" he stopped, jaw dropping. "By Libina the Younger. That was your great-grandmother, Allii. Roaziyan's mother."

Another piece of the puzzle fell into place. I knew where I had seen the book before.

Brunelles was reading. "The sap of sand-kutzi is poisonous to large animals, including humans. This natural toxicity can be enhanced by immersing young thorns in a solution of vinegar, pink-salts, and the flour of sister-killer yams. The level of toxicity can be controlled by changing the quantities and the duration of immersion. A thorn can be turned into a lethal weapon against a human by…" His voice petered out. Behind the half-moons of his spectacles, his eyes bulged.

I looked at Spooky. "When you talked about Bandikutz's bite being poisonous, I remembered sand-kutzi thorns. I've read about them, and I saw them in one of the oases. That was when the idea came to me. I wondered if human agency could enhance the toxicity."

"What are pink-salts?" Spooky asked.

"Salt from the Sea of Roses," Brunelles replied mechanically. He tapped the table with a painted claw. "This is a rare book. How would the murderer know about this?"

"When I saw the cover I felt certain I'd seen it before. I remembered just now. My mother's books are kept in a locked attic room in Father's castle. That was where I saw a copy of this book." I looked from Brunelles to Spooky, excitement slurring my words. "And I now know for certain who Bellizza's killer was. Doktoras Poll. He was mother's friend. It's possible he read her copy. He might even have taken it from the attic room."

Brunelles frowned. "So you think this doctor killed your stepmother?"

"He must have planned it with Sherriz and perhaps Pena. He and Sherriz are very close. Poll would know how to make the poison, where to strike. Bellizza trusted him completely, as I did. He was her physician anyway." I frowned sensing a missing piece. Poll was never allowed to examine Bellizza alone. One of her maids would be in the room all the time. So he would have had an accomplice, maybe more than one.

I turned to Brunelles. "When will your glasses be ready? I feel certain Poll was the killer. But I still want to read Bellizza's letters."

Brunelles chuckled. "I love coincidences. The Stargazers' order is nearly complete. Barring a last minute hitch, we should be able to leave the day after tomorrow."

9
WRITTEN IN THE STARS

"Sallonians wanted that accursed metal. That was why they came to our land. That was why they stole our land. They regarded the metal as an unfailing path to greatness. It turned out to be a path to a living hell."
Histories – Roaziyan the Younger

I HAVE ALWAYS ENVIED THE FREEDOM OF THE BIRDS. When Brunelles agreed to fly us to Mount Mäga, I felt like dancing.

Spooky was of another mind. "The sky is not for us," he grunted. "It should be left to birds. And idiotic dragons."

Brunelles clucked, like a giant hen. "Flying, my dear Spooky, is the only sensible way to get to Mount Mäga. If you walk, it'll take you months. There's no road so you'll probably get lost. Parts are desert, and you might well end up dead from heat. This way, all you have to do is to sit on my back, in the safety of the flying chamber, and enjoy the view." He grinned. "Don't worry. I won't dump you in the middle of our flight. The temptation might be almost irresistible, but I will resist it!"

The reality of flying turned out to be rather different from my dream of it. Brunelles winged his way there. The flying chamber was fixed securely with ropes and didn't wobble even once. Still, the fear of falling possessed me like a sickness the moment we were airborne. I expected Spooky to crow, "I told you so," but he was as petrified as I was. Companions in terror, we huddled on the floor of the chamber, eyes closed tight, shivering.

Eventually, and in slow stages, we became accustomed to the avian experience. We opened our eyes and sat on the wooden bench at the back of the flying chamber. Spooky refused to look down, but I did, staring avidly at a landscape alternating between mountain ranges and deep valleys, naked but for a few stunted trees. It would have been a bleak, forbidding terrain for walking. But seen from the sky, it had a beauty of its own, a place of stark colors and clean lines.

We reached our destination close to sunset. Mount Mäga towered over its fellows, its peak wreathed in a cirrus cloud. The mountaintop was bare, except for a single tree and a cluster of buildings.

Brunelles landed on the tabular summit with practiced ease. Several people ran forward. Some helped me out of the flying chamber while others took out the boxes of distance-seeing glasses.

Brunelles adjusted his flying-hat, a concoction of

dark blue linen trimmed with multi-colored glass birds. He patted Spooky on the back with a giant claw. Then he wrapped his arms round me. I sank into an embrace different from anything else I've experienced before, feeling both lost and safe.

"Send for me when you are done. I'll take you wherever you want to be taken to," he murmured. "Happy hunting, my friends."

)\(

I woke up to a pounding headache.

I was in a room with stone walls and a stone floor. All around me was a white light, clear and painful. The panting sound I heard as I woke up was coming from me. I was breathing through my mouth, emitting a whistling noise with each breath.

Spooky, who was sniffing at a corner, raised his head. He looked as bad as I felt.

I hauled myself up and trudged to the window. Walking had never felt this hard, even in the desert. Each step required a conscious effort, as if I were bearing a huge load on my back. When I finally reached the window and peeped out, the view was of clouds, clouds above and clouds below. It was like being suspended in nothingness. I stumbled back to the bed and sat down, gasping for breath.

"It's the thin air and the height." Spooky's bark sounded hoarse. "Remember how bad the flying felt at first?"

I was trying to recall what I had read about altitude sickness when a knock rang. The door opened and a young woman of about my age peeped in. I opened my mouth to greet her and closed it in a hurry as a wave of nausea hit me.

The woman placed the tray she was carrying on the table and turned around with a sympathetic smile.

"I'm Juju. Poor you. Feeling queasy with a vengeance, I'd wager. It'll go away. Just think of something else."

I followed the advice and focused on Juju. She was taller than me and dressed in a baggy orange and blue tunic over loose black trousers. The close-cropped dark blue hair, high cheekbones and golden skin, dangling silver filigree earrings and the matching silver choker gave her a rather glamorous appearance.

Juju's eyes moved from Spooky to me with open curiosity. "I've always wanted to see a daemon-dog. The problem with this place is that we see a lot of the heavens but very little of earth." She smiled. "Do you think you can manage to stand up? I'll show you the washrooms. Here, take my hand, until you feel steadier."

The washrooms were at the end of the hallway. Juju bustled about making sure I had everything I needed—soap, towels, even a scrub-stone. "When you're ready, come down, and knock on the first door to the right. I'll be there."

By the time I was done with bathing and dressing, my stomach had ceased heaving. Walking was still hard, breathing a conscious chore, but I felt able to contemplate food. I removed the cover and gave what looked like a plateful of cooked meat to Spooky.

Spooky sniffed at the meat, gobbled some, and licked his mouth with a satisfied air. "This meat is good. Not doused in sauces like at that insane dragon's. The cooks there made cakes as high as trees, but never could get a dish of meat done right."

I nibbled at a piece of sour-bread. "That's because anything simple is alien to Bruni."

Breakfast over, we hurried down the staircase and found Juju waiting for us by an open door. I thanked her for the food. "I came to meet a stargazer called Kummizza…"

She smiled. "Come."

She shepherded us through a bewildering array of rooms and passageways, and knocked on a door. A clear voice bade us in. Juju opened the door, muttered, "Good luck," and was gone.

Spooky and I entered a large chamber full of sunlight. Its sole occupant was a woman. She rose from her chair.

"Welcome to Mount Mäga. I'm Kummizza."

I studied the bony face and the shortly cropped blue hair and made a discovery. "You are Juju's mother."

Kummizza smiled. "I am. It's good to meet you finally, Allii. I've heard so much about you, I feel I already know you."

"This is Spooky," I began and stopped. Kummizza would have been informed that Princess Albalia killed Queen Bellizza.

"I didn't kill Belle," I burst out.

Kummizza's eyes were shadowed. "I know you didn't. That was why I told Brunelles I'd be happy to receive you and help you in any way I can. Sit down and tell me your story."

I did.

Kummizza listened as still as a graven image. When I

was done, she leaned forward. It was as if a statue were coming to reluctant life.

"My brother and I are in regular contact, so I know… The day after the murder, your father wrote to my brother asking forgiveness for failing to protect Bellizza. That was his last communication. His Chief Minister, on the other hand, has been writing to my brother daily. In his first letter, he promised the culprits would be found and dealt with, irrespective of rank or position. In the next one he wrote it was his sad duty to inform my brother that Princess Albalia was the main suspect. The letters continued, informing my bother about your incarceration and Bellizza's last rites. About three months ago, he sent an urgent message saying Princess Albalia had escaped after killing a guard."

Spooky nudged me with his muzzle. "Ask if she knows the exact wording of your father's letter." I did.

Kummizza reached into one of the drawers and fetched a wooden casket. She opened it, and took out a folded piece of paper. "I asked my brother for a copy. Here it is."

I opened the letter and read it out to Spooky.

Most honored brother,

Your sister and my wife, Queen Bellizza died last afternoon. Though the details are not yet known, the royal physician suspects foul play. I assure you a full investigation will be undertaken and the culprits apprehended and punished.

I deeply regret my inability to protect Bellizza from her enemies. I beg your forgiveness for my failure.

Walterin

Spooky's eyes gleamed. "Hmm. He apologizes for his inability to look after your stepmother from her enemies. That doesn't sound like an accusation against you."

I reread the letter. By the time it was written, I was already a prisoner. Yet Father makes no mention of me. Perhaps Spooky was right,

A third-reading made me see something else. Father attempted no pretense of a grief he obviously didn't feel. He made no effort to hide his sense of guilt either. Not the guilt of a killer, though, but the guilt of a bystander who had known evil was afoot and chosen not to do anything about it.

I had always regarded Father as a pillar of strength. His gravity, his silences, his solitary habits, his remoteness all contributed to create the image of a man as unmoving as mountains. Now I wondered whether the opposite was true. Was he a weak man who used silence and distance as a cover?

"Father," I began and stopped, not knowing how to continue. If I said what I really felt about him, would that be an act of disloyalty?

Kummizza probably realized my dilemma. "I never met your father," she said gently. I only know him second-hand, from Belli's letters. He may not have had a direct hand in her death. But indirectly, he bears considerable responsibility. Instead of protecting her, he looked the other way. Forgive me, my dear, but your father is a weak man who failed in his duty to his wife and his daughter."

I nodded, thinking 'wives.' He had failed Mother too.

Kummizza placed her hand on the casket. "I have here

every single letter my sister wrote to me since her marriage. You are free to read them. My only condition is that whatever ideas and suspicions you form, you share them with me."

"I will, Mistress Kummizza," I said fervently.

"Call me Kumi. That was what we used to call ourselves, Kumi and Belli. She was the youngest and I was the oldest of four siblings, with more than ten years between us. She was seven when I ran away to escape an unwanted marriage and to become a stargazer. I got in touch with her once I reached here. We've been writing to each other since then."

I remembered Sherriz's question. "Did anyone know about the letters?"

The shadows in Kummizza's eyes deepened. For a second her sharply-etched lips trembled. "No. You see, when she came to your land, she had to leave everything that had been hers behind. At the border of Sallonia, she had to divest herself of every stitch she was wearing, every item of jewelery, every pin, and don clothes and jewels your father had sent her. A symbolic act of dispossession and repossession, I wonder how she could have borne such humiliation. Anyway, she was a stranger in a strange land. She was very lonely. The letters to me were a small act of rebellion, a child's attempt to keep a toy hidden from adults who had taken all other toys away."

"I wish I'd known…"

"You helped her by being there, by being you. We never used mechanical pigeons. We used generias and some trusted intermediaries. Initially it was a whim, a childish game even. Later it turned serious. She was worried about the letters being intercepted. She started using different intermediaries, never the same twice. Towards the end, she was in mortal dread about other eyes than mine reading our letters. I thought she was overreacting. I didn't believe her life was in danger."

Spooky and I exchanged a glance.

Kummizza held out another letter to me. "This is the last letter I got from her. There's one reference to you which might cause you some distress. Please remember, this was written by a woman who feared for her sanity when she wasn't in fear for her life."

I took the letter it had been written on the 18th day of the 13th month in the Year of the Winged-Hedgehog, one month and three weeks before Bellizza's murder. I read it out in a low voice, so Spooky too could share in it.

My dearest sister,

Forgive me for not writing to you for so long. Finding a safe messenger is becoming harder and harder.

I'm more certain than ever I'm being watched. I'd like to place the entire blame for that on Sherriz. But he is only a servant, however glorified. His power and authority are not his own but derived from another. Keeping me under observation might have been his idea, but he still would have needed permission from a higher authority to implement it.

And in the pecking order, there's only one man above Sherriz.

Remember what we were taught from the time we were old enough to understand anything? That as princesses our sole purpose in life was to marry kings and give birth to future kings? (Brood mares in crowns you used to call us.) Well, I succeeded in the first duty and failed miserably in the second.

I have been told, not directly of course but in that language all court officials excel at, my duty is to release my husband from his bondage to me. I should leave, they imply in those honeyed words, and free the king to marry a woman who can give him children. Nothing is said, directly; indirectly, everything is said.

It's humiliating, clinging to a land that no longer wants me. For how long will I be allowed to hang on to my position? Is there a manual detailing how kings can get rid of unwanted wives, apart, of course, from the obvious way?

Had our brother been less powerful, they would have used more direct methods. But our brother is what he is, and officials like Sherriz, who are intelligent and cautious, would be loath to incur the displeasure of a king who is both powerful and quick to take offense. If I go away willingly, then our brother can't blame them.

And I can't go, even if I want to, because our brother won't consent to such a return.

Last week, we had a rare visit by Prince Bernalin. I was surprised when he agreed to come on a little expedition Allii arranged. As I've told you, he never liked me and never bothered to hide his dislike (that much I must say for him). During our journey to the samia wood, from Allii's prattling (she becomes a carefree little girl again in his presence, not the solemn young thing she has grown into). I surmised the destination had been his idea. That should have sounded a warning bell.

It was the season and the samia trees were in full bloom. Have you ever seen a samia tree in bloom? All the leaves are gone, and the entire tree is covered with tiny white flowers. And the fragrance—it can lift even the heaviest of hearts for a moment.

After lunch, Allii busied herself collecting samples for her herbarium, with Nana walking behind her like a brooding hen. To my surprise, Bernalin invited me to go for a short walk in the woods.

When we were away from the rest of the party, within seeing but not hearing distance, he lowered his voice and said, "I'm told they want you to return to your own land, my lady."

I almost choked. Then I understood. He is the next in line to the throne. If I leave and my lord marries again and produces an heir, he'll lose that position.

He must have guessed what I was thinking, because he said, "My lady, my interest in keeping you here is because of Allii. You have been good to her. If my cousin marries again, his next wife might take her in dislike."

"I love Allii," I said. It seemed to be the safest thing to say.

Bernalin coughed. "Then you will readily understand my concern about her wellbeing." He paused and added, "And her safety."

I nodded.

"I have been talking to some interested parties," he went on, his voice almost a whisper. "People who think the way I do, who see no reason why Allii shouldn't succeed her father."

I swallowed. "But your rules…"

"Rules are manmade, even the ones in books considered divine. The Consuetudinal says we must sacrifice a young woman to One God, our purported ancestor, every year. That's Book II, Chapter 12, if I remember right. We haven't observed

that rule for close to two centuries. Tradition decreed the victim be picked by lots. The last one so chosen happened to be a distant ancestress of mine, who was beloved by her father, the then king. So the rule was allowed to lapse. There was some opposition from those who believed tradition was above all else. That was quelled, quite ruthlessly if oral histories are to be believed. In a few decades, the rule was forgotten."

"I had no idea." I murmured.

He gave me a kind of a smile. "My point is, change is possible. It has happened before and it can happen again. All you need is the will. I've tried to talk to Cousin Walterin about this, but unfortunately he is not interested."

"Such an attempt might place Allii in danger," I managed to say. "My lord wouldn't want that."

Bernalin gave a nod. "As you say. But this kingdom needs to change, if it is to survive. If change is not effected from above, it'll come from below, and it'll come with blood. Given the nature of my niece's parentage, she is perhaps better placed than most to effect those changes."

What changes? I wanted to ask, but didn't. I was scared of being overheard, of all this being a trap.

"One of those I have consulted in this matter, my lady, is your esteemed brother. He is outraged by the idea of your marriage being dissolved. He has made it very clear, and not just to me, that any such step will be considered an unforgivable insult, even an act of hostility. He agrees the best possible solution is a change in the law enabling my royal cousin to proclaim his only daughter his heiress. He knows all correspondence between you and him are seen by other eyes, so he wanted me to convey his sentiments to you."

I didn't know what to say. So I said nothing.

Bernalin waited for me to respond. When I didn't, he said, "Your help in this matter would be much appreciated."

I felt my skin crawling with fear. This was treasonous talk.

I said carefully, "I fail to see what I can do, my lord prince. I no longer have any influence with the king. Remember I'm a barren wife, the worst of encumbrances for a king in need of an heir."

"You would know that Walterin is planning to get Allii married off. The purpose is to be rid of her. The Kingdom of Pinutto is almost at the other end of the world. If she is sent there, she'll be lost to us and to this land."

I said carefully, "Allii doesn't want to be married, yet."

"I'm aware. Whatever help you can give in this matter would be invaluable. That, and your steadfast refusal to leave your position."

What do you think, Kumi? Is this a rope a drowning woman could clutch at? Or is this a noose?

The only safe secret is the one that remains buried in one's heart. The secret plans told to me are known by many. Therefore they cannot be secrets. Sooner or later, they'll come to the wrong ears. What then?

I wanted to ask Bernalin why he was so eager to make Allii queen. Is he so fond of Allii he is willing to forego a throne? Or is he using her as a way to clear his own path?

I wish I could talk to our brother. I wish I could talk to you. I wish I knew what I should do. But such wishes are hopeless, situated as I am.

So I live in fear. What if this plan is discovered?

But I did talk to my lord about Allii's marriage. I said she doesn't want to marry into such a faraway land.

He said nothing. He doesn't say anything much to me nowadays. He seemed impatient to get back to his work, the work I interrupted. He was polite. He has always been polite. When I look back, I realize what I took for tenderness in our marriage might have been just politeness.

Four days ago, Nana, slipped me a letter. It was from our brother—or so the signature said. The handwriting was like his. And yet I feel uncertain.

It confirmed what Bernalin told me. And begged me to be of any assistance I can in furtherance of the plan, which, and I quote, "would benefit you as much as it would benefit your stepdaughter."

Kings move in mysterious ways. Is our brother's sole motivation the prevention of my return? Or are there other reasons, such as an assured supply of Sallikan? As you can see, I've become cynical even more than you.

The involvement of Nana gives rise to another set of questions. She never liked Bernalin and encouraged me, very discreetly of course, to reduce Allii's visits to his castle. Not to mention the fact she is one of those hidebound creatures who think tradition cannot and must not be flouted, whatever the reason. So why would she involve herself in this affair? Is it because she wants Allii to be queen? I have to say her love for Allii is probably the only truth in this kingdom of lies.

And what about Allii herself in all this?

I know she believes the only reason she can't succeed her father is because she's female. That was what they told her. I had to continue with the deception because I was adjured to do so when I came here. They don't want her to know about her mother being a Muffic let alone how her mother was treated. Perhaps they are right. Knowing Allii, I think she would be angry. She wouldn't be the dutiful daughter then that she is now.

I realize Allii's face has always been a bit of a closed book. I don't mean she tries to hide her feelings. It's just that only certain feelings appear on her face, like happiness or sadness, and very occasionally, anger. Anything deeper never shows. I can't believe it's for the lack of deeper emotions. She must be having them, yet they never show on her face. I wonder how much she knows about Bernalin's plotting. I wonder if he told her. They have always been such friends.

Can anyone in this place be trusted?

Pay no attention to these ravings, sister. I think I'm not quite sane.

I might not be able to write again for a long while, not until I can find another safe bearer for my letter. I don't know when that will be.

Take care of yourself, dearest. And when you are gazing at your stars, think of me.

I remain as ever,

Belli.

I folded the letter, blinking back the tears.

Poor Belle, poor darling Belle.

Kummizza was standing by the window, her back to the room. She turned around and walked back to her chair. Her face was calm, but the hand with which she took the letter was not. She didn't put it in the casket, but continued to hold it, as if it were a talisman. "What do you think?"

"I suppose someone discovered Uncle Bernii's plans."

Kummizza's voice was strained. "Yes, as Belli put it, a secret ceases to be a secret the moment it is shared."

"If Uncle Bernii were planning to change succession laws and was in communication with your brother, then that would give Uncle Rokkrin a powerful motive to remove me." It was a comforting thought. I clung to it with all my might. Doktoras Poll and Uncle Rokkrin working together to kill Bellizza as a way of getting rid of me.

A neat solution.

Too neat.

Kummizza picked up an onyx penholder and passed it from hand to hand. "You knew nothing about any of it?"

I shook my head, feeling trapped. To anyone looking from outside, it would seem as if I were at the centre of interconnected webs of intrigue.

Kummizza continued to watch me. "I suppose no one bothered to ask you whether you want to be queen?"

I didn't try to keep the bitterness out of my face or my voice. "No one even gave me a hint. Why should they? I was just going to be a figurehead. As for Bellizza thinking I kept my emotions hidden, she was right. All my life I was told I must keep my feelings under control. It was only with Belle I could be myself at least a little bit."

"Ah yes, your Nana was obsessed with that. Bellizza was very fond of Nanarina but didn't approve of some of her ideas. They talked about it, as you will see when you read the letters. Nanarina was one of the few people genuinely kind to Bellizza when she first came to Sallonia. Bellizza was terribly homesick in those first months. She used to burst into tears, and Nanarina would hold her and stroke her head, until she was calm."

I glowed. "Nana is the kindest person imaginable."

Kummizza took a packet from the casket and held it out to me. "Here are Belli's letters. Anytime you want to ask me something or share some insight with me, please don't hesitate. I've given instructions so you'll have access to me whatever time of day or night."

The tabular summit of Mount Mäga was as large as a hamlet. Except for a single cherry tree, nothing grew on its uniform surface. The floor was paved with matte-black stones. A tall iron fence ran the length of the plateau, set with a single gate. A row of steps cut into the mountainside led to the invisible nether regions.

The buildings contained bedrooms, classrooms, observatories, libraries, kitchens, bathing-rooms, and a host of other facilities. A spiral staircase led to the main observatory atop the tower. Since there was no source of water in the plateau, water was brought from the valley below through huge bronze pipes, powered by a Brunelles invention.

"We are given everything we need so we can give the stars their undivided attention," Juju explained.

Mount Mäga had near vertical slopes on three sides. The only way up—and down—was through the fourth side, which was connected to a smaller mountain range via a cirque, a long bowl-shaped verdant valley fed by an abundance of cold and hot water springs. This was the

"Village"—the nursery, infirmary, and retirement home of the Stargazers.

"The children stay here until they are old enough to decide their future," Juju said. "Not everyone wants to be a Stargazer. Most of the children leave because they want to lead normal lives."

"Don't you feel lonely in a place like this?" I asked Juju, feeling that Bellizza had a point about not wanting to spend one's life in a place so isolated from the real world.

Juju smiled. "Not with the stars, not much. Not if you love stars as much as I do, as much as all of us living here do. And you mustn't think there's no practical purpose in our work. We help chart courses for ships and desert caravans. We predict extreme weather phenomena. We are in touch with other learning centers and the rulers of many countries. Bootii, the generia, just returned from taking a message to a principality about a hundred leagues south about a storm brewing several miles away in the sea. The warning will save lives."

Spooky sighed. "We should have checked with these people before we went ambling in the desert, Allii."

I chuckled. The nightmare experience has become an adventure in our memories. It was an interesting phenomenon, I thought, how time had the power to distort events. Maybe it wasn't time. Maybe it was us, by remembering and forgetting as we wanted and needed.

Juju made polite inquiries about Bellizza. "Her death has devastated Mama," she said. "I wish I had known Aunt Bellizza, but she is just a name to me."

"She mentioned you to me several times," I said. "But

she called you Julizza which was why I didn't make the connection."

"My full name. Juju is what my brother called me."

"Your twin. Bellizza said he went to your Uncle's."

Juju's voice was expressionless. "My brother wanted to be a musician. He just couldn't abide it, the life on the mountain top."

I looked at Juju wondering whether every life was sundered in some way because every choice involved some loss.

The first ever letter sent by Bellizza after her marriage to her sister made me cry.

Darling Kumii,

What can I tell you, except I'm happy, happy, happy. You were wrong, my dearest. A marriage can be the greatest blessing. He is good and kind, and I know he will love me with time. I love him already. And his daughter from that earlier union I wrote to you about, Allii, is such a solemn little child. We will be friends, I know it.

I've never felt so happy in my life. Sallonia feels a little strange, but I know I'm going to love it too. My chief lady, Lady Nellin is a bit frightening, but Allii's nurse Nanarina is kind. I will get used to them all in time. And when I have a son, my acceptance will be complete.

I must go. He is taking me to see one of his favorite places in the entire kingdom, a samia forest in full bloom.

I never thought life could hold so much joy.

I love you my dearest sister.
In happiness,
Belli

Letter by letter, I accompanied Bellizza on her journey, from happiness to grief, from hope to disappointment, again and again, until despair began.

It was in the later letters, recording her descent from darkness to even greater darkness, any foretelling of her eventual fate would be present. I started copying out parts I thought were relevant in my Memory Book for further reading.

From a letter written between her penultimate and final pregnancies—

I hear from my maids the army is being expanded. There are rumors that a war with the Muffics is coming. Perhaps it's a good thing Allii knows nothing about her mother. How appalled she would be to hear that her father's people are planning to annihilate her mother's people.

I asked Nana about it, but she looked surprised. She pursed her lips. "It is madness," was all she said.

"But, Nana, I thought you hated Muffics."

She gave me the kind of look she gives Allii, the teacherly one, fond but reproving. "My lady, a wise ruler knows the limitations. We have managed to keep Muffics in their place because we made sure that place was a livable one. You push them too hard, they might fight back. And one never knows what infernal powers these witch-people have."

Nana, the statesman. I suppose she has a point.

From a letter written during the early weeks of her final pregnancy—

Tygyrin paid a call on me. Allii was with me. I ordered cakes and cocolade and we spent nearly an hour talking. To be more precise, Tygyrin and Allii talked, mostly to each other, while I watched.

I've noticed he has begun to call on me when he knows Allii would be with me. There's something in his eyes when he looks at her, something I cannot read.

I asked Nana whether he's interested in her.

Nana gave me a pitying look. "You cannot be more mistaken, my lady."

"Why, Nana?" I asked. "It would not be an improper arrangement. He is an excellent young man, unlike that horrid brother of his. Even you like him."

She repeated the look. "He is a young man of piety and pride, my lady. That is why he will never seriously entertain the kind of union you mentioned."

I was getting angry. "How dare you Nana? And you love Allii."

Nana's expression was withering. "That is why I want the best for her, my lady. She will make a much better marriage. And he will marry someone who is wholly Sallonian."

That was the end of that conversation.

I worry about Allii. She is like a creature in one of those stories she loves reading, a girl trapped in a cocoon. On the outside everything looks calm, controlled. But someday the cocoon will unravel and she'll come out. What will she be like then? I have no idea.

I wish they'd tell Allii the truth about her mother. There is nothing shameful about the truth. Her mother was an intelligent, attractive woman. There is a painting of her in my lord's personal library, the only painting in that stark room. I had a hard time keeping my eyes away from it when I was still a welcome visitor there.

Once, years ago, I was sitting in the library, waiting for my lord to finish some work. Knowing myself to be unobserved I studied the painting, trying to imagine her life. When I looked at my lord to see if he had finished his work, I found that he too was gazing at the picture.

For a moment, our eyes met. I saw the pain in his and the longing, so naked it made me shiver.

I said hurriedly, "Allii looks much like her."

He shrugged. "I hope you don't make that remark in public, my dear. You'll be doing Allii a great disservice."

I flushed and stammered I'd never do Allii any disservice.

(I suddenly remembered. He never called me love or my love. Never, not even in our most intimate moments. For all his faults he is an honest man. He didn't call me his love because that would have been an act of deliberate deception. I'm not his love. She is, even in death.)

Later that day, I related the story to Nana. Her face turned all stony. She said, "My lady, the king gave you good advice. I know you are motivated by kindness. You are good to my baby and I'm forever grateful to you. But it is for her own safety we don't want her to know anything about her mother."

"Someday she will, dear Nana," I said. "Someday she will be married and gone from here. How can you prevent her from discovering the truth then?"

"My lady, when she is married it won't matter. She'll have a husband who'll protect her. And she won't be here. She'll be out of harm's way."

From a letter written during the second half of her final pregnancy—

The court is a hornets' nest of intrigues. The Rokkrin faction becomes ever powerful. Nana is the one who brings me news. She hates Rokkrin, partly on Allii's behalf. He had called Allii a Muffie when she was first brought to the castle. Nana never forgave or forgot. She'll stick a knife into him if she can. It's a funny thought—dear, fussy, proper, kind Nana as a murderess. But she hates him that much. The thought of him on the throne distresses her as much as it distresses me and must distress anyone who cares a whit for Sallonia.

The only time Nana approved of Rokkrin was when he made that decision about poor Kolla. It devastated Allii. He was the older brother she never had, and she cried for days. Nana, who weeps even when Allii has a toothache, was unmoving.

Is it possible to understand people, Kumi, even people you think you know completely?

From a letter written soon after her final stillbirth—

My lord doesn't come to my room at nights anymore. You have no idea, sister, how lonely a bed made for two can be for one person.

I don't know what I would have done without Allii. But my mood is such, at times I wish she wouldn't try so hard to cheer me up but leave me to my misery.

Nellii is as fiercely protective as ever. Sometimes I'm scared she'll say something rude to the king to his face.

Nana often comes and sits with me, especially when I'm alone and feeling as blue as my hair, as Allii puts it. Nana doesn't talk much. But I find her presence comforting. Her calmness is better for me, at least in some of my moods, than Allii's eagerness to help and Nellin's anger. And when my headaches turn unbearable, Nana holds me in her arms and kneads my neck until the pain abates. I cannot tell you how safe I feel in those moments.

I hear Rokkrin spends most of his time in the capital now. His odious wife Amberlina paid a call on me last week, bearing fruits. I wanted her to leave, but she just sat there, making small talk—what a horrid phrase. When she said I must regard her and her husband as friends who are devoted to my interests, I could take it no more. I smiled and asked her whether she had any news of Kollarin. That did it. Within minutes, she was gone.

I wanted to tell the story to Allii. She would have enjoyed it. But she doesn't know Kolla is alive. Why they insist on keeping everything from her, I don't understand. Someday she is going to find out and she will hate us, even me.

From a letter written eight months before Belle's murder—

Sherriz had approached our brother, indirectly, sounding out about a separation between my lord and me. At least that was how our brother put it in his letter. The letter was handed to me personally by a special envoy.

This is what our brother has to say. "Nothing would induce me to consent to a proposal which will bring dishonor to my sister and my house." Quite clear, don't you think?

Of course he didn't mention his interests, but then that'll muddy the pure waters of brotherly love and family honour, would it not?

From a letter written six months before Belle's murder—

Nellii has started sleeping in my room, on a divan between the door and the bed. You can't imagine how comforting that is. Nothing can ward off the nightmares. But when I wake up shivering, she is there to hold me and comfort me.

The story is that Sherriz is in correspondence with several courts, looking for my replacement. But I'm still here and I don't know where else I can go. Our brother doesn't want me home, says it will be a disgrace to our family. Sometimes I think if my lord is willing to make a settlement in 'Salii' (as the miners call the cursed metal), our brother would be quite willing to have me back. Maybe I should drop a hint to Sherriz, since he seems to be in charge of this matter.

Do I sound hysterical, Kumi? I feel hysterical. Sometimes, when we dine together, my lord and I, and he makes polite conversation, I want to laugh, laugh and laugh and laugh until there's no laughter left in me or in the world.

On the afternoon of the fifth day, Kummizza summoned us to her room.

"I've just received a message from Brunelles," she said after a brief greeting. "He is coming tonight to take you home."

I stared, confused. Home? Where? Which home? Why?

Kummizza leaned forward. "There is no good way to say this, Allii. So I'll just say it. Prince Bernalin had sent word to Brunelles. I'm sorry my dear, but your father is dead. He has been killed. Prince Rokkrin has seized the throne, supposedly on the basis of a will left by your father. Bernalin thinks he is planning to march against Muffics as soon as the coronation is over."

BOOK THREE

1
ROCK HER TO DEATH

"They call a Halfling a poisoned vessel. But we say, a Halfling is a sea, fed by different rivers. They seek to shame us. We will not be shamed. They refuse to own us. We own ourselves. They consign us to darkness. We will paint the night."
We, the Halflings – Pamphlet 1

SILENCE. THAT WAS WHAT I REMEMBERED MOST OF THE journey from Mount Mäga.

Brunelles didn't sing or chatter as he had done when he took us to Mount Mäga. Spooky was—or was pretending to be—asleep, curled into a tight ball.

I stared at the starless sky, wishing I had better memories of Father. I dug and dug in search of a time when he and I were close, when he held me in his arms and kissed me, laughed, and played with me. Try as I might, I couldn't find such a past.

I wanted to cry, but the tears wouldn't come. Did it mean I have no love for Father?

To take my mind off my non-grief, I focused on the situation back home. Did Rokkrin kill Father? Or was it someone else? According to Uncle Bernii's message, Tygyrin was unhappy with what had happened. He had expressed reservations about the will and wanted to delay the coronation, or so Uncle Bernii's source had informed him. Tygyrin had always been close to Father. Perhaps he suspected his father had a hand in my father's death.

Brunelles was losing speed, a prelude to a landing. He had insisted on going to his castle first. "I promise to take you wherever you want to go, after you've slept for a few hours, and we've made some plans," he had said.

Sleep was tardy even after the soporific-laced milk Brunelles made me drink. I spent most of the night alternating between lying on the bed with determined stillness, and pacing the room with manic intensity.

Sleep must have claimed me at some point. What woke me up was a sense of alarm.

I sat in bed, certain that Nana was in danger. Nana was supposedly sick and being cared for by Doktoras Poll. Poll had a hand in Bellizza's murder. Nana knew I didn't kill Bellizza. She'd fight for me even at the risk of her own life. That wouldn't suit the murderer's purpose.

I jumped out of the bed. I had to go home. I had to find Nana before she too was killed.

Breakfast was waiting, together with Spooky and Brunelles. I had no appetite but shoveled food into my mouth. There was no time to waste on futile arguments.

"Now, let us plan," Brunelles said. "Bernii wants me to bring you to his castle. Going there would make sense."

"No, I'm going home," I saw the 'Don't be silly,' look in Spooky's eyes, and explained my fears for Nana.

Brunelles tapped the table with a painted claw. "Allii, I promised Bernii I'd ensure your safety. I understand your concern for your nurse. But I can't let you walk into danger."

I swallowed the sudden constriction in my throat. When I spoke, my voice was hoarse and my sentences sounded choppy. "The night I escaped, I looked up and saw a light in my father's room. I wanted to run to him and tell him I wasn't Bellizza's murderer. I didn't. I was scared I'd be caught. It was the right decision. I know that. Still, I'll always wonder what might have happened—if I talked to him—" My throat felt as if it were coated with burning sand. I gulped down some water. "I couldn't save Bellizza, I couldn't save poor Terrii who was killed for a reason that had nothing to do with him. I couldn't reach my father in time. I can't fail Nana too. I understand Uncle Bernii's concern. But I'm not his little Allii anymore. I'll be fine if Spooky is with me." I turned to Spooky who stared back, his expression unreadable. "You'll come with me, won't you?"

He sniffed. "Oh, it's a daft idea. But I'll come."

Brunelles picked a lime-cake with two claws, like a finicky old lady, and gobbled it. "I'm not happy about this.

Still, this is your life and your decision. So I'll take you." He patted his mouth with a lace-edged serviette. "Some questions you need to answer first, though. How are you going to get into the castle undetected?"

"Perhaps Kollarin, my cousin, can help. He is in communication with Panda. Panda should be able to get me into the castle. He got me out of it."

"Then we go to this valley and find your cousin?"

Spooky had been biting a paw, a faraway look in his eyes. Now he said, "Is there any way Allii can be made to look less like a Halfling? Otherwise she'll be recognized the moment she steps into that place, Panda or no Panda."

I smacked my forehead. "What an idiot I'm to have forgotten that." I turned to Brunelles. "I'll need to look brown-skinned and brown or yellow-haired and dressed like a maid if possible, in brown trousers and a long brown blouse. I'll draw it."

I did a rough sketch. Brunelles frowned over it. "My tailor can handle the sewing. Hopefully we have a suitable material. The problem is your appearance. Let's see—"

He bustled out. Spooky stopped his paw-biting for a second. "Dragons!"

I smiled. "By the way, there are no dogs in the castle."

Spooky yawned. "What sort of four-legged creature would attract the least attention in this castle of yours, other than cats?"

I considered the matter. "How about a sikilian-fox? They are allowed in the woods and the gardens because they eat rodents."

"Let's give it a try. Close your eyes."

I did.

After a while, I heard a squeak. "Now see."

I opened my eyes and my mouth fell open. Spooky was gone. Where he had been crouched a creature no larger than my splayed hand. It was grey-coated and stubby, with a broad face, a flat muzzle and a black-tipped bushy tail. A black line ran down the length of its spine.

"Will I do?" The squeak was high-pitched.

I started laughing. "You'll do. If my disguise is half as good as yours, we should be safe."

Brunelles didn't disappoint. As afternoon was wending towards evening, he arrived with a short, stubby man whose excited gait reminded me of Sherriz. The man was an artist from a nearby town specializing in face and body painting for actors and warriors. He worked on me for a couple of hours. By the time he finished, my clothes were ready.

When I looked in the mirror, a yellow-haired, brown-skinned stranger stared back at me.

The night was at its darkest when we reached the little valley.

I slipped to the ground, landing on a patch of gravel, unhurt but badly winded. As soon as my legs felt steady enough to hold me, I stood up and walked towards the cottage. I was halfway there when Spooky overtook me with a bound. He reached the door, sniffed, and turned around.

"There's no one inside. Not even that pesky dog."

I felt a new wave of fear. Had Kolla and Pattii been

discovered by tracker-assassins? Had some other mishap befallen them?

I pushed the door. It opened. Inside everything was orderly, covered, packed away, made ready for a long absence.

Spooky looked up from his sniffing. "Perhaps they left to join the rebellion?"

"Not Pattii."

"She wouldn't want to let Kolla go into danger alone, would she?"

I nodded. That was so.

We hurried back to Brunelles who was sitting with his back against a huge boulder, munching something. "So where are…" he began and stopped, seeing our faces. "What's wrong?"

"They are not here. The house is in order, as if they left voluntarily. Spooky thinks they may have gone to join the rebellion."

Brunelles frowned, the furrows reminding me of sand-dunes. "That complicates matters. What do we do now?"

I tried to think of a plan but nothing came to mind. All I knew was I had to get to Nana before it was too late.

"Home. I mean back to my father's castle, to find Panda."

Brunelles' expression was interrogative. "Do you know where to find this Panda?"

"I know where the foresters' cottages are," I replied. It was not quite the truth. I knew the general direction but had never been to the cottages.

One more thing Princess Albalia wasn't supposed to do, according to Nana.

Brunelles sighed. "I'll take you as close to the castle as possible." His gaze grew stern. "Don't try to go in alone because you are in a hurry to get to your Nana. Get hold of this Panda person, assuming he is still at his duties, and not running around with a sword, howling war-chants."

The thought of the reticent and dignified Panda making such a spectacle of himself made me smile a little. Then the smile vanished. If the rebellion got off the ground, he would be acting more like Brunii's caricature than my memory. In a battlefield, ridiculousness could be as normal as brutality. They probably called it heroism there.

Brunelles landed on a wide ridge to the west of the royal woods. On the other side of the ridge was the canal that irrigated the woods and kept the boating lake filled during the dry season through a series of underground tunnels. Nana used to bring me here to impress upon me "the marvels of Sallonian engineering."

I scrambled off Brunelles' back.

Brunelles bent his long neck bringing his head level with mine and lowered his otherwise stentorian voice to a murmur. "Would this place do? Or do you want me to take you somewhere else?"

I shook my head, waiting for the ground to cease its dance.

"I think you have about an hour of darkness left. Maybe a little more." He patted me with a claw. "Don't take unnecessary risks. I wish I could do more. But by agreements older than me, I can't involve myself in human affairs. If you need to get out fast, try to reach out to me with your mind. Spooky should be able to manage it, even if you can't."

A wave and he was gone.

When I turned around to tell Spooky we too should be going, I found not the daemon-dog but a sikilian-fox.

My laugh was shaky. "Let's go, foxy."

We hurried down the slope towards the tree-wall surrounding the woods. Spooky found an opening and crept through. I followed.

"Which way now?" he squeaked.

I had been mulling over that question during the ride. As we landed, I had caught a glimpse of what seemed like a cluster of small cottages. Maybe they belonged to the foresters. I pointed in what I hoped was the right direction.

If Spooky noticed the tentativeness of my gesture, he didn't comment on it. "I'll go first," he said. "If there's danger, I'll reach out to you. Keep your mind open."

Darkness shrouded the woods. The silence was complete, other than the occasional cry of a striped owl. Rains had ended during my absence. The dry season had just begun. The ground was still soft. The wind didn't burn.

My last journey through these woods seemed to be a different life and a different me.

Spooky paused, his head raised, as if he were listening to something. I stopped too, and focused, but heard nothing other than the strangely symphonic hum of insects.

Spooky's voice throbbed with urgency. *Humans. Two, no three. Headed this way.*

I stepped off the path, and crouched behind a bush, hoping the hammering of my heart was audible only to me.

What do they look like?

Men.

Footsteps became audible, though barely so. These are men used to walking in silence. Then came disemboweled words, the tail-end of a sentence. "…wait for a message?"

"Only till dawn."

I almost cried out with relief. The second voice was Panda's. I couldn't believe my good fortune. All I had to do was to wait till his companions left and reveal myself to him.

"What do we do if Albalia can't be located?" It was that first voice again.

"Then we do without." Panda sounded grim and determined, not a bit like the Panda of my memories. "But she'll be found. We know where she's headed."

A third voice muttered, "She might not want to come back."

"She will be persuaded." Panda's voice was iron.

"We can't wait beyond dawn for whatever reason," the first voice muttered. "It would be dangerous to tarry…"

As they moved further away, the words turned to sounds, and the sounds faded into silence. Somewhere, a flying squirrel screeched. An ill omen, according to Sallonian beliefs.

Spooky's voice had a jagged feel inside my head. *Allii!*

I concentrated and responded. *That was Panda, the tallest one.*

Hmm. The other two are gone. He is alone now. You can talk to him—if that is what you want to do.

My temples throbbed. My stomach felt as if a giant hand was gripping it.

Allii?

I don't want him to know I'm here.

There was a quality of grimness in Spooky's silence. In it I read both acceptance of my decision, and anxiety about this unexpected complication.

I tried to make my inner-voice firm and confident. *We'll head to the castle.*

And then?

The way I'm dressed, I should be able to creep inside and find my way to Nana's room.

Again there was no response from Spooky. This time the silence throbbed with doubt.

Spooky? Shall we go?

Which way to this castle?

There should be a path to the left, I think.

After a couple of wrong turns, I was relieved to discover a familiar paved path. The coiffeur birds started their polyphony, heralding the dawn. Occasionally, I heard a rustle. Since Spooky showed no sign of interest, I presumed it was some nocturnal creature out on its business.

Allii, I get human smells.

I whipped out of sight, huddling behind a hedge of bangella bushes. *A guard?*

No, a woman about your age, dressed the way you are.

It must be a maid.

She is picking flowers.

Star-jasmines, tiny flowers that bloomed for a few hours between midnight and dawn. Court ladies coveted them for their lingering scent. An image flashed before my eyes, bringing with it the sting of tears: Bellizza washing her face and her hands in water scented with star-jasmines.

The footsteps were close. I sneaked a look and recognized the woman with the basket and the covered lamp.

They say a drowning man would clutch at even a fish.

I scrambled out. "Sherby."

The woman turned around slowly and stared, her eyes widening in puzzlement.

"Sherby, it's me, Allii, Albalia."

Sherby's mouth fell open. She closed it with a deliberate snap and held up the lamp, peering into my face. Horror replaced shock as recognition dawned.

"I heard about papa." My breath came in gasps.

Sherby stood as taut as a drawn bow, face tight, eyes hard. "What're you doing here? Are you out of your mind? You'd be dead if they catch you."

"Sherby I must see Nana."

"You'd do better to get out the way you came." Her voice was harsh.

I murmured, "Please, Sherby," and stopped. Perhaps she believed the stories about me. "Sherby, I didn't kill the queen."

Her eyes filled with scorn. "Never believed you did. That's not it. It'd be stupid for you to come in. Rokkrin'd stick a knife into you."

"Sherby, please listen to me."

Sherby spoke through gritted teeth, her voice a hiss. "No. Highness. You listen to me. Rokkrin'll be crowned tomorrow. Then he'll go to war against…Muffics. A war to make him popular or so he'd reckon. Maybe he's right. Chants and slogans, they can fill some stomachs."

"I thought he was crowned."

"They can't, can they, without the ring?"

I stared. "The Ring of Sallonia?" The gold ring with the star-shaped silver pearl, the foremost symbol of Sallonian kingship, placed by One God on the right hand of the first Sallonian king, according to the Song of Sallonia.

"They say the king wasn't wearing it when he—" Sherby's face softened a little. "Wish it hadn't happened. He wasn't a bad man, your father. It's being the king that did him in."

I saw an opening. "Sherby, Papa died before I could see him. I have to see Nana before something happens to her as well. If you don't help me, I'll go anyway and get caught. If you are concerned about my safety, take me to Nana in the safest way you can."

Sherby frowned. "Dame Nanarina's locked up. They say she's mad, but they'd say anything about anyone." She held up the lamp again, studying my face. "You've changed. I don't mean the hair and all. Dame Nanarina helped me once. The queen too. I'd like to help you. But the tower's guarded. I've no way in."

"Do you know Minister Ekko's house? If you tell me where it is—"

Sherby's lips curled. "You'd go and get yourself caught. Won't happen though, 'cos I don't know his house."

My mind darted around desperately, and settled on one name.

"Lord Tygyrin, is he here?" Tygyrin stayed in the castle occasionally.

Sherby nodded.

"Can you take me to him? Please, Sherby." He wasn't like his father, and he would never betray me.

Sherby was silent for a while as if she were considering the merits of my idea. Then she shrugged. "I know nothing bad about him. They say he's unhappy about his father's doings. And he's keeping your garden cared for, and your plant books."

I felt a warm rush of affection.

Her eyes narrowed. "You're dressed right, but—Wait here. If someone comes, hide."

She vanished into the gloom. I waited shivering a little.

Sherby returned, carrying a bunch of reeds. "There, you take that. We bring 'em for the ladies to make fancy things. Useless stuff. Still, it kills time I reckon." She picked up her basket and hurried towards the castle.

Do I come out?

Can you stay in the shadows and follow us?

Easy as pie…How are pies easy?

Sherby entered through a side door, strode down a narrow corridor, and up an uncarpeted staircase. I followed her, clutching the reeds with clammy fingers.

The castle was still shrouded in darkness. There were a few stone-lights in wall sconces but their glow was swallowed by the cavernous spaces. We passed several maids and men-servants hurrying to or from some task, but other than a gruff greeting from a stout elderly woman, no one paid us attention.

We went up another uncarpeted passage. Sherby opened a door, indicating that I should go in. All I could see in the darkness was a couple of chairs and shapes piled up against the walls.

"You stay here," she whispered. "Bolt the door. Don't open it till I call."

I caught her hand and pressed it. "Thanks so much, Sherby."

Her lips curled. "Too early for thanks. Best wait till we're out of this." Then she was gone, swallowed by the darkness.

I reached out to Spooky. *Will you come in?*

I'll stay out and keep watch. In the pause that followed, I could sense the turmoil within him. *Can you trust these people?*

I think so. I hope so.

There was no response from Spooky. I went in and bolted the door. As my eyes adjusted to the darkness, the piles dissolved into recognizable items, old furniture mostly, a copper pot, ornaments, all covered by a patina of dust.

I selected a less rickety looking chair and sat down, mulling over something that had been bothering me for a while, the sense that in Bellizza's letters I read a critical piece of information. The feeling had come to me shortly after we left the valley last night, and nagged me, the way a rotten tooth would, throughout the ride. In the excitement that followed, it receded into the back of my mind. Now that I had nothing to do but wait, it consumed me.

I was still trying to unravel that feeling when I heard Spooky's voice in my head. *She's here, with a man.*

I stood up on trembling legs, trying to hold myself

together, listening, and heard Sherby's voice. "It's me."

Unbolting the door took me a while. Sherby stood outside, and behind her, Tygyrin, carrying a small stone-light. He stared at me for a few seconds, as if trying to decide this was me. Then he gave me a quick smile and turned to Sherby. "Thank you for bringing me to the Princess. Return to your duties and try to act as if nothing unusual happened."

Sherby's mouth thinned and her eyes flashed. But the mutinous expression was gone so fast, I wondered if I imagined it. She bowed to him and turned to me. "Take care of yourself, Highness." Her voice was rough, and there was no smile on her face.

I caught her hand and pressed it. "Thank you so much, Sherby. You saved me. I hope we'll see each other soon."

Her expression softened a little. She nodded and walked away.

A sense of loneliness came over me. I shrugged it away. I was being a fanciful idiot, allowing my disordered emotions a free ride. Things were working out better than I hoped. Soon I'd be with Nana…and…

Tygyrin stepped past me into the room and closed the door. Then he turned around, lifted my chin, and studied my face. "I can't believe this is you I'm seeing. But your eyes are the same." There was no welcome in his voice. "Why did you come? Why in One God's name did you come?"

I tried to smile. "I heard about papa…"

He pulled me into his arms, holding me. "I'm sorry, Allii, I'm sorry."

I could feel the tears filling my eyes. I tried to blink

them back. One fell anyway.

Tygyrin bent his head and kissed first the tear, and then my mouth.

Not very cousinly. But nice. Not melting-my-body nice. But you-can-go-on nice.

He lifted his head. "What am I going to do, Allii? What in Liminalin's name am I going to do?" His voice was hoarse and kind of choky.

Well you can kiss me again, or you can make yourself useful.

"Take me to Nana," I said, opting for the practical. *If we come out of this alive, we'd have all the time in the world to go back to kissing and take it from there—or not.*

"Allii, I'll get you out of this place, get you away to safety. I have protected Nana all this time. I'll continue to do so until this mess is over. But you must leave. You have to."

I pulled myself away. "No. I came to see Nana. I won't leave until I've seen her."

"Allii, please. You don't know what you are up against."

I shook my head. "I must see Nana."

He ran his hand through his hair. "Will you promise me that you will leave once you have seen Nana?"

I nodded.

"Do I have your word?"

I held out my hand. "You can trust me."

He took my hand and kissed it. "I missed you," he said, his voice soft.

Should I say I missed him too? Would it be the proper response? Would it be the truth? I didn't know. So I said, "Thank you so much for looking after my garden and my herbaria."

He smiled again. "How could I not?"

I nodded. Where were words when you needed them most?

He pressed my hand, and released it. "Come, then." Outside the door he paused. "If anyone asks, you are taking those reeds to Dame Nanarina at her request. Don't speak though. I will do the answering." His hand brushed my cheek, soft and fleeting, like a feather. "Your voice is still yours."

I nodded, and reached out to Spooky. *He's taking me to see Nana. I've promised him I'll leave afterwards.*

Finally someone made you see sense. Who's he when he's not squeezing water out of stones?

I gulped back a giggle.

There were guards at the door to the tower, but they didn't ask any questions. I kept my head down. That way they couldn't see my eyes, and I looked properly submissive.

The spiral staircase brought back memories. Kolla and I had played dragons and princes here and catch-me-if-you-can.

Tygyrin climbed fast, as if a company of hell-imps were after him. I clambered in his wake. Soon we were on the topmost floor which contained just one room. I used to hide there, when I wanted to read undisturbed. Nana complained I read too much. "You'll ruin your pretty eyes, my baby," she'd say.

Tygyrin stopped by the massive wooden door and turned to me. "Don't stay for too long. And remember your promise."

I smiled. "Thank you so much, Cousin."

"Do not go wondering on your own, or even if that maid comes. Wait for me."

I nodded, unwilling to trust my voice. Unfamiliar thoughts were churning inside my head. If Tygyrin and I joined forces, wouldn't we be able to unite everyone? And he would make a good…I forced myself to stop.

Tygyrin has been watching me. Now he kissed my cheek, the lingering warmth of his lips turning the familiar chaste salute to something even more intimate than his earlier kiss. "Remember your promise, Allii. I've lost you once. I don't want to lose you again."

I stood on tiptoe and planted a kiss at the corner of his mouth—one open to interpretation. Then I slipped into the room, before he could catch me in another embrace, closing the door behind me.

The room was as I remembered it—a bed, a chair, a washbasin, and a table. The only changes were the remnants of uneaten meals moldering on the table, and the iron bars on the windows. Instead of the clean cool smell of my memory, the room reeked of uneaten food and human waste.

Nana lay curled up on the bed. Her breathing was even, and she seemed to be sleeping. I tiptoed up to the bed, knelt, and touched the veined and wizened hand. Nana froze for a moment. Then she turned, sobbing, "My baby, my baby."

I leaned forward and kissed her cheek. "I missed you, Nana."

Nana was out of the bed, huddled on the ground, cradling me. "My baby. You are here. You are here."

The world vanished as I melted into her embrace. The tears I had been holding back started falling.

Nana rocked me gently, murmuring, "There, there, little Allikin. Nana's here. You are safe. Nothing will happen to you. I'll look after you." Then she started crooning a lullaby.

I wept. The past didn't matter, nor the future. Only this moment. I was too late for Bellizza, for father, for Terrii. But I wasn't too late for Nana.

I didn't care about Sallonians or Muffics or Halflings. All I wanted was to get Nana out of here. Perhaps Brunelles could take us away to some safe place, where Nana could live out the rest of her life in happiness.

Eventually the tears ceased. I breathed in deeply, inhaling Nana's familiar scent, feeling the rough gentle hands stroking my head, the back of my neck, my weary shoulders.

The dream of taking Nana away, of living in happy obscurity in some far off place vanished. Not at once, but layer by layer.

I was late for Nana too. Much too late.

Because, as I rested in Nana's arms and felt the familiar fingers kneading the taut muscles of my neck, the memory that had nagged me the last several hours became clear.

Kummizza talking about how lonely Bellizza was in the early days. "She used to burst into tears, and Nanarina would hold her and stroke her head, until she was calm."

Bellizza writing to her sister, *When my headaches are truly bad, Nana holds me in her arms and kneads my neck until the pain abates a little. I cannot tell you how safe I feel in those moments.*

The truth had been staring at me in the face, again. I had turned my eyes away, again, because I didn't want to know.

I lifted my head from Nana's breast and gazed at that dearly beloved face.

"Nana, why did you kill Bellizza?"

2

LOVE IS DEATH

*"We are the young trees and the eternal
grass. We will bend today, so that we
can stand straight tomorrow."*
We, the Halflings — Pamphlet 1

A TIGHTENING OF THE ARMS HOLDING ME MADE ME LOOK
up. Nana was smiling, her eyes shining like stars.

"My clever baby."

I stilled the shudder of horror. "Was it a sand-kutzi
thorn, Nana?"

Nana laughed; her voice was exultant. "My clever
little Allikin. Yes it was." Her face turned somber. "It was
painless. Just a prick. I insisted on that. Didn't take more
than a few seconds. I held her and sang to her until she was
gone. You mustn't think I left her alone to die. It wasn't her
fault that she had to die. It had to be done, but…"

My body was a block of ice. I wanted to run away, to die, to forget.

"I had no idea they were going to blame you, my baby. They said Doktoras Poll would call it a natural death. Then my boy can have a new wife who'll give him a son, and you'll make a great marriage." She stopped and tilted my chin, staring into my eyes. "She should have gone away. Then I wouldn't have had to kill her."

Her last words were like a body blow. I doubled up, moaning. "Nana, you shouldn't have killed her. She never did any harm to anyone."

Nana shook her head. "She harmed Sallonia. They who harm Sallonia harm the world."

I closed my eyes wishing I could blot out this reality. "She was good to me," I whimpered.

Nana peered at me, her eyes strangely calm. "I know, baby. But I had to do it. Sallonia needed an heir." Her fingers caressed my cheek. "They promised no harm would come to you. They broke their promise. And when you were taken away…" she cradled my head in her arms and wept, dry racking sobs convulsing her body.

Now it was I who held the thin shivering body, I who murmured gentle nothings into the old ear. I sensed Spooky trying to reach me and closed my mind. Nothing else mattered except this woman who had been the only mother I knew, this murderess who killed my truest friend.

I waited till the sobs and the shivering stopped. "How did you get a sand-kutzi thorn, Nana? They grow only in deserts. And they have to be treated."

Her face hardened. "Doktoras Poll. He gave it to

me." She touched my face, staring into my eyes. "You understand, my baby, don't you? I'd kill myself rather than hurt you. I would have never done it, had I known what they were planning to do to you. When they took you away, I went mad. I tried to tell people that it wasn't you, but they locked me up." She started humming a lullaby I remembered from a long time ago.

A suspicion was beginning to form in my mind. "Did Papa come to see you, Nana?"

Nana nodded, her eyes shining again. "My boy, yes he did. He knelt by me, like you are doing. I held him, like I'm holding you. He asked me what happened, and I told him."

"I'm glad, Nana."

Nana smiled. "That's what he said. I thought he'd take me away. He didn't. He said he had things to do first." Her eyes darkened. "I wanted to kill myself. But I had to see you. I had to explain things to you. I knew you'd come. Then he gave it to me."

"Gave what to you, Nana?"

Nana put her hand inside her bodice and brought out a small cloth pouch. "For you, my baby. He said, 'Give it to no one but Allii, Nana.' So I had to live."

I opened the pouch and nearly dropped it.

The Ring of Sallonia twinkled at me. It felt as heavy as a mountain.

Nana stroked my face. "He said to tell you he loved you. 'I'm sorry I never told her that, Nana,' he said."

I had been waiting for those words all my remembered life. Now that I had them, they were like ashes in the wind, blown away by time and events to a shore beyond mind and memory. Perhaps someday, I'd find a way to reach that shore. Not now.

I put the ring back into the pouch and slipped it into an inner pocket.

Nana beamed. "You'll become an empress, and I'll look after your babies. Now we'll go and find my boy. And we'll be happy, you, him, me. He had been unhappy ever since he met that witch."

I rubbed my eyes with the back of my hand, rubbing them until they smarted and my vision blurred. My heart felt as if it was being pressed between two grindstones. "Nana, she was my mother."

Nana went on as if she didn't hear me, as if she was talking to herself. "When he met her, my boy lost his head. He wouldn't listen to anyone. Not even me. I begged him to give her up. I went down on my knees. I wept. But he was lost, tangled in her evil magic. I've hated Bernalin ever since then. He did it all. They say she was his woman before. She…and then you came, my baby." She crooned a lullaby, smiling to herself. "He was so happy, my boy. He brought you to me, looking like he'd won the world. 'She's yours too, Nana,' he said. 'Look after her the way you did me.' Oh we were happy then, my boy, my baby and me. But she wanted to take you away, away from my boy and me."

"How did she die, Nana?"

"Your father sent me a message. He was going to come and get you and me. She found out, with her witch-magic. She didn't want him to have you. Your very first word was *Papa*. You'd stop crying and smile whenever he picked you up. You and he had a bond always. The witch hated it, wanted you for her own. She took you away to that crazy place where her mother lives. Her witch-mother wouldn't let her in. She tried and tried. I think she lost her head then. She decided to flee Sallonia with you. I had to stop her. Your place was with your father. I didn't want the witch to take my baby away." Nana stopped and stared. When she spoke next, it was as if she were reading from a prepared script. "She was driving too fast. Just before the carriage went over the edge, I jumped out with you."

I opened my mouth and closed it. Nana was telling the truth, the truth as she saw it.

Nana's eyes were like those of an anxious lamb. "You understand, don't you, baby?"

I kissed her cheek. "I will always love you."

Nana started to cry. I pulled her into my arms.

The door opened. I turned around, trying to summon a smile at Tygyrin.

The doorway was filled with a tall bulky figure. It was not Tygyrin. It was his father, Prince Rokkrin, soon to be King Rokkrin.

Rokkrin stepped into the room, brown eyes glittering, florid cheeks flushed, fleshy lips open in a smile. He patted his still silken locks and closed the door.

I smiled, surprised at my own calmness. "Good day, Uncle."

"How are you, my little niece?" Rokkrin's voice sounded like bubbling sugar.

I smiled again. "I'm well, Uncle. I hope you are too."

"So the little murderess is well."

"I'm no murderess, Uncle. You know that. The more pertinent question is, are you a murderer?"

"Oh I didn't murder your barren stepmother."

"I know that. But did you murder my father?"

"Your father, my dear niece, was murdered by the Halfling killers who are planning to launch a rebellion in your name and on your behalf."

"You know that's not true."

"What I know is as immaterial as what you know. What matters is what the world chooses to believe." He flashed that sugary smile at me again. "Princess Albalia killed Queen Bellizza and escaped justice by joining Halfling terrorists. Halfling terrorists murdered King Walterin, so that Albalia could be proclaimed queen. A convincing tale, don't you think?"

"As convincing as the one about King Walterin leaving a will, disinheriting Prince Bernalin, and nominating Prince Rokkrin as king?"

Rokkrin laughed. "Good. I never realized you had so much spirit in you. I hope you know I bear you no ill will. This woman will be spared, because, unlike you, she's one of us. You seem rather anxious about her, so I give you my word. She will live out her life, here. No one will believe her blabbering anyway." His face suddenly turned brick red, his eyes flashed. His voice became a snarl. "To think that my own son was conniving with you. I thought he had some sense unlike his brothers. But he is even stupider than them… Bewitched. Bewitched."

So Tygyrin didn't betray me. Of course he wouldn't. He loved me.

Then who did? Sherby? No, not Sherby? Who then?

I kissed Nana and stood up, facing Rokkrin. He was a tall man, and my head came only up to his shoulder. "I met Kolla."

He stared, eyes bulging, lips drawn revealing yellowed teeth.

"He and his Muffic wife are doing well. Had he known I was going to have the honor of meeting you, he would have sent his regards. His respectful regards."

Rokkrin's eyes flashed brown ice. "Kollarin is dead."

"You know he's not. Just as you know I didn't kill Bellizza. Why lie to me? I'm not going to get out of this room alive, am I?"

"For me, he died the day he chose the witch-woman over his family. Like your father. Like…" He clamped his mouth shut.

I smiled, feeling lightheaded, almost happy. "Like my father. Like Tygyrin. Think of that, Uncle, someday you'll have Halfling grandchildren, maybe even a granddaughter like me."

Rokkrin bared his teeth. "There won't be any Muffic spawns to dishonor my line. I'll take care of that. I know when not to stay my hand. I'm not a weakling like your father, or my sons. Your father should have never been allowed to become king. The crown should go to the purest, the one most dedicated to the people, to the race."

"Like you."

"You think I don't know you are mocking me. I don't expect you to understand the importance of blood. You are a Halfling."

"I'm a living breathing creature. Isn't that important?"

"You should have stayed away. I had no hand in killing your stepmother or in implicating you. Killing your father wasn't my idea either. I would have wished you well with all sincerity had you got married and gone away. I didn't mind you escaping. I didn't like you, niece, but I was never your enemy. That changed the moment you returned. Now you are a problem, and I intend to solve that problem."

"You intend to solve the Albalia-problem the same way you solved the Walterin-problem. Murder. My father was also from this First Hundreds you seem to value so much, a pure blooded Sallonian. He was your cousin and your king. You didn't hesitate to order his murder."

"I believe he deserved to die, but I didn't order his death. He betrayed his kind and placed the work of our ancestors in jeopardy."

"And he was going to make a pronouncement, declare me innocent."

Rokkrin's glare turned into a frown. "You seem to be very well informed. I suppose this gibbering fool told you. Or maybe your Halfling cronies. Or even my fool of a son. Amberlina said he was besotted with you, and that was why he said no to every marriage proposal we brought. I didn't believe it. Fool." He pulled himself together with a visible effort. "Your father, yes, he was going to make an official announcement, proclaiming your innocence and naming the killers. Very unwise of him. He made the impossible happen. Sherriz was your father's puppet. Then your father decided to betray him. He turned against your father only to save himself." He smiled. "Everything is working for me.

You are just a gnat…"

Rokkrin lunged at me, a gleaming knife in one hand. I was ready for him and ducked easily. He snarled and leapt at me again. I evaded the knife, but his kick caught me and sent me sprawling. I fell on my back, my head hitting the wall with an agonizing thud. I tried to struggle to my feet as he lunged at me. Nana jumped between us, trying to catch his arm. He pushed her away. She fell next to me, crumpling like a paper-doll.

I cried, "Nana."

Rokkrin loomed over me, hissing in triumph, gleaming knife poised to strike.

The door opened, a shadow appeared, something whizzed through the air, and Rokkrin tottered and crashed, the way a massive tree would.

The shadow turned into Lady Nellin. She walked up to the fallen Rokkrin, bent down, and pulled out the little dagger buried in the back of his neck. She wiped it with a handkerchief, and shoved it into a pocket. She wiped her fingers with the same care, and turned to me. "I had to save you. My lady would have wanted it." For a few seconds her eyes stared into mine. "Until I heard him, I thought you killed my lady. When I was informed you were here, I told him, never suspecting—" She stopped biting her lower lip.

I gulped. "Is he—is he?"

"Dead? Yes. My dagger is poisoned. Like his knife."

I gulped again. "Thank you for saving me. Who told you I was here?"

"I have my sources. That is no matter. You'd do better to

figure out how you are going to get out of here alive. His guards came with us. They are waiting by the landing door. They…"

There was a commotion in the distance, muffled voices, low cries, shuffling, thudding.

Lady Nellin paled. She rushed to the door and started bolting it. I bent to secure the bolt at the bottom and heard Spooky's voice in my head. *We are coming in.* I stood up, elbowed Nellin out of the way, and threw open the door.

Spooky, still in his fox form, rushed in squeaking, "Are you hurt?" Sherby was behind him followed by Panda.

I shook my head.

Sherby looked at me, a grim smile on her face. "I know I was told to mind my own business. I didn't. I went and got Panda."

I caught her hand and squeezed it. "Thanks so much Sherby, for saving me, again."

Sherby shrugged.

"Sherby, do you know where Lord Tygyrin is?" I didn't want him coming in now. He'd think that I had a hand in his father's murder. I didn't want that.

It was Nellin who answered. "He left the castle, after escorting you here. Rokkrin sent some men to monitor him, and delay him, for an hour or so. I'll get word across to him that you are safe, once he returns."

"What if he asks how you know?" I objected.

Nellin's lip curled. "I said I'll get word across to him, not go and tell him myself."

Panda had been bent over Rokkrin. Now he straightened, his eyes moving from Nellin to me.

Nellin said, her voice preternaturally calm, "I killed him."

I walked over to Panda. "She saved my life, Panda."

Panda bowed, but his eyes remained hard and calculating. He spoke slowly, as if he were talking to a child. "I've no idea what you're doing here, Highness. But you can't stay here. The safest place for you is Prince Bernalin's castle. You can return once things are settled."

Lady Nellin had been staring at Panda, her brows drawn together. Now she gave a thin smile. "I suppose you are part of this rebellion I hear of."

There was an element of mockery in Panda's bow. "Indeed, my lady."

I cut in. "Panda, I'm not going to Uncle Berni's castle. I need to meet Minister Ekko. Then I will decide what I'm going to do." I wasn't sure if I wanted to be queen. But I certainly didn't want to get a crown on a platter. I wasn't about to let another bunch of people dictate to me how I should live my life.

Both Nellin and Panda said, "You can't stay here, Highness," and stopped, their eyes meeting. I recognized the glance. They were allies for the moment because they had found common ground—little girls shouldn't be allowed to get involved in adult matters.

But I wasn't a little girl. Not anymore.

"If you would write a note to Minister Ekko, Highness, I'll ensure it gets to him." Panda's voice had changed slightly, as if he were a parent addressing a rebellious youngster. "Take Dame Nanarina with you. In Prince Bernalin's castle she'll be safe."

I smiled to myself. They still thought of me as the old

Albalia. "I know I can't stay here. A search will be mounted for Rokkrin soon, so I will leave the castle. But I won't leave Pinckossia. Panda, you need to think of a way to get rid of my uncle's body. Lady Nellin, I'd be grateful if you can direct me to a safe place in Pinckossia." I allowed my voice to harden. "Else, I'll find some place."

Panda shook his head. "We can't allow you to risk yourself, Highness."

Spooky's voice pricked at my head. *Listen to reason, at least now.*

"Panda, I'm not leaving Pinckossia."

Nana had been sitting huddled into a heap. Now she looked up and smiled a smile both beautiful and terrible. "Ask Minister Ekko to summon the Council, my baby. He has the right. I'll tell them what happened."

Nellin turned around and stared at Nana long and hard. There was hatred in that expression, and something strangely like fellowship.

I suppressed a shudder and addressed Nellin, balling my fingers into fists until my nails dug into my palms, willing myself to speak calmly. "Lady Nellin, do you think you can get me out of the castle and into some safe place in Pinckossia? And arrange for Minister Ekko to visit me?"

Lady Nellin's eyes scanned my face for a few seconds. Then she bowed. "I can manage that, Highness." A ghost of a smile played on her thin lips. "Perhaps this maid can go with you."

"The name's Sherby." Sherby's voice was dry. "I'd join you, happily, Highness."

I smiled back at her. "Thank you, Sherby."

Panda cut in. "Highness, I need to know what you intend doing. I can't let you run into danger. I'll take whatever steps necessary to prevent you from doing so."

I met his eyes. His meaning was clear. I'll have to win him over by convincing him. My first test.

"Panda, you need to dispose of Rokkrin's body in such a way it won't be found for a while. Let there be as much confusion as possible. Confusion will help us. When I meet Minister Ekko, I will ask him to summon the Council, as Nana suggested. If Lady Nellin is willing, she and Nana can tell the Council what actually happened to the queen." I paused to let my words sink in, also because I had been talking a little too fast to be a proper princess. "I'm sure you know the importance of creating dissension in the enemy camp."

Spooky's laugh pinched my mind. *You are full of surprises all of a sudden. Reminds me of someone, you do.*

I ignored him, and waited, my eyes never leaving Panda's face.

Panda started back for a while. Then he flashed a wry smile. "It would be unseemly to knock you unconscious, but I have a feeling that would be the only way I can take you to safety."

I smiled back at him, seeing in the wry smile a kind of victory. "Extremely unseemly, Panda."

He bowed. "You have not convinced me entirely, Highness. But I know a wall when I see one. There are abandoned icehouses with enough ice in them. I'll get his body into one. And his guards too."

I shivered. "Are they all dead?"

Panda shrugged. "You don't coddle the enemy in a battle, Highness."

I gobbled my words of protest. Not only because he had a point. Persisting would have confirmed his opinion of me—a little girl who should be crowned, but not heard or heeded.

But Panda had noticed my horror. That had renewed his doubts about my fitness to decide for myself. I could sense it in the way he stood, the way he stared. If I didn't do something to reclaim myself in his eyes, he might knock me senseless and pack me off to Bernii's castle, unseemly or not.

I walked up to him and lowered my voice. "The rebel forces, where are they?"

He hesitated. "They are stationed in several places, Highness."

So he didn't trust me enough to give me the exact locations. Or perhaps he thought I didn't need to know. "Are any of them near the Sallikan mines?"

His brows drew together. But he didn't answer.

"If they are, if it's possible, I'd like the mines to be occupied, and the miners freed."

His eyes narrowed almost to slits. "Our forces are limited. Such a diversion is not practical. Our goal is occupying Pinckossia and the three regional capitals."

I smiled, marshalling my words. "The war might last a long time. Mines are vital for Sallonian economy. It would make sense to disrupt the mines, make them non-functional. That'll be one more thing for Sallonians to worry about. They'll have to expend resources to get the mines operational again, and that wouldn't be easy. You might also be able to gain some new recruits. Sallonian miners fighting alongside Halfling rebels. They'd be angry enough to do it won't they? That will broaden your base and your appeal."

I thought Panda's stare would never end. Eventually, he bowed. "I'll see what is possible, Highness."

I knew I couldn't expect anything more from him, not now. I knelt by Nana. "I have to leave now. But I will come for you. Will you stay safe until then?"

Nana gathered me into her arms. "My baby," she crooned. Then she let go of me and bowed her head, a strangely formal gesture. "I will, my queen."

3
UNTOLD TALES

"We are the clean slate on which we will write our own future."
We, the Halflings – Pamphlet 1

THE ROOM WAS STIFLINGLY SMALL. DISUSE HAD DAUBED dust on the once white walls. Grime carpeted the wooden floor. Lady Nellin had brought us to this boarded-up and crumbling mansion in her carriage. It was her family home. No one had lived here since her father died, other than a caretaker who seemed a hundred and deafer than a fruit-bat.

"This place is worse than any hole I've ever had to skulk in," Spooky squeaked. His ears were down, his tail had lost its jauntiness. "And I do wish you'd stop going round and round like a crazy wheel that insane dragon invented because he had too much time on his hands."

I ceased my aimless prowling, returned to the room's

only chair. "I'm sorry. Would you like to go out and about for a little?"

"Maybe later. How long do you think we'll have to wait here?"

Sitting was impossible. I walked to the window and ran my hand over the wooden shutters. If only I could open them and let in some fresh air. There was no way, short of wielding an axe. I wiped my grimy hand on my tunic. "I wish I knew."

Spooky scratched an ear. "Do you think you can trust this Nellin?"

I sighed. "I can't be certain. But I think so."

"Why? She betrayed you to your murderous uncle."

"That was when she believed I killed Bellizza. She loved Bellizza far more than I did." Or anyone else, I added silently. "Sherriz and Pena knew she hated me. They must have used that to turn her into their dupe." I started ambling round the room in aimless circles, again. "Believe me, Spooky, no one likes to be fooled. I can imagine how Nellin felt when she heard Rokkrin and realized that she had been lied to and made use of. She'd want to see Sherriz and Pena crushed for murdering Bellizza and for turning her into their pawn. To do that she needs me. She'd like to see Nana dead too, if she could. But she won't make a move until she has Sherriz and Pena where she wants them, which is probably hell."

Spooky had been staring at me. Now he said, "I never realized how dangerous living among humans is, even for humans."

I nodded gloomily.

"What are you going to do about this Nana of yours? She is a killer."

I started walking faster and faster, almost as if I were running away. I wished I could, escape this reality where Bellizza and Father were dead and Nana was a murderess.

I had gone halfway round the world to discover the identity of Bellizza's killer, and all the time it had been my Nana. How blind love and trust could make us.

"Well?"

I brushed the sweat off my brow with the back of my hand and glared at Spooky. "What do you think I should do? Hang her as a murderess? That old woman?" I wanted to say the only mother I knew, but didn't. Spooky was bound to point out that every murderess was probably someone's mother.

"If you become queen you'll have to. You can't punish Sherriz and Pena without punishing your precious Nana."

"I'm not going to be queen."

"Huh?"

I stamped my foot, raising a miniature dust storm. "What do you mean 'huh'?"

Spooky's sikilian-fox tail waved in the air like a feathery fan. "Work it out yourself."

I turned away. "I've got better things to do."

"Like walking round and round?"

"I was trying to think of a plan." The words came out rather sulky. I seemed to be turning into a bad-tempered, whiny brat. It was probably the room. I hoped so.

Spooky's expression was disdainful. "And how far have you progressed?"

I resisted the urge to toss my non-existent hair. "Just a bit."

Spooky cocked his head, a look of weary patience on his face.

The words came out in a rush. "Do you remember Bänge?"

"I thought we were to discuss plans not engage in reminiscences."

"They are connected. Just think of how many disaffected Sallonians there must be in the army, boys like Bänge's Anonn."

Spooky's sigh was long and weary. "Remember the soldier who hammered Bänge with his gun? That's what Anonn must be like now. That's what armies do, take nice boys and turn them into not-so-nice men. I don't know how they do it. Must be another human thing."

I stared at him in dismay. "But wouldn't the soldiers like to be free of their bondage? Anonn would want to go home, wouldn't he? He'd want to return to Bänge and have a life with her, instead of dying in some stupid war, wouldn't he?"

Spooky inspected a paw. "Perhaps he would. Perhaps they all do. Very deep down. Too deep down for your purpose. So if you are thinking of mutiny, think again. Most of them will follow orders, whatever those orders are. A few might not. They'll be shot."

I inhaled slowly. The airlessness was making me nauseous. The taste of bile was unpleasant in my mouth, as unpleasant as Spooky's words. And he was right. I had been too sanguine in my thinking, too careless in my planning.

Still taking the easy way out, still avoiding unpleasant realities.

Yet I persisted. "You remember what Brunelles said. Wars have a life of their own. A war, any war, will devastate Sallonia. And the idea of my father's people murdering what's left of my mother's people is too horrendous even to contemplate. If the army is subverted…"

"Join the rebellion. They want you. That is your best chance of stopping the war."

I closed my eyes thinking, thinking. "I'm scared of what a rebellion could unleash. Halflings have been treated so terribly for centuries. Do you think they wouldn't want revenge once they have power? They might leave Muffics alone, but Sallonians? Will they make a difference between the guilty and the innocent, between Sherriz and Sherby? Remember what Pattii told us about the mob? Mobs don't ask questions about how you've lived your life. They just kill."

"You can stop them if you become queen."

"A symbol is what I'll be. I won't have any real power. How can I, if all I do is skulk in safety while other people do the killing and the dying? If I don't participate, I'll have no authority. Without authority, I won't be able to stop anything."

"Panda listened to you."

"Panda is just one. He has known me all my life. He is fond of me. The others don't know me. I'm just a name to them."

"So you think mutiny is the solution?"

"Solution?" I shook my head. "I don't know. A mutiny might prevent the war. It can give the rebellion a broader base. Halflings and Sallonian soldiers joining together, boys like Anonn who don't want to be in the army."

Spooky stood up and shook himself. "There's something you need to face up to. Whichever way you go, you won't be able to avoid dead bodies. You might be able to prevent a war. I hope so. You might even be able to prevent mobs going berserk. But whatever choice you make, there'll be deaths."

"I don't want any more deaths on my conscience…"

"Stop whining about your conscience," Spooky snarled. "This is no longer about you. It's about a system that has been around for centuries. Do you think it can be upended nicely?"

I almost snarled back, but stopped. Spooky had a point. According to history books, Sallonia was one and a half millennia old. One thousand five hundred years of hatred and oppression: Sallonians oppressing Muffics; Halflings being rejected by Muffics and oppressed by Sallonians; poor Sallonians being oppressed by rich Sallonians. There'd be too many people with scores to settle and injustices to avenge. There'd also be too many people with privileges to safeguard.

I opened my hands in a gesture of surrender. "Sorry. You're right, on both counts…"

There was a knock on the door. It opened and Sherby came in carrying a plate. "I thought you'd be hungry, Highness…I mean Majesty…" Her eyes twinkled. "What'd I call you?"

"Allii would do. Remember I'm a maid. The food is a great idea. We'll share it."

Sherby's eyes widened. "No, no, it's for you."

The black-crust bread was hard, as if it has been around a bit longer than it was meant to. I broke it into three pieces, and gave one to Spooky who gobbled it up. I held a piece to Sherby while biting into my own. She hesitated, then accepted.

Chewing the bread was too much work. I followed Spooky's example and gobbled it, with the aid of some water. Then I turned to Sherby. "I know your sister was a bonded servant. Were you one as well?"

Sherby choked and started coughing.

Spooky sniffed. "What's wrong with her? If it's that atrocity you just made me eat, it's understandable. But I think it was your question."

I bit back a smile. "I suppose bonded labor was one of the many topics Nana ordered never to be mentioned in my hearing."

Sherby gulped. "How'd you know?"

"I was out in the world for months, Sherby. I learned many things I was kept ignorant of, starting with who my mother was."

Sherby stared. I tried to read her expression and failed. Eventually she gave a brief nod. "We thought it was criminal, the way they told you nothing. 'The poor wee thing's going to go off her rocker when she finds out the fibs,' we'd say in the maids' hall." She stopped, as if wondering she had said too much. "Reckon they meant well…"

I smiled. "You were right. I was as mad as hellfire when I discovered how much I've been lied to. Now I want to know everything."

Sherby hesitated, then shrugged a thin shoulder. Her face wore a tight expression. It was as if she had aged suddenly, no longer a girl, but an old woman who had lived too long, seen too much. "Why not? If you're going to be queen here, you'd better know the kind of place this is."

"Yes," I said weakly.

"My parents were farmers. Farming's hard work. See, first there's too much rain, then there's too much sun. Mechanical bulls are too costly for people like us. We have to plough, plant, reap all on our own. I'll never forget what my parents were like after they'd spend a day ploughing… With all that work, harvests are small, almost gone with debts and taxes."

"Tell me about taxes."

Sherby's tone was blank, as if she were reciting from a prepared text. "One tenth to One God, one tenth to king, one tenth if you've no son to give to the army. Daughter-tax is what we call it. My parents had no sons, so that's three tenths gone from every harvest. What's left is not enough to eat. Then you borrow. Lenders can ask their money back anytime. If you can't pay, you lose your land, and your freedom. My parents were taken to the mines. See, no Sallonian would go willingly, and they don't want Muffics." Her voice wavered, but her eyes were brown pebbles. "The judge sent my sister and me to be sold. I was six, Genii five."

I swallowed. "Please pardon me, Sherby, if what I say sounds stupid to you. I have read that when Sallonian parents go away to work in mines, the children are fostered by other Sallonians. I suppose that was a lie?"

There was pity in the glance Sherby cast at me, and contempt. "Oh, they call it fostering. But it's really selling. The buyer owns us. I was lucky. Minister Ekko bought me and gave me to Dame Nanarina to train for a maid." For a second, the tight little voice softened. "He's a good man. He'd do it often. Dame Nanarina and Queen helped."

Shame covered me like a shroud. I lived through it all, and knew nothing; knew nothing because I preferred blindness to seeing.

"My sister wasn't so lucky. Minister Ekko'd have bought her too, but she went first. Bought by a woman in a silver robe. We didn't want to be separated. She clung to me. They had to drag her away. I never forgot the way she screamed my name…"

I wanted to say something comforting. But all I could do was gulp.

"So I became a servant and she became a bonded servant." Sherby's eyes, now burning like fire, met mine. "When you're a bonded servant, you aren't human. Your owners can do anything to you. You can be whipped and burnt and starved and branded, and none of it's torture. They can force themselves on you, and you're blamed. You can't complain to king's courts because you've no right to complain. You can buy yourself out, but you're not paid, so where's the money?" She paused, and whispered, "That was my sister's life."

I had read the Book of Laws a long time ago. The term bonded servants didn't feature in it. Instead, there was a chapter on Guardianship, about how Sallonians who had the means should welcome into their homes those who were in need. The rich guarding the poor and guiding them to prosperity; the poor working with obedience and industry toward their own salvation. I had thought it was a beautiful arrangement.

I had to swallow several times before I could get the words out. "Is it the Guardianship law?"

"That's what they are called. God-made and man-made. Nice words covering a hell." Sherby's voice was a hiss. She was a fire-mountain on the verge of exploding. "All the drivel about Sallonians being one family, the children of One God. Muffics say they've it bad. I know Halflings are planning rebellion. They should try our lot. They should live my sister's life." Her eyes met mine and held them. "What else do you want to know, Allii?" She said my name as if she were uttering a profanity.

My head felt as if it were full of hot coal. I wanted to say something, but didn't know what to say.

No wonder poor little Genii looked as if she were scared of her own shadow.

I didn't want to know anymore. But I knew I had to. I won't be able to look Sherby in the eye ever again if I took the coward's way out and changed the topic; worse, I won't be able to look myself in a mirror, or sleep at night.

"How did you find your sister?" I asked.

Sherby's voice softened again. "I asked Minister Ekko's help. I didn't do it for a long time. I'd ended up in a good place, a safe place. I thought she did too. At six, it's easy to believe in miracles. Later, I wondered. But I didn't know what to do. Also I was scared of doing anything much. Interfering means breaking the law. I guess I didn't want trouble, for myself. See, I was a coward, like you." Her smile was mirthless. "I'll blame myself till the day I die for the time I wasted. But one day, about two years ago, I saw the body of this bonded servant. The same age as my sister, and she'd killed herself. I'd gone out on an errand and saw them crowd… So I found my courage and talked to Minister Ekko. He found where she was and offered to buy her. Her master was a general in the army. He didn't want to sell. Then Lord Tygyrin got involved. I think Minister Ekko must've asked him. He got her out. I don't know how."

"I wish I knew…" The words burst out before I could stop them. I suddenly wanted to join the rebellion, to tear down this horrible edifice, to free the victims, punish the guilty. Death would be too good for them, too good…

"I know you feel bad," Sherby said, in that tight little voice that gave weight to even the simplest word. "You lived with your plants, didn't know what men were like." She caught my eyes again. "Now that you know, you can do something about it. That's why I offered to help you and told no one about this rebellion."

I bowed my head, beyond words.

Spooky squeaked, "We have visitors."

The door opened after a short sharp knock. Lady Nellin came in followed by Minister Ekko. Sherby bowed and went out, closing the door after her. She was back to looking a timid and submissive girl, so unlike the angry, bitter, and passionate young woman of a few seconds ago.

It was like watching a flame snuffing itself out.

Minister Ekko seemed to have aged by a decade since I last saw him. His face was a landscape of lines; his shoulders were hunched; the hand clutching the walking stick trembled. I caught him in an embrace, shocked at how fragile he felt. He gazed into my face, tears running down his cheeks.

"Oh, my dear, dear Highness, the agonies I've been going through, until Lord Kollarin sent that message…"

I let him ramble a little. He needed that. Then I guided him to the room's only chair and made him sit.

He looked around, and tried to stand up. "No, no, you should be sitting here…"

I interrupted him. "No, please. I'm too restless to sit."

Lady Nellin was standing with her back to the door, her face a contrived blank. I put on my best Princess Albalia manner. "Lady Nellin, what is happening in the castle?"

"They have mounted a search for Rokkrin. Lord Tygyrin is handling it. They are being cautious." Nellin's thin lips curled. "They think he might be otherwise occupied, too busy to notice the passing of time. His wife also thinks so. She is angry enough to murder someone." She paused, deliberately, as if to draw my attention to her next remarks. "Chief Priest Pena visited Dame Nanarina and was with her for a long time."

Would Nana have told him anything? She was very pious, and this was the Chief Priest after all. I pushed my misgivings aside and turned to Minister Ekko. "Did Sherriz agree to summon the Governing Council?"

Ekko cast a quick glance at Lady Nellin. I felt relieved that the old shrewdness was back in his eyes. "Chief Minister Sherriz has summoned a meeting of the Council for this evening. If Lady Nellin and Dame Nanarina are willing to testify, that would be the best time to do so."

Nellin said, "I'm willing."

I thought for a moment. "Will you be able to persuade the Council to give them a hearing? Won't Sherriz and Pena suspect something's amiss?"

"The Chief Minister and the Chief Priest might not be happy with my request, but I'm hoping they won't resort to an outright objection. I'll say that I have some important evidence about the planned rebellion to present to the Council." He hesitated. "Since Lord Tygyrin is already aware of your presence in Pinckossia, I might seek his assistance."

I frowned. "I know Tygyrin helped me. But that was before his father was killed. Once he realizes we had a hand in it…"

Nellin cut in. "There was precious little affection between Rokkrin and his sons, Highness. And Rokkrin's death brings his eldest son one step closer to the throne." She flashed me a mirthless smile. "He wouldn't mind that."

I wasn't so sure, but decided not to persist. Instead I voiced my remaining doubt. "Nana is still in the tower. Will you be able to get her to the Council meeting, Minister Ekko?"

Ekko smiled. "The castle is in an uproar. The confusion is bound to grow as time passes and Prince Rokkrin makes no appearance. That will give me the opportunity to get her out of the tower and into an antechamber. We have to act with utmost caution as well as speed. The troops are gathered in the Field of Eternal Glory for tomorrow's coronation. The plan is to march against Muffics as soon as the ceremonies are over." He turned to me. "Highness, if all goes well at the Council, I'll come for you. If you don't hear from us by midnight, leave the city." He put his hand into an inner pocket and brought out a piece of paper. "This has the address of a trustworthy friend. He will get you to Prince Bernalin's." He turned to Lady Nellin. "We should get back to the castle before our absence is noticed."

When Minister Ekko rose to take his leave, I put my arms around him and kissed his cheek. "Thank you for everything. I don't know how I'll ever be able to repay you for your kindness and loyalty."

His smile was tremulous. "Take good care of yourself. Sallonia needs you."

The door closed after them. Spooky flapped an ear. "What do we do now?"

"I want to talk to Sherby some more." I opened the door, but the corridor was empty. "She must have gone down with them."

"What do you want to talk to her about?"

"About the way things are. There's so much discontent in this place, Spooky. It's rotten to the core. Like a tree that looks indestructible from ground up, but with roots eaten by wormites. You think the tree is healthy and strong because you don't see the wormites at work. It all happens beneath the ground. Then with a halfway strong gale, the tree comes crashing down."

"Quite a picturesque analogy. But too simplistic. This is a rotten system, but too many people benefit from it. They'll fight back."

"I know." I pulled a strand of my hair until my scalp

started aching. "It's funny. I even understand the logic of some of these horrible practices. Sallikan is what brings wealth and power to Sallonia. Forcing people into debt is an effective way of finding miners. Logical, but such practices also create weaknesses and dissensions we can exploit to…"

The door banged open. Sherby rushed in, panting. "There were two men on the lane earlier. Doing nothing. Just standing. Didn't seem to belong. Now there's only one."

My stomach started to knot. "Spies?"

Sherby nodded. "They mayn't know about you. But they'll think something's going on here. We've got to get out."

4

EXCURSIONS AND DISCOVERIES

"Birth is not a crime. We did not choose this life."
We, the Halflings – Pamphlet 1

"Don't flee heedlessly," Spooky squeaked. "You might be running into danger instead of away from it. Ask her if there's another exit."

I did.

Sherby nodded. "There's a back gate. Leads to a lane."

Spooky flicked his tail. "Sounds promising. I'll take a look. Where are you going to go once you leave here?"

I shook my head, biting my lower lip.

"Better think of a place. Now open the door."

I did, and he scurried out, the tiny feet moving with surprising speed. I closed the door and turned to Sherby. "He'll let me know if the back entrance is safe. How did you know about it?"

"I snooped a bit. Thought it might come useful."

"Sherby, you're amazing!"

Sherby shrugged. "Where'd we go when we get out?"

"I was wondering, will we be able to find refuge in a temple?"

Sherby smiled grimly. "Huh! You'd better not believe the nonsense in the Holy Book. Succor for strangers!" She almost spat out the words. "Only if you're rich enough to pay the priest." She raised her eyes as if she were addressing her next remarks to the very heavens. "Even gods have their favorites."

"Don't you believe in One God, Sherby?"

"What good did it do me or my parents or my sister, believing in him? Oh, I prayed, till my knees were bloody. Guess he was busy with other things. So I told myself, let him be. He ignores me, and I ignore him. He'd no time for me, and I've no time for him. It's better that way for both of us. I do the rituals or that Pena'll have me flogged. Think of a place to go to, Highness—Majesty—whatever."

"Allii," I said mechanically, taking out the slip of paper Ekko had given me. "No 11, Gerbie Avenue. Minister Ekko said it was a safe place. We'll get there and send him a message."

Sherby frowned as if mulling over the merits of this idea. Then she nodded. "Makes sense. I don't know Pinckossia well. Still we can ask the way. I'll do the talking." She looked over me, a hard measuring expression in her brown eyes. "No one'd recognize you, other than who knows you well. We won't meet such like unless we get caught."

I tried to smile. "In which case it won't matter much." I swallowed. "Sherby, you don't have to come with me. It would make more sense for you to get back to the castle, and tell Minister Ekko what happened."

"I'll go with you."

"I don't want to lead you into danger."

"Danger's nothing new for the likes of me, High-Allii. Nothing'd be more dangerous than another war. I don't care about Muffics or Halflings. But a war'd make things worse for folks like us. A war's a grand excuse for any bad thing." She met my eyes. "I'm not risking my life for you. I like you, always did, but not enough to die for you. I'm risking my life for those like me and my sister."

I had never felt smaller. "I understand, Sherby. I'm glad you are coming with me. Grateful too." I stopped as something occurred to me. "We are both dressed as castle maids. Would that be a problem?"

There was surprise, and a sliver of respect in the glance Sherby shot me. "You'd be right. Attract unnecessary attention, it will."

"I wonder if we can find something else to wear here."

Sherby said, "I doubt not," and ran out of the room.

I looked about the room. There were no telltale signs of our occupation, except for the empty plate and the pitcher. I remembered seeing a cupboard in the corridor and hoped it was open. It was, and filled with odds and ends. I drank the remaining water and shoved the pitcher and the plate into that metallic and ceramic confusion.

Fortunately the floors were so grimy, they showed no footmarks.

Spooky's voice was sharp inside my head. *This gate is safe, so far. Better hurry.*

Sherby went to get some clothes.

I could sense Spooky's annoyance. *What do you mean clothes? You aren't going to a party.*

We are in castle uniforms. It'll attract attention. Sherby went to—

The door swung open, and Sherby rushed in hugging a bundle of clothing. I flashed, *She is here. Be with you soon,* and turned my attention to the haul. "Only mantelots? But…"

"Nothing else. They'll cover the blouses. The rest doesn't matter." A sudden grin flashed across Sherby's face. "They smell something. Like they'd been buried."

I donned a grey cloak that came down to my knee. "Come, let's go."

"Where's that creature? I thought he'd tell us if it's safe."

"He just did. He can reach into my mind. I'm a Halfling, remember."

Sherby went slightly pale round the mouth. Then she smiled. "You're changed, and for the better. Come then."

We hurried through dusty corridors, down an even more rickety staircase than the one we had used on the way up, and finally through a narrow door into a substantial garden that might have been an orchard once but was a miniature wood now. I forced myself to turn my eyes away from an aengal tree, its silver white branches knotted and bent with age, and focus on the path, overgrown, but still visible. It led to a wooden gate. Spooky waited on the other side, back in his dog form.

The road is deserted. Hurry.

The gate was padlocked. I checked for a scalable tree and spotted one a little way away. A mature palukam, with broad boughs, and plenty of leaves for cover, though bare of fruit this time of the year. I walked up to it, saying "Come," over my shoulder. The tree was not hard to climb, still I was careful not to make any mistakes. I wanted to impress Sherby.

Soon we were on the other side of the wall. Sherby made no comment, but I was gratified to see a gleam of respect in the brown eyes.

Spooky was trotting up the road, his nose in the air. I hurried after him, motioning Sherby to follow.

She reached my side and looked around. "Where's that fox of yours? I hope the dog didn't eat it."

"That's Spooky. He is a daemon-dog. He can change shapes."

Sherby went pale again, but rallied fast. "Useful, that."

Spooky glanced back. I could sense his impatience in my head. *Come.*

I nudged Sherby. "Let's go."

"You really hear him in your head?"

"Yes."

"Wish I could do that. I had a dog back at home. Then it happened…" her words petered out.

"I thought Sallonians don't like dogs."

"The First Hundreds don't. Most ordinary folks do. They're useful."

"So that's one thing you have in common with Halflings and Muffics." I wondered whether there were other commonalities. Maybe finding out a few would be a starting point to end this madness.

We reached the top of the lane and turned into a slightly busier one. Sherby had to ask twice to get the directions to Gerbie Avenue.

"Looks like it's at the other end of Pinckossia," she murmured.

"Tell me the directions. I'll communicate them to Spooky. He can walk ahead and warn us of any dangers."

Sherby knitted her eyebrows, but gave the directions. I reached out to Spook and repeated them.

Got it. Now be careful. Don't do anything to attract attention.

I won't.

The narrow, rutted, weed-choked lanes led up to wide, paved streets, the shuttered workshops and tumbling kiosks replaced by shops that seemed to be selling everything under the sun. I had lived almost all my life within seeing distance of Pinckossia, without ever setting foot in it. Here I was, walking the streets, virtually invisible behind my paint and my mantelot.

Sherby whispered, "Don't stare. Keep your head down."

I had been gazing at a glass blower's workshop. I mumbled, "Sorry," and turned my eyes downward.

Tradition was mean to Sallonian girls. When outside home, the proper way to walk was to keep the head bowed and eyes turned groundward.

The urge to look was irresistible, like an itch, because there was so much to see. I ignored it, trying to follow Sherby's example. It was not as bad as walking blindfolded, but close. Several times people snarled at me to look where I was going. The first time I almost stopped to ask how I was supposed to look where I was going if I had to keep my head down.

Spooky's voice inside my head had a warning timbre to it. *Stupid rules. Don't say anything now though.*

I sighed inwardly, and almost walked into a cart piled high with pots. *This place needs to be shaken hard.*

Agreed. There was a laugh in Spooky's voice.

When the third person, an irate woman in a richly worked brocade robe followed by a parasol-wielding maid, scolded me for not looking where I was going, Sherby grunted impatiently, and grabbed my hand.

Since I couldn't look, I kept my ears open. As we waited to cross a road or pressed back to allow a person of consequence to pass, I heard muttered words.

"They say the king has vanished."

"King? Rokkrin's no king."

"Well, there's no one else. And he's one of us."

A low sound between a laugh and a growl—a growly laugh. "And what does that make you? A killer?"

"Shut up. You want to end up in jail?"

"Walterin had no spine."

"Better spineless than vicious."

"Need a strong king to keep us safe."

"There's that."

"Yeah, so who keeps us safe from your strong king?"

Pinckossia, I realized, was a hive of gossip, or a fount of information, depending on how you looked at it. No wonder Nana didn't want me to even ride through the city.

The day had advanced, and the heat was stifling. We were at another four-way junction when I caught a scent. My mouth watered. The tangy-sweet smell of pine-lemon.

I sneaked a look. An old man was pushing a cart piled with fruits. My stomach started rumbling. I pressed Sherby's hand, indicated the fruit seller with a tiny turn of head, my brows raised in a silent question. Sherby wetted her lips with a pink tongue and nodded.

The old man was dressed in clothes frayed and patched up; he had a wispy white beard and a pair of watery eyes. He cut two pine-lemons, and handed them over to us in exchange for a copper coin Sherby fetched out of her trouser pocket.

I bit into the pine-lemon. It tasted heavenly. I wiped the juice off my chin, licked every last drop off the fingers, and smiled at the old man. "This's nice," I said, trying to imitate the way Sherby spoke.

He stared at me, beetle-brows drawn together. Then his lips parted in a toothless smile of singular sweetness.

Sherby nudged me. I bowed, saying, "Good day," and followed her to the crossing.

We waited to cross to the other side, amidst a knot of people. A street guard stood in the middle, on a low platform, directing the stream of mechanical carts and carriages, pedestrians, and horsemen. The streets were clogged, tempers frayed, and horses nervous of the mechanical equipages.

I focused my attention on the muttered conversations around me.

"They hate Bernalin because his mother was one of us."

"I'd rather have the mongrel princess than that Rokkrin."

"They say the—"

The muttering stopped. A sudden hush fell. I could almost smell the unease, the fear. It overrode everything, including the smell of fruits and the odors of humans and other animals.

A troop of mounted soldiers trotted down the street. The road had cleared for them, vehicles moving away from the middle to hug the sides. The soldiers were smart in their blue and silver uniforms, the horses tall and sleek. The officer wore a ceremonial sword and a dagger apart from the standard arrow-gun. His moustache was waxed to a pinpoint.

I had no idea how it happened. Perhaps the fruit-seller's cart hit an uneven patch on the roadside; perhaps he was careless. All I saw was a purple guava, round and luscious, rolling on the road towards the cavalcade.

The officer's mare reared. He managed to bring her under control with some effort. His face had turned red with exertion and anger. His blazing eyes fell on the fruit-seller, standing by his cart, staring with his mouth open, eyes dilated. He pointed with his silver-handled lash. Two of the soldiers rode to the side of the road and dismounted.

A scream rent the air, long and sharp like Bellizza's thread-knitting needles.

People around me started scattering, the way a flock of birds would when they spied a hunting bird. I wanted to run too, but my body had become petrified.

A hand grabbed me. I came out of my stupor and stumbled after Sherby to the shelter of a shop. A crowd had gathered at the entrance, spilling over to the dark interior.

I huddled next to Sherby on the bottommost step, and stared at the horror unfolding, as if in a play.

The soldiers had toppled the handcart. Fruits spilled on to the roadside and rolled down the road, circles and cones of red, yellow and green. The soldiers watched laughing. One of them picked a ripe swallow-cherry, tossed it up, caught it, and took a bite off it. He looked around with a triumphant smile, as if expecting applause.

The fruit seller wailed again, a wordless sound that made me shudder from inside. The second soldier turned around and slapped him on the mouth. The man reeled, slipped on a bunch of yellow grapes and fell, wailing all the time.

The officer said, in clear clipped tones, "Shut that noise up."

The old man was kneeling, hands clasped together, praying to One God for protection. A third soldier rode up and hit him on the head with the butt of his arrow-gun. The fruit seller fell back. The soldier raised his gun again with playful slowness.

Don't.

"Don't."

I ran and clutched at the gun with both hands. The force of the averted blow pushed me off my feet and sent me sprawling. For a second, it was as if I were flying. Then the world went black. When sight returned, it was accompanied by a sharp throbbing pain. I touched my forehead, felt something warm and slightly sticky. Blood.

A low moan brought the rest of the memory back. I crawled to where the old man lay, his head pillowed in a pool of red, his body twitching slightly. The gun had cracked open his skull.

"Get out of the way, woman."

I ignored the command and crouched by the old man feeling for a pulse. It was there, as faint as the flutter of a moth's wing.

The same clear, clipped tones said, "If he's anyone of yours, take him and get out."

Take him away, Allii.

The old man opened his eyes. I read the awareness of death in them. For some incomprehensible reason, it reminded me of Father.

Had Father seen his death coming?

He would have been alone, with no one to hold him or comfort him.

I looked back into the fruit-seller's feverishly bright eyes and touched the brow with a gentle hand. He tried to say something.

Or perhaps it was just the last rattling breath.

I eased him back gently and placed his hands on his still chest. I wanted to stand up, but my legs felt like water.

Suddenly, Sherby was kneeling by me. "He's dead," I muttered, before tears choked me.

Then, a pair of arms was circling me, and I was being pulled into a tight embrace. Sherby stroked my head, murmuring, "There, there." I hid my face on her shoulder, trying to stifle my sobs.

A kind of silence had fallen around us, as if time had stopped. I gulped down the final sob and looked. The mounted soldiers stared at us, their faces blank walls.

The clear clipped voice broke the silence. "Get out

of here." There was something new in it, a strain; it was spider-web thin, probably as fragile, but it was there. The officer didn't look at us, nor did he wait to see his order obeyed. He turned around and trotted off.

The people who had watched the bloody spectacle from the relative safety of shops rushed to us once the soldiers were gone.

Spooky's voice rasped in my head. *Are you in one piece?*

Yes.

Not the most intelligent thing to do, was it?

I supposed it wasn't. But it felt right.

People crowded around, exclaiming and muttering. Women helped us to our feet. Someone pressed a handkerchief to the cut on my forehead. An argument broke out about what to do with the dead fruit seller. Children gathered round the cart, grabbing fruits.

It happened so fast, with no warning. By the time Spooky's, *Horsemen*, reached me it was too late.

Four riders, richly clad, stopping, one of them asking, "What is going on here?"

I took an instinctive step back into the crowd, trying to still the shivers. I knew that voice, oily or insolent, depending on the occasion. Now it was all insolence. A transformation to be expected. After all, Tawnilin, Rokkrin's second son, Tygyrin's younger brother, and my most unfavorite cousin, was within striking distance of the throne.

All movement had stopped. It reminded me of a painting. I looked for Spooky in that still life but couldn't spot him. But his voice resounded in my head. *Get out of sight.*

I took one more step back and bent my head for good

measure. Nothing to be seen from the lofty height of a thoroughbred's back, just a head of ruffled yellow amidst other heads of ruffled yellow.

The troop of soldiers had returned to the scene. The officer rode up to Tawnilin, and saluted. "There was an accident, my lord." He stopped and twitched, as if he was sitting not on a horse but on an anthill. "Pardon, Highness. There was an accident, but now things are under control. Highness." He almost shouted the second Highness.

Someone in the crowd said, "It was murder."

Tawnilin turned his head around, trying to spot the speaker in the crowd. He obviously failed, because he asked, "Who said that?"

No one answered.

"Don't be afraid. Speak up. Tell me. What was the murder?"

A tall elderly man stepped forward. He was pale and a little stooped. His faded brown robe was of high-thread cotton. He reminded me of father's minor officials, the anonymous men who carried out orders, reported back, and generally made the castle, and probably the kingdom, work. Perhaps he was such a person, because he spoke in the clear economical manner of a man used to reducing a page into a sentence.

"A soldier hit the old man with the gun, Highness. That was how he died."

Tawnilin's fleshy lips narrowed into an angry pout. "Let me inform you, my good sir, the glorious soldiery of Sallonia is incapable of murder. When our glorious heroes kill, it is in protection of our glorious land, and her, umm—glorious people."

Silence followed his words. I felt a wave of hysteria rising in me. I repressed an insane urge to tell Tawnilin to find another adjective apart from glorious.

Tawnilin broke the silence. He asked the officer, "What is your name?"

I could see the fine sheen of sweat covering the officer's face. But his voice was steady. "Captain Ciillan, Highness."

Tawnilin smiled and pointed his saber at the elderly man. "You heard this man accuse the glorious soldiers of Sallonia of murder. He is clearly a traitor. Arrest him, take him to the Field of Eternal Glory, and give him a public flogging. Tell the commander it's my personal order. We need lessons in obedience. Things have been too lax for too long. Not anymore."

The officer twitched some more. But he gave the order.

A soldier rode up. The elderly man had gone pale, but he stood his ground. Suddenly a young woman broke through the crowd and ran to him. She caught his hand crying, "My father is sick. You can't flog him. He'll die."

The elderly man tried to pull his hand away and to push her back into the safety of the crowd. She clung to him. I felt a stinging in my eyes, a tightening in my heart.

Tawnilin watched the father and daughter, as if they were actors putting up a performance especially for him. Then he turned away with a shrug. "Take him," he ordered, in a dispassionate voice. "If she wants to, take her as well. They will probably have some use for her at the Field of Eternal Glory." He smiled, flashing even, white teeth. "Everyone must make a contribution to the war effort."

It was as if the father gained some superhuman strength

from Tawnilin's words. He managed to wrench his hand free, and push her back into the crowd, shouting, "Go, Jaku." He stepped forward and said, "I'll come."

Jaku cried, "Papa, no," and tried to get to his side. But she was beaten to it by another woman, middle aged and in a blue tunic. She caught Jaku by her arm, as easily as if the girl were a ragdoll. Her eyes moved around and stopped when they reached me. She gave a brief nod, as if she had found what she was looking for, and pushed Jaku in my direction. I caught her to me.

The middle-aged woman smiled. She stepped between the elderly man and the soldiers, arms akimbo, eyes flashing. She had both height and girth and stood the way a tree would.

Tawnilin's voice was cold, but I sensed the first notes of panic in it. "Arrest them all. Jail them. Now."

A soldier dismounted. Before he could take more than a step, the woman pushed him back with a hand as thick as a knotted branch. He collided with his own horse. The horse screamed in fear and fled down the road.

"Arrest her!" Tawnilin screeched like an angry owl.

The soldier tried to hit the woman with his gun. She pulled the weapon away with one hand, and twisted his arm with the other. I heard the sickening sound of crunching bones. The air reverberated with the soldier's screams. The woman looked over her shoulder saying, "Get out, all of you." Her voice was low, but somehow it resonated.

People started fleeing. Sherby and I tried to join them, pulling Jaku along. She resisted with a strength that surprised me, shouting, "Papa, Papa." Sherby pushed me aside, pulled

Jaku around, and slapped her face. Jaku blinked, her eyes vacant, and didn't resist when Sherby dragged her away.

I looked back for a second. The mounted soldiers had plowed into the battle, thrashing with their muskets, and lashing with their whips. The woman and several other people were trying to defend themselves and fight back at the same time.

I didn't realize I'd joined the melee until I kicked a soldier in the back, enabling his opponent to fell him with a blow. Then I was holding a gun, hitting another soldier with it. Excitement possessed me, a strange bloodlust. My body was in command, as if it belonged to someone else. My heart sang every time my wild blows reached their target.

Three shots rang out. A tumult followed, people screaming, horses neighing. A voice rose above it. It was Tawnilin's. "Silence. Captain, get your men to stop. These are our glorious people. They have been misled."

The melee ebbed. The soldiers moved back, and those who had battled with them moved away. I dropped the gun and started to follow them when a warm trickle on my cheek distracted me. My wound must have reopened in the melee. The handkerchief was gone. I wiped the blood with the sleeve of my mantelot.

I heard the sound of silence before I heard the sound of hooves. I looked up, and my eyes met the clear brown ones of Tawnilin.

Running away won't work. The soldiers flanked Tawnilin.

Tawnilin brought his horse forward, until he was within

touching distance of me. He bent over the saddle and smiled. "Well, well, well, so the Witch's spawn has returned disguised as a Sallonian."

5

FACE TO FACE

"Let them keep the past and the present.
We claim the future."
We, the Halflings – Pamphlet 1

I STOOD UP SLOWLY AND FACED TAWNILIN. A SPACE HAD been cleared around us. We were alone in it, two wrestlers in a pit.

I summoned a smile. "How are you Cousin Tawni?"

He didn't answer. His eyes, hard and bright, never left me. Emotions played across his face the way lightning does, each flash so fast, it wasn't possible to see them properly let alone know them.

Unfathomable wasn't an adjective that could have been used in relation to the Tawni I knew—or thought I did. This Tawnilin was different, unfamiliar, worrying.

The crowd bothered me even more. I sensed wariness

and waiting, like a troupe of actors ready to play their part but uncertain as to what it was.

The emotional dance on Tawnilin's face ended with a smile of triumph. He straightened on the saddle and faced the crowd. Then he bowed, a strange, and oddly convincing gesture of humility, like an errant acolyte before a master. His voice was neither arrogant nor oily. It was solemn. "Glorious people of Sallonia, forgive me."

Whatever I expected, whatever the crowd expected, it wasn't this. My jaw dropped. Behind me, there were wavelets of gasps.

Tawnilin bowed again. "Forgive me, dear brothers and sisters, for mistrusting your faith in your god, and your loyalty to your king. I should have known that mischief-makers were at work when I came upon the disturbance."

A sickening feeling settled in the pit of my stomach. He was planning to turn the crowd into a mob and make them tear me apart, like another mob in another place did to Pattii's brother. I focused on my breathing, willing myself to be calm, reminding myself that two could play at that game.

I'd wait for the right moment to enter the fray. Now would be premature. Now they wanted to hear him.

Tawnilin raised his eyes to the empty sky. "One God is merciful. He caused the real traitor to be exposed. Glorious people of Sallonia, look well at this Halfling disguised as a pure Sallonian. She is Albalia, the bastard princess. You've hardly ever seen her. My late uncle kept her hidden. She was a living reminder of his greatest shame, of that brief inglorious hour when he succumbed to his baser instincts, and betrayed his god and his people."

Bastard, I almost cried out. I'm not a bastard.

Then another piece of the puzzle that was my life fell into place. My parents couldn't have married even if they wanted to. No one would have married them.

Bastard—the word felt like a slap on my face. But what hurt me more was Tawnilin's depiction of my parents' forbidden love as a fleeting outburst of lust.

I dug my nails into my palms, as questions swirled inside my mind. Why did Father bring me to Sallonia to become the locus of so much scorn and hate? Why didn't he abandon me the way he did Mother?

Focus. Spooky's voice thundered inside my head. *Focus, you stupid idiot. Do you want to be torn to shreds?*

I shoved the new revelation aside with an effort. I'll deal with it later, if there were a later.

Tawnilin was staring at me, a mocking smile on his lips, almost as if he knew how much the discovery of my bastard-status hurt me. That smile needled me and spurred me to bring all my attention on the here and now. I even managed an answering smile. "Do go ahead with your tale, cousin."

A few titters greeted my words. Tawnilin's smile vanished, and his lips tightened for a second, making him look like a younger, less generously proportioned version of his father.

I waited for him to lose his temper and start screaming. He didn't. He turned away from me and faced the crowd.

"A Halfling disguised as a Sallonian is crime enough. But that I would have overlooked. Murder is something else." He paused, his expression turning sad and stern.

"She killed the good queen Bellizza and escaped justice by joining Halfling terrorists. Now she has returned in disguise to aid Muffics to invade this sacred land, to desecrate its holy places, to butcher its glorious people."

The mood of the crowd reminded me of shifting sand; it was changing fast, from wary and expectant to shocked, frightened, and angry. I had always regarded Tawnilin as a lightweight, someone who cared little for anything other than his appearance. Here he was, conducting himself like a trained provocateur.

Tawnilin's eyes gleamed with triumph. His fleshy lips parted in a smile. He pointed a hand at me, theatrical and effective. "This Albalia disguised herself, using magic, to pollute the minds of the glorious people of Sallonia, to make them rebel against their natural protectors." The smile vanished. His eyelids dropped and a look of deep piety fell on his face. "One God is watching over us. He caused me to come here, so that I may recognize her and expose her evil plans. Look at her, brothers and sisters. See how the accursed coppery skin is visible where she had wiped her face."

The mood of the crowd was like a pot nearing the boiling point. I had to speak up now. One more speech from Tawnilin, and it would be too late, forever.

I turned around. Exposing my back to Tawnilin was not a good idea, but there was no choice.

"Lord Tawnilin told you a few truths and many lies," I said, trying to get my voice right, loud enough to be heard, but not too loud, lest they thought me hysterical. "I am Albalia, the daughter of late King Walterin and his Muffic mate, Filliana. I'm a bastard, but I prefer the term love-child, because I was the result of a love so great that my parents were willing to risk everything for its sake."

I paused for a reaction. There was none. The sense of waiting was back though.

"Lord Tawnilin is correct about another thing," I said. "I ran away. I was accused of killing the queen. He was wrong though when he called me a murderess. I didn't kill my queen," I paused, and added in ringing tones, "or my king."

"Your father, my dear cousin, was killed by Halfling terrorists." Tawnilin's voice had lost none of its suavity.

I didn't turn around. "My father was killed by those who want his throne."

A voice broke the silence. "Witch's spawn."

Tawnilin chuckled. My skin crawled, the way it did once when we were both children and he put a centipede down my back.

"I loved Queen Bellizza," I said, trying hard to keep my voice steady. Tears wouldn't help me. Had Tawnilin managed some, the crowd would have thought him sincere. If I cry, they would dismiss me as deceptive or infantile. "I didn't kill her. Lord Tawnilin had no hand in her death. Neither did his father, Prince Rokkrin. Her death was the work of others, Chief Minister Sherriz and Chief Priest Pena."

Spooky's voice was searing inside my head. *And your precious Nana. Say it, you fool, tell the whole story, if you want to be believed.*

She was their pawn.

Huh.

I blanked out Spooky and focused on the crowd. "Queen Bellizza was murdered because she failed to give birth to an heir," I said. "And the blame was put on me. When my father discovered the truth, he decided to proclaim my innocence and reveal the true killers. When Chief Minister Sherriz and Chief Priest Pena heard of my father's plan, they formed a pact with Prince Rokkrin. They killed my father and produced a fake will nominating Rokkrin as heir."

"You're lying!" Tawnilin's voice had lost some of its assurance, probably because he could sense what I did—the crowd and even the soldiers were listening with real interest.

I ignored him. "When I escaped, I didn't join any rebellion. I went to see Queen Bellizza's sister. She is the head of a colony of stargazers. I met Lord Kollarin on the way." I allowed my glance to roam, meeting an eye here, an eye there, seeing interest and fascination. "You have been told that Lord Kollarin died. Some of you may have even seen his tomb. He is not dead. Like my father, he fell in love with a Muffic woman. He was banished. His parents claimed he was dead."

Someone in the crowd sniggered, "Look at the little lordling's face." I risked a quick glance. Tawnilin's face had turned a brick red. He obviously had no idea about the actual fate of his brother.

I felt that stab of pity. It must be hard being the son of those parents.

"You lie…" Tawnilin shouted. Then his voice turned quieter. He eyed the crowd, addressing them. "Don't get lost in her stories, dear glorious people of Sallonia. Forget not that she is the pawn of Halflings and those Muffic devils. They sent her here to turn you against your One God mandated rulers. Even as we bandy words here, Muffics are savaging our borders, and Halfling hordes are rising against us. They…"

"The princess is right." The voice, high and harsh, stopped Tawnilin short. His eyes bulged and his mouth closed into a tight line.

Sherby stepped out of the crowd, ignoring my horrified, "No."

"The princess is right," she repeated, her voice shaking a little. Whether it was from anger or fear I had no idea, but the hand that took mine in a tight clasp was cool and dry. "The queen and the princess loved each other. Like mother and daughter they were. They—"

"Shut up, slut," Tawnilin spat out the words. "You are a servant." He turned to the captain. "Take her away and lock her up."

Sherby inclined her head in a little mock bow. "I sure am sorry, your lordship. But I'm not a Halfling, like the princess. I'm a Sallonian and glorious as you call us."

There was a wave of low muttering and some titters. A man's voice cried out, "Ay, let the girl speak."

Tawnilin had managed to regain control over his anger. He shrugged an elegant shoulder. "Speak then."

Sherby nodded. "I served Queen Bellizza for fifteen years. A good kind lady she was. My parents were farmers. They lost their land. They were sent to Sallikan mines. My sister and I were sold. My sister went to a master as nasty as any Muffic we hear tell of. He…"

"You can tell your life story some other time, girl." Tawnilin's voice was suave, even a little mocking. He met Sherby's angry eyes and chuckled. "The princess is a good actress, I grant you that. She took you in, didn't she?"

Sherby's eyes glittered. "If anyone's trying to take anyone in, it'd be you." She turned to the crowd. "Think about it. He was ready to murder every one of us, till he recognized the princess. Now he wants you to kill her. Brothers and sisters, he says. But his kind treats us worse than any Muffic. My sister was…"

Tawnilin's arm flashed. The whip caught Sherby on the side of her head. She might have fallen had I not caught her. I wrapped my arms around her, screaming at Tawnilin, "How dare you, you miserable coward!"

He didn't bother to respond to me. Instead he turned his full attention on the crowd. "I'm sorry, brothers and sisters, for employing such an unhandsome method to silence this poor duped creature. But the situation is dire, as I was revealing to you when this deluded pawn interrupted me. Let me repeat. Muffics are invading our borders, and Halflings are menacing our towns. Even Pinckossia is in danger. My father and my brother think the extent of our plight should be kept secret lest you panic. I disagree. I think they should have confidence in you. After all, we are the children of the same god."

Sherby pulled herself away from my arms, her eyes on Tawnilin. "He's good," she muttered to me.

I had to agree. Had I heard his speech before I knew about my Halfling status, I would have been scared out of my wits, seeing a murderous Halfling or an evil Muffic in every shadow. I would have hated Halflings and Muffics, without knowing a thing about them.

Tawnilin was picking out individuals in the crowd, pointing to them, addressing them. "You, my brother, will be murdered. That baby you are holding with such love, sister, they will…"

"You know that is not so, my lord."

The voice was not loud, but it stopped Tawnilin.

Jaku's father stepped into the ring and stood facing Tawnilin. His robe was torn and muddied, his face bruised. Despite his battered appearance, there was a quiet dignity about him. Jaku had her arm through his, a determined expression on her fawn-brown face.

The man bowed, first to me then to Tawnilin. "My name is Hikkary. I worked for Minister Sherriz as a clerk for forty years and retired just a fortnight ago. Ask His Excellency, my lord, and he will tell you that I discharged my duties with competence and diligence. I'm lacking neither in obedience to my god nor in loyalty to my king. What I say, I say with knowledge because for the last ten years, my remit included searching for possible Muffic threats. I've also studied the work of my predecessors going back centuries. I tell you, my lord, there's no Muffic threat. What you say about Halflings might be true. Indeed we have been hearing similar rumors for a while. But Muffics are not attacking us. They abhor war, and indeed bloodshed of any kind. They are opposed to killing even animals." He turned to Tawnilin, a grave look in his eyes. "My lord, whoever told you about a Muffic invasion was telling you a lie."

Tawnilin leaned forward, staring down at the old man. When he spoke, his voice was calm and authoritative. "I remember you well, Master Hikkary. You are the man who accused our glorious soldiers of committing murder. No wonder, if you spent years studying Muffics. What did they seduce you with? Magic? Or was it women?" He turned to the crowd. "Now you see how clever our enemies are. A trusted official turned an enemy-agent, tasked with sowing discord among us. Let us not be too harsh in our judgment. If a king can fall, why not a mere clerk?"

The crowd was silent.

Tawnilin's manner grew more assured. "Think of what you stand to lose. Do you want your homes invaded? Your men murdered? Your women violated? If that is what you want, then listen to this nonsense. If you want to save yourselves, heed me. Do you think Halflings and Muffics will treat you kindly if they have power? Do you think they will be generous and gracious in victory? Do you think they will forgive and forget?"

A sound erupted. It had no words. Or perhaps there were too many words screamed by too many mouths. A mob didn't have to make sense.

Get out now, before they tear you to pieces. Spooky's voice flamed inside my head. *I'll cover for you.*

No. Don't show yourself. You'll only frighten them into greater madness.

The mob started pressing in. Their excitement had the smell of raw meat. Hikkary and Jaku were hugging each other, the father's head bent over the daughter's as if to shield her.

The idea came in a flash. I put my hand inside the mantelot and into my tunic pocket, pulling out the thread-knitting needle slowly, the remaining one.

The sound now had words. "Get them. Get them."

Tawnilin smiled, like a benevolent father, his attention absorbed by his baying children.

I whirled around and stabbed his thigh, driving the thread-knitting needle into his ample flesh. Blood spurted, splattering my face, filling me with a savage joy. He screamed. I grabbed the reins from his slackened grasp, looked the mare in the eye and murmured, "Run." She bolted, with Tawnilin barely hanging on.

As the sound of his screams receded, silence returned.

A mob has no mind of its own. Once its director was gone, the mob began to retreat like a tidal-wave, no longer a tower of water, but individual wavelets.

The soldiers were another matter. The officer, perhaps scenting rapid promotion and glory, shouted, "Arrest the traitors."

The soldiers started moving forward. The mob ceased its retreat.

A gunshot exploded. When its echoes died, a deathlike silence descended.

I thought a soldier had fired the shot. Then I saw the actual shooter: the woman who had played such a star role in the earlier melee. She stood with the same tree-like stillness, an elegant mini-gun upraised in one hand, the other hand holding the officer—probably the rightful owner of that weapon—by the scruff of his neck, his kicking feet a good six inches above the ground. She caught my eyes and smiled, mouthing a word, *Run.* Then she swung the officer in a perfect arc and threw him in the direction of his men.

Havoc followed. The horses neighed madly and fled headlong, some with their riders, others without. The mob scattered into terrified individuals whose only care was to flee.

I grabbed Sherby's hand, hearing Spooky's voice in my head. *This way. This way.*

Guided by Spooky's voice, I found a narrow opening between two buildings, an overgrown footpath smelling of human waste.

Come. His voice was urgent.

Where are we going?

To the end of this. Then we wait.

Wait for what?

For that woman.

Surprise made me speak the words. "Do you know her?"

No, but she is a Muffic. She reached out to me and showed me this place. I think she plans on joining us.

6

A CURIOUS CABAL

"We are Halflings. In our veins run the blood of Sallonians and Muffics. They can disown us, but can we disown them? They can expel us, but can we escape them?"

We, the Halflings – Pamphlet 2

THE FOOTPATH ENDED AT A DILAPIDATED BRICK WALL.

Sherby's eyes narrowed. "There's no way out."

"Spooky says we must wait here."

Sherby cast Spooky a suspicious glance. "Why?"

"He says that woman who broke the mob is a Muffic. He thinks she'll join us here."

Sherby's face paled. Then she drew a deep slow breath. "Muffic, eh? Wish I'd that kind of strength. Could've done with an arm like that many times, I could've."

I cast Sherby a look of respect. The girl was a veritable

mistress of understatement. Perhaps Sallonia needed a bit of Sherby's shrug-of-the-shoulder acceptance of the new and the different.

I smiled. "I wish I got to know you earlier."

She raised her thick eyebrows. "No use wishing for impossible. Dame Nanarina'd had my hide if we tried to talk friendly like. How long do we wait?"

As if in answer, I heard Spooky's voice in my head. *The Muffic woman says to go back up the passage. There is a turn to the left we missed. Come.*

I turned to Sherby. "Spooky is going to take us to that Muffic woman. She has reached out to him and given directions."

She pointed to her head with a finger in a silent question. I nodded.

Spooky had stopped about halfway up the passage, his body radiating impatience. *Here.*

Tendrils of ivy hid an opening so narrow that we had to slide in. Inside, it widened by several feet into a tunnel-like passage with moss-covered brick walls. The high roof was of tiles. Slime and wild grasses fought for predominance on the stone floor. The air reeked of mildew.

Sherby said, "Bah, smells like a grave." She paused and added, "Dark like a grave too."

I took her hand. "Come."

"You can see?"

"A bit."

The passage led to another dead end, probably the outer wall of a building. Spooky backed up a few feet, nosing the floor. He stopped, and placed his paw on a patch of grass dotted with pearl-stalks—mushrooms, as white and as tiny as pinheads.

Remove this stone. There's a tunnel underneath.

He was already at work, using his paws to weed out the grass. Sherby and I joined him. Soon the square stone was bare. Prising it open was a messy affair involving torn nails and bleeding fingers. Spooky, unable to help, hovered, exuding impatience. I tried to shut him out, but his irritation bristled like a hedgehog inside my head.

Finally the stone was dislodged, revealing a square of deep blackness.

Spooky trotted to the edge and peered down. I was about to tell him to be careful when he vanished into the darkness below.

"Spooky!' I scrambled to my feet and would have tumbled in too, had Sherby not caught my hand. I crouched by the hole, fighting my fears. A sob of relief escaped me when I heard his voice in my head.

No steps. You'll have to jump too. Don't worry. It's not high.

You gave me a scare, I flashed.

Sorry, I—eh—missed my footing.

I gulped down a hysterical giggle, and turned to Sherby. "Spooky wants us to jump in."

Sherby looked about wildly. "What?"

Before Sherby could object, I lowered myself into the hole and let go. The fall was short. I scrambled away, calling. "Sherb, come. It's quite safe. The floor is all sand."

Sherby jumped, landing on hands and feet. She sat back with a groan. "Nothing broken I hope. How're you?"

"Nothing broken." I peered. "It seems a proper passage.

We won't have to crawl. Sherb, give me your hand. Spooky, should we leave the entrance open?"

Spooky was silent for a few seconds. "She says she'll attend to it. Come."

The ground was dry and sandy. The air smelled stale, as if it had been lying unused for too long. Silence whirled around us, broken only by the sound of our panting breaths. We turned from tunnel to tunnel, until I lost all sense of direction.

Our journey ended in a stone chamber, bare except for a pile of sacks in a corner. Before I could ask Spooky what to do next, a blade of light bisected the darkness. I blinked trying to adjust my vision.

There was an open door where the sacks had been, with three shallow steps leading up. The Muffic woman stood on the doorstep, holding a lamp.

Spooky tripped up the steps and vanished into the light. Sherby and I followed. The woman closed the door, and placed the lamp on a table. "Dollin's my name. My Sallonian name. You are Albalia."

"Please call me Allii, and this is Sherby. Thank you for…" I stopped, staring.

The room was brick-walled, stoned-floored, and capacious. The lamp illuminated only a sliver of it, leaving large swathes in shadow, probably why I didn't see them at first.

Master Hikkary and Jaku walked into the circle of light. Sherby's indrawn breath and Spooky's *What* were reflections of my own incredulity. I turned to Dollin. She stood, arms folded, a sardonic gleam in her eyes.

"I crave pardon for this intrusion, Highness." Master Hikkary's manner was calm, as if this encounter was the most normal thing in the world. "My daughter and I want to pledge you our allegiance."

I closed my gaping mouth. Behind me, Sherby muttered something, too low for me to hear. In my head, I heard Spooky. *What do we have here?*

"I'm afraid I had little choice in the matter." A smile softened Dollin's stone-hard face. "They insisted on coming with me. The old man says he had developed a great admiration for Muffics and wished to meet one for years."

I sought and found my Princess Albalia voice. "It is very kind of you to want to join us, Master Hikkary and Jaku. But it will place you at risk, and I don't want that."

Hikkary said with unruffled calm, "Since I identified myself to Lord Tawnilin, it would be an easy matter to discover where we live. You are not placing us in danger, Highness. We are already in danger."

"That's that," Sherby said, in a voice of finality. "They can't return even if they want to, any more than I can." She grinned at me. "When there's no going back, best to go forward."

Dollin gave Sherby an approving look. "You got that right. Looks like none of us have a choice. I'm known in this area. They'll get my details soon enough. It would make sense for us to work together to find a way out of this mess."

Spooky studied each face in turn. Then he turned to me. *Better accept the offer. Alone we'll never manage, not with you running into every danger you see.*

I smiled. "Spooky tells me I should say yes, and he is rarely wrong."

Hikkary and Jaku had been staring at us. Suddenly Jaku cried out, "You talk to each other in your heads? I wish I could too."

"I wish I can too, but being a glorious Sallonian, I can't." Sherby chuckled. "Not so glorious, I guess."

Laughter greeted Sherby's words. It lightened the air and made the idea of 'working together' seem doable.

I turned to Dollin. "Where are we?"

"This is the cellar of my late husband's shop. He was a Sallonian. His nephew owns it now. We are safe here, but not for too long. As I said, I'm known in this area. Enough people would have recognized me. Some might speak to the authorities, voluntarily or under compulsion. The soldiers will get here then." Her eyes met mine. "What were you doing walking the streets in broad daylight?"

I glanced around the room and made a decision. It was an ill-assorted group, but at this moment it was the assorted part that mattered.

I narrated my story in concise form, careful to keep names out of it. It wasn't distrust, not quite. We could be intercepted and arrested. I guessed torture would be used to extract information from everyone, but me. I didn't want to place Minister Ekko, Lady Nellin, or Panda in greater danger than they were in already.

"Pardon me, Highness, but it's dangerous for you to remain in Pinckossia." Hikkary's tone was grave. "They'll tear the city apart looking for you." He paused, as if for consideration, and added, "You mentioned a plan to reveal the conspiracy at a meeting of the Governing Council. But what happened a little while ago might change everything. Your friends might not be able to convince a majority. That's why you must not stay here to be discovered."

Spooky barked. *He is right. Listen to reason for once, for wolf's sake.*

I didn't want to leave Nana. I wasn't going to run away to a safe place, leaving her in danger. She was the only witness to Bellizza's murder. If Sherriz and Pena felt it was necessary, they'd murder her too, whatever Tygyrin's objections.

Then a way out occurred to me. I'd go to this house on Gerbie Avenue and send messages to Minister Ekko and Tygyrin.

I smiled at Hikkary. "I have been given the address of a house I can use as a refuge. We will go there as soon as the night falls. From there we can…"

Dollin cut in. "Night is hours away. To sit here until then isn't sensible. Nor is it necessary. I should be able to alter your appearances enough to get by."

"Do you mean paint our faces like the princess, ma'am?" Jaku's voice had a ring of excitement to it. Her cheeks were flushed.

Dollin gave her quick up-and-down. "She needs paint 'cos she looks what she is, a Halfling. For you, a different hair arrangement and a new robe would do."

There was silence as each of us absorbed the new idea. I broke it. "I'm willing."

Sherby nodded. "Me too."

Jaku turned to her father. "Papa?"

He bowed to Dollin. "I don't think you will have to work very hard where I'm concerned. We, the clerks working for Minister Sherriz, are called 'gray men' for a reason. We are expected to look like nonentities, and I've had a lifetime of practice."

Dollin opened a door half-hidden in shadows and went in.

Hikkary cleared his throat. "Highness, would you mind telling me the address of this house we'll be going to."

I did.

Hikkary frowned, as if trying to summon a memory. Then he shook his head, his face clearing. "I have been thinking whether the address you mentioned came to my notice during the course of my work. I'm certain it didn't."

I could feel my brow furrowing as I tried to process what I just heard. "What was your line of work, Master Hikkary?"

He hesitated. "Sallonia is not the stable place it seems on the surface. Underneath her facile quietness, there are currents of unrest. There is discontent among Sallonians, including at the highest level." His gaze was steady. "Minister Sherriz makes it his business to discover what these pockets of discontent are."

"You mean he spies on all of us?" Sherby's voice throbbed with anger. Her eyes flashed. "So all that talk about, 'Trust and Love are the cords binding us,' is another lie."

Master Hikkary's expression was that of a stern schoolmaster. "My dear young lady, gathering information about their subjects is what rulers do everywhere. I assure you that such practices are not limited to Sallonia."

Sherby cast him a scornful look. "Ay, I'd no doubt it's as you say. I still don't like it. But that's no matter what folks like me want and don't. It's not as if we count, apart from in speeches and stories and such like." Her anger vanished. She smiled at Hikkary, a genuine smile full of amusement. "No need to blame you either, Master Clerk. You're a servant like me. We do what we're told to do. That's that."

Hikkary had been staring at Sherby, a frown of disapproval on his face. At her last words, the frown evaporated, replaced by a smile, a thin smile, but one as real as hers. "Indeed, young lady, we are both tools in the hands of our masters."

"I thought you had the look of a spy." Dollin had come into the room, carrying a pile of clothing and a small wooden box. She dumped them on the table and turned to Hikkary. "I always thought that a good spy is just a step away from being a rebel." She gave a low chuckle. "I've devised a story to suit our new looks. You can tell me if it works."

Hikkary bowed gravely. "It'll be my pleasure to do so, Mistress."

Dollin told her plan quickly. Hikkary would go first, accompanied by Spooky. The rest of us would follow in the guise of a party of worshippers visiting a shrine in the vicinity of Gerbie Avenue. Dollin would be Mistress Kolee, the widow of a well-to-do merchant. Jaku would be her daughter. Sherby and I would be maids.

Hikkary listened closely as Dollin explained the details, dates, addresses. At the end, he bowed to her. "There's nothing I can possibly add. I know a master when I see one. It's part of my training."

Dollin favored him with a hard stare, but said nothing. She selected a bright green robe from the pile and gave it to him. "You can change in the underground room."

Once Hikkary was gone, I took off my muddied and tattered clothes, my mind a whirl of questions. The trousers and blouses given to Sherby and me were patched and faded. Jaku's robe was almost new, blue satin with white flowers. The clothes fit even though none of us were of the same size; Jaku was short and rather plump, Sherby as thin as me, but taller.

I put on my new attire, wondering how Dollin managed to find robes to fit all of us and probing the meaning behind Hikkary's cryptic remarks about Dollin being a master.

Dollin, now arrayed in a brocade robe as gorgeous as a peacock's tail, selected a hairpiece and turned to me. "Sit over there." A grim smile played on her mouth. "You are wondering why I have such an array of disparate clothing."

Hot blood rushed to my face. "Please it's not that I'm suspicious—"

"You should be suspicious." She ran a brush through my hair, telling Jaku over her shoulder, "Call your father in."

"Please don't be offended," I said. "I thought perhaps they belonged to your children…"

Dollin interrupted me. "I've no children. If we had any, they would've been Halflings. You can't disguise babies or even toddlers. That would've given our secret away."

"I'm sorry."

Dollin shrugged. "Choices involve losses as well as gains. My husband and I agreed that having each other was more important than having children with different partners." She picked up a pot of paint and a brush and started coloring my face with sure swift strokes. "I have a collection of clothes to rival a theatre troupe because you are not the first fugitives I've helped. It started years ago with a neighbor who got into debt. He wanted us to save his wife and baby daughter from being sold. We sheltered them until my husband could smuggle them out with a trading caravan. That was how it began. Naturally, it wasn't meant to be a beginning. But once the first step is taken in any direction, the rest often follows. Soon there were others—two soldiers running away from the army, a Halfling maid who had been uncovered and was about to be arrested…a drop, a trickle and then a river—as we Muffics say."

Sherby said, softly, "I wish I'd known you."

Dollin had finished with me and was working on Jaku. She smiled gently at Sherby. "I wish it too." She sighed. "What we did was nothing compared to what we couldn't do."

Jaku shook her head, almost upsetting the hairdo Dollin was working on. "No, Mistress." Her voice quivered. "What you did was great. I wish I had done one hundredth of it. I wish I had your courage and your kindness. It's not as if I didn't know about Sallikan mines and bonded servants. I often prayed to One God to end it all. The rest of the time I forgot because remembering made me sad and uncomfortable."

Dollin's voice was a little rough, "Don't blame yourself, child. There is a tipping point for most of us. Until we reach that, we do little. When we get there, well, that's when we take a new turn or deaden ourselves and live a lie. You and your father reached that point today. And made the right choice."

I wetted my lips and asked the question that had been uppermost in my mind for a while. "Did you know my mother, Mistress?"

Dollin replaced pots and brushes in the box and picked up the only piece of clothing left on the table—a long length of blue silk. She started winding it around her head. "No, but I've heard of her. She had courage. Going against your grandmother must have been like trying to dam a raging river with bare hands. Have you met your grandmother?"

"She saved me when I ran away."

"So you went into that bubble of hers?"

I nodded.

"That's what they do." There was bitterness in Dollin's voice. She wielded pins like knives. "Those Muffics who possess the most power have recreated a bit of the past and live there. Well, to each his or her own. If some people like to live in bubbles all their lives, that's their affair. The problem is that they try to control the rest of us from those bubbles. They don't understand that time moves, with or without them." She nodded at me. "People like your grandmother don't allow us to change or to rebel. All we are allowed to do is to vegetate in our own anger." The length of silk was now a turban covering Dollin's hair, giving her an entirely different appearance. "There, we are done. Let's practice our stories once and leave."

The streets were simmering cauldrons. The heat came from the sun at its worst during its downward trajectory, and from the milling crowds. Hushed voices swirled like the wind. There were mounted soldiers, foot soldiers, and even a company of temple guards. The air pulsated as if a killer storm was in the brewing.

Hikkary walked first, in a faded ochre robe and a cap of the same color. Spooky ambled a little way behind. Dollin and Jaku were next, each carrying a fan and a wire basket full of flowers. Sherby and I followed close, holding parasols over their heads. No one stopped us even though we saw soldiers questioning other pedestrians.

We left the busy centre behind and moved toward quieter outskirts. "We are almost there," Dollin murmured after a while. "It's the left turn at the second fold."

We passed the first fold. A crowd was gathered at the next fold, all of them peering at the left turn.

Hikkary checked in his stride. Spooky overtook him with a run. Soon I heard his voice in my head. *Something's wrong. Soldiers crawling all over the lane.*

Hikkary stopped near a small knot of people. Dollin walked on. As I passed the turnoff to Gerbie Avenue, I sneaked a quick look. It was a largish lane lined with mature gerbie trees, their bottoms bare, their tops lush and cone-shaped. There were houses on both sides.

Soldiers blocked the entrance to the lane.

Dollin stopped at the margin of the crowd and asked a man next to her, "What's happening, Master?"

He gave her an interrogative look and relaxed. "Soldiers, Mistress," he said in a voice as low as hers. "They've surrounded a house down there."

I reached out to Spooky. *Be careful.*

He chuckled. *No one pays attention to dogs. There are several here. I'll be… They are coming out. Your cousin's there.*

Tawnilin?

Yes, looking rather worse for wear. Sheep-faced too. Oh my tail!

Spooky?

It's that minister fellow of yours. Ekko. And another man. They seem to be prisoners.

Minister Ekko a prisoner?

He wouldn't be wearing manacles for fun, right?

I felt as if someone had kicked me in the stomach. Despite the heat, I was cold, almost shivering. Sherby was looking at me, face pale, eyes wide with anxiety.

Spooky's voice was a warning. *They are coming your way.*

Sounds filled the air. The trotting of horses, voices shouting orders, indrawn breaths of tens of people.

Three mounted soldiers came first and turned left, followed by the rest of the cavalcade.

My cry of horror was lost in the surprised gasps of people around me.

In the middle of the cavalcade, Tawni rode. Behind him, rode a soldier, holding the bridle of Minister Ekko's horse with one hand. Ekko's hands were manacled. I stared, unable to believe my eyes.

Then I saw Uncle Bernii and every other consideration fled from my mind.

His hands too were manacled. His robe was even more crumpled than usual. Sweat poured down his face and his eyes were puffed, as if he hadn't been sleeping for days. But he sat on the horse straight, his head held high, staring ahead. Another soldier rode next to him, holding the bridle of his horse.

I bit back a sob. Sherby made an inarticulate sound, as if she was choking on something.

Who's the fat one?

Uncle Bernii. I tried to gather my whirling thoughts. "I must go."

Dollin muttered, "Go where?"

After them," I remembered to whisper at the last moment. "I can't let Uncle Bernii go into danger and just stand here. Minister Ekko too."

Dollin inspected the road, now deserted except for an occasional passer-by. She gestured at Hikkary with her head.

He hurried over. "What shall we do now?"

"She wants to go after Prince Bernalin."

Hikkary frowned. "It is not advisable in my opinion. What we must do now—"

I cut in. "I'm going. You don't have to come with me."

Sherby had been picking fruits from a clump of beetleberry bushes. She gave me a handful of red-and-black-striped berries and shoved some into her mouth. "I'm coming," she said, chewing the fruits with obvious relish.

Dollin nodded. "I'll come too."

Jaku said, "And me." She turned to her father. "Papa?"

I was about to object, when Hikkary stopped me with a smile. "Indeed."

7

A WAR OF A KIND

"We are moths flying against two headwinds."
We, the Halflings – Pamphlet 2

THE CAVALCADE MOVED PONDEROUSLY, AN UNDULATING snake, its tail growing ever longer as more and more people joined in.

Spooky's acerbic voice rasped inside my head. *Your mind feels like a midden.*

I gave a mental shrug. *I'm trying to plan something.*

Huh! Think you'd be able to do that before they murder the lot of us?

I did try to think of a plan, but questions trapped my mind. Why was the arrest of Bernalin and Ekko turned into a spectacle? It was not in the nature of Sherriz and Pena to act in the open. They preferred darkness, concealment, obfuscation. Are they losing their nerve, because of the continued, and inexplicable, absence of Rokkrin? Or have they found Rokkrin's corpse? What was Uncle Bernii doing here? Did he come in secret to meet other Sallonian dissenters or did he come openly to attend tomorrow's coronation? Did Ekko go to Gerbie Avenue to meet him? Where was Tygyrin? What was his role in all this?

Spooky's voice cut through the confusion in my mind. *Where are we going?*

I looked about and drew a blank.

Perhaps Dollin sensed the unasked question; or Spooky, tired of waiting for my answer, asked her. She turned to Jaku, saying impatiently, "We are right out of our way, child. To get home from the Temple of Seven Blessings it'll take more than an hour."

Jaku pouted. "We can hire a mechanical carriage, Mama."

The Temple of Seven Blessings was the largest and the most important temple dedicated to One God, supposedly built in the place where One God crowned the first king of Sallonia. Since then, every single Sallonian ruler had been crowned there. I had visited the temple once, for Bellizza's crowning as queen-consort. Bellizza had been dressed in a robe of magenta silk, the color of royal bridals. It should have clashed hideously with her blue hair but didn't. She had looked radiant.

I suppressed the memory and focused on matters at hand. The temple was a public place with forty-nine entrances and forty-nine exits. Perhaps it had dungeons, and the prisoners were going to be held there instead of in the castle. That would make sense. Pena had absolute control over the temple while the castle was a maze of conflicted loyalties.

Is that your god? Spooky sounded puzzled. *Why does he have four heads?*

Because he's All-seeing. He can see our past lives, our present lives, and our future lives.

That's three. What does he do with the fourth?

Study the Cosmic Void.

Weird.

I know.

The temple came into view. Seven was the number sacred to One God and everything here was in sevens. The temple was built in seven concentric circles, using marble blocks of seven different colors. Outside were seven fountains and seven statues of One God, each one depicting an aspect of his Being—creator, destroyer, warrior, peacemaker, lover, lawgiver, and protector.

As our part of the cavalcade rounded a bend, I had a clear view of the marble platform fronting the temple. It was crowded with people. This far I couldn't see the faces properly, but that was no bar to knowing who they were —the entire court, ministers and generals, courtiers and officials, the men who ruled Sallonia.

Jaku said, in a puzzled voice, "What are they going to do, Mama?"

"A trial," Dollin answered.

"The traitors," a woman said, her eyes flashing. She wore a striped robe, and a turban like Dollin's. She waved a silk fan about, making her bangles tinkle. "They'll be tried and punished. We have been summoned as witnesses."

"An ancient tradition," a man in an ochre and red robe added. "What concerns Sallonia concerns all Sallonians."

A chorus of ayes followed.

Night was falling. The massive stone-lights on their tall plinths illuminated the ground with a golden glow. The huge incense blocks perfumed the air with the scents of seven sacred flowers—star roses, kadoopul, conch shell flowers, bee roses, butterfly jasmines, atria, and blue dove flowers.

Bells in the seven bell-towers started ringing. As their polyphony faded, a figure rose and walked to the voice-enhancer at the centre of the platform. It was Pena. He was in full High-priest regalia, including the blue conical hat with its nodding plume. He bowed his head and began to intone the Commencement Prayer.

"Most High, Most Merciful Divinity, Our Creator, Sustainer and…"

I clasped my hands and bent my head. The prayer would take at least five minutes. I closed my ears to Pena's sonorous voice and tried to think of some plan, any plan. I needed to save Uncle Bernii, Ekko and Nana…

Nana. How could Nana take the poisoned thorn, jab it into Bellizza's unsuspecting neck, and hold her while she died?

Until now, the thought that Bellizza didn't die alone, that Nana was with her to the end, had comforted me. But Nana was Bellizza's murderer. In her dying moment, Bellizza would have known that. She wouldn't have wanted to be cradled by her murderess.

Nana holding the dying Bellizza, crooning to her, wasn't comforting. It was preposterous, obscene.

Nana didn't see anything wrong in what she did. She

had no remorse. If time could be rolled back, she'd do it again, after ensuring the blame wouldn't be foisted on me.

And Nana didn't hate Bellizza. Nana was fond of Bellizza. If Nana could kill someone she was fond of because of her loyalty to her tribe, what about others like her? Wouldn't that…

A nudge from Sherby brought me back to the present. Pena had finished with the prayer and was reading out from a document.

"…of conspiring with Halfling terrorists and Muffic demons to overthrow the rightful king of Sallonia and to place on the throne Albalia, the bastard daughter of the late King Walterin and his Muffic concubine. With this intent, they have been meeting in secret with other traitors of similar mind. The aforementioned Albalia was found guilty of murdering the late Queen Bellizza. She escaped…"

That was the moment I knew what I had to do.

There was no time to think through the idea. I shoved the parasol at Sherby, whispered, "I'm going to the front," and started threading my way toward the platform.

Have you gone barking mad? Spooky's voice sounded near hysterical.

I considered the question on its merits. *I don't know. I guess I'm tired of running away.* Mostly from myself.

When I reached the edge of the crowd, I stopped and peered over the shoulders of those standing in front. On the far side of the platform I saw Bernalin and Ekko, seated on a bench. Four temple guards, in their purple and silver attire, stood behind them. Sherriz sat on the centre-front of the stage, his short wiry body hunched. He had changed almost beyond recognition. His vitality was the thing I remembered about him most. That crackling energy was gone. He had the appearance of a sick man.

He had been loyal to Father. Did the knowledge of his betrayal sap his being and turn him into the lifeless creature he seemed to have become?

To the right of Sherriz, Tawnilin slouched in his chair. He looked subdued. His mother sat on his other side, her body rigid, her face set, her bejeweled fingers gripping the arms of the chair. Amberlina's fury was probably explained by the empty chair to her right, the High Throne that should have been occupied by Rokkrin.

Tygyrin should have been sitting with his mother and brother. There was an empty seat, but no Tygyrin. I looked about wildly and saw him, seated alone on a chair to a side. The message he was conveying was clear—he wanted to have nothing to do with the proceedings.

If only I could catch his attention. But his face was turned away from me.

A hand gripped my shoulder. I tried to bunch a fist but my fingers were as stiff as sticks. A voice whispered in my ear, "Listen, you fool."

The hand left my shoulder. My mobility returned. I turned around to face Dollin. A glare from those flashing eyes silenced the words on my tongue.

Dollin grabbed my arm and placed something on my palm. Something cold. A wet handkerchief.

I caught her hand and pressed it, smiling my thanks. Dollin nodded and turned her attention to the stage.

I looked around. Sherby and Jaku were standing a few feet away. As I stared at my friends, trying to master my emotions, Sherby turned her head and winked.

A patina of tears covered my eyes. They had not abandoned me. I wanted to embrace all of them, including Master Hikkary, who stood a little to the right his eyes riveted on the stage. How shocked he'd be if I embraced him! The thought brought a smile.

The future looked promising. Assuming any of us had a future.

Pena was still speaking. I moved laterally, focusing on his words, realizing I had missed a vital part, his justification of an immediate trial.

"This gathering will constitute itself into a court of law. That court will hear the charges against the accused and the evidence against them. It will also listen to whatever words of defense the accused see fit to utter, if any. It will then give its verdict. With Halfling terrorists and Muffic devils massing against us, we live in a time of emergency which permits, indeed requires, drastic measures in the interest of public safety."

The crowd was silent. It was the silence of approval.

Pena resumed speaking. "I must reveal to you a disturbing development which happened this very afternoon. Albalia was seen in Pinckossia, trying to subvert the people. She was arrested but managed to escape using her dark arts. We believe she is, at this moment, reunited with Halfling terrorists who are gathering outside this very city…"

"I'm Albalia and I'm right here."

Surprise was my ally. It enabled me to move past the guards before they knew what was happening. I stood alone in the empty space between the crowd and the platform, wiping my face vigorously with the wet handkerchief, hearing Spooky's voice in my head.

Take care of your silly self. I don't want to lose you.

I smiled feeling like a bird, light and free. *I don't want to lose you either, Spooks,* I responded, as I started walking towards the platform. *We've still things to do, you and I.*

The guards were too well-trained to panic. The ones forming the human barrier, keeping the thousands of Sallonians in their place, didn't move an inch. The crowd, coming out of their stupor of surprise, had begun to swell, like a wave, but the guards held them back. I was grateful for that. I feared the crowd far more than I feared the guards; better a single poisoned knife than hundreds of knife-like hands.

On the platform too there was chaos, people rising from their seats, shouting. Uncle Bernii tried to stand up, but Ekko restrained him. Tygyrin sprang from his chair, but stood still, staring.

Pena gave a hand signal. Next moment several temple guards appeared, as if from nowhere, and surrounded me, cutting me away from both the court and the crowd.

I said, loudly, "The holy traditions prevent you from touching me," and realized that the said holy traditions didn't prevent them from sticking a poisonous something into me.

The words did have an impact, though. The guards continued to surround me, but they didn't touch me.

"Arrest her," Pena said, the voice enhancer turning his order into a thunderous roar. "Arrest her."

I held out my hands, palms upward. One of the guards snapped a manacle into place.

Pena said, "Take her away. Hold her inside the temple. We will hear the case against her later."

I spoke in the loudest voice I could manage. "You have charged Minister Ekko and Prince Bernalin of conspiring with me. I'm therefore a co-accused. I'm here of my own free will to seek justice for myself and for my murdered father."

Tygrin, who had been staring at me, a look of horror on his face, walked to Pena and started talking to him. Pena frowned and shook his head. Tygyrin persisted. Going by Pena's taut face and Tygyrin's clenched fists, they were both angry.

Eventually, Pena shrugged and gave a brief nod.

Tygyrin climbed down the steps and walked towards me, slowly, as if he was weighed down by an invisible burden. The guards parted for him.

I smiled, not bothering to hide my relief. He tried to smile back, but his face looked too weary for it. He caught my hand, his fingers closing over mine in a grip tighter than any I've ever known. "Allii, Allii…" He stopped biting his lip. "Come."

We walked to the platform, up the stairs, side by side, hand in hand. Not quite. He walked one step ahead and was holding my hand in his. A child being led to—

"Take her away!"

The shriek broke the spell. Rokkrin's wife's eyes were on

fire. Her ample bosom was heaving, but the accusing finger she pointed at me was steady.

"As Queen, I order her to be imprisoned."

Tygyrin muttered something under his breath. I pulled my hand away from his, and stepped forward, bowing. "You are not yet queen, Aunt."

"You vicious bastard!"

"Allii, come." Tygyrin's voice was urgent.

I ignored the urgency in his voice and evaded his attempt to grab my hand.

"I order her to be…"

"Your…er…Majesty, a word please."

The voice made its mark because it was low, smooth, the voice of someone in control. It was a tall man with stooping shoulders, in a gleaming silver uniform, a general, going by the gold chain lying across his bare chest.

He walked to the centre-front of the stage. "Highness, I'm General Soodda. I assure you, the justice you seek is yours, so long as you submit willingly to the judgment of this court." He turned to Pena. "My Lord, I don't think there's any cause for hasty action."

General Soodda, the name seemed familiar. Then I remembered. He had helped Kolla and Pattii escape the tracker-assassins.

Amberlina cried, "She's a traitor and a murderess…"

General Soodda's smile was as smooth as his voice. "All the more reason to try her without delay, Your Majesty." He turned briefly, looking at the assembled court. "I'm certain you would agree, my lords."

There was a murmur of assent.

What do you think this creature's game is? Spooky's question reflected my own misgivings.

No idea. He was the one who helped Kolla and Pattii. He must be having some purpose in mind. I'll go along, for now.

Be careful. Might as well go along with a crocodile. At least you'll know where you're with a crocodile. I wish we never came to this place.

I bowed. "I will be happy to abide by the judgment of this court."

General Soodda nodded. "Please be seated, Highness."

I wanted to walk over to the bench where Bernii and Ekko sat, but Tygyrin guided me to the other corner where he had been sitting. Amberlina called him, but he ignored her, just as he ignored his brother's hissed words, "Witch's dupe!" He offered his chair to me and made a guard bring him another chair. He sat next to me.

I smiled. "Thank you, cousin."

He said nothing. His eyes moved like restless moths. The hand he placed on mine was icy cold.

Pena stood watching us, his eyes glittering, as if he were looking forward to a pleasurable experience. Then he addressed the court and the crowd, the voice-enhancer carrying his words to every corner.

"This court will now recommence its proceedings. May One God guide us in this endeavor and enable us to complete these proceedings with justice to all…"

I shivered. Tygyrin's fingers pressed mine in a gesture of reassurance.

Pena read out the charges against me. The murder of Bellizza and Terrii, I was prepared for. "The murder of King

Walterin," I wasn't. "Our late revered king," Pena added, "Her own father."

I looked down to avoid meeting anyone's eyes and saw Tygyrin's totemic ring, with its engraved stone.

And the world rocked like a swing gone mad.

Many years ago, Nana invented a game called 'Piece the Story' to keep me occupied during the rainy season. She would give me ten slips of paper, each with a single sentence. I had to arrange them in the right order so that they become a coherent story—in twenty seconds. Towards the end, I could manage in just ten.

"The soldiers who nearly caught me the night I escaped," I whispered almost to myself. "They were wearing a uniform with that insignia." As suspicion solidified into certainty, the world vanished. I was back in my familiar nightmare, fleeing across a barren plain, pursued by a figure who was no longer faceless but wore a face as familiar as my own.

Tygyrin was watching me, his expression unreadable. I returned his gaze. "It was you all the time. You and Pena. Sherriz was your dupe. You planned everything. Bellizza's murder, scapegoating me, Papa's murder." I paused searching his impassive face. "Even Uncle Rokkrin didn't know the full plan. I suppose it was you who informed him of my arrival, through Lady Nellin." I blinked, feeling bludgeoned by the discovery. "You removed every snag in your path to the throne, one by one. I suppose Pena will be the last to go."

He smiled at last, his thumb stroking my manacled wrist. "Being a fugitive has done wonders for you, my dearest Allii. You have blossomed in more ways than one. I wish we had more time together. Believe me, I'm going to miss you."

8
VERDICT

"If we create a new world, do we make it like the old, with oppressors and oppressed, some with too much of everything and others with nothing of anything?"
We, the Halflings – Pamphlet 3

FEAR HAD A TASTE. MY MOUTH WAS CLOGGED WITH IT, brackish and sour.

I turned away from Tygyrin and stared at the waves of moths circling the massive stone-lights, their gossamer gray wings fluttering with mad intensity. How many of them would be dead by tomorrow? Did they not see the pathetic remains of their fellows? Were the black eyes on those ghostly wings blind? Was that why they always returned, night after night, returned to die? Or was it the way they were built inside, to seek death by battering their futile wings against an elemental force?

Fool, fool, a part of my brain mocked me; fooled once by Nana, fooled again by Tygyrin. Fooled so much, I was beginning to imagine a future with him and liking the idea.

I wanted to pull my hand away from his clasp, to run away from his presence, but didn't try, knowing he wouldn't let me. Instead I fixed my attention on Pena who, finished with praying, had summoned the first witness.

A nondescript looking man in a gray robe walked on to the stage and stood by the voice-enhancer. He identified himself as Dämiyan, an official working for Chief Minister Sherriz, said his prayer, and took his oath.

Pena consulted a piece of paper. "Did you uncover a plot to murder King Walterin and place his bastard daughter Albalia on the throne?"

Dämiyan bowed. "I did, my lord. Thanks to the vigilant faith of Sallonian servants in the castle, I found secret communications between Prince Bernalin, Minister Ekko, Queen Bellizza, and her brother."

"Tell the court the contents of these communications."

"The letters from Prince Bernalin and Minister Ekko were about changing the laws of succession to enable Princess Albalia to replace her father. The queen's brother advised her to lend her support to these plans."

"What did you do once you uncovered these letters?"

"I handed them over to the Chief Minister."

Pena held up a sheaf of papers. "These are copies of those letters. The court will examine them once the testimonies are over."

The crowd drew a collective breath.

"Tell the court what happened this morning."

"Minister Ekko arrived at the castle around 7:30 in the morning. He left about half an hour later, accompanied by a woman."

"Who was the woman?"

"She wore a cloak, my lord, one with a hood and a heavy face veil."

Pena nodded. "Continue."

"I and a colleague followed the carriage. It went to a boarded-up house on Kata-kaloo Road. Minister Ekko and the veiled woman went in and spent about an hour there. Then they left. I ordered my colleague to follow the carriage and kept guard outside the house."

"Did anyone else come into the house or leave it?"

Dämiyan hesitated. "Not through the front entrance. After I got reinforcements, I examined the place and discovered a back entrance."

"An unpardonable error on your part." Pena's voice was ice.

The witness paled.

"Who owns the house?"

"My colleagues are checking out that information, my lord. We will know soon."

"Was there anyone in the house?"

"No, my lord."

The caretaker must have hidden himself. I wanted to laugh with relief.

Pena nodded. "Continue."

"I continued my vigil outside. At about four, Minister Ekko returned but left almost immediately. I followed him. He went to a house on Gerbie Avenue. I sent a mechanical pigeon to inform the Chief Minister of this development. Then Prince Tawnilin arrived with a troop of temple guards and surrounded the house. The Halfling terrorists guarding the house attacked us, but the prince managed to repulse them with no loss of life on our part. All four terrorists were killed. We went in and discovered Minister Ekko and Prince Bernalin there."

Uncle Bernii tried to get up but was yanked back by a guard.

The crowd hissed.

"That's a lie," I muttered. "There was no attack. They just killed some innocent people."

Tygyrin smiled with unimpaired calm. "Try telling that to the crowd, cousin."

I realized, to my horror, he was right. No one had heard the sound of any fight. That didn't matter. The crowed believed. That belief was kindling to their fear and their anger.

Pena announced the name of his next witness. Prince Tawnilin.

Tawni had been slouching in his chair, his face a pout of discontent. As he walked up to the voice-enhancer, he became a changed man, the same man I saw a few hours ago whipping up a mob.

Tawni made some adjustments to the voice-enhancer, said his prayer in a resonant voice, and took his oath. Pena asked him to inform the assembly of the events at the Natta-kota Street earlier in the day. He answered in a measured voice. As his narration progressed, I understood that I had underestimated my foppish cousin again. He was trying to focus attention not on the event but on me. "I had expected her to be affected by the death of her father," he said at one point. "He was a good father to her. He brought her up as a Sallonian princess. She didn't express even the slightest grief about his murder. There were no tears, no lamentations. She was intent on completing her fell mission."

The crowd sank into a deeper silence.

I leaned towards Tygyrin, "He's good. At this rate, he'll beat you."

Tygyrin had been staring at his brother, his eyes narrowed to slits. Now he looked down at me. "So you are impressed by his theatrics? You disappoint me."

I smiled at him. "Theatrics do matter. Your father used them to claim the throne which should have been Bernalin's by rights. Tawni can use them too to upstage you."

He flashed his even white teeth. "He will never be king."

Tawni continued, sounding shocked and saddened in turns. "It pained me deeply, because she was brought up with the greatest care, in the best traditions of Sallonian womanhood. But she leaves her father's house without a word to him, and spends months in unknown places with One God knows who. I tried to appeal to her sense of honour. She laughed in my face."

When his testimony was over, Tawni walked back to his chair with cocky steps. Before sitting down he flashed a triumphant look at his brother.

Pena had begun to speak, "In the name of One God and the King, I summon…"

Tygyrin was too focused on his brother to pay me attention. I sprang to my feet before he realized what was happening, saying in a loud voice, "You err, Lord Pena. You can't speak in the name of the king. There is no king. My father is dead. His successor is yet to be crowned."

In a second, Tygyrin was by my side, his hand gripping my arm so hard, I feared he would break it the way a man would break a twig. Pain coursed up my arm, like lightning. Then his grip relaxed, still unbreakable but no longer punitive. I swallowed a sob of relief.

Pena had been watching the little byplay between us, his expression mocking. Now he said, "I'm referring to King Rokkrin."

"Prince Rokkrin. The coronation is yet to happen."

"One God makes allowances for special circumstances when his people are threatened. I performed the necessary rites of kingship yesterday. Rokkrin is now the sovereign lord of all of us."

I listened to the indrawn breaths and the mutterings and watched the looks of surprises on official faces—flashes of annoyance in ministerial eyes, the slight tightening of priestly mouths. The court didn't like what it heard. Next to me, Tygyrin muttered something.

Pena had taken a wrong step and given me an unlooked-for opening.

I arched my brows. "Was this strange coronation approved by the Governing Council? Or even by your own priests?" I paused. "Who else was present at this coronation?"

Pena's eyes snapped hate, but his demeanor remained calm, his voice steady. "I'm not bound to answer your questions. I order you…"

"One moment, Lord Pena." General Soodda had risen from his chair. He walked to the front and spoke into the voice-enhancer. "If you crowned Prince Rokkrin, I and everyone else here would like to know who was present at this ceremony." He paused and added, "I'm also perturbed by the continued absence of King Rokkrin. He…"

Tygyrin and Pena exchanged a quick look. Pena said, "His Majesty is attending to matters of utmost importance…"

Soodda cut in. "I'm hearing that your temple guards are searching for him in the castle and even in the woods."

Someone, I had no idea who, tittered and turned it into a cough.

A voice rose, clear, precise, demanding attention. "Lord Pena, did you obtain the consent of the people for the coronation by sending out heralds?" It was Minister Ekko.

Pena gave a dismissive shrug. "It's a mere formality…" He stopped, his face paling. He had been standing by the voice-enhancer, thereby rendering his words audible to every single member of the crowd.

It was not the words so much that angered the crowd; consent was indeed a mere formality and every little child knew that. Still, maintaining that formality was important because it enabled Sallonians to believe that they had a say in how their country was run. Pena had taken a cudgel to those illusions. He knew it too, going by the dismay on his face. He had made a misstep, and he had done so publicly, something unimaginable in a man who was so controlled, so in command.

After a moment of stunned silence, the crowd erupted into a wave of hissing. Above the sound of hissing came a shout. "No Rokkrin." My heart raced with excitement and anxiety, for it was Dollin. "No Rokkrin."

Suddenly the crowd erupted, like a wave breaking a sand fortification.

"No Rokkrin. No Rokkrin. No Rokkrin."

Tygyrin swore under his breath. He released my arm, moved to Pena's side and muttered something. Pena nodded, bent his head and began a prayer, asking One God for guidance. As his voice continued to intone the familiar words, people started to join. At one point the shouting voices and the praying voices vied with each other for predominance.

The latter won.

Tygyrin guided me back to the chair. I allowed him, trying to think of a way out. Pena and Tygyrin had One God on their side; centuries of blind belief formed their ramparts. They couldn't be defeated without breaching those walls first. Going by the rapidity with which the crowd changed from injured fury to mindless piety, I wondered whether it was doable at all.

The prayer over, Pena resumed the proceedings. He summoned Doktoras Poll.

Poll's testimony began with the murder of Bellizza. Tygyrin's hand tightened on my arm, the message from those iron-hard fingers clear.

"It grieves me to say that the rose-apple came from Princess Albalia," Poll said. "It was poisoned with nivati…"

"You know nivati doesn't kill instantly," I cried. "You know it was a sand-kutzi thorn…" Realization hit me and stopped my mouth. Everyone on stage was regarding me with surprise, liberally laced with suspicion. I had shown myself to be knowledgeable about poison, too knowledge-able.

Poll waited for me to say more. When I didn't, he continued detailing his discoveries and how they implicated me. I didn't interrupt again. He was a physician, known to be my father's friend and mine. His words carried weight. The crowd's echoing silence was inimical. The court too was silent, regarding me with tight-lipped disapproval. I stared back defiantly, until it dawned on me that my behavior was likely to be interpreted not as a sign of innocence but as a sign of brazenness. So I trained my eyes on Poll, trying to keep my expression blank.

Tygyrin's thumb caressed my wrist again. "A clincher, don't you think, cousin?" he whispered.

I ignored him. I also agreed with him. Poll had almost sealed my fate. Unless—unless…

Spooky's voice sounded like a shot inside my head. *What is she doing here?*

I looked up and froze. Lady Nellin was walking up to the voice-enhancer.

That blasted priest of yours summoned her. Spooky's voice flashed. *She is going to give evidence against you.*

Nellin was dressed in the deepest of mourning, a robe of dark green. Her face had more lines and shadows than it did this morning. I tried to catch her eyes, but she didn't look in my direction or in anyone's direction.

Fear was a monster inside me, eating away at my courage, filling me with rage. I wished I had enough faith to pray to One God for deliverance. I tried and understood, consciously, what I had known for a while. I no longer believed.

With no One God to lend me a helping hand, I was on my own.

Pena began by questioning Nellin about Bellizza's murder. His voice was courteous, his manner respectful. She answered his questions promptly, her voice clear and precise.

"So you found the rose-apple?"

"There was a half-eaten one by her side. I kept it and gave it to Doktoras Poll."

"Why did you do that?"

"Because I suspected that the queen had been poisoned. And I knew there was only one person in the castle who was interested in poisons."

"Who was that?"

"Princess Albalia."

The collective gasp sounded like a freak storm.

"Why do you say that?"

"I've heard Dame Nanarina, and even the queen, cautioning her about handling toxic plants."

"So you surmised that Princess Albalia might have had a hand in what happened?"

"I thought the princess killed my lady. I thought so until this morning. I stopped thinking that when I heard the real killer confess." Her lips parted in a smile that would have terrified the dead. "Now I know the princess didn't kill the queen."

What? Spooky shrieked inside my head.

I slumped with relief.

Tygyrin swore under his breath.

Pena recovered fast. He grabbed Nellin by her hand saying, "Lady Nellin, you are not yourself…"

She pushed him aside so hard that he almost fell. Her voice was no longer cool and unemotional, but seething with fury. "No, I'm finally myself. I fell for your lies and became your tool. I know the truth now." She whirled around, pointing an imperious arm, like the lead actress in a melodrama. "Dame Nanarina, please come forward."

Tygyrin cursed under his breath. "Blast that old biddy."

I would have slapped him, had I a hand free. "How dare you? How dare you insult Nana?"

His look made my innards curl. "I saved her life, my dear cousin. They wanted her killed. I saved her."

Nana walked to the front of the platform ignoring the swelling chaos around her. She was dressed in a clean robe of faded green. She looked like the old Nana, except for an added gauntness.

"What is this mad woman doing here?" Pena cried. He turned to the guards. "Take her away."

General Soodda was on his feet. "Don't touch her."

Pena eyed him. "May I remind you, General, that you have no authority in this holy place?"

"This is the king's court, and as a member of the Governing Council I have the same authority as you do, my lord. All I'm saying is that Dame Nanarina, who is the last of an illustrious family and the one-time nurse to King Walterin, should be allowed to speak."

"She was also Albalia's nurse. She'll tell any lie to protect Albalia."

"My lord, are you saying the king's court is incapable of

knowing the truth from lies?" The general smiled a little. "Surely not? And if we do fall into such an error, you can lead us in another prayer, asking One God for guidance."

Nana had been listening to this interchange, a grim smile on her face. Now she said, "May I speak?"

There were nods of assent.

"I killed the Queen," Nana said. There was something terribly convincing about her calm expression. Her voice sounded distant, as if it were coming from far away. "I was fond of her because she had always been good to my princess. But the king had to have a son. He had to marry again, and the queen was refusing to go away. She was being stubborn. There was no other way to secure Sallonia's future, to save the work of our fathers." She paused, and her voice dropped a little. "I spent the night before in this holy place, praying for steadfastness. Lord Pena gave me absolution." She put her hand inside the robe and took out a silver talisman and kissed it.

No sound, no movement. Everyone seemed petrified. It was as if Nana's admission had taken them to a place beyond words and deeds.

"She was seated thread-knitting when I went in. A white tree. She was having headaches all the time. I used to knead her neck. It gave her relief." For a second her voice wavered and an expression of horror crossed her face, as if she saw, really saw, what she had done. Then she squared her shoulders. "I had a sand-kutzi thorn with me. Doktoras Poll had prepared it. He gave it to me and showed me where I should strike. I feared my hand would waver, miss its mark when the time came. But my hand was steady."

I groaned. Lady Nellin's face was like a mask used for the demon dance.

Nana continued to speak, in that strange distant voice. "She touched the wound and said, 'Nana, what sharp nails you have.' She picked up her knitting again and dropped it. It was fast. I waited till she died. I didn't want her to die alone. Afterward, I went and reported to Lord Pena. He gave me absolution again. Doktoras Poll promised me he would pronounce it a natural death. A burst blood-vessel in the head, because of all those terrible headaches. I believed him. Then they arrested the Princess. They planted false evidence.

"They locked me up in the tower to silence me. Last week, the king visited me. I told him the truth. He accepted it. He forgave me. He gave me the Ring of Sallonia and told me to give it to the Princess. I was scared. I believed that touching the ring would harm my baby. The book says if anyone other than a Sallonian who is pure of blood touches the Ring of Sallonia, One God's punishment will be swift and terrible." She paused and looked around. "But my boy, my king, he said, no, it was just a story."

Pena cried, "Shut up, you ninny. You are accusing our late revered king of sacrilege. He will never give the Ring of Sallonia to his Halfling bastard." He turned to the temple guard. "Arrest her. She has confessed to murder. Arrest her."

Nellin placed herself before Nana. "If you arrest Dame Nanarina, you have to arrest those who planned the murder as well." She jabbed a finger at Pena and at Sherriz. Pena stood unmoved, but Sherriz shrank into his chair, cowering like a hunted animal.

Tygyrin walked up to Nana and spoke to her, his voice

calm and authoritative. "Dame Nanarina, I promise you that this court will give your words the most serious consideration and do its best to investigate the charges you have made."

His words seemed to have a soothing effect on Nana. She smiled at him. "You do that, Lord Tygyrin. You are faithful. See that justice is done."

Tygyrin gave Nana a warm reassuring smile and turned to Pena. "My lord, if you permit me, I will take charge of the proceedings and bring this trial to conclusion."

Pena's eyes narrowed. I felt a sudden urge to laugh. Did Pena think that Tygyrin was planning a final double-cross? I watched their little tiff with bated breath. If Pena won, I could see a way out. If Tygyrin did, death would be the only way out.

Tygyrin said, "The credibility of this court and its…"

Pena cut in. "There's no need for you to take charge of the proceedings. These are lies concocted by embittered women. They should not be taken seriously. Hadn't One God said that a woman must be seen, used, but never heard?"

Tygyrin's eyes flashed with irritation. "Let me remind you…"

Pena cut in, his eyes on me. "Where is this ring?"

"I have it with me."

"You are lying. The Ring of Sallonia cannot be touched by a Halfling. You are polluted from birth. If you wear the ring, One God's wrath will be on you."

His words were having an effect. There were looks of fear, of hurried prayers.

With my manacled hands, I couldn't reach my pocket. If I asked for the manacles to be removed, Pena would call it a ploy. "Nana," I called. "Can you please get the ring out for me?"

Nana hurried to my side and took out the pouch. I extended my manacled hands. She laid the ring on my right palm. I picked it up with the fingers of my left hand and raised it. The ring's star-shaped silver pearl, believed to be the only one of its kind in the world, glittered in the golden glow of stone-lights.

Pena cried, "That is a fake."

I said, "You know it is not."

"The terrorists who killed the king took it. They gave it to you. You are in cahoots with them, planning the downfall of Sallonia."

I ignored him and turned to face the court and then the crowd, my eyes moving over the faces, expectant, fearful, shocked.

"This is the Ring of Sallonia. If Lord Pena is correct, I can't even touch it. But I'm touching it. And I will wear it, as my father wanted me to."

With theatrical deliberateness I put the ring on the middle finger of my right hand. The manacles made it hard work, but the slowness added to the dramatic tension.

When the deed was done, there was a collective gasp, followed by silence.

I allowed that silence to stretch. When I sensed the first mutterings, I spoke.

"Nothing will happen to me, because this ring has no divine power. Its only power is the power given to it by you, with your unquestioning belief in Lord Pena." If the conflict were between One God and me, I didn't stand a chance. But if I could depict it as a contestation between Pena and me, I might win.

A muscle twitched in Pena's face. He called out to the commander of the temple guard. "Take the Halfling bastard away."

Tygyrin cursed under his breath and stepped forward. But Soodda was already at Pena's side. "Let me remind you, Lord Pena, such an order would be highly irregular."

"There is nothing irregular, general."

I turned to the court. "I didn't come here to grab the throne. I came here to ensure that those who plotted the murder of my father, my stepmother and the palace guard Terrii don't benefit from their crimes." I held out my hand. "And if any of you doubt the authenticity of the Ring, I invite you to come and check."

Ministers, priests, generals, and lords looked at each other. After a silence of many seconds, a priest stood up. I remembered him from the old days as a key acolyte of Pena's, though I couldn't recall his name.

He bowed to me. "If you would permit me, Highness?"

I smiled, took off the ring, and held it out to him.

He picked it up, peered at it, held it up, held it down. I almost expected him to smell it. He returned it to me with another, deeper bow. "This is the Ring, Highness."

Pena opened his mouth, but was stopped by the sound of a scuffle below, several voices raised in anger. A soldier climbed the marble steps and stopped. Pena, Soodda and Tygyrin said, almost in one voice, "What is it?"

The soldier looked at the three faces, unsure as to who he should report his news to. Then he compromised by speaking to all three. As a result his voice was louder than it would have been otherwise and the voice-enhancer carried it to the crowd. "My lords, Halfling terrorists have attacked the Sallikan mines. They've—they've released all the miners."

Exultation swept over me like a wave. After the bitterness of failure, the first success tasted like Bellizza's honey-infused cocolade. The memory sobered me. One step forward didn't mean victory.

All three men were talking at once. I sidestepped them and reached the voice-enhancer. "You heard the news," I said. "The Halfling rebels have liberated Sallonian men and women forced to labor in Sallikan mines. I have never been to a mine. I know you haven't either. Those who are taken to the mines rarely return alive. But you have heard the songs." I paused to refresh my memory and sang my favorite miner's song.

"A moth
Caught in a dark vale
I flutter, searching for a light that never is
The stars that glitter
Are illusions
Traps
To catch my wings and tear them
Teeth
To consume my body.
But I will not fall.

I will paint the night…"

Frogs probably had better singing voices, but it didn't matter. As I neared the last line, some of the crowd started mouthing the words with me.

"I was told that the miners are heroes," I said. "But they are slaves, like the bonded servants working in the cities. Those fates can befall any one you, if your workshops or your farms fail, if you lose your livelihoods. As Princess Albalia, I lived a life of luxury, thanks to Sallikan. But what had Sallikan brought you, other than fear and pain? There has to be a better way to live. There has to be a better way to run this country."

Pena was at my side, his eyes venomous. I could smell his breath, the scent of sweet oranges and something acidic underneath. "You, a Halfling, you think you can tell us, true Sallonians, how to run our country? The Halfling murderers are on the march…"

I ignored him. "We have a choice. Do we choose war or peace? During my time on the road, I saw young Sallonian men taken away from their loved ones and forced into the army. Most of you would have a son or a brother or a husband or a father in the army. It is they who will die, if there's war. You will lose irrespective of who wins. Just as the riches from the Sallikan mines go to a few people at the top, the spoils of the war too will be denied to you…"

Pena tried to grab me. I stepped aside to avoid him. My foot became entangled in something. I lost my balance, fell, and was caught in mid-fall.

"Steady, Allii," Tygyrin said, his hands holding me.

I tried to twist myself free. Tygyrin let go of my shoulder.

His hand brushed my cheek.

Spooky's voice exploded inside my head.

A line of ice seared my cheek. I clutched at Tygyrin's arm. He tried to shake me off. I clung tighter. The ice in my cheek was spreading, like hot-cold lava. I tried to scream. But my mouth wouldn't open. The ice was all over my face. The sound began to fade. Tygyrin's fingers were silver. Mist was everywhere. Uncle Bernii cried my name. Spooky howled. Howled. They were gone. There was just me and Tygyrin's arm, cold flesh, hard sinews…My fingers were ice. I clutched, and clutched. I couldn't let him go. I couldn't…

9

OF ALL THE POSSIBLE ENDS

"We need to create a world where lives matter more than myths, and happiness is a greater value than tradition."
We, the Halflings – Pamphlet 4

FINGERS TRAILING MY BROW, WORK-HARDENED, YET AS gentle as a baby's breath.

I murmured, "Nana?" It wasn't Nana. It lacked something Nana's touch had.

Love.

A voice I knew but couldn't place said, "Allii?"

No, not Nana at all…

I opened my eyes and focused. Braided red hair, onyx complexion, gray eyes. Strange but familiar…

The waterfalls. Kolla, my dead-but-not-dead cousin. His Muffic mate who taught me how to make bamboo paper. Patriana, Pattii…

"Pattii?"

A smile lit up Patriana's face, turning the gray-on-gray eyes into stars. "Welcome back."

"How did you get here? What happened to Spooky, and Kolla?" I glanced around and recognized my old room. That answered the where of it.

"You are still far from well." Pattii's eyes danced a little and sobered. "But from what little I know of you, you are unlikely to take 'later' for an answer. How about the war was averted? Short, but captures the essence of the events of the last five days."

"Five days?" My left cheek throbbed. I touched it and felt not flesh, but soft cloth. "What happened to me? Why is…"

The door opened slowly. Sherby entered, carrying a covered bowl. Her eyes met mine, a glow of happiness lighting them from within.

"Sherby. How are you?"

The smile broadened into a grin and broke into a laugh. "Me, I'm fine. But we've been worried about you."

"How is everyone? Where is Spooky?" A sense of dread was clogging my heart. Was this what drowning felt like? "Is he injured? Is—is he—"

Sherby chortled. "Skulking outside, and sulking."

I fell back, my breath a sob.

The sense of dread lingered, though, like a nightmare waiting to pounce.

Sherby picked a sachet from the bedside table, emptied its contents into the bowl, stirred, and held it out to me. "Pattii's teaching me to heal people."

Pattii's moonlight smile dawned. "An excellent pupil."

The smell made me gag. The taste was worse. I gulped the brownish liquid down and made a moue of distaste. "My injury can't be worse than this."

Sherby took the bowl. "You don't remember what happened?"

The memories were all jumbled in my head. "I remember putting on the ring, and the Sallikan mines are liberated, and—oh, I sang a mining song…"

Sherby perched on the side of the bed. "Pena tried to grab you. You ducked. Your foot caught on something and you fell. Tygyrin caught you. That's what we saw. What really happened wasn't that. Tygyrin made you fall. Then he caught you and tried to jab your neck with his ring. It had a poisoned needle inside. You turned at the last moment, so it slashed your cheek. He tried to do it again, but you hung on to his arm. Then Spooky was on Tygyrin and all of you fell, you still clutching at his murdering arm." She shook her head. "It could've worked. We didn't know he was a plotter. You would've died. He would've cried. We would've believed him too. Then he becomes king…"

"When Bernalin's message reached us, Kolla and I left everything in Panda's charge and rushed here." Pattii smiled a little. "I kept you in a state of sleep, to prevent the poison from clogging your heart, and administered potions to dilute the toxin, through a cut in your arm."

I touched her hand. "Thank you for saving my life."

The eyes were gray pools again. I allowed myself to be lost in them for a while.

"We went to your valley on the way here," I said at last.

"Panda and Bernalin sent messages summoning Kolla. I didn't want him to go into danger alone. And I thought my healing abilities might be useful."

"Did—did many people die?"

"Mercifully not. There were a few skirmishes, but no major battles. Many are imprisoned—Rokkrin's sons, Sherriz, Pena, Poll…I find Sherriz fascinating. He seems to be inhabiting a different reality. He talks as if your father is still alive."

I felt a stab of sadness. Sherriz was my enemy, but he had never been Father's enemy. Having to connive in Father's murder must have destroyed him.

Pattii's fingers caressed my brow. "Very few people saw how rotten the system was behind the façade of strength and unity. It was a monolith, but all hollow inside. You somehow managed to push it at its weakest point when you told Panda to liberate the Sallikan miners. That and your possession of the Ring changed things around. Tygyrin did the rest, when he tried to kill you."

I tried to raise my brows but a stab of pain in my cheek stopped me.

Pattii smiled. "Many rescued miners came to Pinckossia with the rebels. I think the sight of them, the stories they told, did much to reconcile Sallonians to the idea of change." She paused and added, with a touch of grimness, "For now."

Sherby's lip curled. "'Tis one thing to know, another to see. Still, I won't say reconciled. They're quiet. They're watching. Best we can expect, given everything."

A memory struck me. I turned to Sherby. "You parents?"

Sherby's expression was rock hard. "Dead. Very few

survive long there."

"But how do you know?

She shrugged. "They keep records."

I caught her hand and pressed it.

Her eyes turned misty and dried up again. "Bernalin ordered the mines to be closed for now, in your name."

I frowned. "Have I become queen in my sleep?"

"Why not?" Sherby's voice throbbed with anger. "Kings and queens, rather useless if you ask me. Just take up a lot of space and create heaps of trouble too. But some people can't do without them. It's a kind of sickness. They like to be told what to do." Her smile mocked the world. "So better you than all the others."

"Inexperienced, malleable."

Pattii shook her head. "Don't underestimate the intelligence of men like Soodda. The court saw you in action. They'd hope to influence you, certainly. But they would know that you won't be clay in their hands."

I said nothing. I had nothing to say. A terrible sense of weariness weighted me down.

Sherby walked to the door, saying over her shoulder, "It's all right not to be certain about things. If you ask me, the problem with this place's that everyone was too certain about everything."

I marveled again at Sherby's capacity to boil down an entire speech to a couple of sentences.

Pattii smoothed a non-existent crease in the linen sheet. "When most descendants of the First Hundred Families are willing to make you—a Halfling and therefore a bastard, not to mention a female—their ruler, that means many of the laws and traditions that shaped, regulated and guided Sallonian existence from year zero are gone."

I tried wrinkling my brow and gave up. That hurt too. "Have you bought into Kolla's wonder-tale?"

"No, I haven't. Even if all Sallonians, Muffics, and Half-lings become sincerely reconciled with each other, other problems will remain. And new problems will come up. As long as there is conscious life, there will be pain, suffering, discontent, injustice, winners, losers. Don't let anyone tell you otherwise, because that is the wonder-tale. Still we can try to ensure that winners don't take everything and losers aren't left with nothing."

"One drop more or less—what's that to an ocean?"

"Don't despise little improvements, Allii. They are important. One bonded servant less is better, infinitely better, than one bonded servant more. Sallonians and Halflings and the few Muffics who are around are not killing each other. The mines are closed. Bonded servants are being freed. The priests are still powerful, but after Pena's treachery, they are not dominant. The planned war against Muffics has been shelved." Her shining smile dawned. "And everyone has taken to Bandikutz."

The heaviness in my head lightened a little. "Is she here?"

"Complete with a gold collar, from Bernii. She has developed a passion for carriage rides. I fear…"

The door opened to the sound of a bark. Spooky bounded in, all laughing mouth and wagging tail.

I tried to sit up. Pattii pushed me back gently. "You can't get out of bed yet. You can't dance on your bed either. If you don't behave, I'm sending Spooky out."

"I'll be as still as dead," I murmured, my fingers combing Spooky's shaggy coat, tears blinding me. "Thanks for saving me, Spooks."

He licked my uninjured cheek, the plumed tail a blur. "You saved yourself. If you hadn't bent your head in that second, you would have died. That cousin of yours…is killing each other a tradition in your family?"

A well remembered voice said. "A pardonable surmise, don't you think, my Allii?" A pair of familiar arms circled me. I laid my head on Uncle Bernii's chest, feeling like a little girl again, wishing I were back in that past before death came calling.

When I sat back, we were alone in the room.

Uncle Bernii wiped his eyes with a crumpled sleeve.

I watched him. "Nana is dead, isn't she?"

He rubbed his baldpate and nodded.

I fought back the tears. "Who killed her? Was it—Nellin?"

Bernii's voice was heavy. "Yes. She is being detained in her rooms. She refuses to go out anyway. Some people consider her a hero because she killed Rokkrin and spoke up for you."

"Did…did Nana suffer?"

"Nellin says Nana didn't resist. I believe her." Bernii sighed. "I agree with Spooky. Humans bewilder me."

Grief and horror were claws, tearing me apart. Had Nellin killed me, Nana would have killed Nellin. Both of them dealt with absolutes. In their world, which was also the world of Tygrin and Pena, limits had no place, nor did gradations.

A new fear laid its icy hands on me. Would I become like them, if I stayed here?

"Nellin confessed to another thing. She was the one who betrayed our plan to rescue you from incarceration. She discovered the details through her spies and informed Sherriz and Pena." He rubbed his baldpate again. "If not for you taking the other route, they would have killed you that night. What made you suspect a trap?"

"Minister Ekko warned me not to trust anyone. I don't know why he said it. But he sounded so desperately in earnest—"

"We looked for you everywhere. Finally I convinced myself that you must have gone Roaziyan's way."

I narrowed my eyes. "You know her?"

"Know of her."

I hesitated. "I found Mama's things. A long time ago. Books, the distance—seeing glass you gave her…"

He swallowed as if struggling with a memory and a decision. "Your mother was a very special person. Intelligent, strong, courageous, and kind, so very kind. I got to know her by chance, and we became friends. That was how your father met her. I'll never forget the way they looked at each other that first day, as if they had found the most precious thing in the world. He let her down. But he never stopped loving her." He paused as if mulling over his next words. "There were those who said your mother and I were lovers. We loved each other, but not that way." He added softly, "I don't love women that way."

Another piece of the puzzle that was the past fell into place. I understood why Bernalin had always seemed something of an outsider, why he lived away from the court, why Sallonian nobles didn't want him to be Father's heir.

One God might have four heads and seven manifestations, but he sanctioned only one kind of love.

I wasn't allowed any more visitors that day. I didn't mind. Sometimes the only company you could bear was your own.

And there was something I needed to do.

I waited until Pattii had given me my nightly medication, until she and Sherby were gone, until all human sounds ceased. Then I opened the door and peered. No one was about. I stepped out and closed the door quietly.

Going anywhere?

I jumped at the voice in my head. Spooky emerged from the shadows, red eyes shining in the dark.

I didn't see you.

That was the idea. I don't think you are allowed out of your room yet.

I have to see Nellin.

There was a pause.

Only if you let me come with you.

I smiled. *What are companions for?*

We walked towards the staircase side by side.

Each step was a step away from the present into the past. I stopped on the landing, certain that I heard a scream. I clutched the banister with a clammy hand, listening. There was nothing for my ear to hear, just silence.

The floor where Father and Bellizza had their apartments echoed with emptiness. No maids, no guards, not even a scurrying mouse. I opened the silver-studded door leading to the Queen's apartment. The passage smelled musty. The door to the sunroom was closed.

When I knocked on Nellin's door, she answered at once. Despite the lateness of the hour, she was fully dressed. She nodded at me. "I knew you would come."

I sat down in the chair Nellin indicated, and waited.

Nellin stood before me, as straight as a pillar. Her eyes never left mine, and she spoke in her usual clipped tones. "I killed Nanarina. I knew you'd never punish her. I understand. She was the only mother you knew. But she killed my queen and I couldn't let her escape justice. I went to her room with my dagger. She bent her head and bared the back of her neck to me. I waited with her until she died. She was a good woman in many ways, a descendant of the First Hundreds. I didn't want her to die alone." She went to her dressing table, opened a drawer, and took out a necklace, yellow stones with a sparkle of green. "She left this for you. She said to tell you it belonged to your mother."

I took the necklace. Inside me was a volcano.

"I have admitted my crime, Highness." Lady Nellin held her head high. Her eyes were as hard as rocks. "I await your judgment and your justice."

I put on necklace. The cool stones settled on my burning flesh. The volcano inside me died slowly, until only ashes were left.

I stood up. "You took your revenge. Now you want me to take mine." The necklace reached my waist. My fingers played with the stones. "Goodbye, Lady Nellin. Thank you for saving my life. And thank you for telling me the truth. I appreciate it."

I was allowed out the day after.

The castle had changed from the quiet orderly place it had been. It was cheerfully noisy, with all sorts of people coming in and going out. The howl of a cloud wolf or the hoot of a pink owl would not have seemed alien in it.

But in my workroom, time had stood still. Everything was in its proper place. There wasn't even a mote of dust on the table. No cobweb ornamented the walls. Tygyrin had made certain that one part of my life stayed unchanged, even as he created the maelstrom that upended the rest.

I had been yearning to check my herbaria, my plant presses. Now that I was here, in this place where life had stopped moving, all I wanted to do was flee.

I closed the door behind me and hurried down to my indoor garden. It too was flourishing; Tygyrin again. The rose-apple tree had grown into a mini-giant. I ran my hand over its trunk, feeling the shape of the whorls under my palm. The tears filled my eyes and spilled over. I leaned my forehead against the trunk, and wept.

I spent that day and the days which followed walking about, feeling like the ghost of a dead past. Sometimes I heard voices and even thought I saw people. But it couldn't be. How could I hear Father's quiet voice, or Nana's firm footsteps? How could I see Bellizza sitting by the glass wall in the sunroom, knitting a white thread-tree? They were dead. Yet they felt more real than the marble walls or the granite floors or me.

My ramblings took me to parts of the castle I had never known—kitchens and cellars, servants-quarters and pantries, unpainted rooms and musty passages. It was during one of those aimless walks I saw a familiar face. Sherby's sister, Genii, whose name I had claimed for myself during my encounter with Bänge.

"Genii."

The girl stopped and bowed.

I had always thought of Genii as little. Now standing face to face, I noticed she was actually a hand's width taller than me. It was the way she held herself that gave the impression of smallness. She stood as if she were shrinking into her own body, turning herself as insignificant as possible, as unnoticeable.

"How are you, Genii?"

She didn't look up. Her words sounded too jumbled to make sense.

We stood, me staring at Genii, she staring at the ground.

Suddenly she looked up, her eyes meeting mine. "Do you need anything, Highness?"

That look threw me, as did the tone of the voice. She sounded resigned, as if she was used to people demanding from her what she didn't want to give, as if she were habituated into giving whatever that was demanded of her.

"No, no—"

I stood aside. She bowed and walked away. Her treads were heavy, like earth was pulling extra hard at her.

⋀

That evening, I walked into a meeting of the informal Governing Council.

When I opened the heavy door, a blast of sound hit me, the clamor of many voices raised in anger. By the time I closed the door behind me, silence shrouded the room.

I bowed.

The silence was broken by a scraping of chairs and a chorus of welcomes.

When I sat down, Bernalin pushed a piece of paper towards me. The day's agenda, law, order, finances, international treaties…

I looked up. Every eye was on me. I fixed my own on the inscrutable face of Dollin, who was seated opposite. "I'd like to know what is being done to help former bonded servants and miners."

Dollin lowered her head, not before I noticed her lips curl in a smile. Bernii cleared his throat, and said, "I'm afraid we haven't discussed the matter yet."

There was another silence. General Soodda broke it. "Highness, may I express my delight at seeing you here? I hope this is the first of many visits." His voice had sincere written all over it.

I smiled at him. "Thank you, General. You'd be delighted to hear that henceforth I intend to attend these meetings regularly." I held up the piece of paper. "I'd like the issue of former bonded servants and miners to be included in today's agenda, as a matter of special interest."

General Soodda's lips thinned. He exchanged a quick look with the man next to him. The man's face was familiar, though his name escaped me. He bowed with exaggerated humility. His voice had enough oil in it to fry me. "Highness, it is indeed an important matter, but the precarious state of the royal treasury…"

I raised my eyebrows. "Pardon me, but would you mind introducing yourself please…"

The man said, without missing a beat, "My name is Jujian. I was a minister to your honored father, Highness."

I nodded. "Ah yes, you used to come with Chief Minister Sherriz to interrogate me when I was imprisoned."

There was the hiss of indrawn breaths, the sound of a laugh being turned into a cough. Jujian went from brown to red to pale. "Highness, we were all deceived by the traitor Sherriz. I was deeply unhappy about the injustice done to you, as Minister Ekko would bear witness. But I had to do my duty…"

I smiled. "Indeed, Minister, we must all do our duty. That is why I'm here. And that is why I think the relief of former miners and bonded servants should be treated as a matter of priority. That is a duty Sallonia owes her mistreated sons and daughters."

General Soodda nodded. "An important matter, Highness. But first we must secure Sallonia. Afterward, the matter must be prioritized, as you very correctly proposed." He bowed his head to me. "The defense of the realm cannot be compromised, Highness."

"Pardon me, General, but as you know I had been out of things for a while due to my injury. Please enlighten me about the current threats to the realm."

"We have many enemies, Highness."

"I want to know who they are, since it's a matter that concerns me closely."

Soodda's eyes hardened, though his voice never lost its politeness. "These are confidential matters that cannot be discussed in a forum such as this, as I was explaining to Prince Bernalin."

I looked at Bernalin. He continued to study some papers before him.

I shrugged. "General, I'm not proposing that you deliver a speech in the main square listing the names of our enemies. I understand the need for confidentiality. But this is the informal Governing Council, the right and proper forum for such a discussion."

Soodda's eyes darted to Panda, who was leaning back, arms folded, facing a closed door. "If you permit me, Highness, I will pay a call on you and explain matters further."

I smiled at him. "General, I look around this table, and I see a glimpse of what Sallonia is capable of becoming. Some of you have been on this Council for decades. Some are new to it, including myself. But all of us sitting here are guarantors of Sallonia's present peace. In this forum, openness is possible, indeed necessary."

Soodda inclined his head. His expression reminded me of the desert.

I looked around the table. "I'd like to put the matter to

a vote. Those who are for including my proposal in today's agenda, please raise your hands. We can then take a count."

Some hands were raised even before my words ended—Bernalin, Ekko, Panda, Kolla, and Dollin. Jujian was next, followed by three other ministerial types, and two nobles I recognized as distant relatives of Father. Soodda was the last.

Kolla cleared his throat. "A unanimous vote." There was a very slight tremor in his voice.

I bowed my head. "I thank all of you. Let my proposal be the last item on the agenda."

The meeting ended past midnight. I managed to win approval to set up a small group of my choice to provide relief to former miners and bonded servants.

⋊⋉

Unfamiliar days followed, full of strange challenges.

The proposal to end the daughter tax passed easily. But the proposal to end Sallikan mining didn't.

In the end, it was Sherby who won that battle, and Genii.

Sherby talked. She talked in private to ministers, priests and generals; she spoke in public to soldiers and to ordinary Sallonians. Every time, she told her story, of what happened to her parents and her sister. "No one'll want to work in those hells," she'd say at the end of some public gathering. "Raw Sallikan kills. If the mines are open, and no one wants to work in them because it's killing work, the king and ministers will find other ways to get workers. They'll once again turn us into slaves. They'll find some line in a holy book, and then there'll be a new law, and it'll be back to the old days again. And no one'll be safe, except the king and the First Hundreds. You can be rich today, but your shop can fail or your farm, then you are in debt, the next thing's you are sent to the mines."

At first, Sherby went for those gatherings alone. One day she told me that Genii wanted to go with her. She thought getting out of the castle might do Genii good. I wasn't so certain. Genii reminded me of a snowflake that'll dissolve into nothingness in the sun and the air.

Genii used to listen in silence, Sherby told me, until the day she stood up and spoke, about her life as a bonded servant.

Soon others joined them, men and women, even children, who had known mines and servitude. Their words won the battle for me. When we held the first referendum in the history of Sallonia asking people whether mines should be reopened, the no side—our side—won a resounding victory.

Acts and laws were not my only concern.

There were personal tasks to complete. I made inquiries, and discovered that Anonn, Bänge's friend, had left the army and gone home. I visited the guard Terrii's family in their little home on the outskirts of Pinckossia. His widow embraced me. "He liked you, Highness. I knew you wouldn't do him harm."

I went sightseeing in Pinckossia, not as Albalia but in

disguise. Master Hikkary was back in service, functioning as Minister Ekko's deputy, but his daughter Jaku had no official designation or duties. She was working with former miners and bonded servants and found time to accompany Spooky and me on our meanderings in Pinckossia. She knew the city well and took me everywhere. As Albalia, I would have been uncomfortable, perhaps even fearful. But in my disguise as a Sallonian, I could walk the length and breadth of the city, visiting shops, workshops, eating places and parks. Sherby joined sometimes, but she was busy with new tasks, learning healing from Pattii and administration from Ekko and Hikkary.

The complexion of Pinckossia had changed. There were many Halflings around, and even some Muffics. The city felt free and tense, on the verge of something unknowable. Sallonians aired their grievances openly, and their grievances included the open presence of Halflings and Muffics. "Can we trust a witch's spawn?" was a constant refrain, as was, "We've known worse. She hasn't done too badly…so far."

Jaku was working with the freed miners and bonded servants, trying to connect families together and setting them up in new occupations. I went with her often. Amongst these Sallonians who had experienced the darkest side of Sallonia, I felt at home.

Busy, that was what I was those weeks, busy with papers, laws, decrees, discussions and arguments. Busy was a barrier against memories, a rampart against plans. Running from one meeting to next, I had no time to wonder how my Nana became a murderess. Studying drafts and writing letters, I had no time to think where I was headed.

I was studying a draft law to regulate borrowings when Sherby burst into the room.

"Lady Nellin is dead."

We ran to Nellin's room. Pattii was already there, kneeling by the bed. She looked up when the door opened, her face ashen. "She killed herself."

I turned to Nellin's maid who huddled by the bed weeping. "What happened?"

"She told me to get some notepaper," the girl whispered, through sobs. "When I came back—when I—"

"She came running to me." Pattii's voice was toneless. "Nellin was dead when I reached her." She paused and added, her voice heavier than I had ever heard it, "She had used her own dagger."

I knelt by the bed, partly because my legs could no longer hold me. Nellin's face looked as hard in death as it had been in life, the lips pressed tightly together, the muscles taut.

I turned away, feeling like a used cloth, washed and wrung dry too many times.

⋈

That evening I paid the visit I had been evading with no conscious thought.

Tygyrin was being detained in his own apartment in

the North wing of the castle. He was terminally ill and not expected to last until the end of his trial. Spooky's bite wound wasn't healing. Since Spooky was a daemon-dog, the wound needed something more than what Sallonian physicians could give. "I wanted to try," Pattii had told me with a lopsided smile. "But he doesn't want to be touched by me."

He greeted me in his usual manner, kissing first my hand and then my cheek, the one he stabbed. The wound had healed, but the scar remained, and would remain—a diagonal slash of angry red, puckering my skin and making one eye seem smaller than the other. "Cousin, it is good to see you. You look well."

I noticed that he limped a little and caught the faint smell of rotting flesh.

"I wish you'd allow Pattii to treat you," I said in a rush.

An eyebrow went up. "Dearest Allii, I might be a captured lion, but not a tamed one."

"You know you are being silly." I used the adjective deliberately; I wanted to make him feel infantile.

His nostrils flared, and his lips thinned. But when he spoke, his voice was even. "My principles are sacred. They don't change depending on circumstances, unlike my foppish brother."

I hid a grin. Tawni had written to me, several times, expressing eternal fealty.

"I'm not trying to undermine your principles," I said. "I'm just telling you to allow a Muffic to treat you."

"Not allowing myself to be profaned by the touch of a witch is one of my principles."

"You touch me. You even kissed me."

"I didn't mean to."

"I had the impression you rather liked it."

His eyes flashed. "You are my uncle's daughter. We share ancestors, we share blood. We are kin." His eyes caught and held mine. "I wouldn't have touched your mother."

Anger bubbled inside me. Since I didn't trust myself to say the right thing, whatever that was, I said nothing.

"I don't see the point of being healed," Tygyrin said. "I have been told that the death penalty is not operative in this new Sallonia of yours. Very disobliging of you, my Allii. I would have welcomed a public execution. The idea of spending a lifetime in prison doesn't appeal to me."

This conversation was going nowhere. I changed the topic. "Was it you who set tracker-assassins after me?"

"Ah, you learnt about that. And lived to tell the tale. I'm impressed."

"So it was you."

He bowed. "My idea, certainly. But it wasn't just my doing." He paused, watching me. I knew he was waiting for frenzied questions and said nothing. Just sat there, my hands resting on my lap, giving him look for look.

He waited some more and shrugged. "Sherriz kept your father informed. Your father approved the funds. Sherriz told him, 'Sire, the princess will be taken care of.' Interesting phrasing, don't you think, one that is open to many different interpretations? Sherriz meant one thing and your father probably understood something else. Probably." He smiled. "Ruling is not a fit occupation for the faint-hearted. You will come to understand these compulsions, someday."

I remained silent.

Tygyrin shrugged again. "Sherriz thought Pena and he were a team. He didn't know that Pena and I were working together. Pena was my religious instructor. We had been allies for a long time, even when old Hiro was Chief Priest."

I couldn't help myself. "Ideological soul-mates?"

He smiled. "We were appalled by the growing laxity in Sallonian society. We felt that a strong hand was heeded, and a pure one."

"Father loved you like a son."

Tygyrin flushed. "At first we had no intention of going against your father. We were willing to wait. Then we heard about Bernii's plans to change the succession laws. We had reason to believe that even some of the First Hundreds were willing to consider the idea." His smile was wry. "Anything to keep my father away from the throne, I suppose. It's a sentiment I fully understand and even sympathize with. Still it turned waiting into a non-option."

"But why did you have to kill Bellizza? Why not just arrange an accident for me?"

He gave that wry smile again. "The idea was discussed, and dismissed as impractical. Nanarina guarded you too well. We were also uncertain of your father's reaction."

"So you killed Bellizza who had showed you nothing but kindness," I cried. "I thought you liked her."

His gaze turned contemptuous. "Like and dislike never came into it."

"What came into it then, Tygyrin?"

He stared, his eyes flashing, then shrugged. "I suppose all of this will come out in the trial. Pena will vomit out whatever he thinks will help him."

"You can defend yourself. You will have every chance."

If looks could shrivel, this one would have. "Do you think I care about your mongrel justice?"

"Then just tell me why you got Bellizza killed. I have a right to know."

"We had to get rid of you in such a way that both you and your father were discredited. The witch's spawn killed the queen. How did the witch's spawn come about? Because the king betrayed his own kind."

"So for that you arranged the murder of a woman who never did you any harm?"

"I don't expect you to understand my reasons. How can you? You are not a Sallonian. But let me tell you, cousin, your father did."

"Don't lie. Papa had no hand in Belle's death."

"When Sherriz showed Bellizza's brother's letter to your father, his response was, 'Get the queen away.' His exact words. Pena then showed the letter to Nana. After that Nana was putty in Pena's hands."

I lowered my eyes and dug my nails into my hands, the pain distracting me from the questions I didn't want answered.

Still a coward. But sometimes survival needed a dose of cowardice.

Tygyrin noticed. Of course he noticed. He smiled, that slow smile. "You played right into our hands, cousin, with your rose-apples. The rest was easy. The only loose end was Nana. Sherriz and Pena wanted her silenced. I insisted that her life be spared."

I said, softly, "Thank you."

He shrugged. "She was one of us. I was fond of her. I presume you know by now how she died."

I nodded, pursing my lips to still their trembling.

He waited, his eyes never leaving me.

"Why did you speak against Uncle Rokkrin taking the throne?" I asked at last. "Was it to deceive people into thinking you had no hand in my father's murder?"

He flashed a look of contempt. "There was no need. No one knew of my involvement. I was sincere when I spoke against my father in the Council. He was being unpardonably stupid. He faked a will. He didn't have the Ring. He was in an unseemly hurry. It wasn't the way. I wanted to defeat the Halflings and finish off the Muffics. That way no one would have opposed my father claiming the crown. But the fool thought he knew better."

"Would you have killed Uncle Rokkrin next, to make way for King Tygyrin?"

I had hoped to needle him; he just shrugged. "There was no need. Provide my father with some distractions and he would have allowed us to run things our way."

"I suppose you got one of your spies to inform Nellin about my presence in the castle. You would have known that she'd tell your father and he'd get rid of me."

"Guilty as charged." His smile turned warm, caressing. "I did it with utmost regret though."

I repressed a shudder.

"I should have known my father would botch it," Tygyrin's voice was low, musing. "Thanks to his criminal incompetence, Sallonia has fallen to her enemies."

I frowned. "I understand you wanting to defeat the

rebellion. But why go to war with Muffics? They were not a threat. You would have known that."

"Not a threat, but a hindrance. We are running out of Sallikan. The remaining deposits are in the lands the Muffics occupy. They must be removed to free the land. War was the only way. But your father wouldn't permit it. Had he allowed it, none of this would have happened. We had to get rid of him because he was standing in the way of Sallonia's continued greatness in the world."

"You talk about Sallonia's greatness. You knew of the horrors visited on miners and bonded servants. You helped save Sherby's sister. A country that enslaves its own people has no greatness."

He nodded. "For once, Allii, I agree with you. That was one of the reasons I wanted power. I was going to change things, end bonded servitude, free miners…"

"But you want to continue with the mines. You just said so."

He leaned forward, and spoke slowly, as if he was talking to an intellectually disabled child. "Allii, I was going to free Sallonians, compensate them for past injustice, secure their future. We don't need Sallonians to run mines. There are enough Halflings. And perhaps Muffics, once the land is liberated from them. Sallonia owes all Sallonians a decent, safe life. But for Muffics and Halflings, Sallonia owes nothing."

I couldn't bear it any more. I got up.

He too rose to his feet, with some difficulty. "I never liked the way they lied to you. It was stupid and I don't like stupid."

"Which is why I wish you'd allow Patriana or some other Muffic to take a look at your leg."

"It will get worse, and I will die. Probably suffer too. Do you think I'm a weakling like my brothers? I've done my duty by my kind and my God. I will be reincarnated to complete my God's work, to bring Sallonia back to him in a state of sanctity. Why should I fear death when the future is mine?"

I stared at him, unable to believe my ears. "You mean you truly believe that the First Hundreds keep on getting reincarnated in the same set of families?"

"Of course, Allii."

There was no mistaking the fervent glow in those eyes. I had always thought Pena was the true believer. Now I realized it was Tygyrin.

I held out my hand. He took it "So the Ring of Sallonia has become a woman's trinket."

"Better a woman's trinket than a symbol of oppression and intolerance."

His fingers tightened on my hand. His eyes were brown fires. "What is a man—or a woman—without blood and faith?"

I extracted my hand from his grip, but didn't avert my eyes from his burning gaze. "Human."

Nellin's suicide cracked my cocoon of busyness. Tygyrin's revelations obliterated it, forcing me, freeing me, to confront the past and face the future.

"I need to think through things and make some decisions," I told Spooky that evening.

He stared at me for a while. "Don't rush into anything."

The next six days, I limited myself to the work that I had to do, giving myself time to remember and think. As the sixth day dawned I made a surprising discovery.

When I did things only I could do, I had nothing much to do.

That evening, I sought Minister Ekko. He and Master Hikkary were seated in what had once been Sherriz's official chamber, working on some documents.

"Must we always have kings or queens?" I asked in a rush.

Ekko and Hikkary both looked at me, their gazes sharp. Hikkary glanced down quickly. Ekko said, "Well, that is the norm."

"I've read about places which do quite well without."

Hikkary said, his voice carefully neutral, "You are probably referring to the city-state of Sammalore, Highness. I'd call it an exception that proves the rule."

"Why do you say that?"

"Highness, they've had eight centuries of practice."

I turned the pages of a ledger near me. "But for them too, there would have been a day one and a year one."

No one said anything. The only sound in the room was the steady clicking of an air-clock.

Ekko said, "You want to talk to me, Highness."

I turned some more pages before getting up. "Yes, some-day soon."

※

The evening after the law banning Sallikan mining came into effect, I visited the dead—the tombs of Father and Nana in the First Hundred Cemetery and Bellizza's tomb in the Consorts' Cemetery.

That night I went in search of Bernii. He was alone in his room, writing a letter.

"I talked to Tygyrin last week."

He nodded.

"He wanted me to believe that Papa indirectly ordered Bellizza's murder. I don't think so. But I think he knew it could happen and did nothing to stop it. Just as he did nothing to stop me from being persecuted for a crime I didn't commit."

Bernii passed the pen from hand to hand. "You can't live in the past, love. It's all over and done with."

"It's over, yes. But not done with. The past is hardly ever done with. I don't want to live in the past. But I can't stop the past from living inside me. If I don't face it, it will possess me, and I won't even know."

Bernii's brows went up. "So?"

I could feel myself getting angry, whether with him or with myself I had no idea. Probably both. "So, I had to make sense of why Papa and Nana did what they did."

"And have you done so?"

I felt the anger seeping out, leaving in its place a curious sense of emptiness. "No. I've thought about it and thought about it, but it makes no sense." I licked my suddenly dry lips with a tongue that was not too moist either. "But I might, if I become the queen and remain queen for long enough."

"You are talking in riddles now."

I ignored the intervention. "If I accept the crown, I claim Sallonia for my own. My property. My possession. And the worst part is I want to be queen. I've come to like the idea. Too much. If there are challenges to my rule, as there will be, I'm scared of how I might meet them—violence, spying on people, things I abhor now. Staying here is not a risk I can afford to take. If I do, I might end up becoming someone I don't like, another Nellin, another Nana, another Papa, maybe even another Tygyrin."

He shook his head. "Never that, love, never that. There's too much of your mother in you."

"Papa loved Mama. You said so. He was fond of Bellizza. I think he cared for me a little. Yet he betrayed all three of us, because for him tribe mattered most. Nana was the kindest creature in the world. She wouldn't harm a fly, literally. Yet she killed Bellizza. What guarantee do I have that I won't turn out the same way some day?"

Bernii's gaze moved away from me.

I chose my words carefully. "A girl I met on the road said that kings never helped anyone but themselves. Sherby recently told me that kings and queens just take up a lot of space and create heaps of trouble. I think they are both right. I've been thinking about this. Must Sallonia have a king or a queen? Surely there are other ways of governing a country?"

He said, "Well kings are the norm."

"We have done the unthinkable. Why not continue

along that path for a while more and see how it works? Why not let the Governing Council govern? It has performed quite well so far. Its composition needs to be changed of course, to include more Halflings and Muffics. That way it can be representative of the new Sallonia."

He stared hard at me. "There won't be any agreements only arguments."

"We've had too much conformity in this place. You know where that got us. There's nothing wrong with arguments. And sooner or later, there'll be agreements."

He sighed. "And what will you do?"

"If I stay here, Sallonia can never be free to grow into a republic. I will be in the way. My stances would weigh too much, either positively or negatively. I will also be a figure of contention, queen to some, usurper to others." I smiled. "There is another reason, a very selfish one. When I was on the road, all I wanted was to discover the identity of the killer and get back home. Now I'm here, I realize I was never happy here. I was happiest while I was a fugitive, running for my life. I never felt so alive, so free, ever. I want that feeling again, that sense of being alive, being free."

He sighed again. "Are you certain about this?"

"As certain as I can ever be about anything. Papa, Nana, Nellin and even Bellizza, they all allowed birth to dictate their lives. I will not. I don't want my birth to limit me to a preordained path. I want to find my own way, to succeed and fail on my own terms." I grinned. "Only stories have neat ends. Life is too messy, too confusing."

Bernii leaned forward to kiss my brow. "Well, that's not a conclusion I can quarrel with."

The hardest part was telling my friends about my decision.

Each took the news in different ways.

Spooky was skeptical. He didn't think leaving made much sense. "Take a holiday by all means," he said. "You've earned it. But your place is here, queen or not. Don't run away."

"I'm not running away."

"Of course you are. The responsibility scares you. You don't want to make hard decisions. So you are copping out."

I shook my head. "You are right about me being scared of the responsibility, or not wanting to make certain decisions. But that's not the real reason I want to leave. I want to leave because I don't want to be bound. Here I will always be a princess and a Halfling. Here I'm like a camel, carrying my birth like a hump on my back, for good or ill. But on the road, I'm whatever I can make of myself. Maybe I'm nothing if I'm not a princess and a Halfling. Maybe I'll fail at everything I do. How can I know one way or the other, unless I try it out?"

Spooky flapped an ear. "Seems daft to me. I was born a daemon-dog. I can't become a cat, simply because I like the idea of being a cat. Not that I want to, of course. I'm just trying to tell you that you can't run away from yourself."

"I'm not running away from myself, Spooks. I'm running away to find myself, whether I can be something more than a Halfling and a princess. Maybe I'll return with my tail between my legs. But I have to try. If I don't break out of the confines that bind me, I'll never find out what I can be. And

I can never break out of those confines, if I stay here."

Spooky said nothing. I wondered if he didn't want me to leave, because he didn't want to leave.

"You don't have to come with me, you know," I said.

He threw me a contemptuous look and walked away.

"You don't, you know," I cried after him. "I can manage on my own. You are not bound to me." I stopped, my voice on the verge of breaking, my eyes smarting.

He didn't turn. But his voice thundered inside my head. *Good luck.*

Sherby wanted to join me.

"I'd love your company, Sherby. But there's work here to do. I've nominated you to the Governing Council in my place." I smiled at the shock on her face. "That is my gift to the new Sallonia, you."

Panda proved to be more understanding than I feared. He listened to me in silence and said, "You are doing the wrong thing by Sallonia. But this is probably the right thing for you." His smile was rueful. "Your mother would have approved."

I gawped at him. "You knew her?"

"I worked for her and your father when they were together. Then your father became king and you were born and she died…Your father got me down here. I always kept an eye on you, partly because of her." He turned his face away.

I gulped. "Did my father know——?"

He finished the question for me. "That I was a Halfling? I've no idea. If he did, he didn't let on. He was a weak man, but he tried in his own way."

I nodded, grateful for that epitaph.

Kolla tried to stop me. And failed. Pattii just asked, "Where will you go?"

"There are forests no one has ever explored. They should keep me busy for a long time. But before I leave Sallonia, there's someone I must visit."

The gray eyes were pins, holding me down. "Will she let you in?"

"She owes me a life. My mother's." I didn't wait for a response but walked up to Bandikutz. The little dog was seated on a cushioned chair licking a fat paw with fastidious care. "I hope you won't be too disappointed in me, Bandikutz."

Bandikutz glanced up from her task. "Not at all, Allii. I understand. Some people are not born to rule."

10

A BRIDGE OF LIGHT

"Only we the Halflings can become a bridge between Sallonians and Muffics, because they are our parents and we are their children."
We, the Halflings – Pamphlet 1

As a dying sun turned the sky into a medley of red and gold, I followed Spooky through a thick wall of vegetation and emerged onto a meadow of unruly grasses and butter-yellow wildflowers. The single dead tree, its branches twisted into bird-shapes, stood like a sentinel over the stone and timber cottage. The curtains were drawn and the chimney smoking.

I stared at the cottage for a while and turned around to ask Spooky if he were coming in with me.

He wasn't there.

We hadn't talked much since we had that argument

about me leaving. The subject never came up again. He didn't say he'll join me. I didn't ask.

Now he was gone, without even a word of goodbye.

Anger, hurt, a grief that was sharper than every other grief I had known assailed me. I wanted to howl like a wolf.

I stood still, until the urge to turn myself into a spectacle faded. After all, Spooky had done enough for me. If he wanted to return to his life, how could I blame him? I pretended to believe it, because it felt noble, because I had no other choice.

One of the curtains twitched a little. I looked about. The trees were still.

I squared my shoulders, walked to the cottage and rapped at the dragon-knocker.

Roaziyan opened the door. She looked like herself, tall, thin, angular with the sharpness of knives.

I met those depthless eyes, not gray pools like Pattii's but black holes. "Thank you for letting me in, Grandmother."

She nodded and stepped away from the door.

There was no food on the table.

"So your nurse killed your stepmother," Roaziyan said after I sat down. It was a statement, not a question. I wondered how long she had known it.

"Pena put her up to it. But the real author of the plan was Tygyrin." Still making excuses for Nana, I thought. Perhaps I always will.

"Rokkrin's eldest son." Another statement.

"He thought things were getting lax. He wanted Sallonia to return to purity. I never suspected him because he wasn't ambitious for himself. He was just consumed by an idea.

Spooky bit him when he stabbed me. The wound never healed. He died two days ago."

Silence filled the room.

Roaziyan broke it at last. "I see you are wearing that accursed ring."

I smiled a little. "My father left it to me. By taking it off before he died, he freed himself from the burden of kingship. By giving it to his Halfling daughter, he freed Sallonia from its past."

Roaziyan said nothing.

"Sallonia is not a kingdom anymore. It officially became a republic last week. We have created a new set of laws. We have set up a new way of ruling. But for these to work, more Muffics are needed. If Muffics aren't adequately represented in the new Governing Council, their voices will be faint, and their interests neglected. That will be a pity because this is the only chance any of us have."

The claw-like nails tapped the table. "Why are you telling me this?"

"Because you, and others like you, should not stand in the way of your people. Let them come out and join the new Sallonia." I took a deep breath. "We have to pay our debts. I've paid mine. Now it's your turn, Grandmother. My mother died because you rejected your daughter. You owe me a life. Get out into the real world. Sallonia cannot belong to Muffics alone, anymore than it can belong to Sallonians alone. Cleaving to the past will not help anyone. The world is not a bubble."

Roaziyan's glance was withering. "I see that you have a fondness for platitudes, like your mother."Like my mother!

I could feel the smile tugging at my lips. "I think platitudes are platitudes because they contain timeless truths." I sobered. "Pena and Tygyrin were planning to unleash a war on Muffics. Everyone thought it was a political ploy to unite Sallonians behind a King Rokkrin. That was one of the reasons, but not the most important one. Sallonia is running out of Sallikan. The remaining deposits are in the lands occupied by Muffics. Mining is banned now, but who can know the future? If there are enough Muffics on the Governing Council, they can fight against any attempt to restart mining."

The silence was long, or perhaps it just felt so.

"What will you do?" Roaziyan asked at last.

"That's what I want to find out. Maybe discover new plants, something I've always wanted to do. Maybe investigate crimes. Maybe just see the world and get back to Sallonia when I'm done with being a vagabond." I spoke the next words both to her and to myself. "Sallonia is trying to find a new identity for herself. I too want to know who I really am."

Roaziyan went up to the window and stood with her back to me. When she spoke, it was as if her voice were coming from another world. "Do you want me to erase your scar, make it disappear?"

The scar started throbbing, and I put my hand to it. When Pattii's attempts to efface it failed, I had been devastated. Now I had a chance to get rid of that disfigurement.

My fingers lingered on the puckered skin. The deep line had a familiar feeling, as if it were a part of me, the new me.

"I think I'll keep it." I walked up to Roaziyan and kissed

her cheek. "Thank you for letting me in, Grandmother. Will you please let me out now?"

One moment, I was walking in a flower-draped meadow. The next moment I was on a sun-baked plain staring at a dragon and a daemon-dog.

I knelt on the dusty ground and cried, with relief, with happiness. Spooky came up to me and licked my hand. I put my arms around him, feeling whole.

Brunelles said, "Bernii sent me a message. Thought you could do with a ride to wherever you are going. And this pesky dog says he is going with you."

I turned to Spooky. "Are you certain you want to come with me? You don't have to. You've more than paid your dues to Roaziyan."

"This is nothing to do with her. This is between you and me. Dues don't come into this. Neither one of us owes the other anything, except friendship." His mouth opened in a canine grin. The tail blurred. "I decided I like this idea of pushing boundaries. Who knows what I might discover about myself?"

I laughed and clambered to my feet. We walked, side by side, toward the waiting dragon.

SOMEDAY, SOMETIME

THE TREE HAD A DELICATE BEAUTY, WITH SMALL BLUE-green leaves and clusters of feathery white flowers. Its branches twisted and curved into works of art.

But it was the trunk that held us spellbound. The tall column was streaked in a symphony of blues.

Spooky circled it, his eyes glittering in the gloom of the forest's evening. "I knew trees could be pretty strange, but this?"

I touched the trunk, soft and grainy. "Neither did I. I have never read of a tree like this or even heard of one."

He looked at me. "Ah, so you've discovered your first new tree. How will you name it?"

Mother died and took the memories with her. Bellizza died and left the memories behind her, her gift to me.

I blinked back the tears, turned around, and bowed to

Spooky, one hand resting on the trunk of the tree. "Meet Anumata Bellizza."

"And what does it mean?"

This time, tears didn't blotch my smile. "Beloved Bellizza."

ACKNOWLEDGMENTS

Fairytales were the first tutors of humanity, Walter Benjamin said in Illuminations. Fairytales, in their original versions, are stories of crime and punishment, suffering and redemption. The world they depict is the world we know, a place where dysfunctional families are as common as murder and betrayal, homes could be both havens and traps, and kindness—or its absence—to even an ant could be life-changing (the first inkling of the Butterfly effect?). But fairytale does more than depict dark gritty reality; it also offers the leaven of rebellious hope calling magic to its aid.

I will paint the night was born from every fairytale I know. My first thanks go to my grandmother who introduced me to the terrifying and wonderful world of fairytales. You showed me the way in and the way out. The stones you left behind still guides me.

If I mention all the critique partners and beta readers who helped me make this book that might become a book in itself, at least a novella. But I must mention Cez Apello who showed me many of the ropes of fiction writing and Joe Williams who read and commented on every version of this book and every story I ever wrote. Thank you, Cez,

Joe, and everyone else. Without your time and care, this book would never be.

For a literary unknown to find an agent/publisher is a bit like Sisyphus and his labors with the rock. My eternal gratitude to the team at Fractured Mirror Publishing for taking this chance on me. Thank you especially Emily for the instructive editing and Allison for your patience and forbearance. It has been a learning process in more ways than one.

Most of the characters in this book lived their first lives as dogs. A few were mine (or rather I was theirs). Many I knew. This is a minute return for the light and the happiness you brought me.

Like most families, mine is functional and dysfunctional. Good or bad, I need you. To my found family, my indispensable friends, life wouldn't be life without you.

And thanks above all to FP, who makes the impossible possible.

Please…

A million thanks for buying *I Will Paint the Night* and another million for reading to the end. Hope you loved it, liking is fine too, even hate is ok. Please consider leaving an honest review on your favorite store and sites and social media

ABOUT THE AUTHOR

Sam Muller loves dogs and books and spends much time saving one from the other. *I Will Paint the Night* is her first novel. She is currently finalizing the second installment of investigative adventures of Allii and Spooky.

Her short stories can be found in Cosmic Roots and Eldritch Shores, Voyage YA by Uncharted, Apparition Lit, Pedestal Magazine, Wyldblood Magazine, anthologies by Third Flatiron, Deep Magic, Brigid's Gate Press, Air and Nothingness Press, Sans Press, Worldstone Publishing, and Water Dragon Publishing, among others.

CONTINUE READING FOR
AN INSIDE LOOK AT THE
NEXT PART OF ALLII AND
SPOOKY'S JOURNEY IN

PEOPLE OF DUST

THE NIGHT BEFORE

ENTRE — THE BLUE MOON

"Lu stares at the ember screen, at the innumerable pinpricks of fire. Her hands scrub the marble floor. Sights and sounds from the afternoon throb in her mind, like a freshly-opened wound. The hanging trees, the echoing words: People of dust, Obedience, Humility, Hard work…back to Obedience, the chorus of their lives."
Unwinged – Page 1

HE SMILED AT THE BLUE MOON, ALWAYS HIS FAVORITE. EVEN during his distant childhood he had loved nights like this when the red and the yellow moons were absent and the sapphire queen owned the sky.

Across the white-stone road the eatery, *Pegala on a Plate,* was beginning its busiest hour, tables in the large garden sloping down to river Akash filling up already. The place was famed for its range of dishes from across the world, including rarities like black rosewater toffee from Salliyan Kingdom and purple truffle salad from the Republic of Sheebatiya. He had not been there since he hired Allii as part-time help. Her dishes had a spontaneity the curated fare of the eatery lacked. She played with ingredients making them sing. Like the dessert she created with parrot-mangoes and sugarcane yesterday. For the duration of that sweet, he had even forgotten the skeletal fingers of danger throttling his life.

Several air-clocks in the chronometers three doors down rang the hour in perfect melody. Eight. He stepped inside the bookshop and closed the door, locking and bolting it. The new ritual. In the thirty-eight years of bookselling, he had never bothered to lock doors. Sammalore was a safe city. And his shop didn't stock valuable books, only new releases. Any book published in any country within one year, he had in his shop. An oddity and a boast that also gave the bookshop its name, *Common Place*.

Inside, he locked and bolted the windows before picking up his copy of *Unwinged,* the cover depicting a white feather falling from a gray sky. A book was a feast, and not just for the mind. A book appealed to every one of the senses— the sight of the colors, the touch of the paper, the crinkly sound, and special smell. Books were his first and greatest love: bookselling the only occupation he ever wanted. A predictable and a safe life, until Patz disappeared on the ten-minute walk from *Bookends*, his ocean front bookshop, and his home by the beach full of childish laughter and dog barks. Two weeks later, Frika had vanished while on her customary night-stroll. Last month it was Jube, spirited away from her locked and guarded home. Gone, neither dead nor alive, but vanished like snowflakes melting into the general sludge.

He extinguished the central illuminator, picked up the small firestone, and went to the living quarters, bolting and checking doors, thinking, *Soon I'd see nothing abnormal in living like a cornered animal.*

The air-clock was chiming nine by the time he finished his bath and headed to the kitchen. Allii had kept the windows open, and the kitchen was cool with river breeze. His mouth made a moue of distaste as his gaze settled on the iron grilles imposed on the windows. The city guards had been in the shop and the house three times, checking for vulnerabilities, making polite suggestions which were really orders: *Why don't you get some grilles set up over your windows, Master Khuti. Let the wind in and keep the troublemakers out (ha, ha!). And we know just the woman for the job. She'll be coming this way tomorrow morning, at your convenience of course.*

His dinner was on the table. Allii came every evening, leaving his dinner on the table, his breakfast and lunch neatly packed in the cold cellar. The monetary payment was only a part of the arrangement; what she really wanted was a chance to borrow books from his library. Telling her to make enough food for two and take her share home had been his idea.

Beside the covered dishes of food was a bowl of water filled with star-jasmines, their subtle scent a relaxant. It was a tradition from her homeland, Allii had told him. More an act of kindness, he mused. The young woman wasn't always truthful, but she was invariably kind. She hadn't seemed all that different from everyone else who fled the fires of Kharimi, the same faraway look in the eyes as if they had seen too much, the same unwillingness to talk about what she had experienced, the same wariness and weariness.

It was Spooky, her dog, who had given her away, if dog he were.

The three dishes were labeled in Allii's neat hand, the hand of someone at home with writing. Fiery mushroom ismoru, the finely shredded pink fungi floating lazily in a dark red gravy, saffron rice balls in a smaller dish, and on a side plate two treacle and gingerly cakes with a small jug of cream by it. He inhaled the combined scents before breaking the rice balls into the gravy. Allii had once said that she learned cooking on the road, a matter of survival that turned into a pastime and something else. "A way of gaining little control over life, I suppose. I love reading, but when you read you are adrift in somebody else's creation. Cooking is the opposite. You decide what goes in and therefore what comes out. Cooking also gives me a chance to play with plants. I once kept a..." Her voice had trailed off and her face tightened, deepening the lines on her scarred cheek. "Plants are fascinating, aren't they?"

He scraped the last of the food with a forefinger, stacked the dishes in the stone trough for later, heated the pot of cinnamon cream in the clay oven, and took it into the reading bay. He had lit the incense block earlier and the subtle sense of jasmine filled the niche. He relaxed into the rocking chair and picked up *Unwinged*. The book had made The List when it was nothing more than a rumor in publishing circles. The notoriety had driven up sales, unsurprisingly, for many wanted to know why Pegala's greatest power would bother its imperial head over a work of fiction.

He inhaled and exhaled deeply a few times and took a long sip of the cinnamon cream. He opened the book, giving his mind over to prose that reminded him of the sea, slow and sleepy for a page or two, other than the occasional choppy sentence, then with scarce warning rearing and roaring, like a monster demented. He was currently in a placid place. *The mountainsides are covered with snail-grass, and in that green sea finding kanga herbs needs patience and commitment. But patience and commitment are functions of freewill, and Lu, made a slave by a war waged when she was a babe, possesses neither. She has no memories of freedom having lost it with the home she was born into and the mother who bore her…*

DAY ONE

1

A NEW PATCH TO CLEAN

"Lu brushes the covers and the spine of each book with the cloth-duster. Books are universes, Sabha once told her. She yearns to visit them, to know them. He is teaching her how to read, but the progress is slow. For their time together is short and illicit, the fear of discovery a menacing shadow over the joy of being with each other."
Unwinged – Page 13

YESTERDAY, THEY ALLOCATED ME A NEW PATCH TO CLEAN, from the Sailor's Colonnade through the College of Mechanists, from the Black Swan Bridge to the Silent Grove, the city's main cemetery. Twice the size of my previous patch which stretched from the Gateway Bridge to the Theatre of the Souls. In that place, old hands maintained, one could find anything, from a dead body to a purse of gold; all you had to do was to look hard enough and dig deep enough. Two bodies were discovered in my seven months there, but of that fabled purse of gold there was no sign.

My new supervisor glared at me when I peeped into his narrow office after knocking on the half-open door. He had been checking a list. Now his pen hovered like a weapon over the piece of paper. His brows, thick and pale yellow, formed a bridge above a flat nose. His reputation as a hard taskmaster was well known. No surprise in that. He was in charge of the political heartland of the city, where the rulers lived and ruled. They deserved nothing but the best, at least in their own estimation.

"I have been assigned to Districts 21 and 22," I said.

His eyes narrowed, as if he couldn't believe my words. "What is your name?"

"Allii."

He peered at the long distance as if he were considering my name for measure and finding it falling short by yards. "Just Allii? Nothing more?"

"Nothing more." Allii had the advantage of being as common as sand in a desert. When you were Allii, you could be from anywhere in Pegala.

Albalia was another matter. It was a product of my birthland's history. After a princess of that name became an empress of Kikilonia, it became a popular choice for daughters, be they princesses or peasants. It wasn't a particularly beautiful name, not the name I would have chosen for myself had I the opportunity. But in a culture where marrying up was a woman's greatest achievement, that original Albalia had reached the pinnacle.

My new supervisor's gaze was hovering around me like a vampire-moth. I stood my ground, an attitude I was good at.

He pulled another piece of paper toward him and studied it. His face grew graver. "You are here to replace Hiro." He sounded as if Hiro's death was somehow my fault.

I said nothing. Silence was another thing I was good at.

His abrasive gaze flitted over my scar and crawled over my face, probably trying to identify my origins from my appearance. I responded with a polite smile, knowing he would fail. Copper hair and copper skin, I've discovered, was a common look in north-eastern Pegala, a vast stretch of territory ranging from the windy Kangha plains to the Belzo mountains, all of its many lands menaced by the rapidly elongating reach of the Kikilonian Empire.

He shrugged, opened a drawer, and threw a small card and a badge at me. I caught both easily, thanked him, left.

The dawn air rippled with the contrasting smells of the river and the sea, flower farms and forests. I pinned the badge to my brown tunic and headed to the depot next door to collect my cleaning equipment. The depot manager, bushy haired and goateed, barely glanced at me. He peered at the card and waved a vague hand in the direction of a row of cupboards before returning to his book. As I walked past I peered over his shoulder and caught the title: *Unwinged.* The latest entrant to The List.

The man turned around, vagueness gone. "What are you peeping at?" He had closed the book and was covering it with his arm.

"Sorry," I said hurriedly. "I didn't mean to pry. It's just

that I've been wanting to read that book ever since I heard about it. The price is too steep though." I shrugged and smiled, waiting for conversation to get off the ground and fly, about *Unwinged* and everything else, related or not. A good way to start the day. Maybe even the beginning of a friendship.

In Sammalore, books were bridges.

There was no returning smile, no offer to lend the book once it was finished. Instead, the depot manager looked me up and down, put the book inside a drawer, and started studying a ledger.

What in the name of stars is this? I wondered, opening the cupboard with the right number. Have I come across that rarest of rare things, a Sammalorian who rejected an open invitation to share his or her view of the world?

Or was Sammalore going the way of Kharimi? Maybe Spooky was right in his unvarying opinion, expressed in his driest tone: *The only safe place is the jungle, even for a human.*

For most Sammalorians, the day was still an hour away. Other than a few pedestrians and two or three mechanical carriages, the streets were deserted. In my pervious patch, the noise would have begun by now, carts, animals, people. This area had more trees than buildings. The litter was mostly leaves and twigs; the bird droppings made incomprehensible patterns on the smooth stone blocks.

The work fell into its own rhythm soon: sweep, short deep strokes; gather the leaves into neat pile; dump them in the cart; use the dust snapper for final mopping up, scrub the bird droppings off. As I worked, the familiar sense of peace descended on me. Having immersed myself in my task, I could also escape it. Normally my mind would roam deep and far, from ocean depths to deep space. Today it settled on fate of booksellers, one among them in particular. He'd be safe, he had to be safe in a house turned into a fortress…

The Black Swan Bridge marked the beginning of District 22, a tiny commercial enclave of shops and cafes, a miniature woodland, and the cemetery. The last building, just before the tree line began, was a café, *Happy Tummy.* Hiro, who had handled this patch for years, often recommended its excellent beverages, saying that they were better pick-me-ups on a bad morning than any alcohol.

Maybe I'd take a look in once I was settled into my new routine.

The next was the cemetery, the metropolis of dead within the metropolis of living. Not all the dead. Getting buried there was expensive business if you didn't have a family plot.

Like in life, you got a head start in death if you had the right connections.

The main entrance to the cemetery was an ornate affair, wrought iron gates painted in bluish-green flanked by two gate houses done in pale yellow marble. As I waited for the gatekeeper, I tried to calculate the cost of this construction. The marbles would have been brought from the quarries in the Klemmii District, two days drive away even in the fastest mechanical carriage. The cost would have covered the upkeep of the city's army of street cleaners for several years.

The gatekeeper examined my badge. He was an old man, a little bent, skin wizened like the barks of ancient trees, eyes slightly milky. His expression was not unfriendly. "So Hiro's gone," he rasped, pausing to cough and to inhale deep from a long clay pipe. A merry-go-weed smoker by the smell. When you lived in such close proximity to the dead, you probably needed an escape route to get through life.

"He was a good man." I said.

The gatekeeper stared at nothing for several unnerving seconds. I was wondering what I should do to bring him back from wherever the weed sent him when his gaze returned to me, no longer wooly but needle-sharp. He chortled and opened a narrow side gate, his movements slow.

I went in, my mind focused on maneuvering the cart through the confines. As soon as I was done, he closed the gate and was gone, his movements no longer slow.

If the streets had been silent, the cemetery existed in a place before sound. The effigies were worse. Life-sized, they reared from every plot, watching the world with blank regard. Turning one's back on them was impossible; they were more numerous than trees.

No wonder the pay was higher.

A line from *Mesmerizing*, a poetry collection by Galz, the newest star in Sammalore's firmament of authors, came to my mind.

"You are not alone. You are never alone. When you reach that place, look behind, and I will be there..."

I had been elated at the new allocation since it was a promotion with higher pay, but in this moment I wished I were back in my old patch, in the company of other living beings.

I had moved deeper into the old part of the cemetery and was piling leaves and twigs into the cart before taking them to the compost heaps, while trying to keep my eyes away from a lifelike effigy of a toddler, when I felt it. I turned around, my gaze brushing past the three feet of pink marble, a toy dragon clutched in one small hand.

Two people, heading this way. Gray tunics and gray trousers, meant officials of some sort.

My heart did a summersault. This wasn't good.

"Are you Allii?"

The speaker was a woman, in her early twenties, her tiny turned up nose contrasting with the pin-sharp eyes.

In that moment I knew who they were. Maybe it was the tone or their glances which seemed to roam wide and sink deep.

City Guards had a uniform, green trousers, green tunic, green cap. But the investigative branch of the Guards, the Kruptos, dressed like all other city officials in unobtrusive gray.

I gripped the broom tighter. There's only one reason they'd bother to come looking for me.

"Master Khuti, they got him?"

The woman tilted her head. The sharpness of her gaze would have put an eagle to shame. "Now how do you know that?"

I shrugged, wondering why they equate menial with

stupid. "Why else would two members of the elite Kruptos come looking for a lowly street cleaner?"

The woman exchanged a glance with her companion before stepping closer. She was shorter than me, her cleft chin on par with the breast pocket of my blouse. "He vanished last night."

I nodded dully. Poor Master Khuti. I had got to know him well in the three months I worked for him, over conversations about books and food.

Death came to all of us. Disappearing as if you've never been was quite another fate.

At least Master Khuti wouldn't leave behind a grieving family. Only Bhan, his assistant, a few friends, and me.

"You are to come with us," the woman said. "We have already talked to your supervisor. He'll be sending someone to take over for the day."

They waited patiently as I washed my hands and my face. The woman watched me while pretending to study a piece of paper. The man walked in a wide circle around me pretending to look at the effigies. He even gave a realistic shudder, saying, "These give me the creeps." Since he said this while looking at the effigy of the toddler, the shudder was probably real.

As we set off, I faced reality. If Master Khuti had vanished from a house that was more like a fortress, then there'd be two prime suspects for that crime—his assistant Bhan and me.

2

SEASON OF REBIRTH

*"Fear, the more irrational the better, Lu thinks
watching the Lord striding from the stables into the
palace, the silver-handled whip caressing a booted leg.
Then it can spread faster and undermine deeper. Isn't
that how the few control the many?"*
Unwinged – Page 22

WALKING DOWN TREE-LINED STREETS, I FELT THE DAY HAD
the feeling not of warm Grisma, the fructification season,
but of mild Vasantha, the season of rebirth and flowering.
The air still retained enough of the departed night's
coolness. The thick foliage of marah and organza orange
trees absorbed the sun's heat, allowing only a pleasant
goldish-green light through.

I didn't dare to ask where I was being taken. But once
we passed the Cosmic Tower, the headquarters of the

Stargazer Collective, I knew our destination was neither the prison nor the Guard Headquarters. When I caught a glimpse of the huge marble statue of the Twin God and the Peerless Pool by it, popularly and irreverently known as Twinie's Dip, I guessed that I was being taken to Diaochrisi Hall, the massive complex which housed Sammalore's administrative buildings.

The Hall stood on a hillock backing the meeting place between river Akash and the Zeeba Ocean. I've seen the white sandstone complex from afar but never been anywhere close, maybe because it was surrounded on two sides by rose-apple orchards. Every time I saw a rose-apple tree, I thought of my murdered stepmother.

The two officials ignored the main entrance and took a paved path that ran round the complex. I focused on feet, theirs and mine, glad that this was not the flowering season. Bellizza often talked about the scent of rose apple flowers. The flowers never gave a hint of their coming arrival, she said. They didn't bother with buds. They would appear fully unfurled one morning, tiny pink stars covering every inch of every branch of rose apple trees. For three days the world would be pink and perfumed. On the fourth day the flowers would be gone, leaving behind the fertilized carpel of the coming rose apples.

I knew reality was not quite so picturesque, but preferred to cling to my memory of Bellizza's memory.

The journey ended at a plain wooden door. The woman opened it, motioning me to follow her into a white-walled narrow hall. A wooden staircase rose from it at mid-point. At the far end, under an anodyne painting of a flowery meadow, a young man sat reading a book. The wooden desk before him was innocent of even a scrap of paper. The book he was reading seemed to be a work of fiction, going by the colorful cover depicting a man in a rich blue robe, and the title, *The Lost Butterfly*. He looked up when we entered, nodded, and returned to his reading.

Up three floors, the staircase ended in a spacious hall, sunlight and fresh air streaming in through windows looking on to the sea. The white walls were hung with more bland paintings, flowers, animals, birds, and babies. Chairs and tables were arranged in the manner of a reception room in a mansion. On one side of the hall were doors in serried brown ranks, all of them closed.

The two officials walked up to the corner-most door. The woman knocked. A youthful voice bade us enter. The woman opened the door and indicated I should go in. I did, and the door closed behind me.

The room was large, the near-floor length windows making it seem even more capacious. One set of windows led to a balcony on which reposed two mola trees in large ceramic pots. The other set gave a captivating view of the sea. The walls were white, but there was nothing standard about the single painting in the room. Though I had not seen it before, I recognized the hand immediately, the distinctive style of Koomari, Sammalore's preeminent painter, being unmistakable. This one depicted a woman in a purple and blue costume, long hair braided and garlanded, face in repose, caught in that precise second between motion and stillness.

"*Dancer Before the Dance*," the same youthful voice said. "You feel it, don't you, that any moment she'll begin to move and you will hear the tinkling of the bangles?"

I turned around to stare at the biggest surprise of this day of surprises. The youthful voice belonged to an old man, bald headed and wrinkled.

"Do sit," he said, indicating the chair opposite him. "I took the liberty of ordering two lunches." His smile was friendly, guileless. "They are quite passable. Nothing like your fish thiyal though."

I clamped my teeth on my lip, throttling the gasp at birth. Master Khuti ate neither flesh nor fish, like me. The only time I made a fish dish was when he had a friend over for dinner about two weeks ago.

"You were Master Khuti's dinner guest," I said.

"Please sit," he said again. "I was. Dinner guest and old friend. We grew up together. He was six years my junior in age, but sixty years my senior in intelligence. I always looked up to him, metaphorically of course." He got up as he spoke, revealing a tall figure, in which thinness indicated a wiry strength. "May I give you something to drink? It is my invariable practice to have a glass of sand lemon before a meal. Excellent for digestion." The smile dawned again, an inviting one. "Not as young as one used to be."

I nodded, not trusting my voice. He disappeared behind a side door. I was glad of the reprieve. I was in the hands of a master. If he wanted to pin this or any other crime on me, he'd probably succeed well enough to convince even me.

Who was this man? Did he summon me as a suspect? Or because he knew enough of my investigative past, my tendency to poke my long nose into dead people's affairs, as Spooky phrased it?

Everyone was aware of the hierarchy of the Guards. Kruptos was a closed book. Street cleaners were founts of information for they knew a side of a city unknown not just to ordinary citizens, but also to rulers, guards, and even spies. Had I wanted to know the insides of the Kruptos, all I would have had to do was to ask the right question, the right way, from the right street cleaner. But the subject had never interested me. So the only information I had was what Master Khuti said about his dinner guest.

"A childhood friend has asked himself to dinner," he had explained after asking me whether I would object to making a fish dish. "I have seen him around of course after we grew up and went our separate ways, but this is the first time we are meeting for a meal. I would like something special. He likes fish. Are you certain it wouldn't be a problem?"

"Not at all," I assured him with perfect truth. "I'll do my very best. Two old friends having a meal together after many decades should be a joyous occasion."

He smiled wryly. "My friend is an important city official. While I have no doubt that personal factors play a role in this projected visit, the real purpose would be to see how secure this place is and how it can be made even more secure."

Two days later, he said his visitor loved my fish concoction.

"Now," said the youthful voice as a thin hand handed me a glass, "why would a young woman with such a turn with a fish work as a street cleaner?"

I took a sip of the drink. "I'm sure a person as highly placed in the Kruptos as you would know that street-cleaning in

Sammalore pays well. By helping to rid Sammalore of her detritus, I make more money in a week than I would have done as a cook's or a bookseller's assistant in a month."

He chuckled softly. "Thanks to which fact we are probably the cleanest city in Pegala and have not had to contend with even a minor plague for centuries. A clean city is a strong city."

I nodded, taking another sip. "This drink is very pleasant."

The childlike smile flashed. "Thank you. Now it occurs to me that I have been rather remiss in a basic matter of courtesy. I know your name, yet never bothered to introduce myself. My long name is Mufhilah. Friends call me Mufh, as I hope you will."

I bowed, murmuring it was an honor. I never forgot a name or the face it belonged to and I've never heard this one before. All the more reason to step with care. One did not rush headlong in any direction when crossing a quicksand.

A knock made him look up, eyes bird-eager. "Ah food. Now we can eat and talk."

He went to the adjoining room, and after a brief time returned with a laden tray which he placed on his desk.

The lunch was pumpkin and fire-chili bake with sweet-potato drizzle and a honey mango jubab, quite passable. Throughout the meal, the talk ran on ordinary channels, food types, produce, and of course that perennial topic without which humanity would be lost, conversationally, weather.

Food done and cleared away, he sat down once again, after pouring both of us two cups of coffee. "Now to the matter at hand. Master Khuti vanished sometime last night. His assistant Bhan went to work as usual at seven thirty in the morning and found the place still locked up. He rang the bell, receiving no answer, sounded the alarm. Two Krupto operatives were watching the place in normal clothes, an arrangement we have made for all bookshops. They had seen nothing, heard nothing."

"Had Master Khuti finished his dinner?" He had his dinner around nine. If he hadn't, the time could be narrowed down considerably.

"Yes, but not his breakfast, which we found untouched in the cold cellar." The guileless eyes met mine for a second, a twinkle in their blue depths. "Fortunately for you, there were enough traces left in the used crockery for our searchers to test. The food and the drink were clear, which cleared you, considerably."

"The dinner dishes were not washed?"

"No. The dishes were in the washing trough, a pot of cinnamon cream and a half-filled cup on a table in the reading bay adjoining his bedroom." He leaned back, fingers intertwined on the desk, watching me.

"He washed and put away everything before going to sleep. Invariably. He was a precise man who ran his life with clockwork exactitude. He would eat, read a book for about an hour sipping cinnamon cream, then clean the kitchen before going to bed. I think he had other part-time help in the past. You can check with them. Bhan should know their names." I paused as I remembered the account book. "No, actually he recorded all domestic expenditures, in a separate book with a bright yellow cover. It should be in his library."

Mufhilah smiled a little. "Yes, we found the account book. But your revelation about his nightly habits opens up an interesting avenue of exploration."

"One more thing," I said. "Was the bed slept in?"

"Yes. It was more than a matter of ruffled bedclothes. Our people found some hairs on the pillow and some dandruff. He had been plagued by dandruff from his childhood. So we can safely assume that contrary to his set-in-stone routine, my friend went to bed suddenly. He lay down and fell asleep, even though, in my opinion, his intention was not to sleep but to take a brief rest, before returning to his habitual groove. The illuminator in the reading bay had died out, as had the one in the kitchen."

"I put used firestones on the sun-disk and placed new ones every evening." Spurred by the wealth of information, my mind sprinted, a mare given her head in open country. "Master Khuti was a light sleeper. No one could have entered his room without him waking up. He also had difficulty falling asleep, thus the warm cinnamon cream. Even with that he often had bad nights. On such days he'd be prone to headaches and bouts of irritability." A tight ball of pain formed in my throat as I remembered the warning Master Khuti gave me on my evening at work as his part-time help. "I should tell you, young lady, that after a bad night's sleep, I'm like a porcupine with too many quills." A wry smile had taken the sting out of the words without diminishing their seriousness.

I blinked back the tears and dashed off a stray drop, sneaking a look at Mufhilah, hoping he didn't notice.

Mufhilah seemed to have no eyes for me. He had turned his gaze away from me to the faraway sea, a coverlet of blue under a white sun. "So his sudden urge for a short rest couldn't have been due to the usual causes like tiredness or old age?"

"They can't be ruled out entirely," I said, careful to cover all possibilities. "But if he fell into an untimely and deep sleep, the most likely reason would have been a soporific."

He ran a hand over his bald pate, clearly a leftover habit from the days when he had hair, the color of warm brown going by the eyebrows. "But the food is clear, the drink is clear, so what was the medium used? Every door was bolted from inside, every window was properly closed. Yet someone came in, introduced a soporific into his system, waited till he fell asleep, and left carrying him along. How did any of it happen?"

"Wait," I cried. "You said all the windows were closed. What about the kitchen windows?"

He pulled out a piece of paper from a sheaf and studied it, though I had the feeling he didn't really need to refer to anything. "All closed. Why?"

"That window was kept open the whole day. Master Khuti closed them himself in the night, once he had finished putting away the dinner dishes."

Mufhilah smiled a little. For some reason I felt it was the first spontaneous smile I saw in him, and he was smiling not at me but at a memory. "The kitchen window was his little act of rebellion, I presume. Yes, true to form."

"He said it was to let the river breeze in." I paused to gulp an unexpected sob. Where was he? Was he being kept in the company of the other abducted booksellers, all friendly competitors, or alone? Where? In the city? The surrounding countryside? Or had he been taken beyond Sammalore's borders?

Whatever the truth, the entire operation pointed to a vast network of spies. I failed to repress the sudden shudder but did manage to prevent myself from looking over my shoulder, at what I knew not.

Mufhilah cleared his throat. "If my old friend didn't wash the dinner things, then that window was closed by whoever took him. Perhaps the one mistake they made in an otherwise flawless plan." He extracted a long envelope from the sheaf of documents and held it out to me. "Have you seen this before?"

The envelope was cream colored and heavy. Master Khuti's name was written on it in thick ornate letters, the long name, Khutibanda. It contained a single sheet of paper of excellent quality, like the envelope. The brief note was written in the same ornate hand.

It has come to our notice that your esteemed bookshop stocks items which offend human decency and divine morality. It is our earnest hope that you will take steps, within the course of the next three days, to remove these pollutants from your shelves and your stores.

I read the note twice before folding and returning it to the envelope. "Did the other bookshop owners who vanished receive similar letters?"

"They didn't vanish, Allii. They were abducted. And yes, they did. Identical. You could safely call them quintuplets."

I wondered how many bookshops there are in Sammalore

and how many more letters were ready waiting to be sent.

"Eleven more bookshops. Including some of the biggest ones. But I have a feeling many will be removing the 'objectionable' items from their shelves by tomorrow the latest."

Suddenly a memory enveloped me, Master Khuti coming into the kitchen, placing a book on the table, title page up. "This is new and I just finished reading it. You may want to take this today."

I had peered at the book while slicing a honey melon for a salad, the sweet juice covering my fingers in a patina of molten gold.

Refugees from Time, by Meeshkin, the Chief Priest of the Twin God.

"Oh!" I cried looking at him with a smile. "I've been wanting to read this ever since I read that review in *Literary Sammalore* by Meaya saying Meeshkin's deity couldn't have written a book so original, yet so familiar."

He touched the book caressingly. "Quite accurate. Meeshkin always had a way with words. His *Reflection on History* is something you should read. It's in my library." His index finger traced the cover picture, a sun over a desert, with exquisite slowness. "This must be on the top of The List. I hear that one or two bookshops are not happy about stocking it." He had shaken his head, his face grave. "That's a bad beginning. If there's anything worse than censorship it is self-censorship. Enslavement of the body could be overcome, but enslavement of the mind?"

I blinked as the memory faded.

Mufhilah was watching me his well-shaped head

slightly tilted like a bird, a predatory bird in the plumage of a songster.

I needed to escape that gaze. "The book he was reading, was it there on the folding table? *Unwinged.*"

"Only the cover, carefully torn into two." Before my horrified *oh* was over, he handed me a thin folio. "These are the contents of his bedroom. Will you check and see if everything is in order?"

I glanced through the sheets. The missing item sprang at me.

"There was a packet on incense blocks on the table in the reading bay. It had two blocks left. It is not mentioned here. There was an incense burner as well. That is not mentioned here either." The spiky letters moved about on the page in a spider-dance. "The incense was a relaxant. He'd use a block every night."

Mufhilah held out his hand. I gave him the folio. His gaze moved rapidly over the sheets. "No, you are right. Give me a moment."

He vanished through the connecting door. I closed my eyes, trying to imagine the packet. Oblong, red background, a cluster of white star-jasmines.

There was a supply of incense blocks in the kitchen cupboard. I frowned, trying to recall when I took a packet from there. It was several days ago. Which meant the new packet came not from the stores but from some other source.

Mufhilah came in, closing the connecting door behind him. "I've sent a message asking about incense blocks and the burner."

I told him briefly of my conjectures. He listened to me in silence, returned to his desk, and took some more paper from the sheaf. "Two days ago, he bought a packet of incense blocks from an old salesman going door to door. It was mentioned by Bhan in his statement. The transaction was crosschecked with the account book and confirmed." He leaned against the table, shoulders hunched. "So the soporific was in the incense. We would have never known without you."

"Placing a new packet of incense blocks on the folding table every three days was my job. Yesterday I noticed that one was already there and didn't think anything about it." *Fool, fool!*

Mufhilah gave me an admonishing smile. "If you are going to assist us with this investigation, and I hope you do, I'd insist on self-criticism but not self-blame. The one comes from reason, the other from self-pity."

I bowed my head in acceptance of his stricture. My heart was soaring with relief. Free, for now at least. Free to walk out of this place, free to take the cliff path up to my home, free to tell Spooky the events of the day, free to attend the lecture on animals in the evening, free…I stood up bowing. "Is it possible for me to visit Master Khuti's house?"

"Perfectly in order. Our people will be done with it by evening. I too am thinking of paying a visit. Why don't we meet there? Would ten be all right with you?" He paused, his eyes on me, their gaze glittering, "Albalia?"